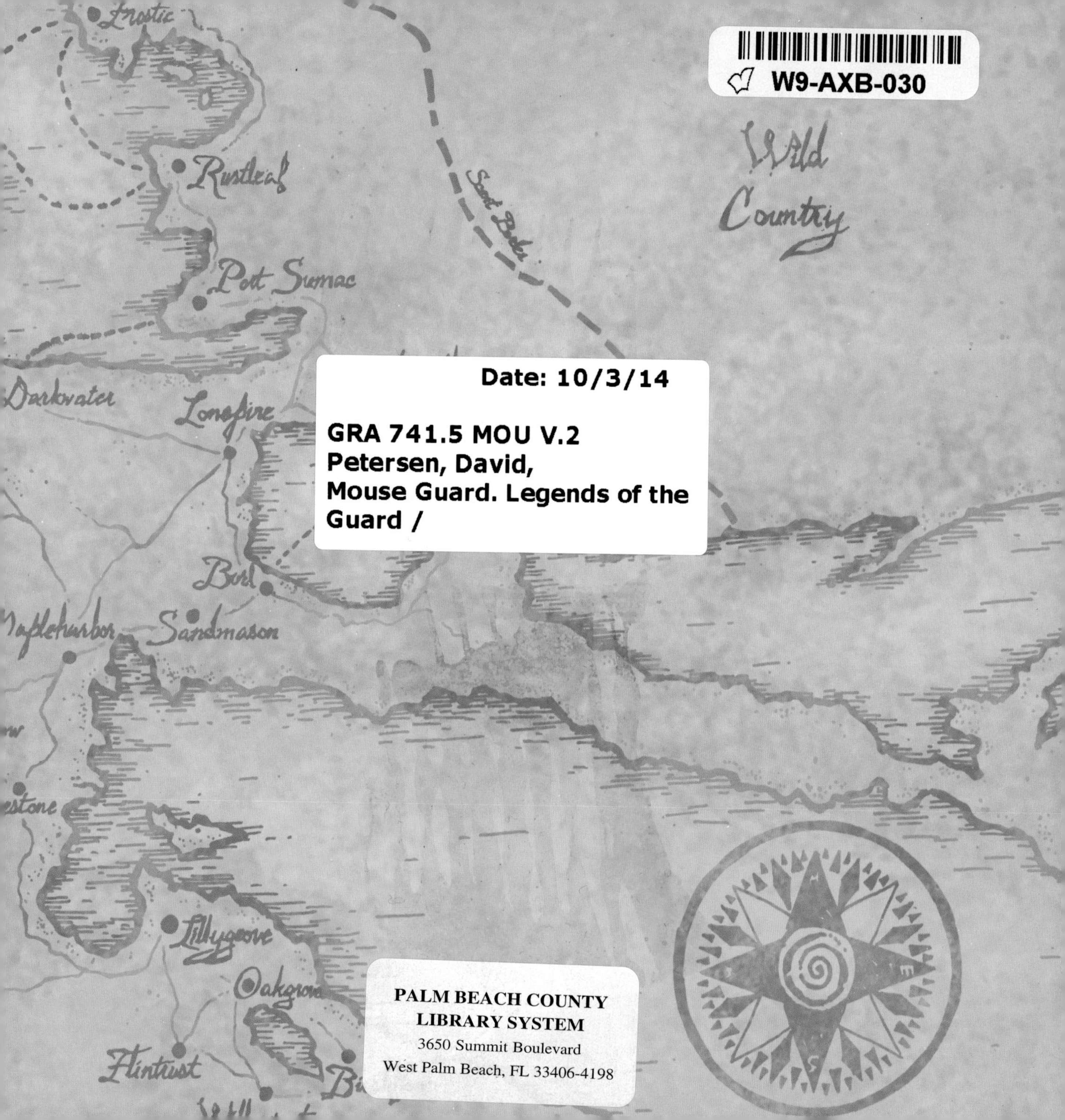
Frostic
Rustleaf
Port Sumac
Scent Border
Wild Country
Darkwater
Lonepine
Sandmason
Lillygrove
Oakgrove
Flintrust

FOR THE FANS OF MOUSE GUARD

SPECIAL THANKS TO:
STAN SAKAI, ALEX ECKMAN-LAWN, NICK TAPALANSKY,
BEN CALDWELL, CHRISTIAN SLADE, RICK GEARY, JEMMA SALUME,
C.P. WILSON III, CORY GODBEY, ERIC CANETE, BILL WILLINGHAM,
JACKSON SZE, JUSTIN GERARD, CLIFF MONEAR,
DIRK SHEARER, & PAUL MORRISSEY.

MOUSE GUARD:
LEGENDS OF THE GUARD

VOLUME TWO

Published by
ARCHAIA

MOUSE GUARD:
LEGENDS OF THE GUARD
VOLUME TWO

DAVID PETERSEN, *EDITOR*

PAUL MORRISSEY, *EDITOR*

REBECCA TAYLOR, *MANAGING EDITOR*

 **ARCHAIA**™

Published by **Archaia**
A Division of **Boom Entertainment, Inc.**
WWW.ARCHAIA.COM

BOOM! Studios
5670 Wilshire Boulevard, Suite 450
Los Angeles, California 90036-5679

ROSS RICHIE CEO & Founder • **JACK CUMMINS** President • **MARK SMYLIE** Chief Creative Officer • **MATT GAGNON** Editor-in-Chief
FILIP SABLIK VP of Publishing & Marketing • **STEPHEN CHRISTY** VP of Development • **LANCE KREITER** VP of Licensing & Merchandising
PHIL BARBARO VP of Finance • **BRYCE CARLSON** Managing Editor • **MEL CAYLO** Marketing Manager
SCOTT NEWMAN Production Design Manager • **DAFNA PLEBAN** Editor • **SHANNON WATTERS** Editor • **ERIC HARBURN** Editor
REBECCA TAYLOR Editor • **CHRIS ROSA** Assitant Editor • **ALEX GALER** Assistant Editor • **WHITNEY LEOPARD** Assistant Editor
JASMINE AMIRI Assistant Editor • **STEPHANIE GONZAGA** Graphic Designer • **MIKE LOPEZ** Production Designer
HANNAH NANCE PARTLOW Production Designer • **DEVIN FUNCHES** E-Commerce & Inventory Coordinator
BRIANNA HART Executive Assitant • **AARON FERRARA** Operations Assistant • **JOSE MEZA** Sales Assistant

MOUSE GUARD: LEGENDS OF THE GUARD Volume Two, Original Graphic Novel Hardcover, November 2013.

FIRST PRINTING.   10 9 8 7 6 5 4 3 2 1   ISBN: 1-936393-26-3   ISBN-13: 978-1-936393-26-8

FOREWORD

AS PAUL MORRISSEY & I WENT UP TO ACCEPT THE 2011 EISNER AWARD FOR BEST ANTHOLOGY, I SAID TO HIM, "LET'S DO THIS AGAIN SOMETIME." THE TRUTH IS, PAUL AND I WERE ALREADY WELL INTO ORGANIZING A SECOND ROUND OF THE *LEGENDS OF THE GUARD* ANTHOLOGY. IN FACT, SOME ARTISTS WERE ALREADY DRAWING PAGES. AND WHY NOT? MICE IN A TAVERN TELLING TALL TALES COULD ONLY GET STALE IF IT WERE POSSIBLE TO RUN OUT OF TALENTED PEOPLE TO CONTRIBUTE TO IT.

"DON'T YOU HAVE A HARD TIME TURNING OVER THE KEYS TO YOUR WORLD TO OTHER PEOPLE?" I'M OFTEN ASKED. THE *LEGENDS* BOOKS ARE TREMENDOUS FUN TO WORK ON, AND IT'S *BECAUSE* THEY ARE IN ANTHOLOGY FORMAT. I GET THE PLEASURE OF WORKING WITH VERY TALENTED PEOPLE WHO I ADMIRE AND GET TO WIDEN THE WORLD OF *MOUSE GUARD* AT THE SAME TIME. *THE CANTERBURY TALES*-ESQUE NATURE OF THE CONTRIBUTORS' STORIES BEING THE FABLES OF MY WORLD MEANS THAT THE FANS AND I GET WONDERFULLY CREATIVE STORIES THAT DON'T NEED TO PERFECTLY FIT INTO MY MAJOR MOUSE CONTINUITY.

EACH CONTRIBUTOR IS SOMEONE I CHOSE BECAUSE I LIKE THE WORK THAT THEY ALREADY DO. I TRUST THEM TO MAKE GREAT STORIES. PAUL AND I TRY TO STAY OUT OF THEIR WAY EDITORIALLY AND LET THEM FEEL FREE TO DO THEIR BEST WORK. AND WHILE THE VISUALS MAY LOOK DIFFERENT THAN MY MOUSE STORIES, I LOVE HOW THE DIVERSITY OF DRAWING AND COLORING STYLES SERVES AS A VISUAL REPRESENTATION OF THE SOUND & TONE OF EACH MOUSE STORYTELLER'S VOICE. PLEASE ENJOY THE RICHNESS THESE TALENTED FOLKS HAVE BROUGHT TO THE WORLD OF *MOUSE GUARD* AND ITS FANS.

David Petersen

DAVID PETERSEN
MICHIGAN, 2013

Story and Contributor Index:

Autumn Tale: art & story: Stan Sakai

Leviathan: art: Alex Eckman-Lawn, story: Nick Tapalansky

A Bone to Pick: art & story: Ben Caldwell

Love of the Sea: art & story: Christian Slade

Over the Falls: art & story: Rick Geary

The Shade: art & story: Jemma Salume

The Mouse Generals: art & story: Eric Canete
colors: Scott Keating

When Moles Are Around: art & story: C.P. Wilson III

The Thief, The Star-gazer, The Hunter, & The Tailor:
art & story: Cory Godbey

The Veteran: art & story: Bill Willingham
colors & letters: Brad Thomte

Back & Forth: art & story: Jackson Sze
letters: Nate Pride

The Timber Mice: art: Justin Gerard
music: Cliff Monear, lyrics: mouse traditional

Just a Printer: art & story: Dirk Shearer

Additional pages by David Petersen

Legend Cover Gallery & Extras

On the Cover:

The Guardmouse pair of Leire and Morton gained fame beyond their standard duties under the matriarch Dayana for three things. The tending, care, and training of quail for cart racing; the largest harvests of mushrooms anymouse ever retrieved; but for more than these two, for their daring escape from four dangerous mink chieftains. The lyric "...quickest carts in all the wood, towed by bird with feathery hood, to a crop where chief weasels greet, a-get-a-way quick that is a feat..." from the ballad "Gatherers in the Dale" is a reference to their legend.

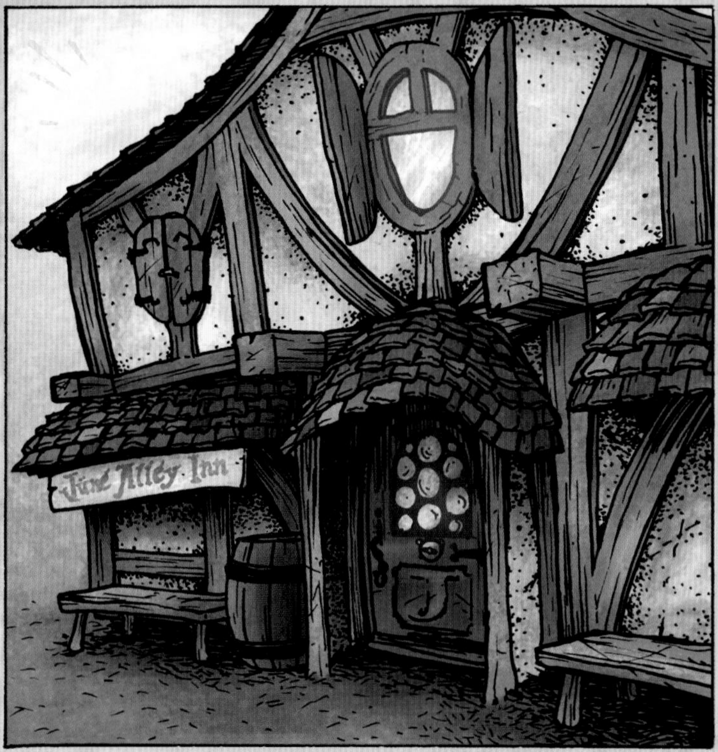
Jüne Alley Inn

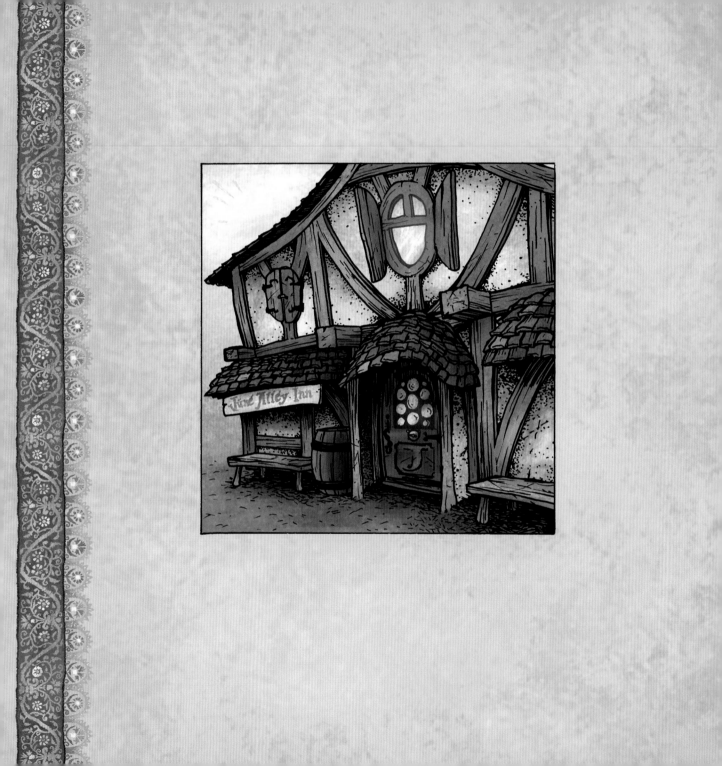

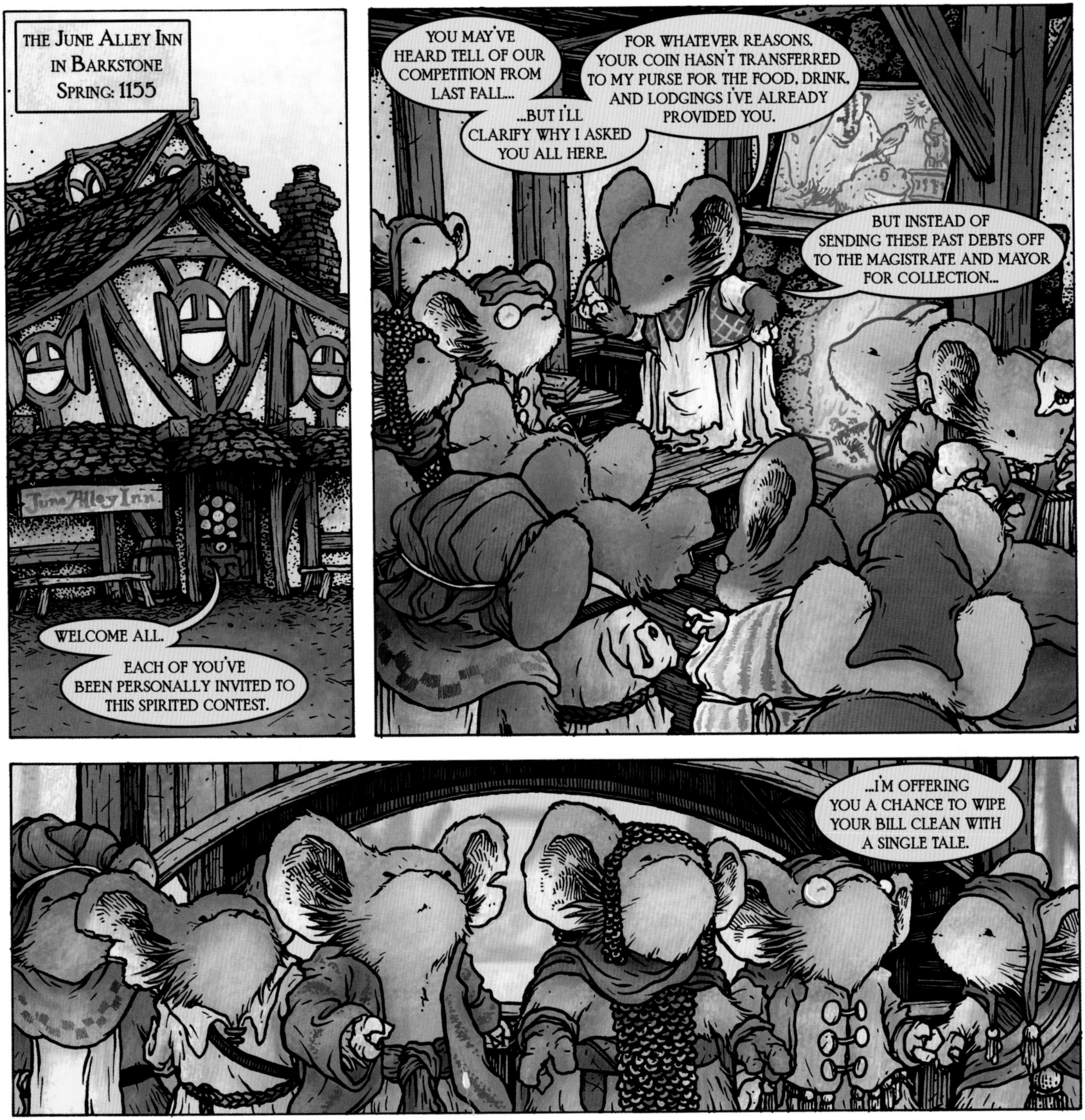
THE JUNE ALLEY INN IN BARKSTONE SPRING: 1155
June Alley Inn
WELCOME ALL.
EACH OF YOU'VE BEEN PERSONALLY INVITED TO THIS SPIRITED CONTEST.
YOU MAY'VE HEARD TELL OF OUR COMPETITION FROM LAST FALL...
...BUT I'LL CLARIFY WHY I ASKED YOU ALL HERE.
FOR WHATEVER REASONS, YOUR COIN HASN'T TRANSFERRED TO MY PURSE FOR THE FOOD, DRINK, AND LODGINGS I'VE ALREADY PROVIDED YOU.
BUT INSTEAD OF SENDING THESE PAST DEBTS OFF TO THE MAGISTRATE AND MAYOR FOR COLLECTION...
...I'M OFFERING YOU A CHANCE TO WIPE YOUR BILL CLEAN WITH A SINGLE TALE.

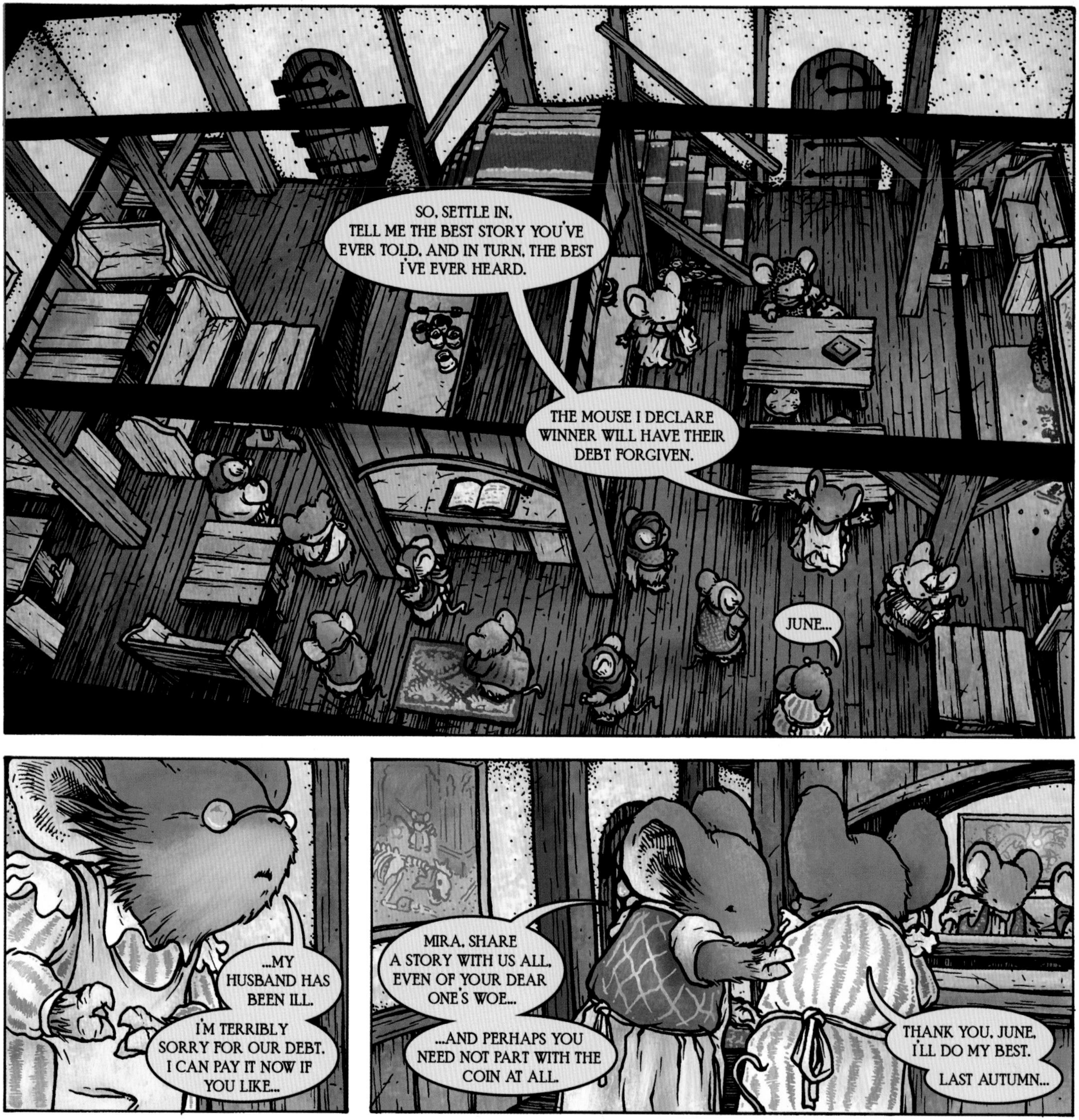
SO, SETTLE IN. TELL ME THE BEST STORY YOU'VE EVER TOLD, AND IN TURN, THE BEST I'VE EVER HEARD.
THE MOUSE I DECLARE WINNER WILL HAVE THEIR DEBT FORGIVEN.
JUNE...
...MY HUSBAND HAS BEEN ILL.
I'M TERRIBLY SORRY FOR OUR DEBT. I CAN PAY IT NOW IF YOU LIKE...
MIRA, SHARE A STORY WITH US ALL, EVEN OF YOUR DEAR ONE'S WOE...
...AND PERHAPS YOU NEED NOT PART WITH THE COIN AT ALL.
THANK YOU, JUNE. I'LL DO MY BEST.
LAST AUTUMN...

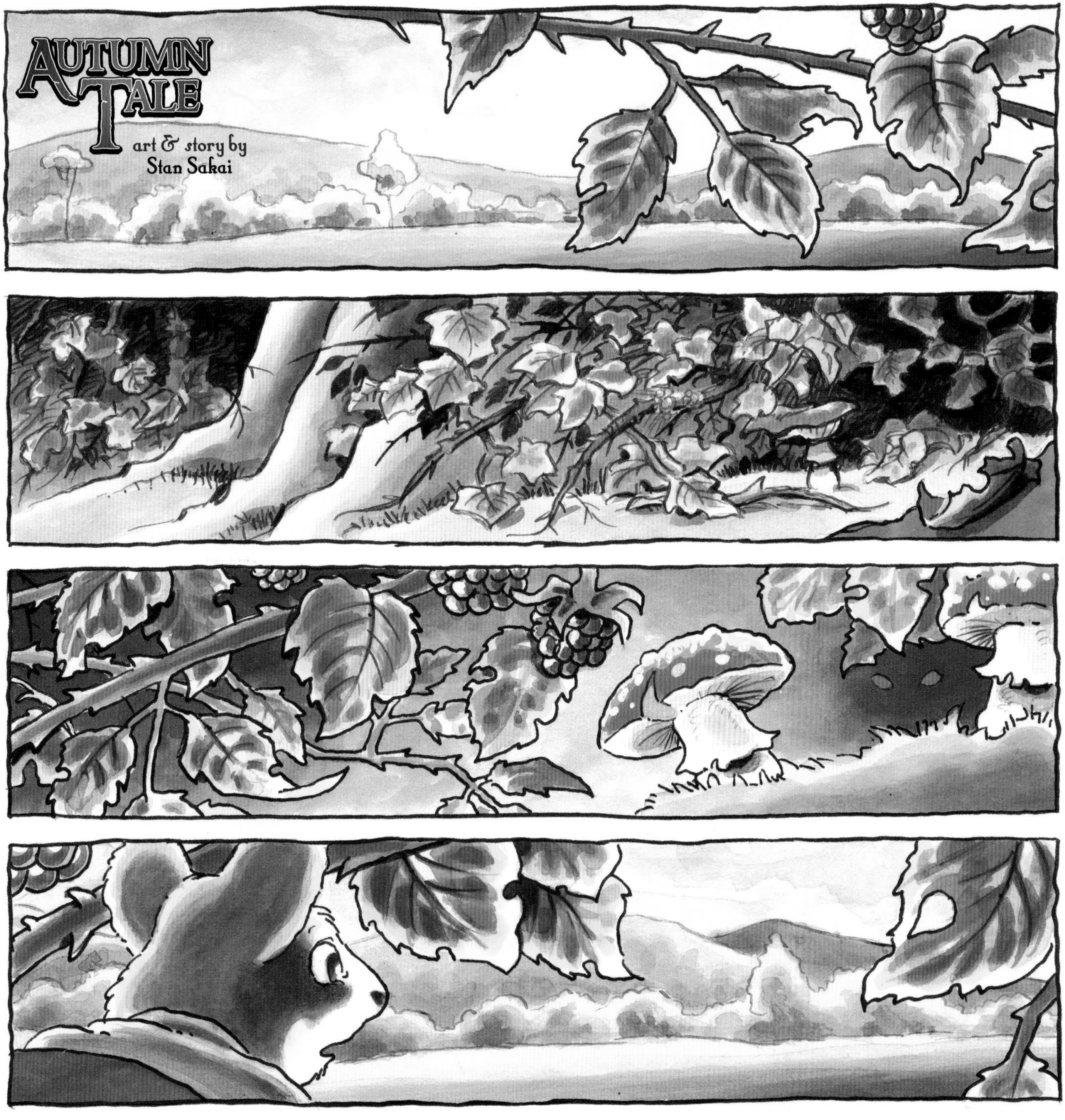

AUTUMN TALE
art & story by
Stan Sakai

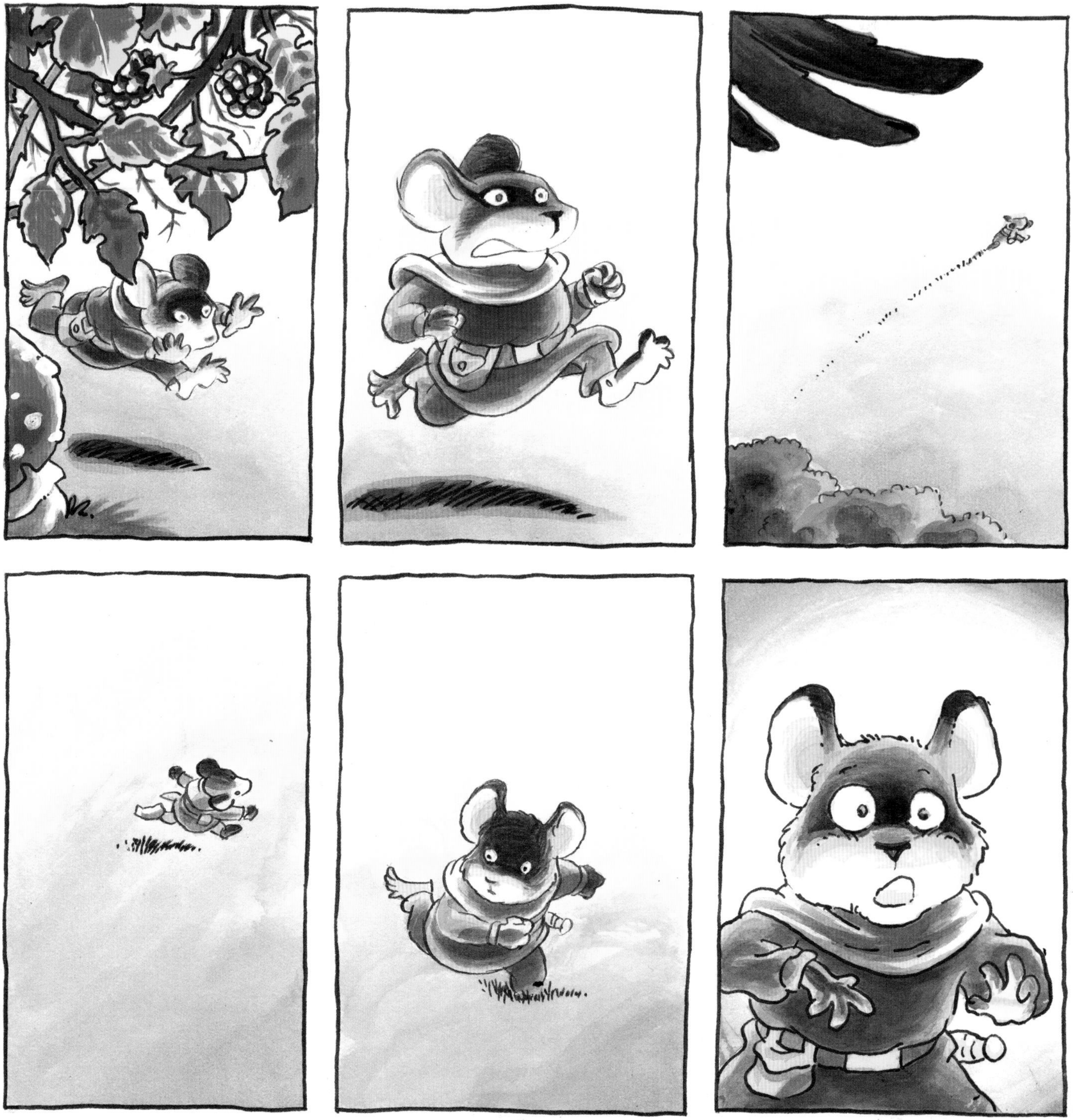

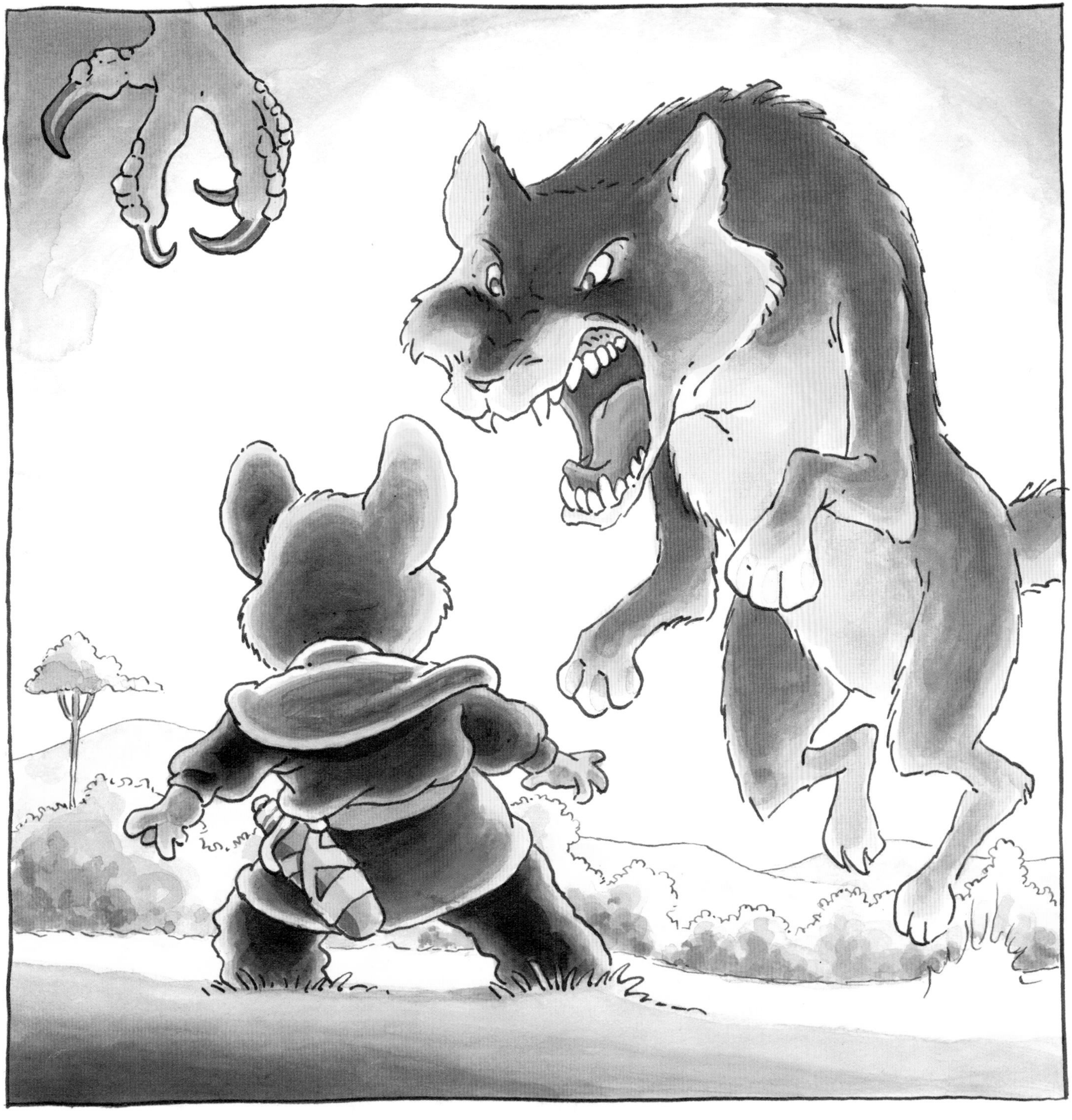

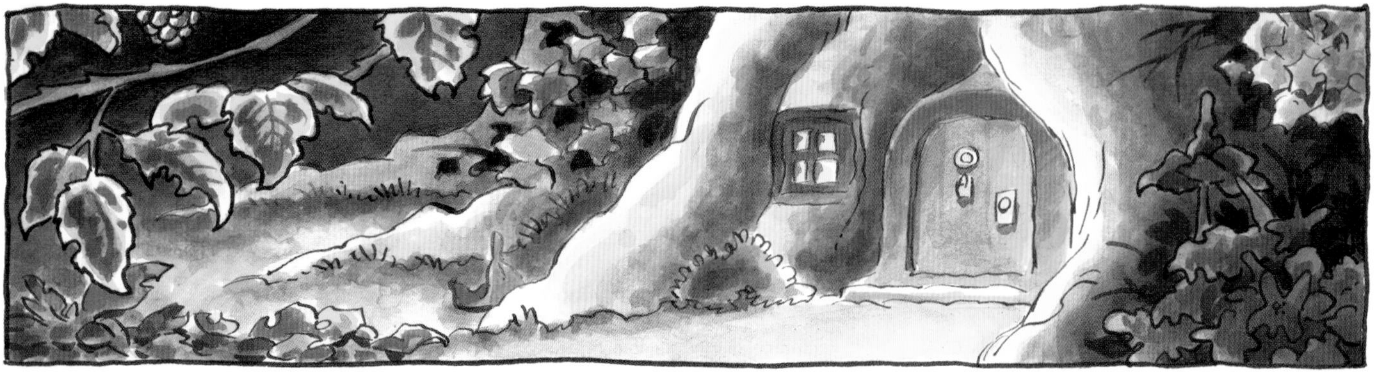

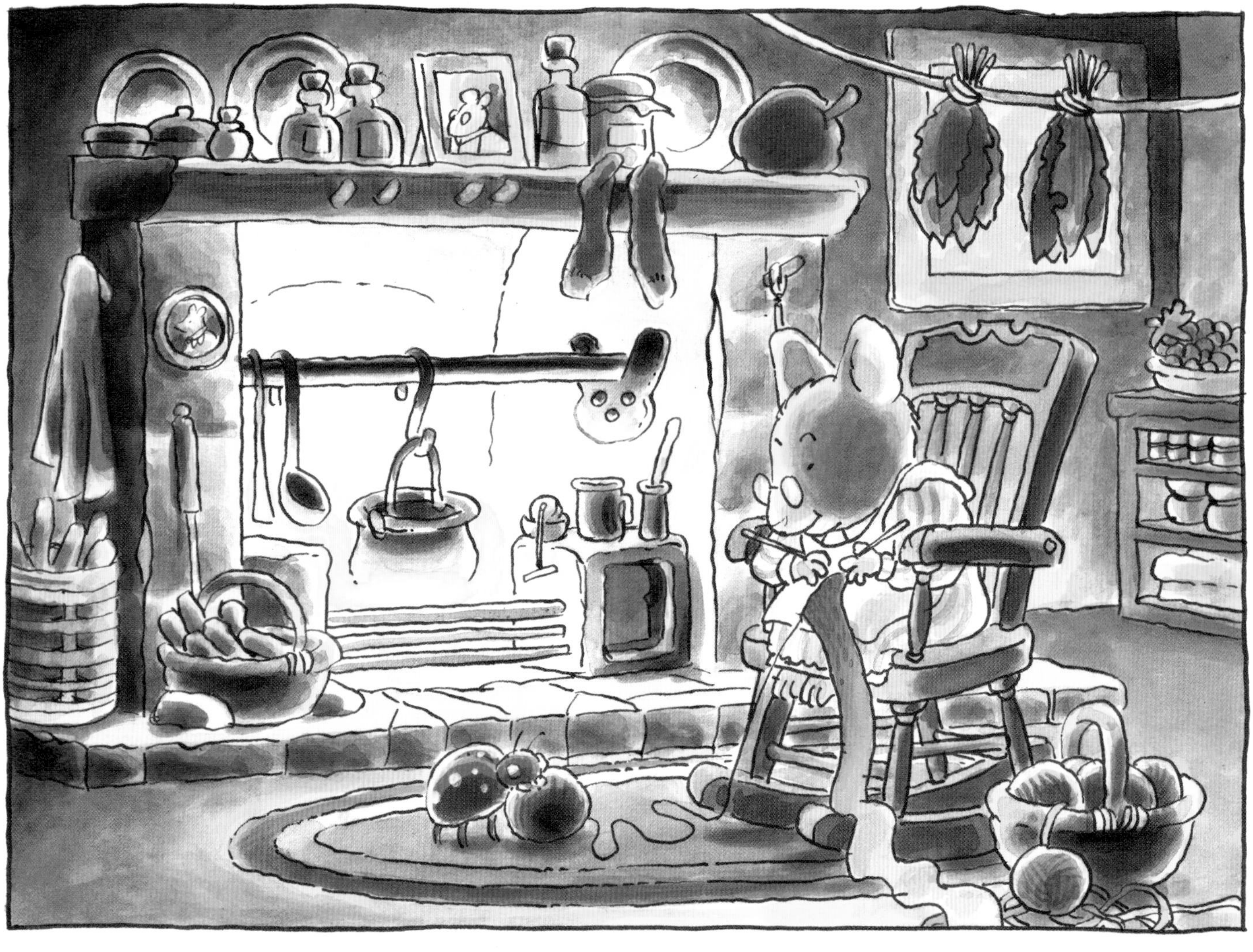

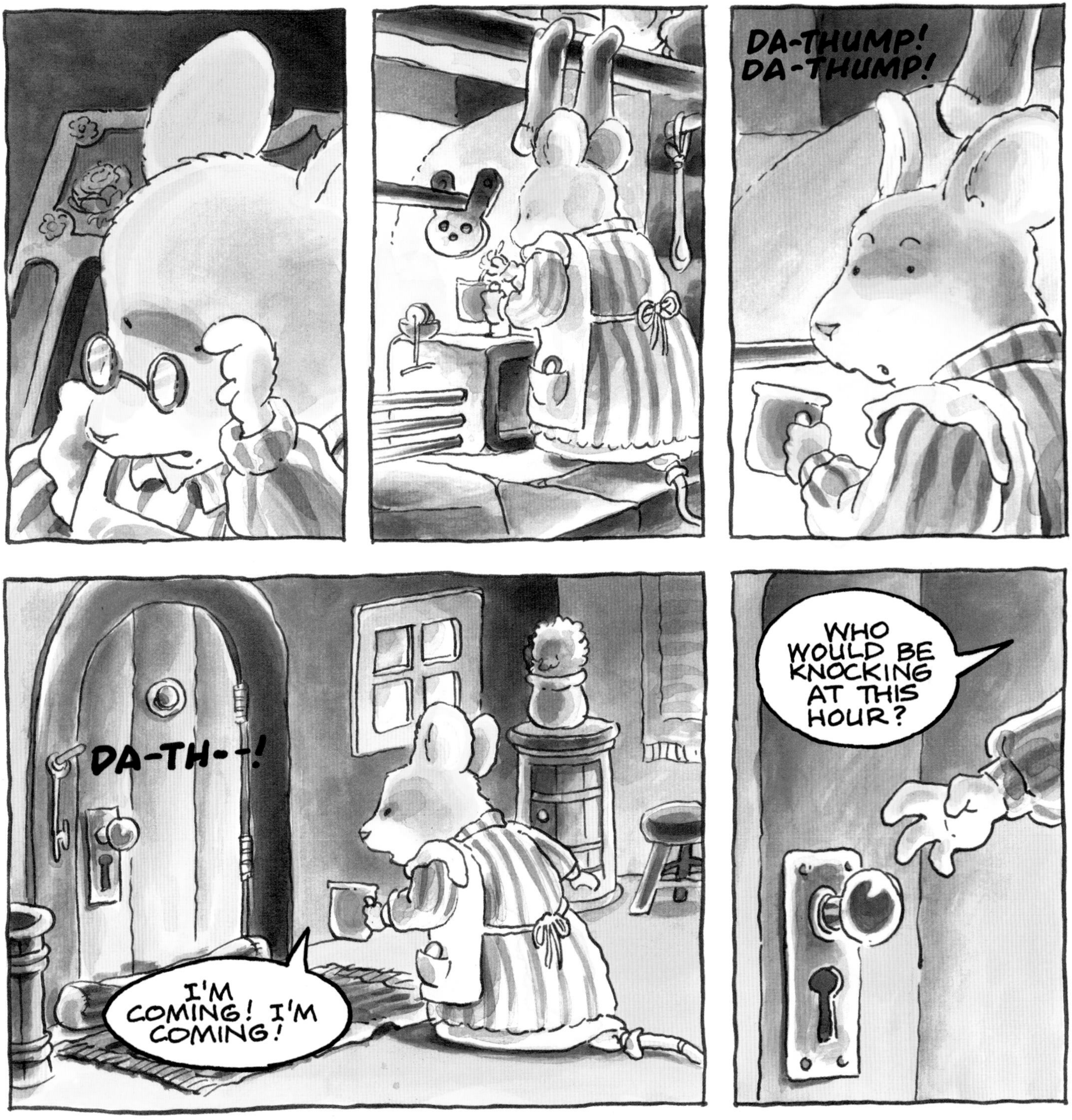
DA-THUMP!
DA-THUMP!
DA-TH--!
I'M COMING! I'M COMING!
WHO WOULD BE KNOCKING AT THIS HOUR?

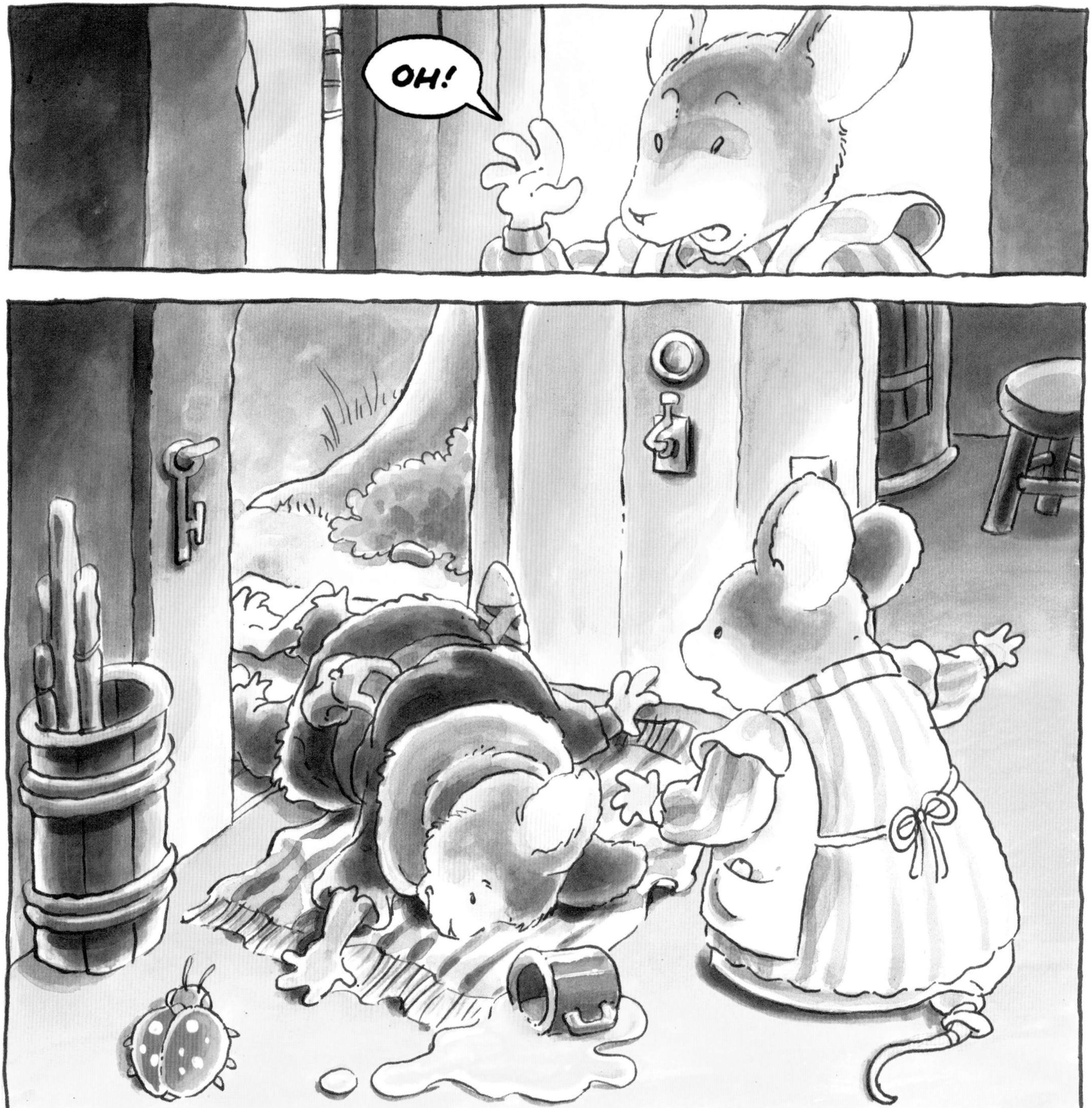
OH!

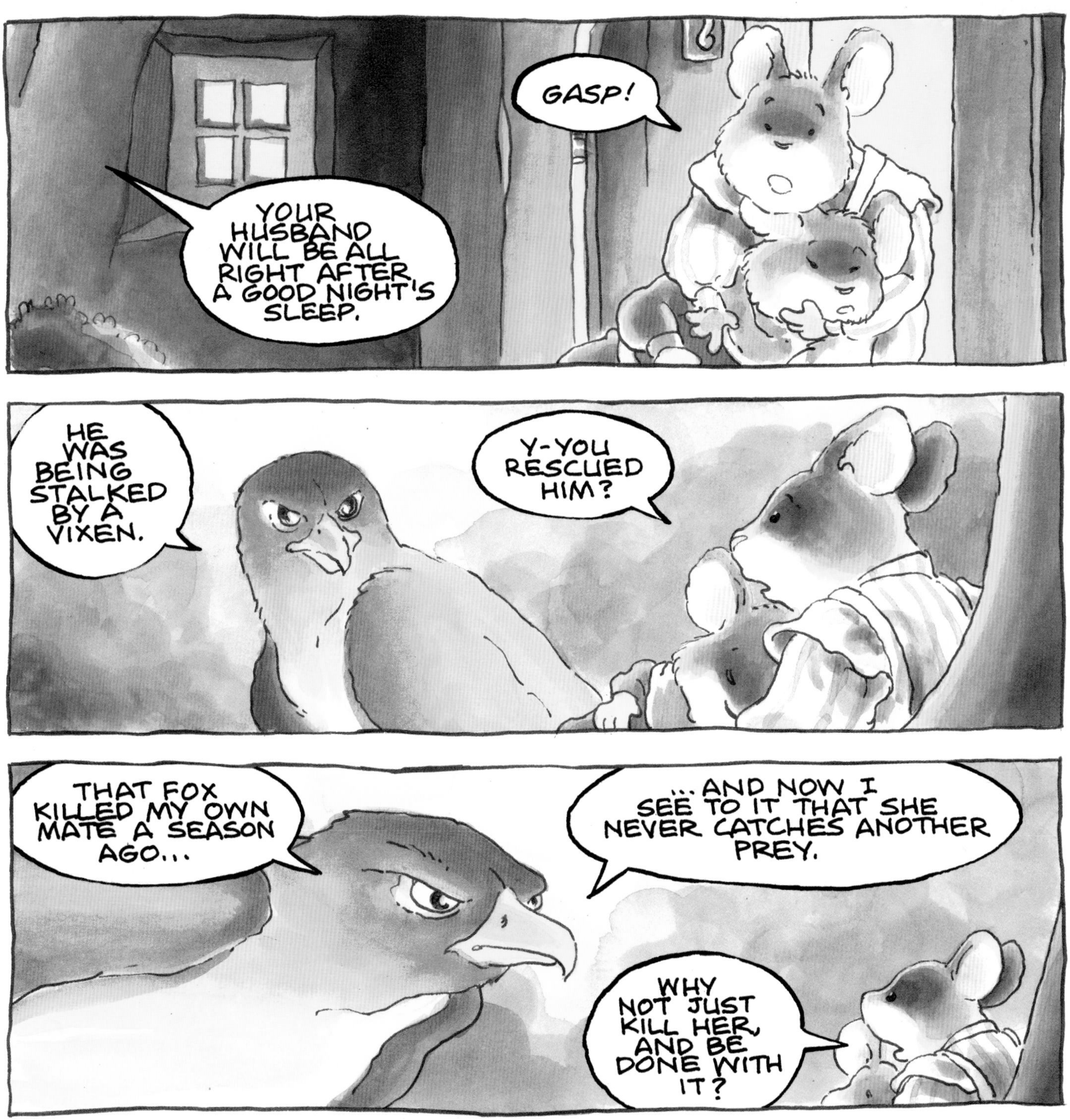
GASP!
YOUR HUSBAND WILL BE ALL RIGHT AFTER A GOOD NIGHT'S SLEEP.
HE WAS BEING STALKED BY A VIXEN.
Y-YOU RESCUED HIM?
THAT FOX KILLED MY OWN MATE A SEASON AGO...
...AND NOW I SEE TO IT THAT SHE NEVER CATCHES ANOTHER PREY.
WHY NOT JUST KILL HER, AND BE DONE WITH IT?

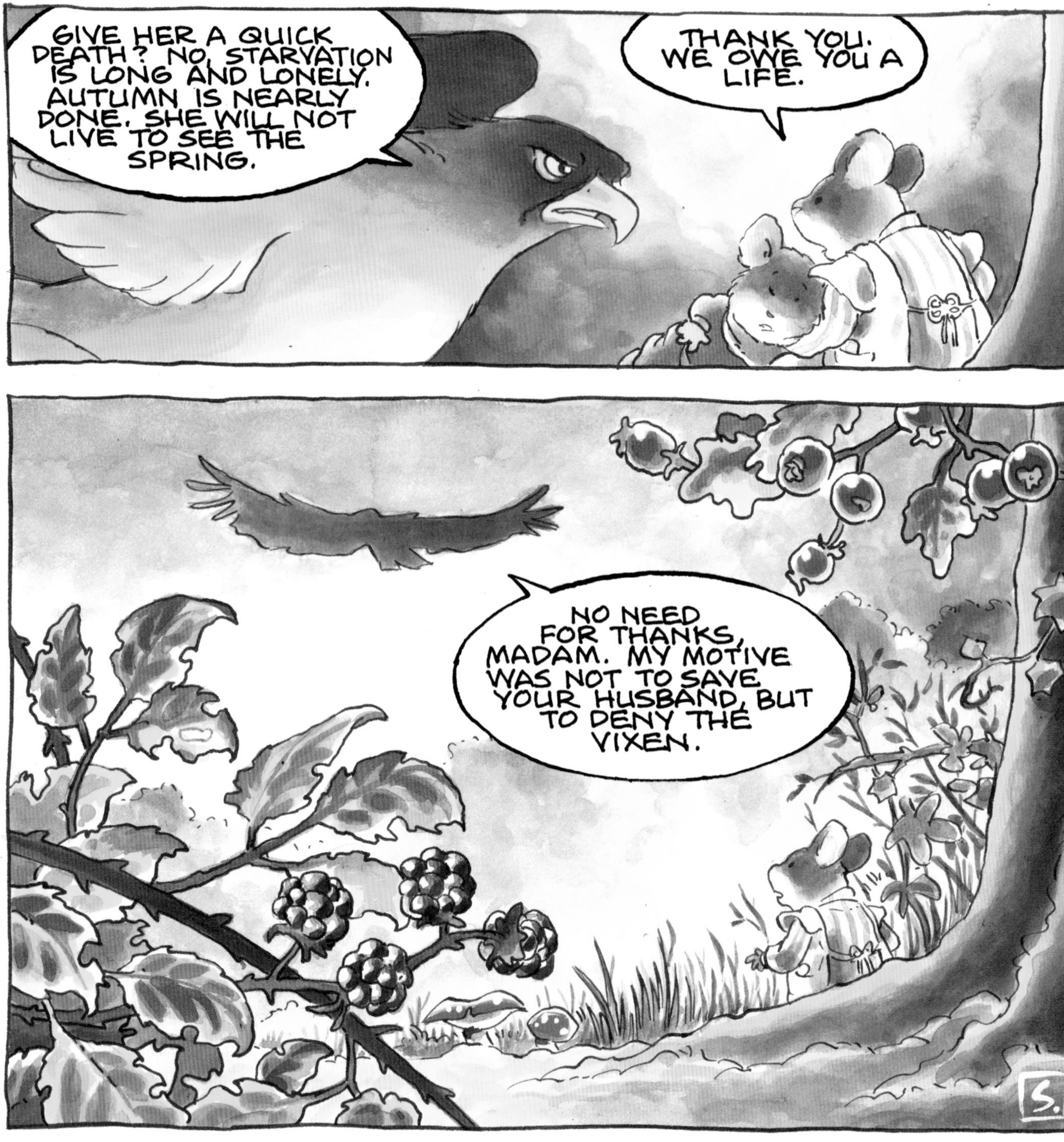
GIVE HER A QUICK DEATH? NO, STARVATION IS LONG AND LONELY. AUTUMN IS NEARLY DONE. SHE WILL NOT LIVE TO SEE THE SPRING.
THANK YOU. WE OWE YOU A LIFE.
NO NEED FOR THANKS, MADAM. MY MOTIVE WAS NOT TO SAVE YOUR HUSBAND, BUT TO DENY THE VIXEN.
S.

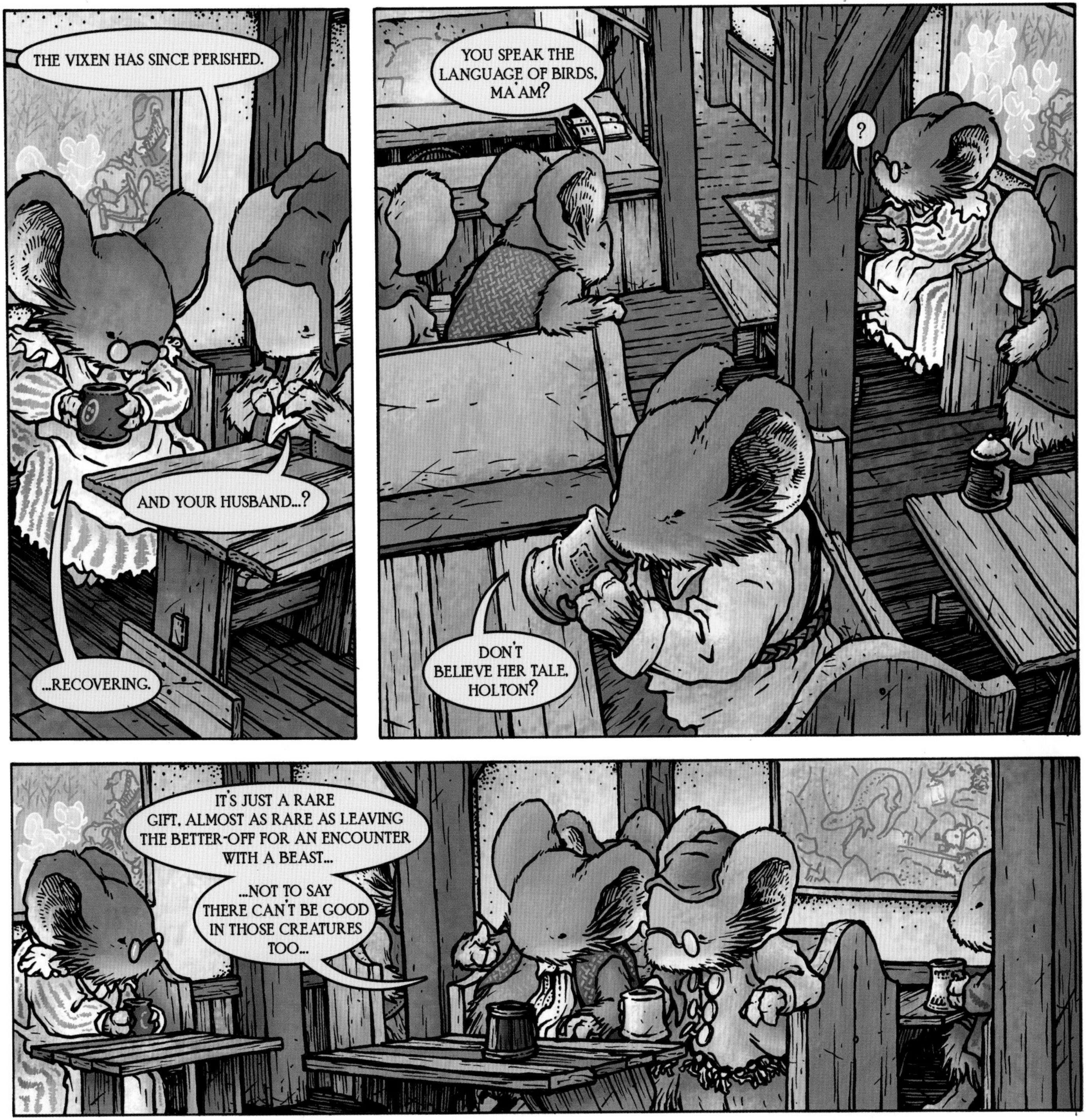
THE VIXEN HAS SINCE PERISHED.
AND YOUR HUSBAND...?
...RECOVERING.
YOU SPEAK THE LANGUAGE OF BIRDS, MA'AM?
?
DON'T BELIEVE HER TALE, HOLTON?
IT'S JUST A RARE GIFT, ALMOST AS RARE AS LEAVING THE BETTER-OFF FOR AN ENCOUNTER WITH A BEAST...
...NOT TO SAY THERE CAN'T BE GOOD IN THOSE CREATURES TOO...

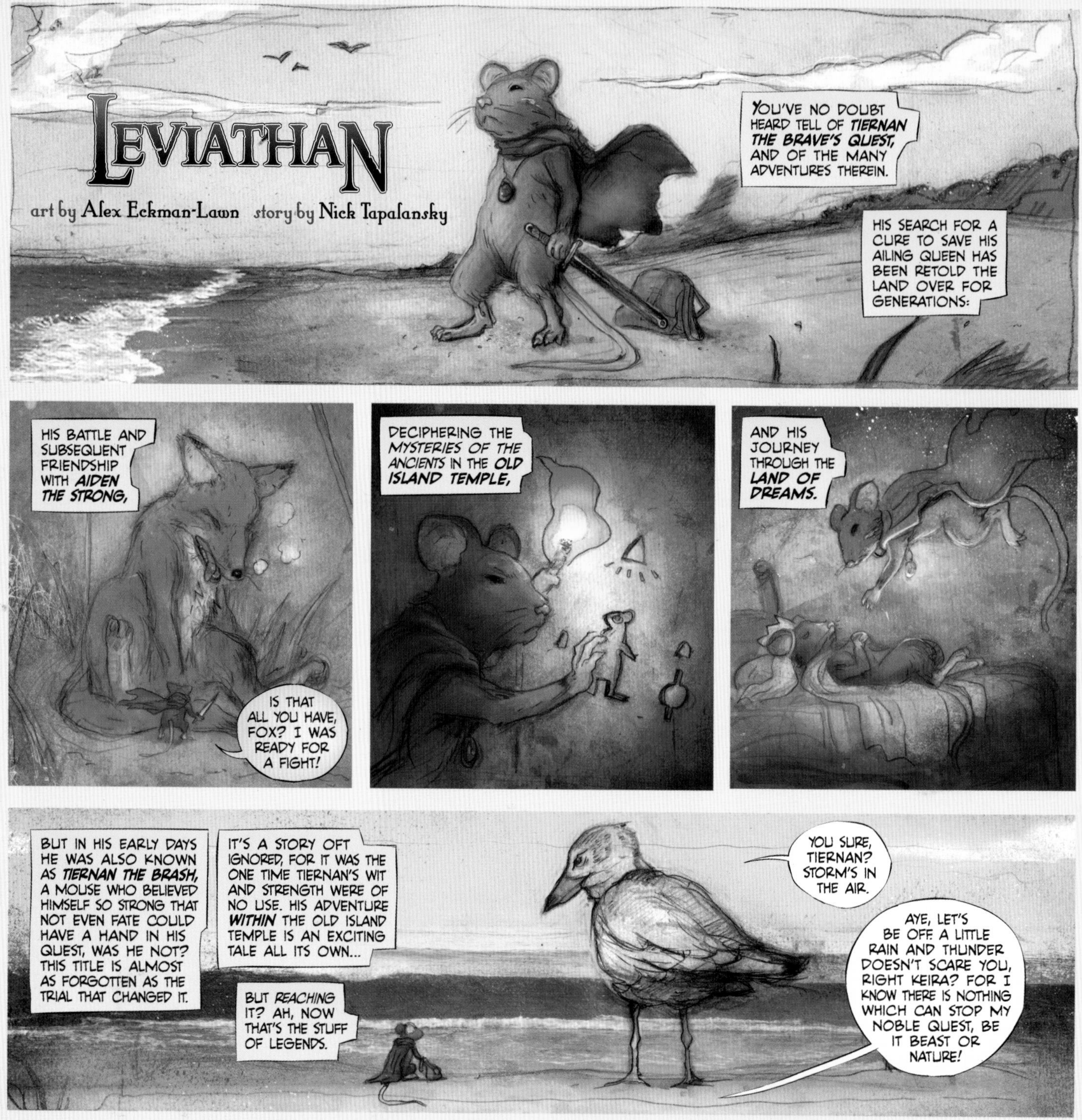
LEVIATHAN
art by Alex Eckman-Lawn story by Nick Tapalansky
YOU'VE NO DOUBT HEARD TELL OF TIERNAN THE BRAVE'S QUEST, AND OF THE MANY ADVENTURES THEREIN.
HIS SEARCH FOR A CURE TO SAVE HIS AILING QUEEN HAS BEEN RETOLD THE LAND OVER FOR GENERATIONS:
HIS BATTLE AND SUBSEQUENT FRIENDSHIP WITH AIDEN THE STRONG,
IS THAT ALL YOU HAVE, FOX? I WAS READY FOR A FIGHT!
DECIPHERING THE MYSTERIES OF THE ANCIENTS IN THE OLD ISLAND TEMPLE,
AND HIS JOURNEY THROUGH THE LAND OF DREAMS.
BUT IN HIS EARLY DAYS HE WAS ALSO KNOWN AS TIERNAN THE BRASH, A MOUSE WHO BELIEVED HIMSELF SO STRONG THAT NOT EVEN FATE COULD HAVE A HAND IN HIS QUEST, WAS HE NOT? THIS TITLE IS ALMOST AS FORGOTTEN AS THE TRIAL THAT CHANGED IT.
IT'S A STORY OFT IGNORED, FOR IT WAS THE ONE TIME TIERNAN'S WIT AND STRENGTH WERE OF NO USE. HIS ADVENTURE WITHIN THE OLD ISLAND TEMPLE IS AN EXCITING TALE ALL ITS OWN...
BUT REACHING IT? AH, NOW THAT'S THE STUFF OF LEGENDS.
YOU SURE, TIERNAN? STORM'S IN THE AIR.
AYE, LET'S BE OFF. A LITTLE RAIN AND THUNDER DOESN'T SCARE YOU, RIGHT KEIRA? FOR I KNOW THERE IS NOTHING WHICH CAN STOP MY NOBLE QUEST, BE IT BEAST OR NATURE!

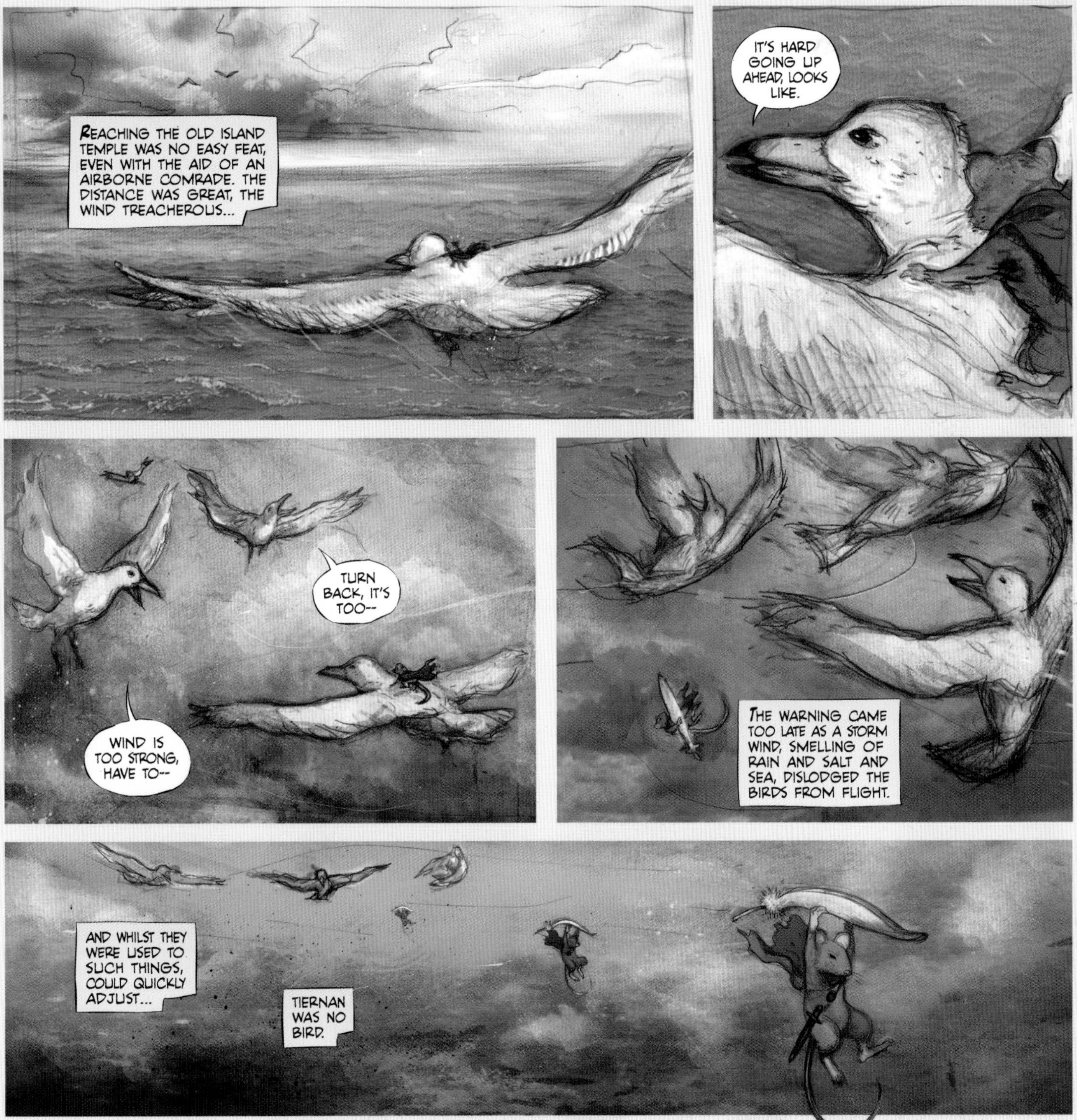
REACHING THE OLD ISLAND TEMPLE WAS NO EASY FEAT, EVEN WITH THE AID OF AN AIRBORNE COMRADE. THE DISTANCE WAS GREAT, THE WIND TREACHEROUS...
IT'S HARD GOING UP AHEAD, LOOKS LIKE.
TURN BACK, IT'S TOO--
WIND IS TOO STRONG, HAVE TO--
THE WARNING CAME TOO LATE AS A STORM WIND, SMELLING OF RAIN AND SALT AND SEA, DISLODGED THE BIRDS FROM FLIGHT.
AND WHILST THEY WERE USED TO SUCH THINGS, COULD QUICKLY ADJUST...
TIERNAN WAS NO BIRD.

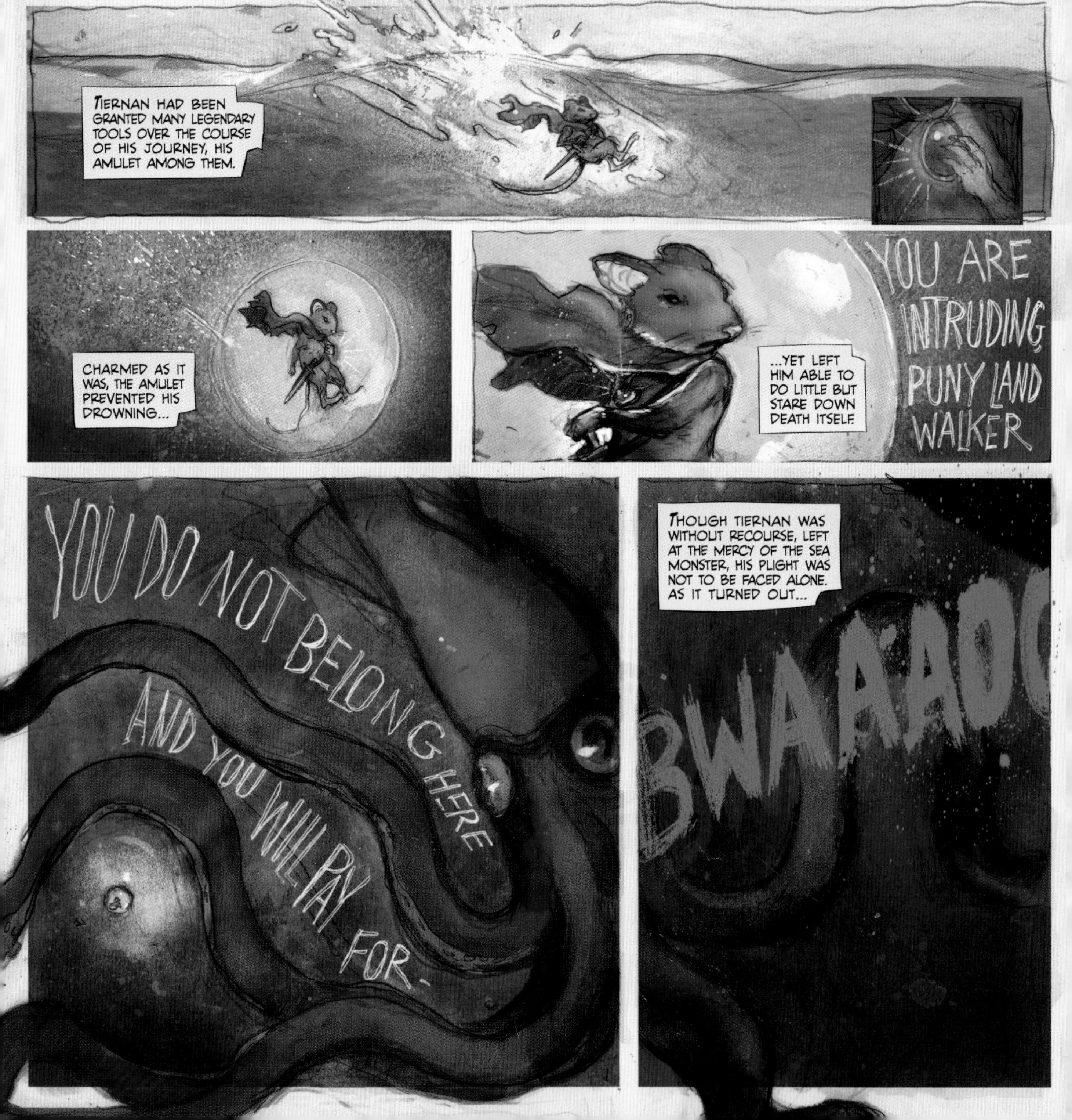
TIERNAN HAD BEEN GRANTED MANY LEGENDARY TOOLS OVER THE COURSE OF HIS JOURNEY, HIS AMULET AMONG THEM.
CHARMED AS IT WAS, THE AMULET PREVENTED HIS DROWNING...
...YET LEFT HIM ABLE TO DO LITTLE BUT STARE DOWN DEATH ITSELF.
YOU ARE INTRUDING, PUNY LAND WALKER
YOU DO NOT BELONG HERE
AND YOU WILL PAY FOR-
THOUGH TIERNAN WAS WITHOUT RECOURSE, LEFT AT THE MERCY OF THE SEA MONSTER, HIS PLIGHT WAS NOT TO BE FACED ALONE. AS IT TURNED OUT...
BWAAAO

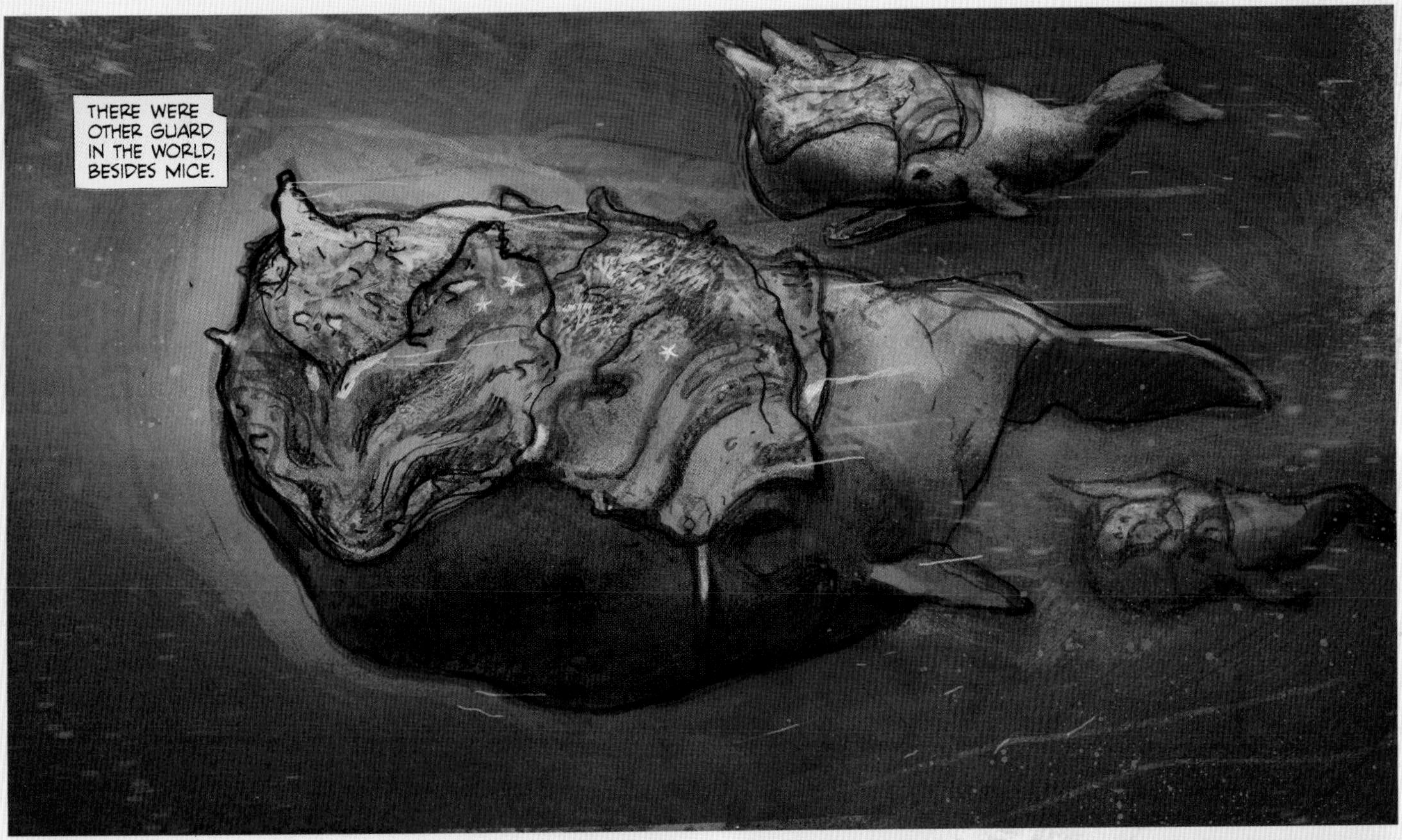
THERE WERE OTHER GUARD IN THE WORLD, BESIDES MICE.

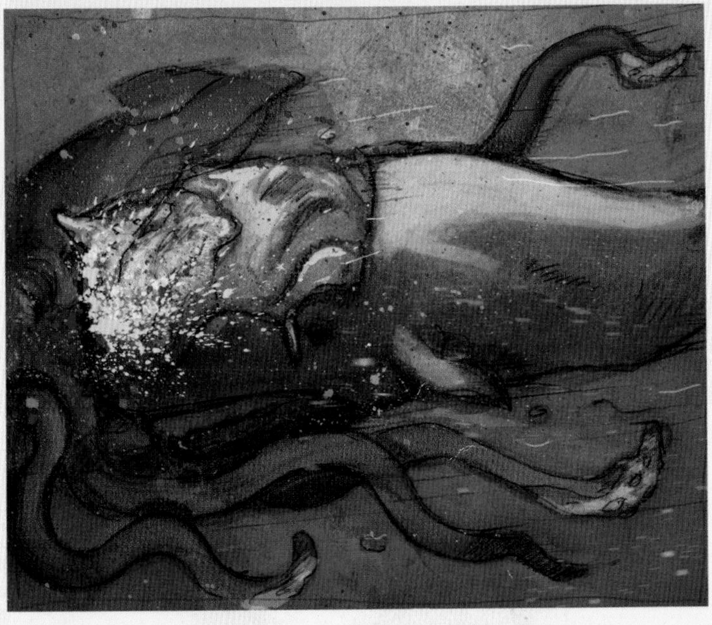

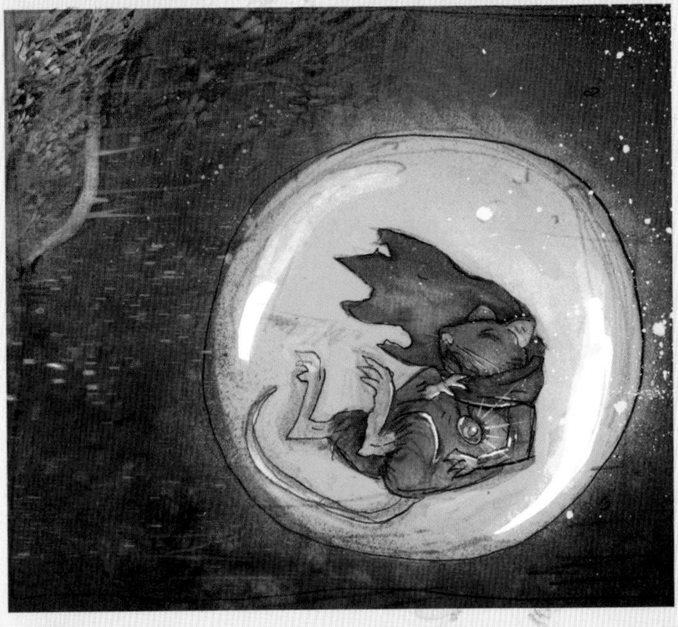

THERE IS GOOD IN EVERY WORLD, JUST AS THERE IS EVIL; SAFETY IN EACH LAND, JUST AS THERE IS DANGER.

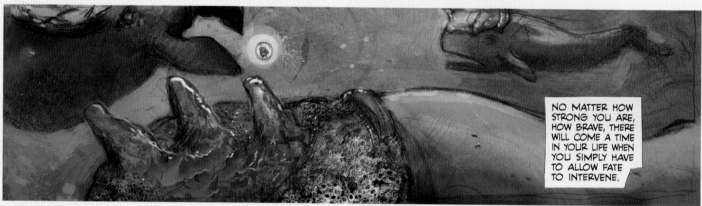

NO MATTER HOW STRONG YOU ARE, HOW BRAVE, THERE WILL COME A TIME IN YOUR LIFE WHEN YOU SIMPLY HAVE TO ALLOW FATE TO INTERVENE.

AND TRUST THE GOOD IN THE WORLD.

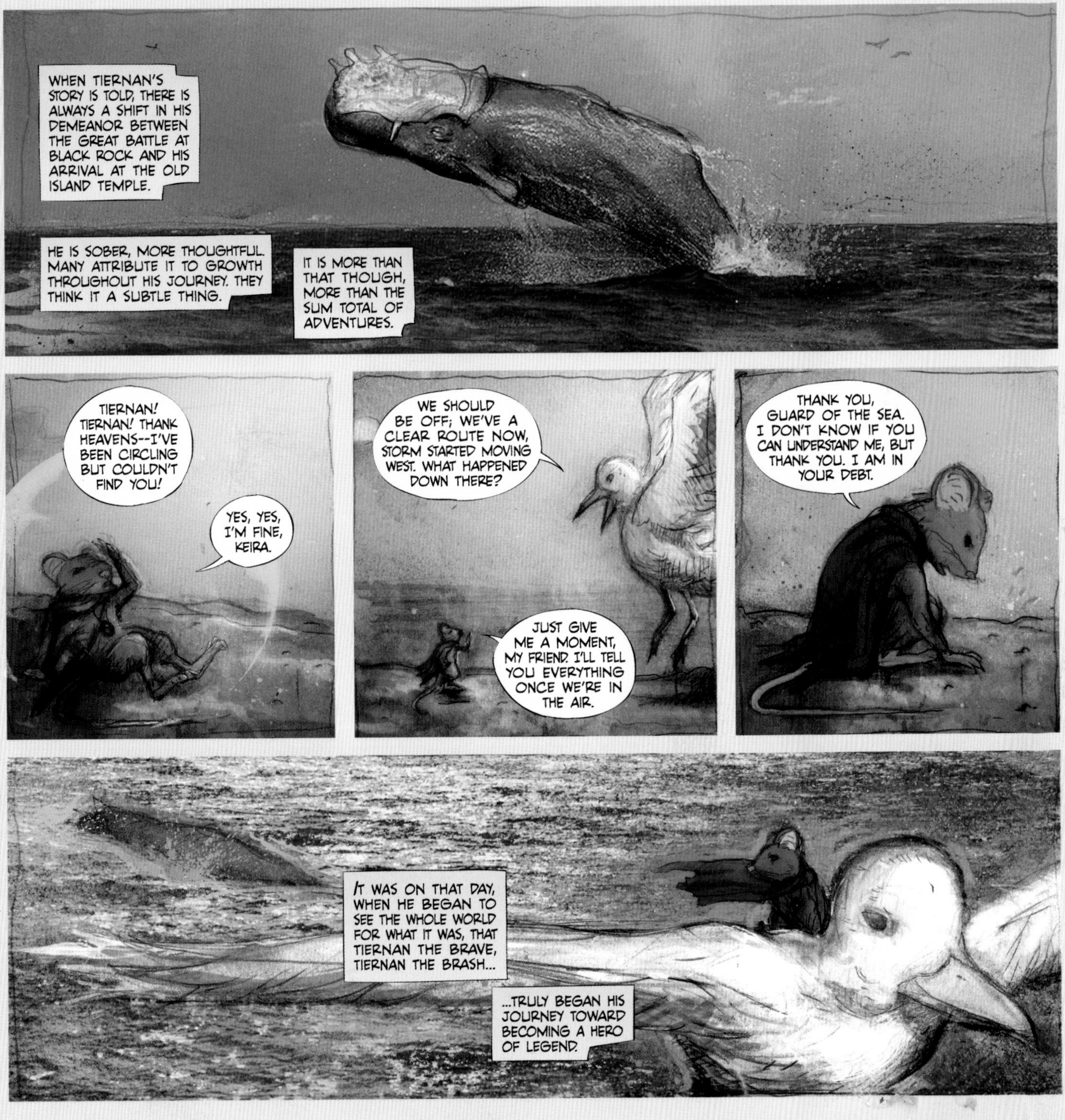
WHEN TIERNAN'S STORY IS TOLD, THERE IS ALWAYS A SHIFT IN HIS DEMEANOR BETWEEN THE GREAT BATTLE AT BLACK ROCK AND HIS ARRIVAL AT THE OLD ISLAND TEMPLE.
HE IS SOBER, MORE THOUGHTFUL. MANY ATTRIBUTE IT TO GROWTH THROUGHOUT HIS JOURNEY. THEY THINK IT A SUBTLE THING.
IT IS MORE THAN THAT THOUGH, MORE THAN THE SUM TOTAL OF ADVENTURES.
TIERNAN! TIERNAN! THANK HEAVENS--I'VE BEEN CIRCLING BUT COULDN'T FIND YOU!
YES, YES, I'M FINE, KEIRA.
WE SHOULD BE OFF; WE'VE A CLEAR ROUTE NOW, STORM STARTED MOVING WEST. WHAT HAPPENED DOWN THERE?
JUST GIVE ME A MOMENT, MY FRIEND. I'LL TELL YOU EVERYTHING ONCE WE'RE IN THE AIR.
THANK YOU, GUARD OF THE SEA. I DON'T KNOW IF YOU CAN UNDERSTAND ME, BUT THANK YOU. I AM IN YOUR DEBT.
IT WAS ON THAT DAY, WHEN HE BEGAN TO SEE THE WHOLE WORLD FOR WHAT IT WAS, THAT TIERNAN THE BRAVE, TIERNAN THE BRASH...
...TRULY BEGAN HIS JOURNEY TOWARD BECOMING A HERO OF LEGEND.

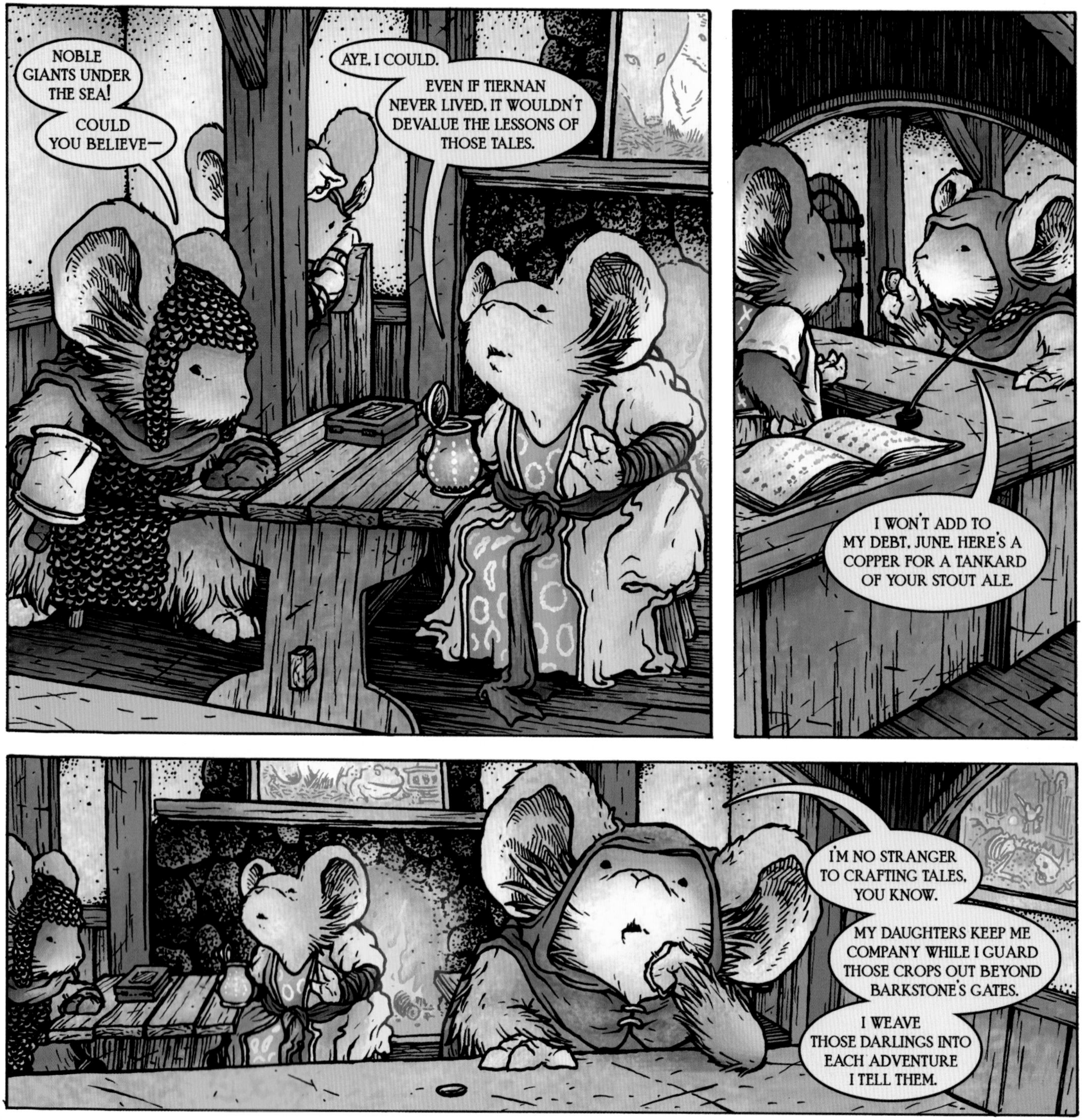
NOBLE GIANTS UNDER THE SEA!
COULD YOU BELIEVE—
AYE, I COULD.
EVEN IF TIERNAN NEVER LIVED, IT WOULDN'T DEVALUE THE LESSONS OF THOSE TALES.
I WON'T ADD TO MY DEBT, JUNE. HERE'S A COPPER FOR A TANKARD OF YOUR STOUT ALE.
I'M NO STRANGER TO CRAFTING TALES, YOU KNOW.
MY DAUGHTERS KEEP ME COMPANY WHILE I GUARD THOSE CROPS OUT BEYOND BARKSTONE'S GATES.
I WEAVE THOSE DARLINGS INTO EACH ADVENTURE I TELL THEM.

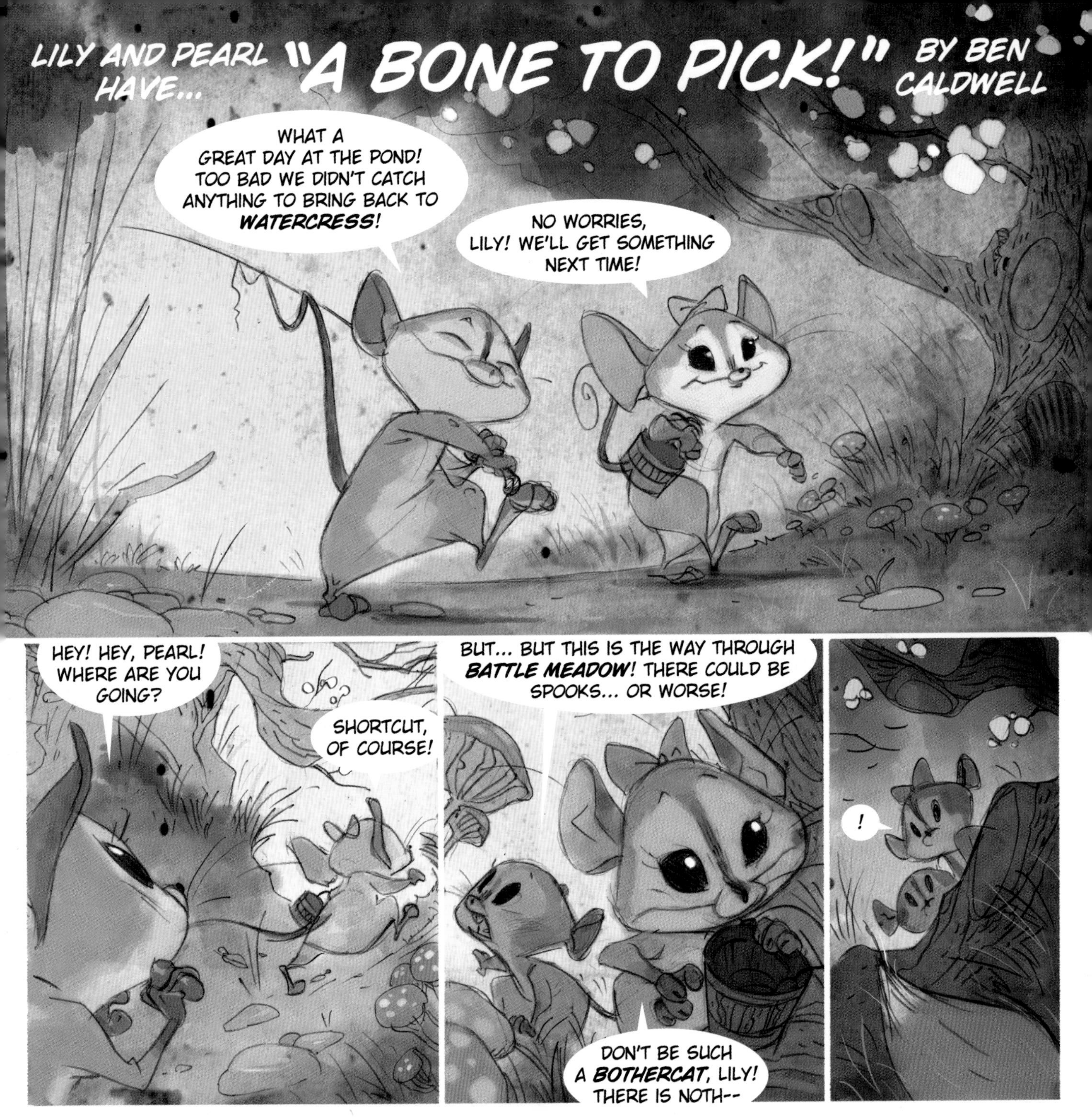
LILY AND PEARL HAVE...
"A BONE TO PICK!"
BY BEN CALDWELL
WHAT A GREAT DAY AT THE POND! TOO BAD WE DIDN'T CATCH ANYTHING TO BRING BACK TO WATERCRESS!
NO WORRIES, LILY! WE'LL GET SOMETHING NEXT TIME!
HEY! HEY, PEARL! WHERE ARE YOU GOING?
SHORTCUT, OF COURSE!
BUT... BUT THIS IS THE WAY THROUGH BATTLE MEADOW! THERE COULD BE SPOOKS... OR WORSE!
DON'T BE SUCH A BOTHERCAT, LILY! THERE IS NOTH--
!

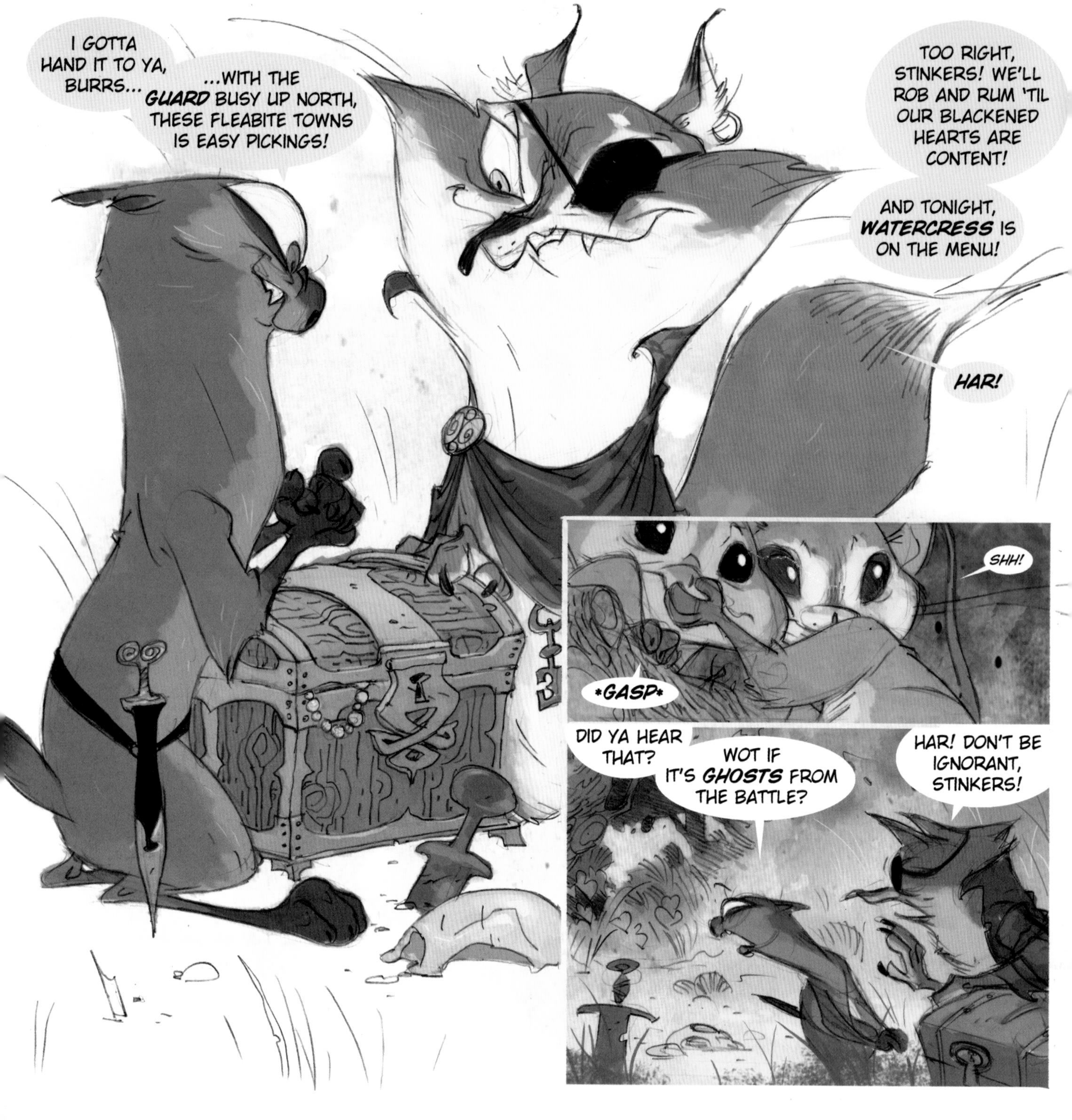
I GOTTA HAND IT TO YA, BURRS...
...WITH THE GUARD BUSY UP NORTH, THESE FLEABITE TOWNS IS EASY PICKINGS!
TOO RIGHT, STINKERS! WE'LL ROB AND RUM 'TIL OUR BLACKENED HEARTS ARE CONTENT!
AND TONIGHT, WATERCRESS IS ON THE MENU!
HAR!
SHH!
GASP
DID YA HEAR THAT?
WOT IF IT'S GHOSTS FROM THE BATTLE?
HAR! DON'T BE IGNORANT, STINKERS!

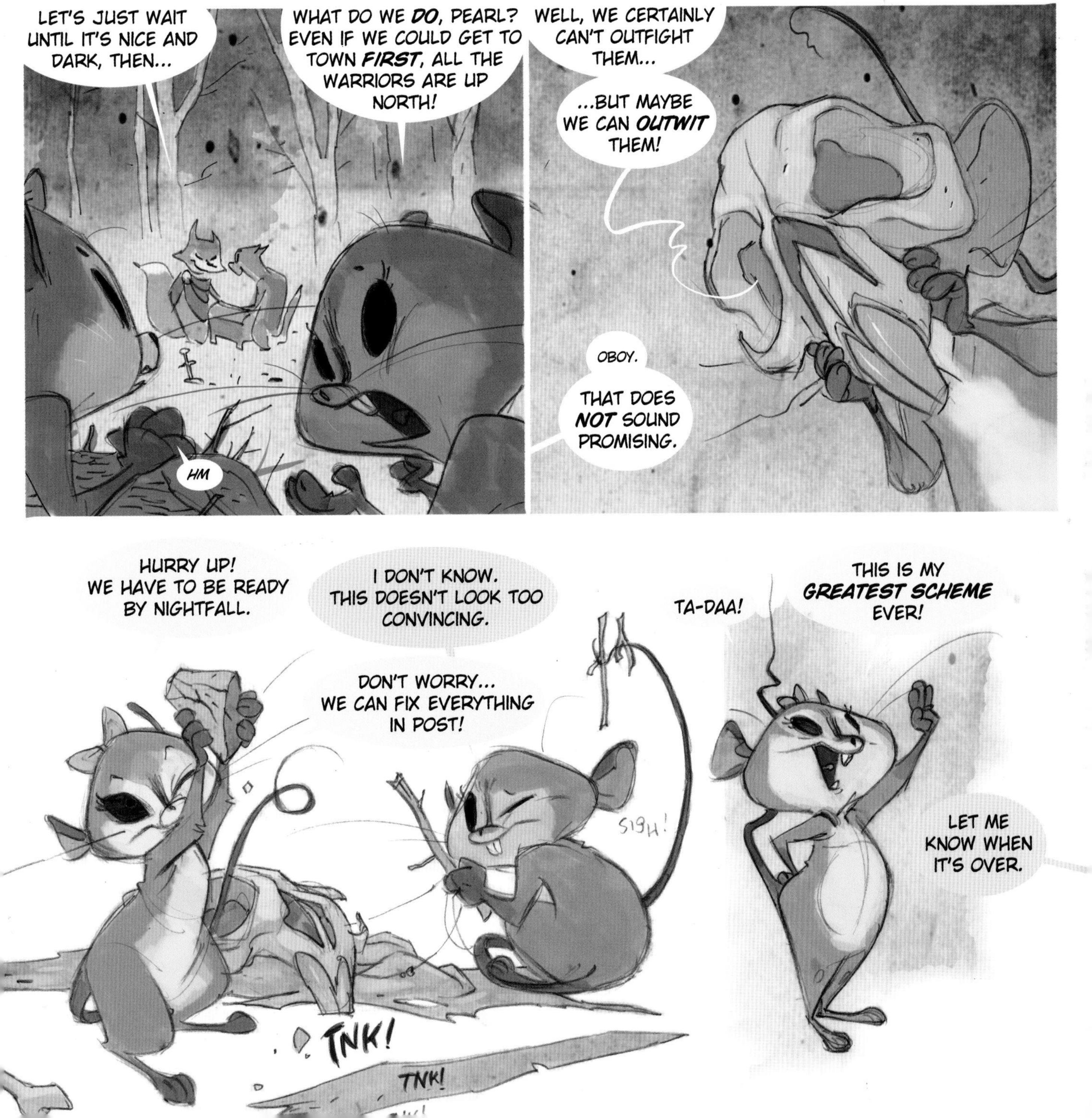
LET'S JUST WAIT UNTIL IT'S NICE AND DARK, THEN...
WHAT DO WE DO, PEARL? EVEN IF WE COULD GET TO TOWN FIRST, ALL THE WARRIORS ARE UP NORTH!
HM
WELL, WE CERTAINLY CAN'T OUTFIGHT THEM...
...BUT MAYBE WE CAN OUTWIT THEM!
OBOY.
THAT DOES NOT SOUND PROMISING.
HURRY UP! WE HAVE TO BE READY BY NIGHTFALL.
I DON'T KNOW. THIS DOESN'T LOOK TOO CONVINCING.
DON'T WORRY... WE CAN FIX EVERYTHING IN POST!
SIGH!
TNK!
TNK!
TA-DAA!
THIS IS MY GREATEST SCHEME EVER!
LET ME KNOW WHEN IT'S OVER.

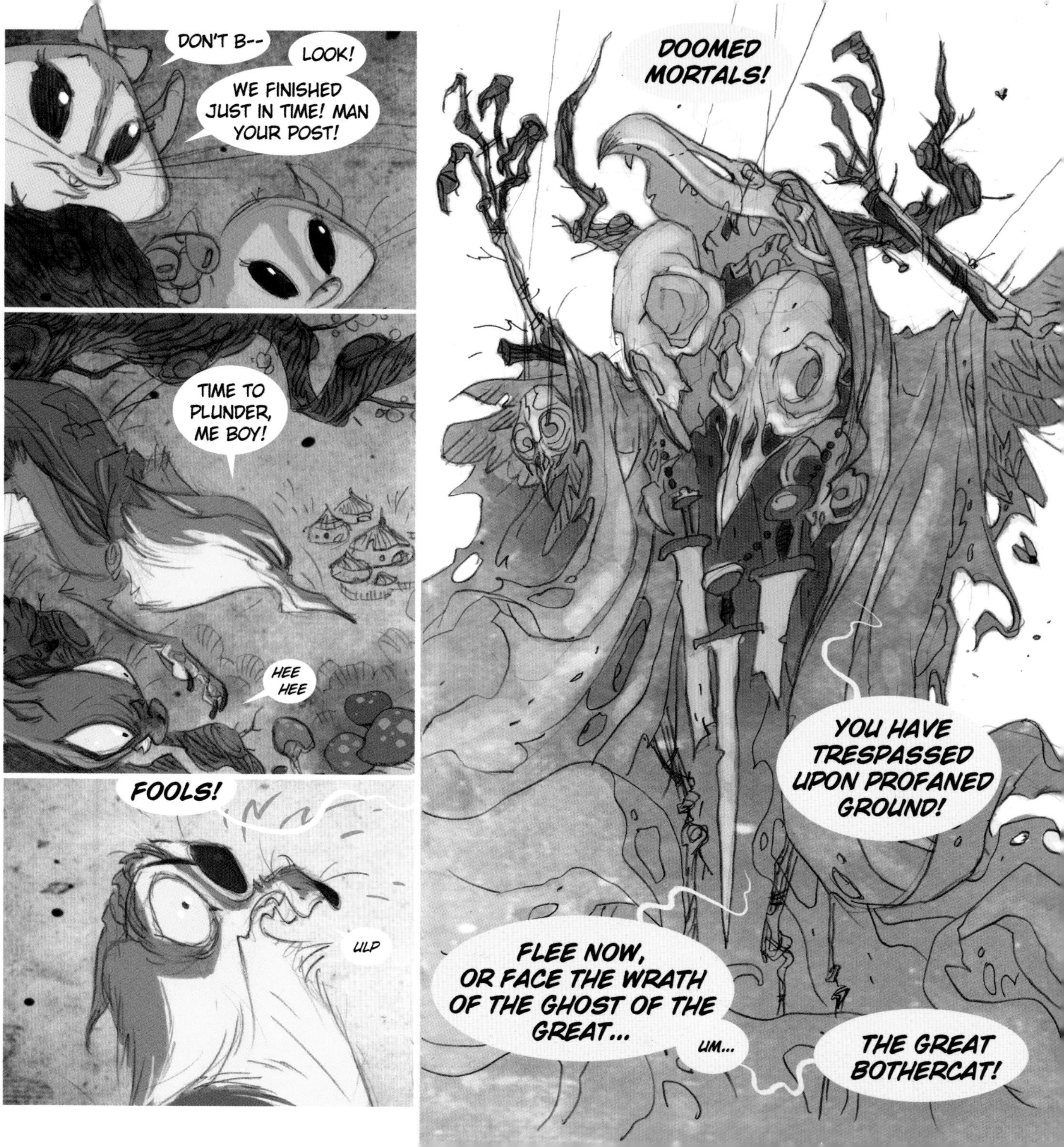
DON'T B--
LOOK!
WE FINISHED JUST IN TIME! MAN YOUR POST!
TIME TO PLUNDER, ME BOY!
HEE HEE
FOOLS!
ULP
DOOMED MORTALS!
YOU HAVE TRESPASSED UPON PROFANED GROUND!
FLEE NOW, OR FACE THE WRATH OF THE GHOST OF THE GREAT...
UM...
THE GREAT BOTHERCAT!

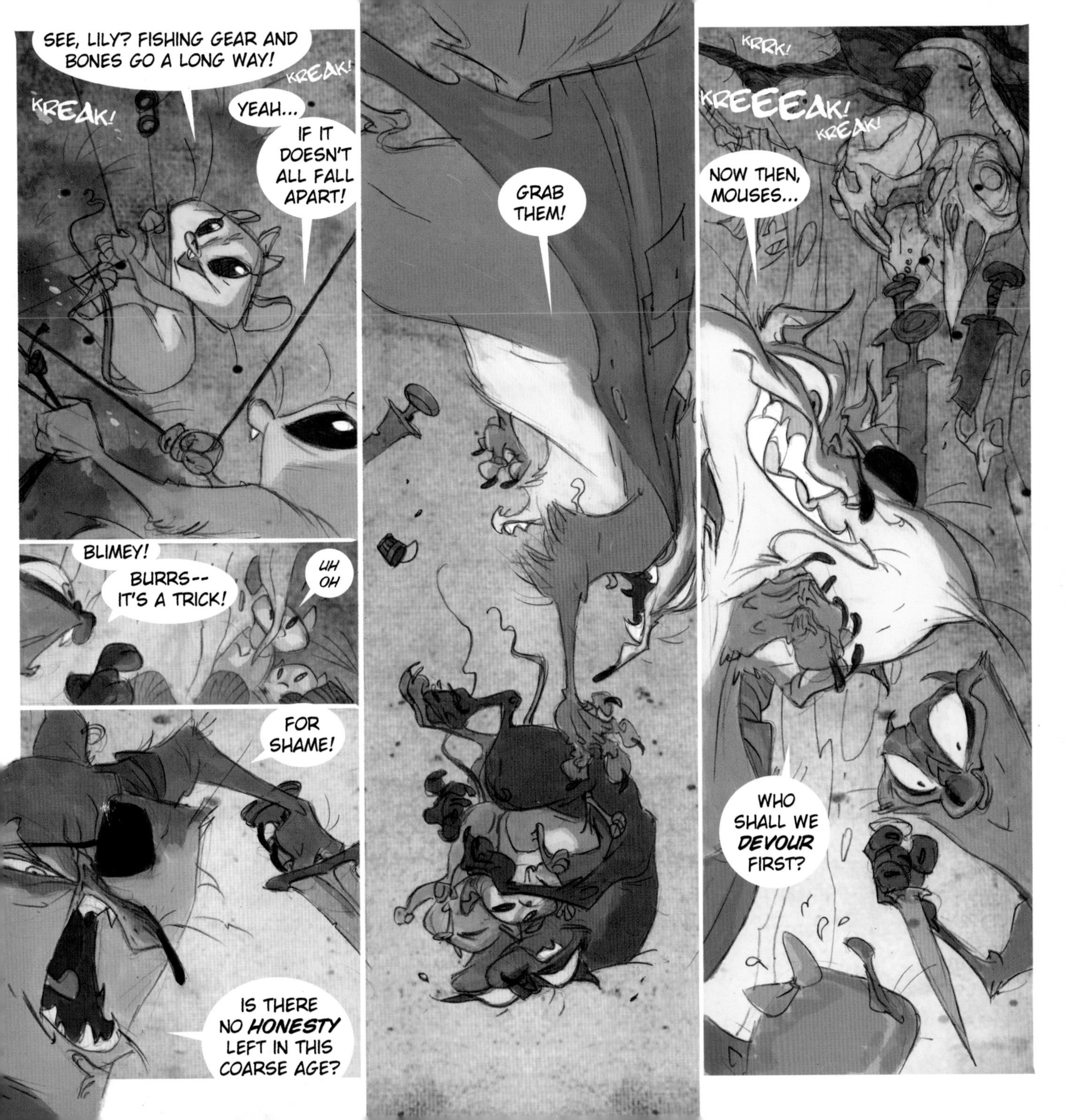
SEE, LILY? FISHING GEAR AND BONES GO A LONG WAY!
KREAK!
KREAK!
YEAH...
IF IT DOESN'T ALL FALL APART!
BLIMEY!
BURRS-- IT'S A TRICK!
UH OH
FOR SHAME!
IS THERE NO HONESTY LEFT IN THIS COARSE AGE?
GRAB THEM!
KRRK!
KREEEEAK!
KREAK!
NOW THEN, MOUSES...
WHO SHALL WE DEVOUR FIRST?

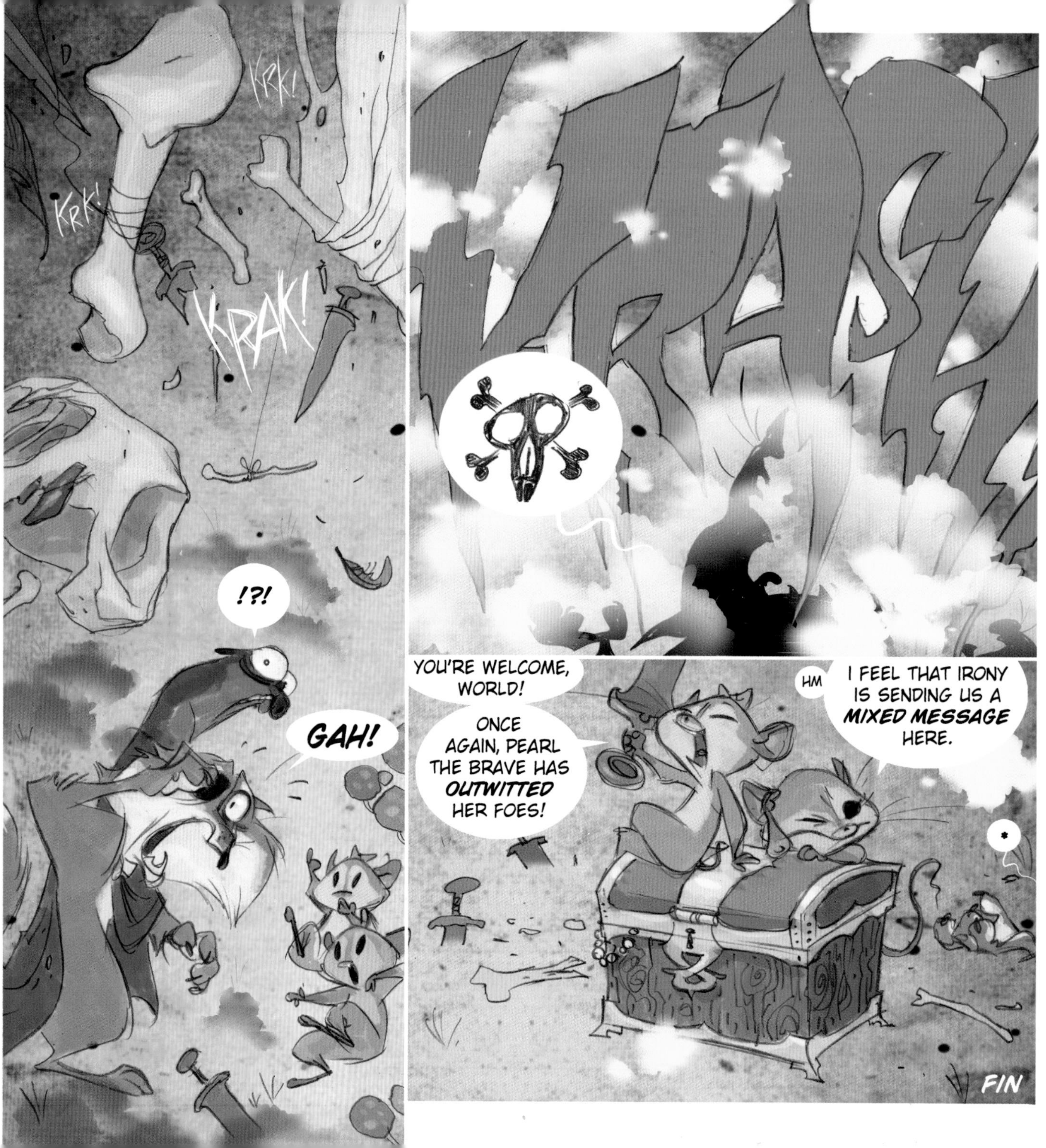
KRK!
KRK!
KRAK!
!?!
GAH!
YOU'RE WELCOME, WORLD!
ONCE AGAIN, PEARL THE BRAVE HAS OUTWITTED HER FOES!
HM
I FEEL THAT IRONY IS SENDING US A MIXED MESSAGE HERE.
FIN

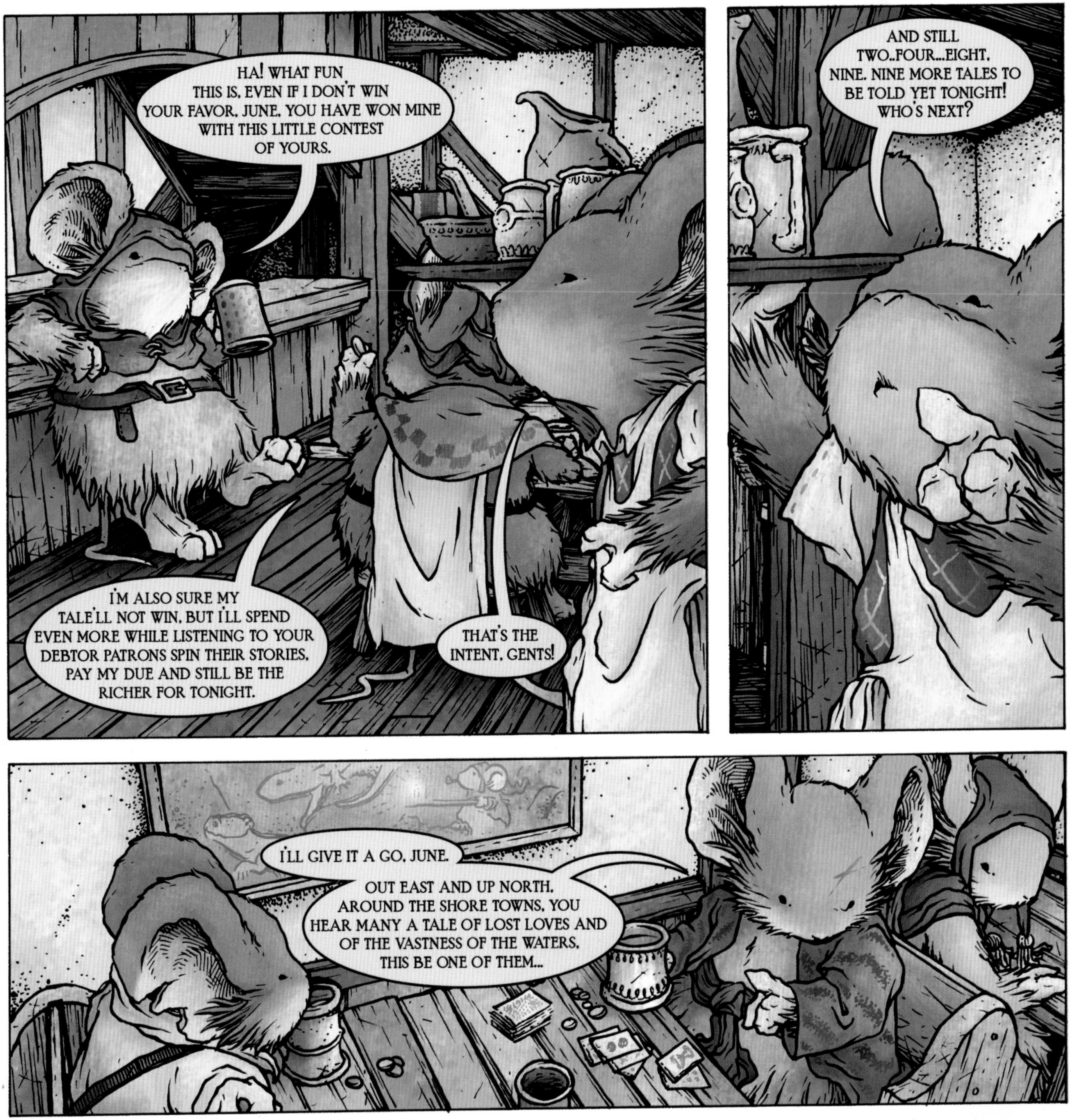
HA! WHAT FUN THIS IS, EVEN IF I DON'T WIN YOUR FAVOR, JUNE, YOU HAVE WON MINE WITH THIS LITTLE CONTEST OF YOURS.
I'M ALSO SURE MY TALE'LL NOT WIN, BUT I'LL SPEND EVEN MORE WHILE LISTENING TO YOUR DEBTOR PATRONS SPIN THEIR STORIES, PAY MY DUE AND STILL BE THE RICHER FOR TONIGHT.
THAT'S THE INTENT, GENTS!
AND STILL TWO..FOUR...EIGHT, NINE. NINE MORE TALES TO BE TOLD YET TONIGHT! WHO'S NEXT?
I'LL GIVE IT A GO, JUNE.
OUT EAST AND UP NORTH, AROUND THE SHORE TOWNS, YOU HEAR MANY A TALE OF LOST LOVES AND OF THE VASTNESS OF THE WATERS, THIS BE ONE OF THEM...

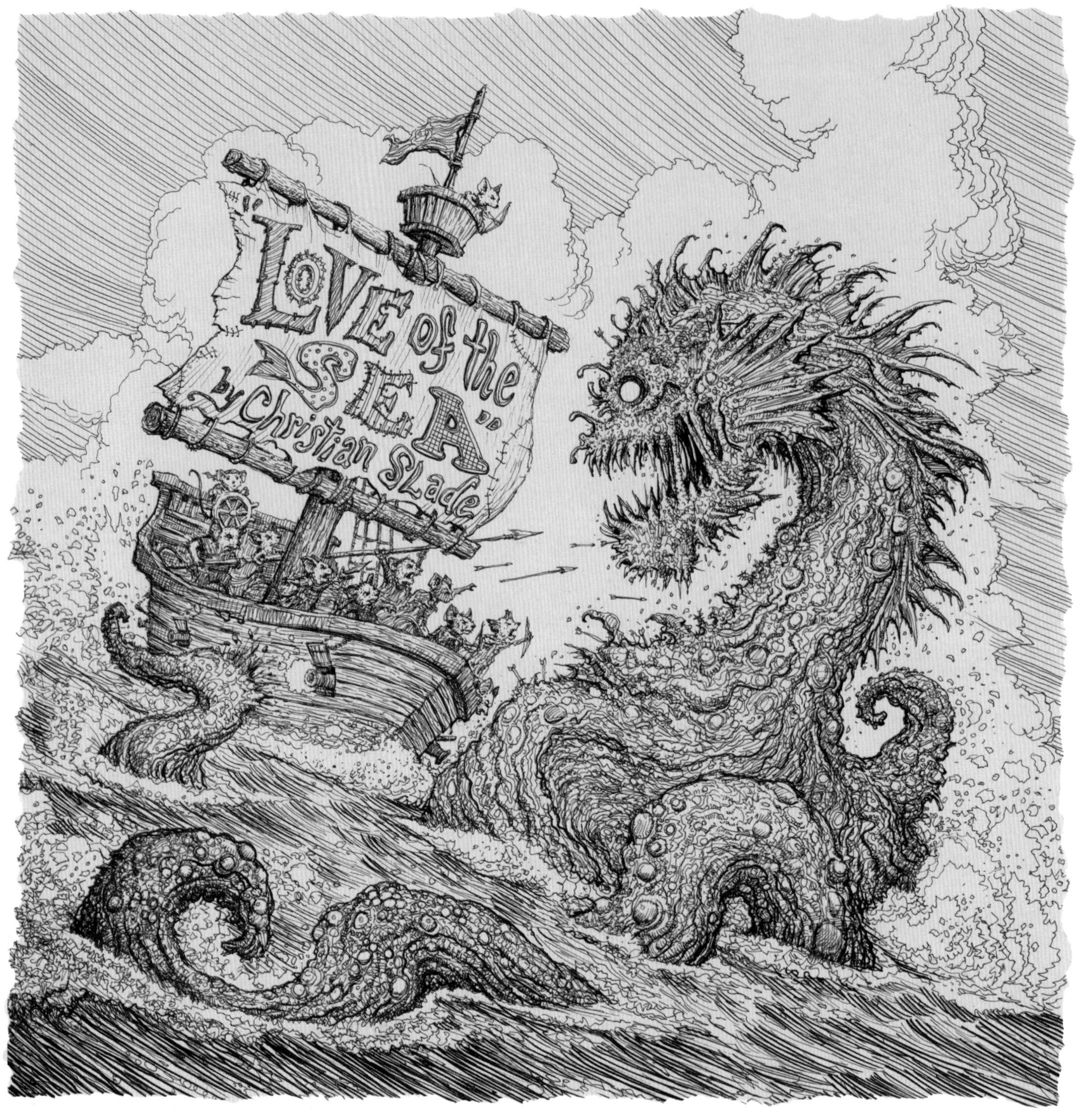
"LOVE of the SEA"
by Christian Slade

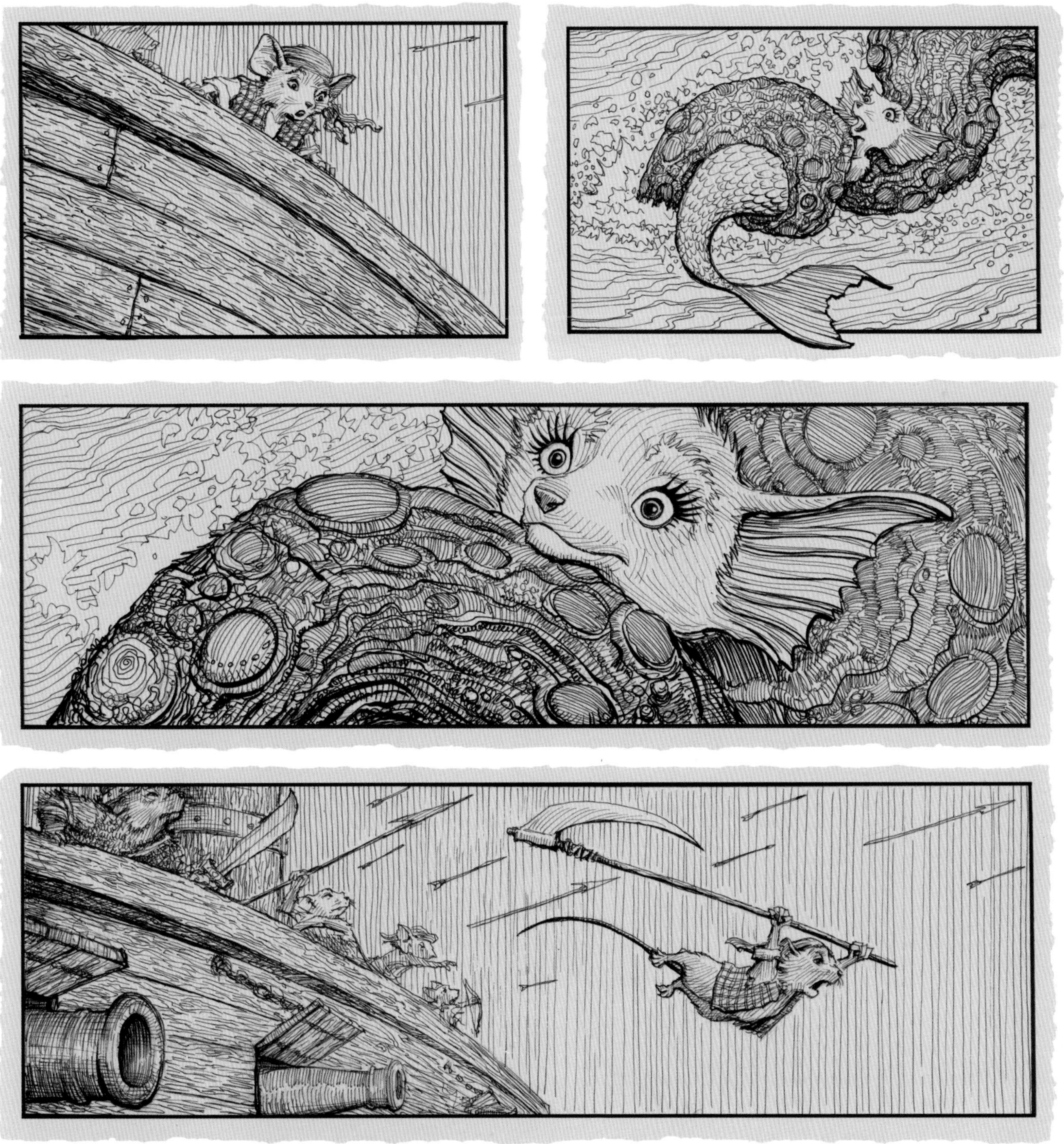

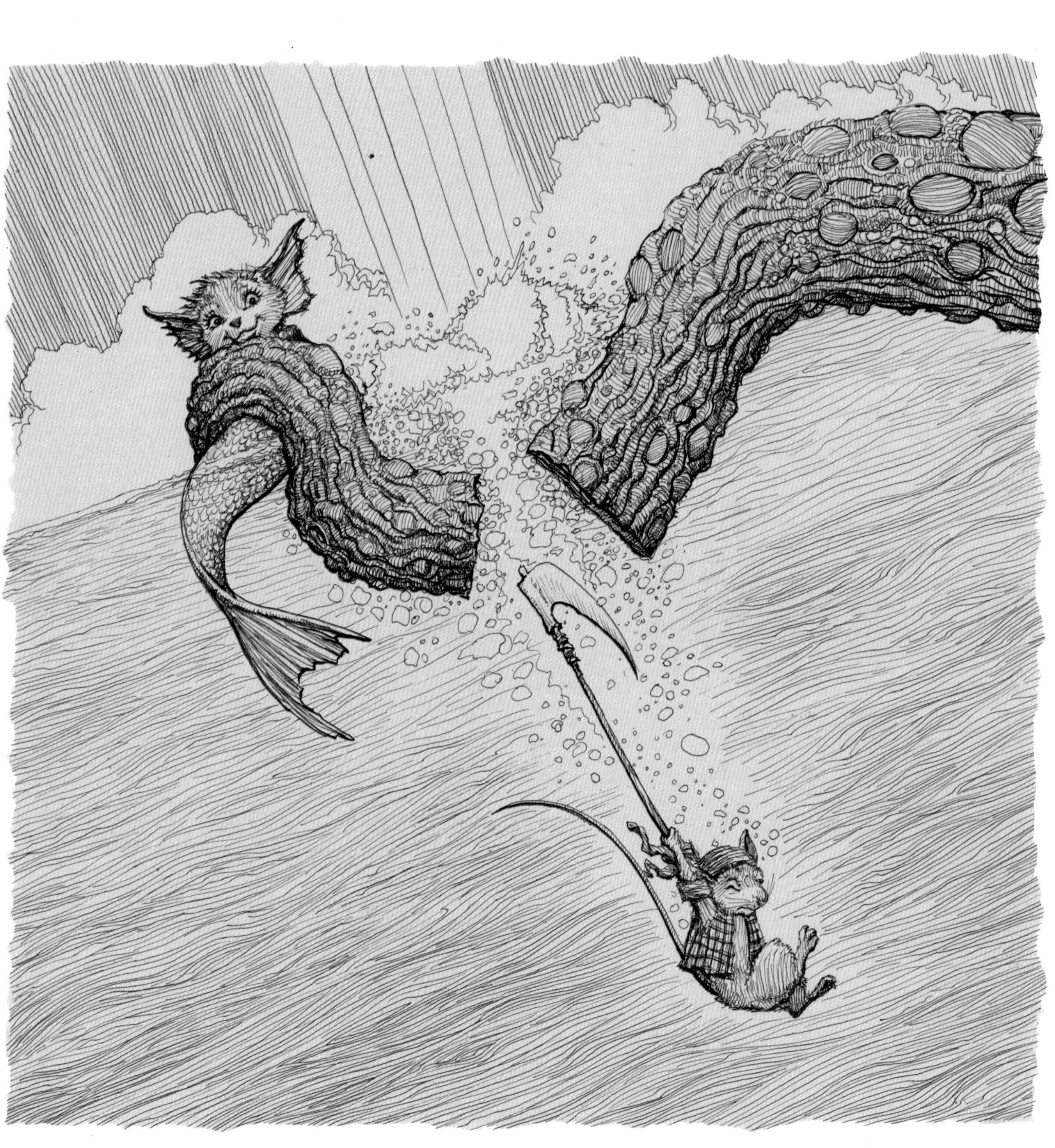

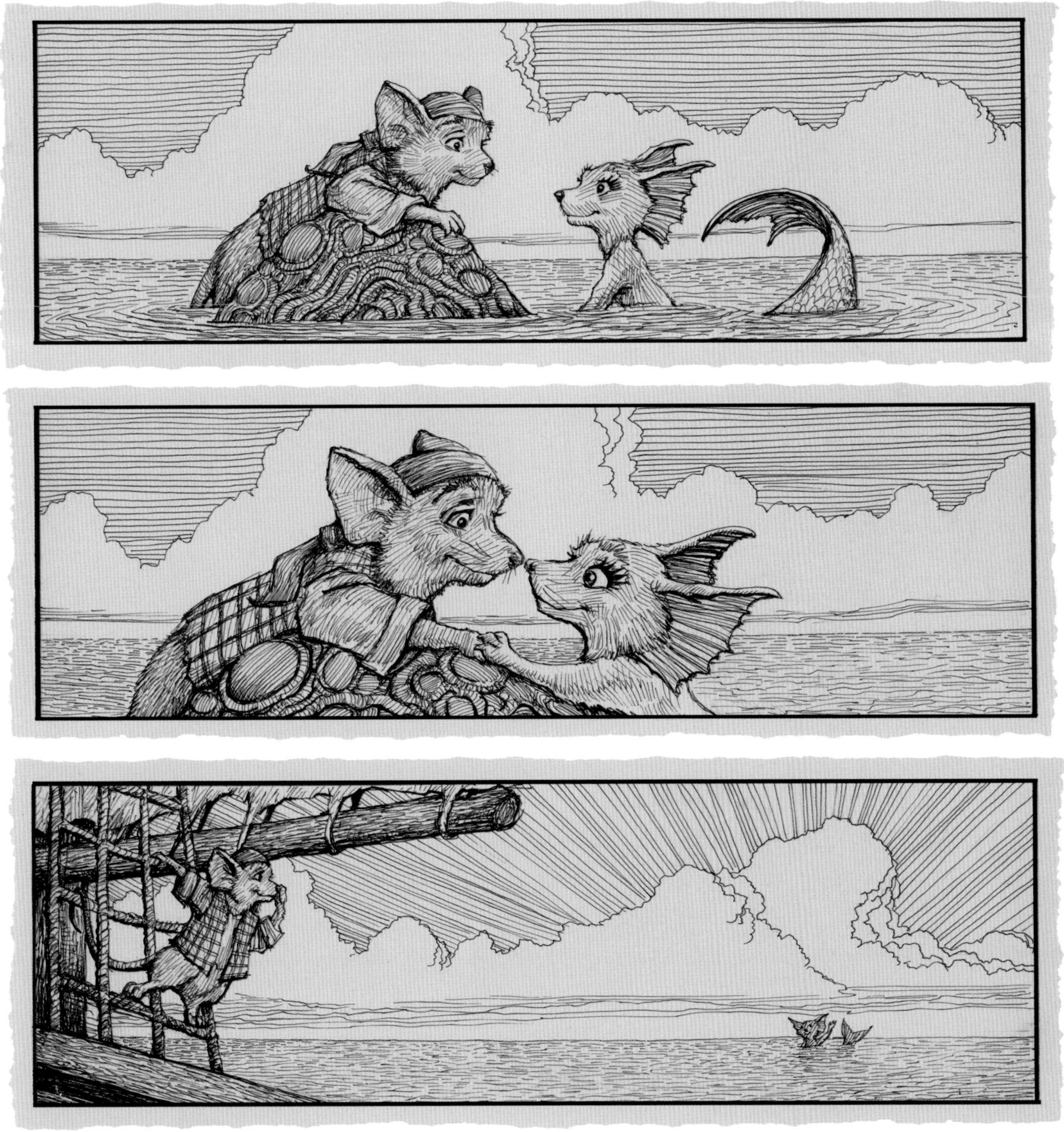

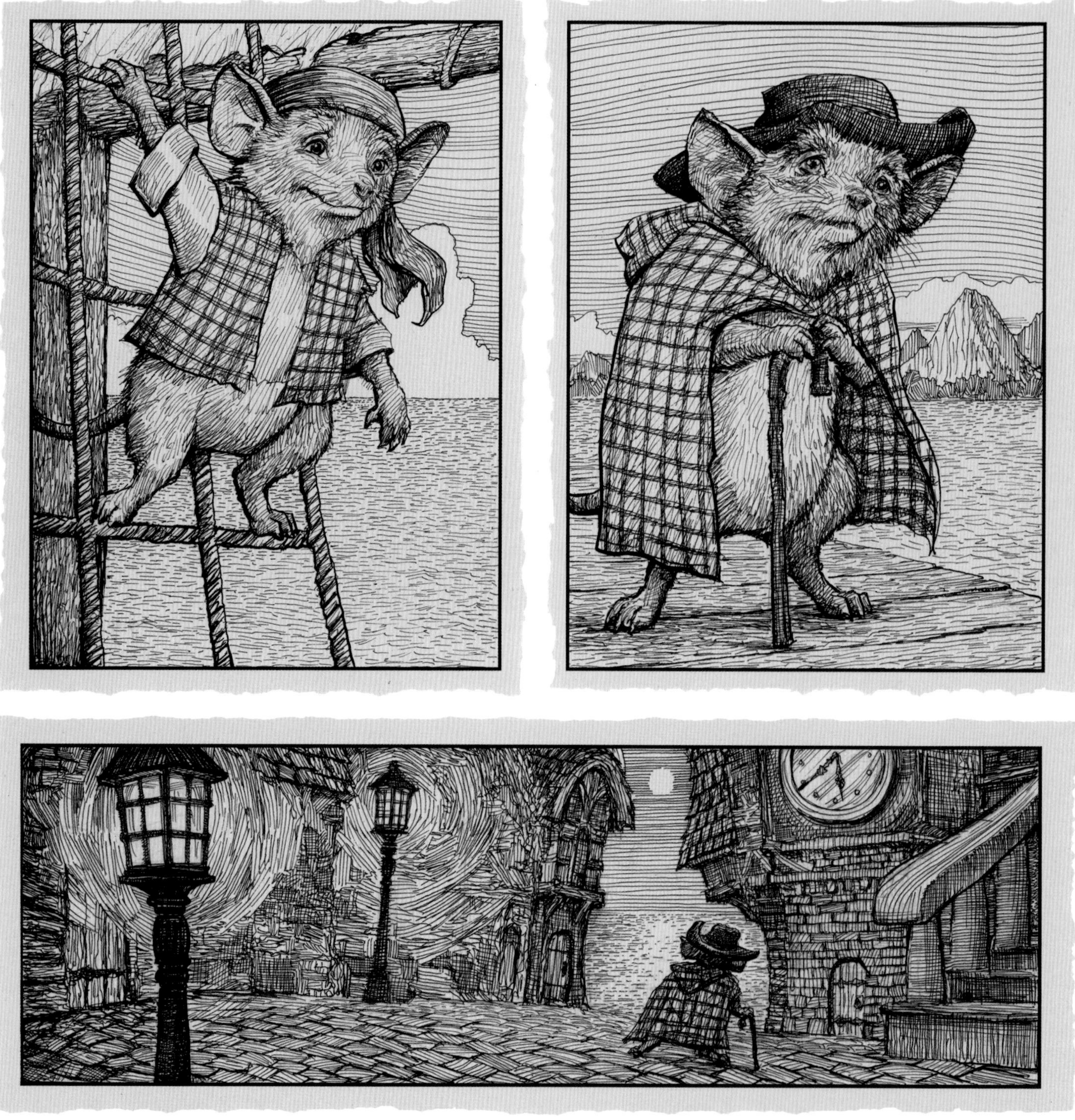

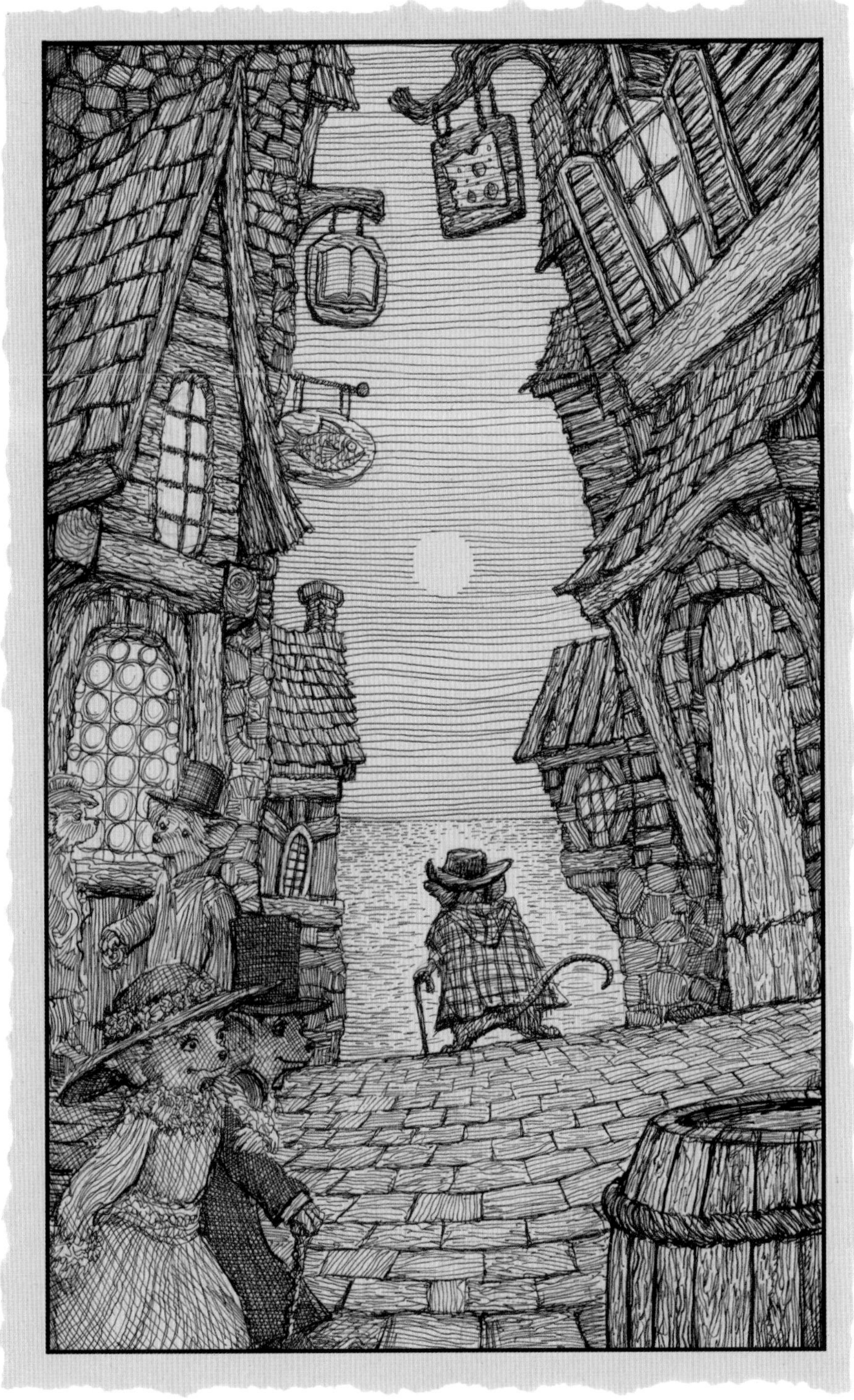

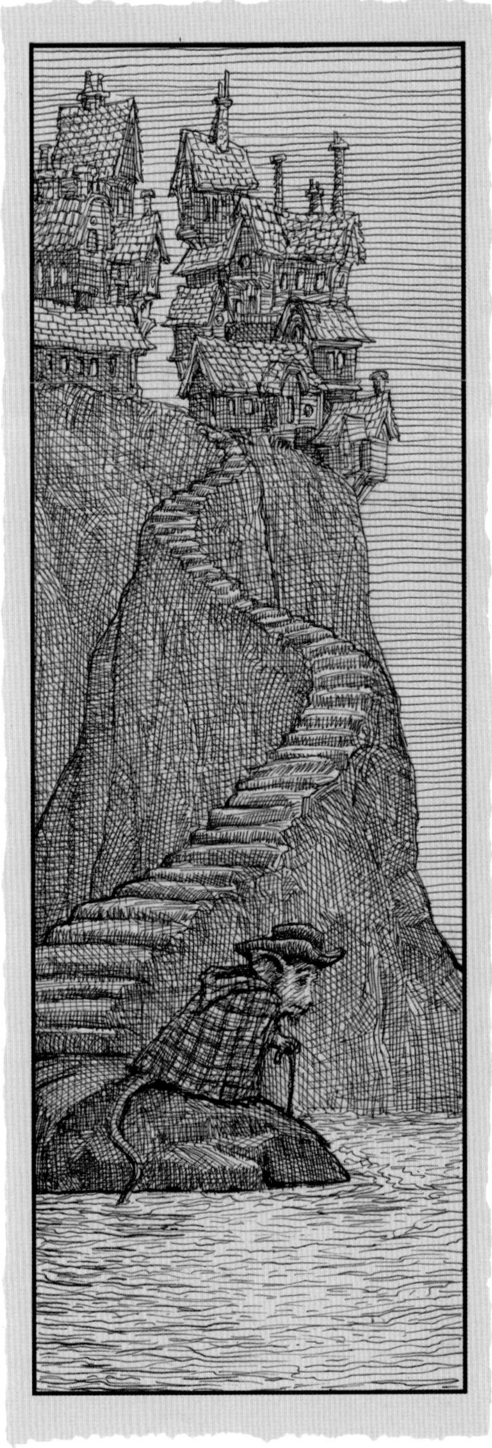

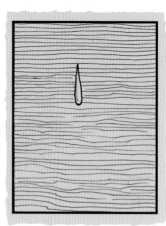
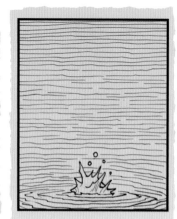

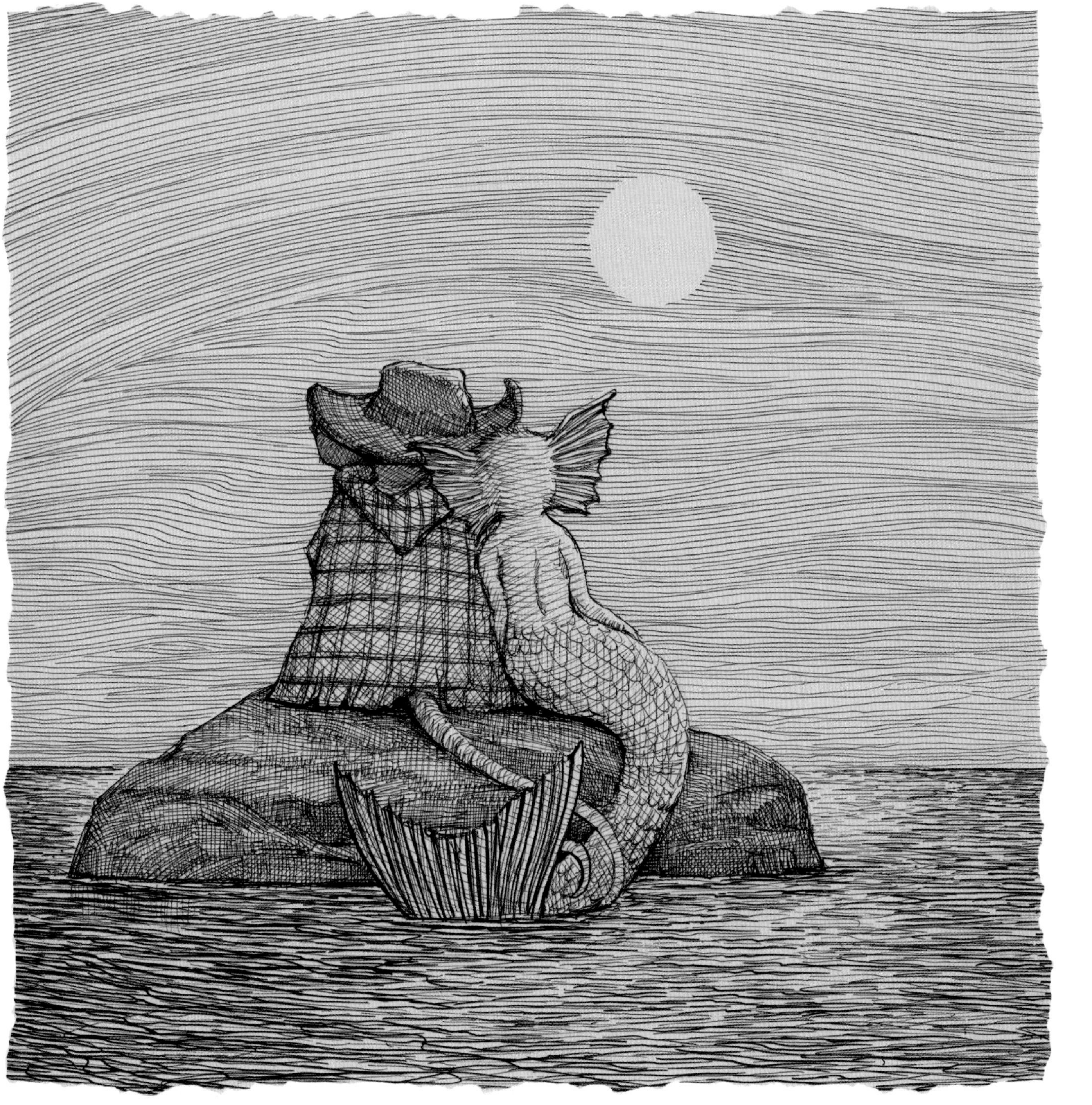

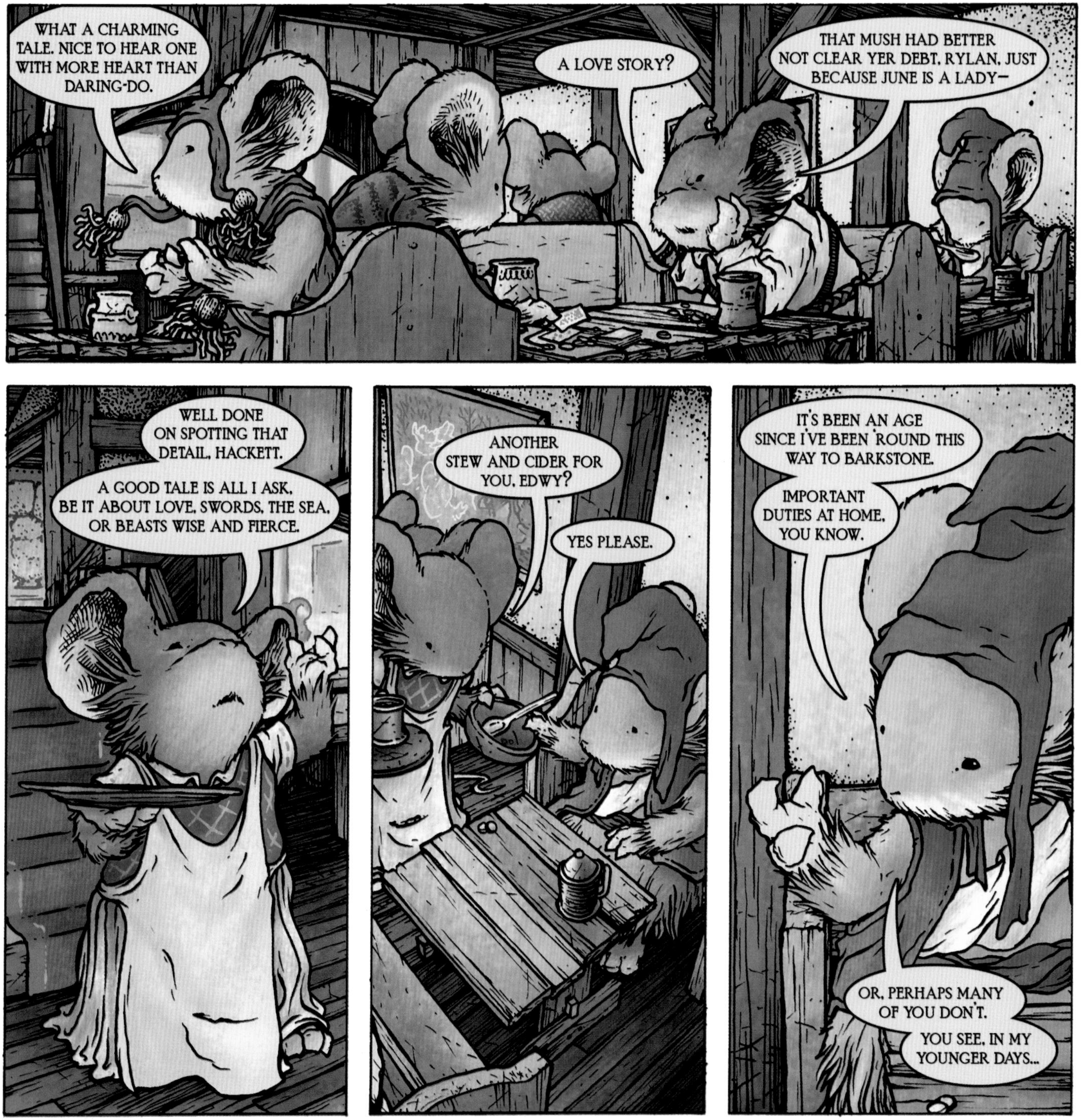
WHAT A CHARMING TALE. NICE TO HEAR ONE WITH MORE HEART THAN DARING-DO.
A LOVE STORY?
THAT MUSH HAD BETTER NOT CLEAR YER DEBT, RYLAN, JUST BECAUSE JUNE IS A LADY—
WELL DONE ON SPOTTING THAT DETAIL, HACKETT.
A GOOD TALE IS ALL I ASK, BE IT ABOUT LOVE, SWORDS, THE SEA, OR BEASTS WISE AND FIERCE.
ANOTHER STEW AND CIDER FOR YOU, EDWY?
YES PLEASE.
IT'S BEEN AN AGE SINCE I'VE BEEN 'ROUND THIS WAY TO BARKSTONE.
IMPORTANT DUTIES AT HOME, YOU KNOW.
OR, PERHAPS MANY OF YOU DON'T.
YOU SEE, IN MY YOUNGER DAYS...

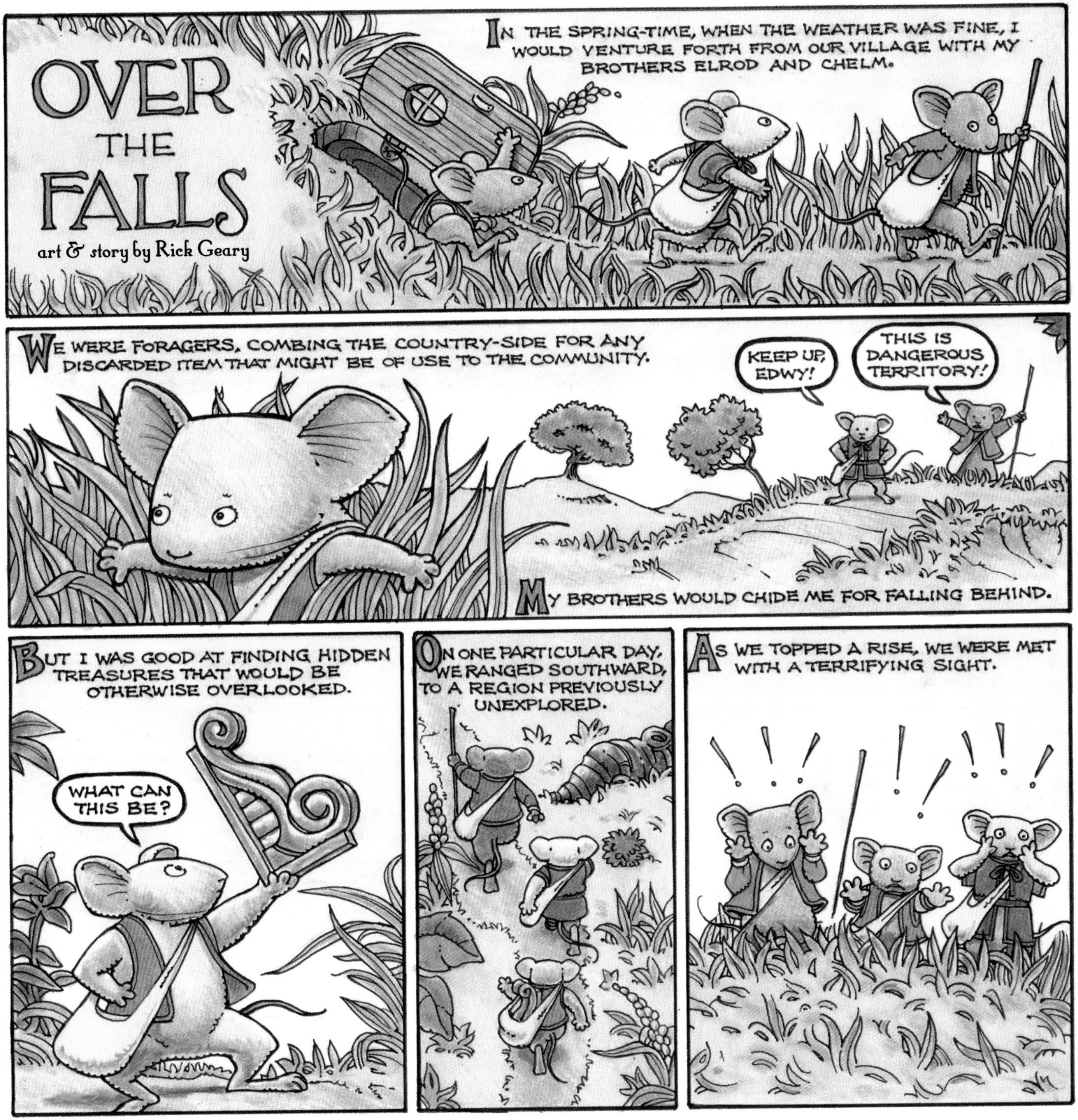
OVER THE FALLS
art & story by Rick Geary
IN THE SPRING-TIME, WHEN THE WEATHER WAS FINE, I WOULD VENTURE FORTH FROM OUR VILLAGE WITH MY BROTHERS ELROD AND CHELM.
WE WERE FORAGERS, COMBING THE COUNTRY-SIDE FOR ANY DISCARDED ITEM THAT MIGHT BE OF USE TO THE COMMUNITY.
KEEP UP, EDWY!
THIS IS DANGEROUS TERRITORY!
MY BROTHERS WOULD CHIDE ME FOR FALLING BEHIND.
BUT I WAS GOOD AT FINDING HIDDEN TREASURES THAT WOULD BE OTHERWISE OVERLOOKED.
WHAT CAN THIS BE?
ON ONE PARTICULAR DAY, WE RANGED SOUTHWARD, TO A REGION PREVIOUSLY UNEXPLORED.
AS WE TOPPED A RISE, WE WERE MET WITH A TERRIFYING SIGHT.
! ! ! ! ! ! ! !

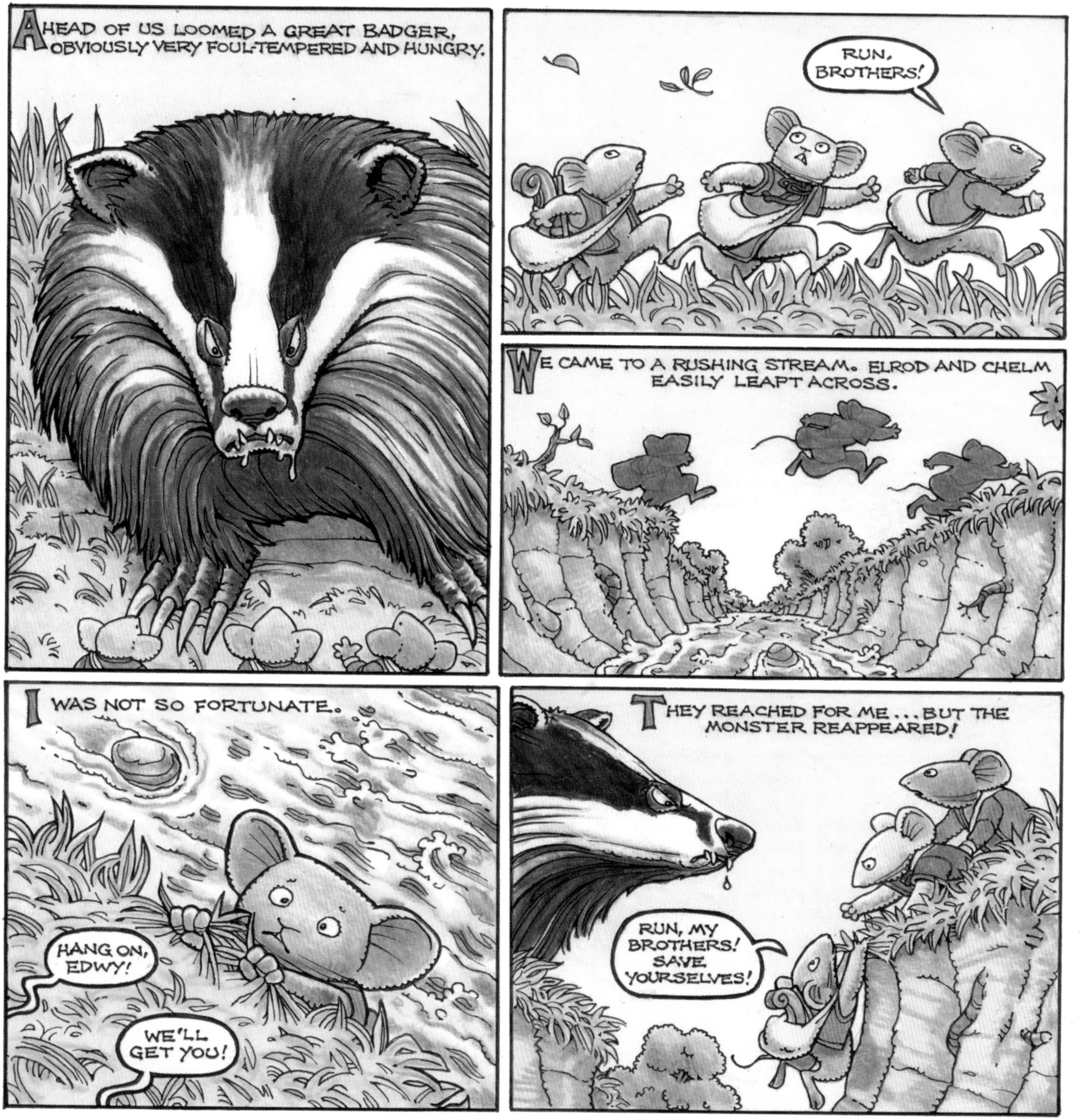
AHEAD OF US LOOMED A GREAT BADGER, OBVIOUSLY VERY FOUL-TEMPERED AND HUNGRY.
RUN, BROTHERS!
WE CAME TO A RUSHING STREAM. ELROD AND CHELM EASILY LEAPT ACROSS.
I WAS NOT SO FORTUNATE.
HANG ON, EDWY!
WE'LL GET YOU!
THEY REACHED FOR ME . . . BUT THE MONSTER REAPPEARED!
RUN, MY BROTHERS! SAVE YOURSELVES!

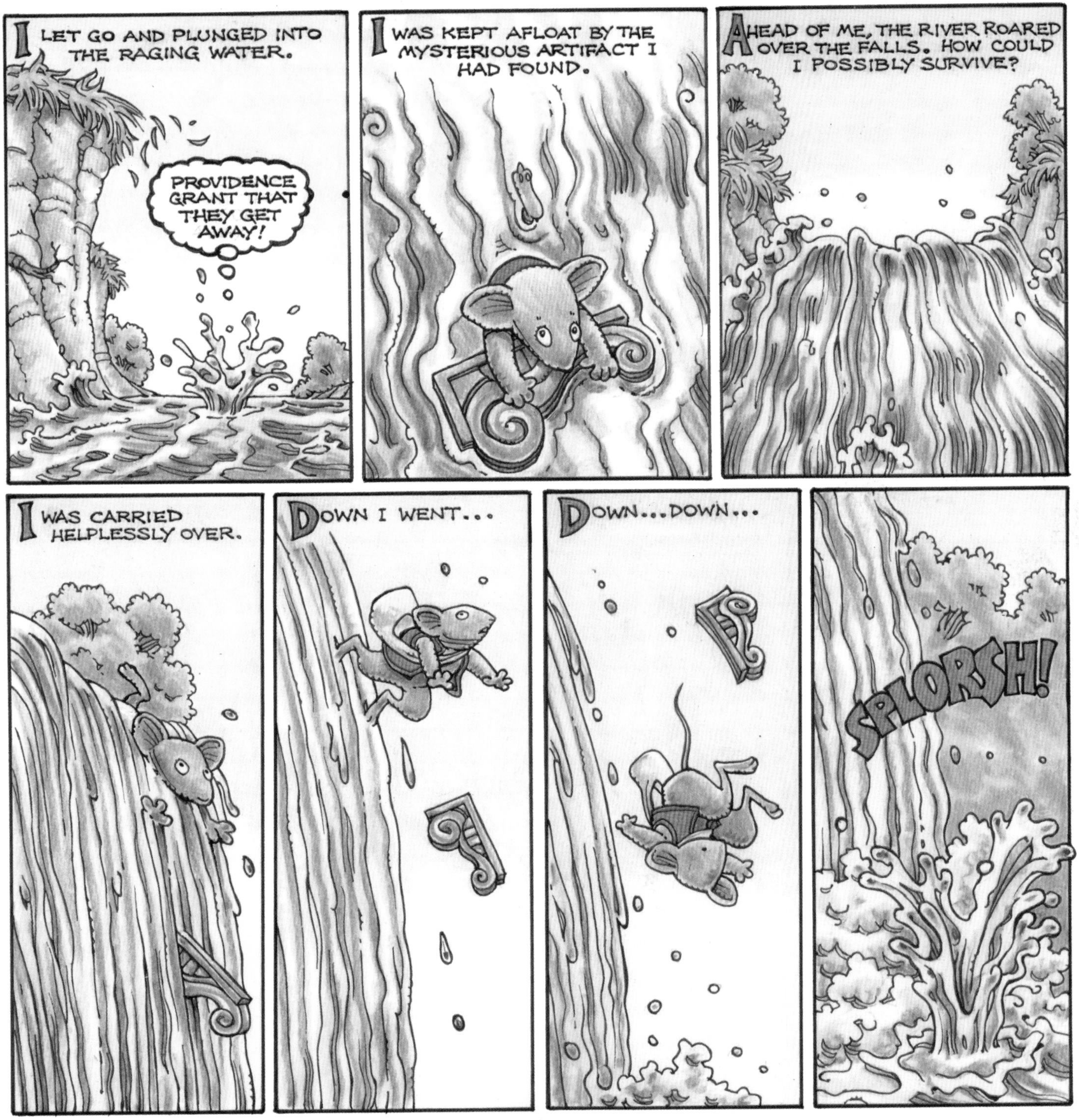
I LET GO AND PLUNGED INTO THE RAGING WATER.
PROVIDENCE GRANT THAT THEY GET AWAY!
I WAS KEPT AFLOAT BY THE MYSTERIOUS ARTIFACT I HAD FOUND.
AHEAD OF ME, THE RIVER ROARED OVER THE FALLS. HOW COULD I POSSIBLY SURVIVE?
I WAS CARRIED HELPLESSLY OVER.
DOWN I WENT...
DOWN...DOWN...
SPLORSH!

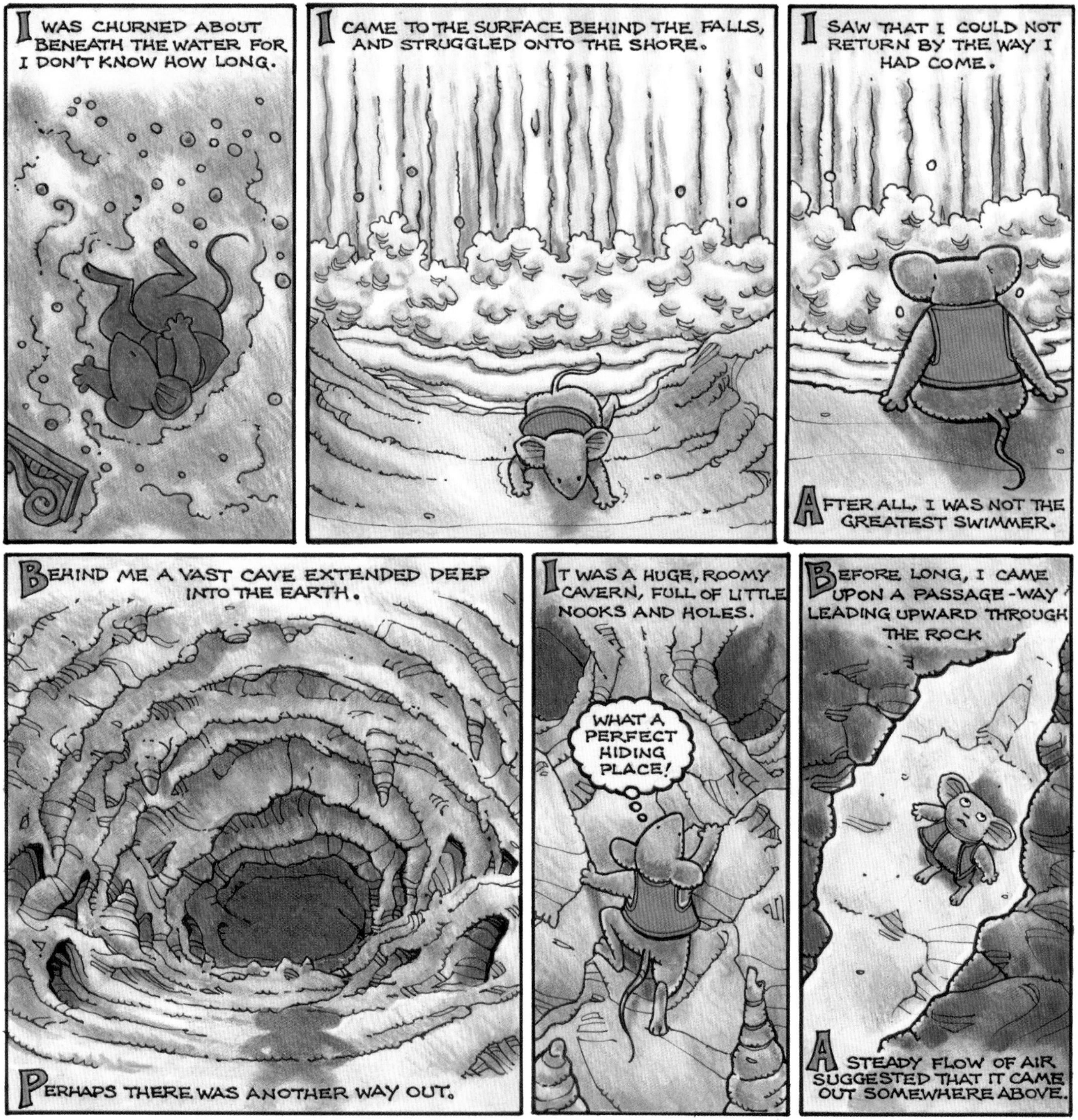
I WAS CHURNED ABOUT BENEATH THE WATER FOR I DON'T KNOW HOW LONG.
I CAME TO THE SURFACE BEHIND THE FALLS, AND STRUGGLED ONTO THE SHORE.
I SAW THAT I COULD NOT RETURN BY THE WAY I HAD COME.
AFTER ALL, I WAS NOT THE GREATEST SWIMMER.
BEHIND ME A VAST CAVE EXTENDED DEEP INTO THE EARTH.
PERHAPS THERE WAS ANOTHER WAY OUT.
IT WAS A HUGE, ROOMY CAVERN, FULL OF LITTLE NOOKS AND HOLES.
WHAT A PERFECT HIDING PLACE!
BEFORE LONG, I CAME UPON A PASSAGE-WAY LEADING UPWARD THROUGH THE ROCK
A STEADY FLOW OF AIR SUGGESTED THAT IT CAME OUT SOMEWHERE ABOVE.

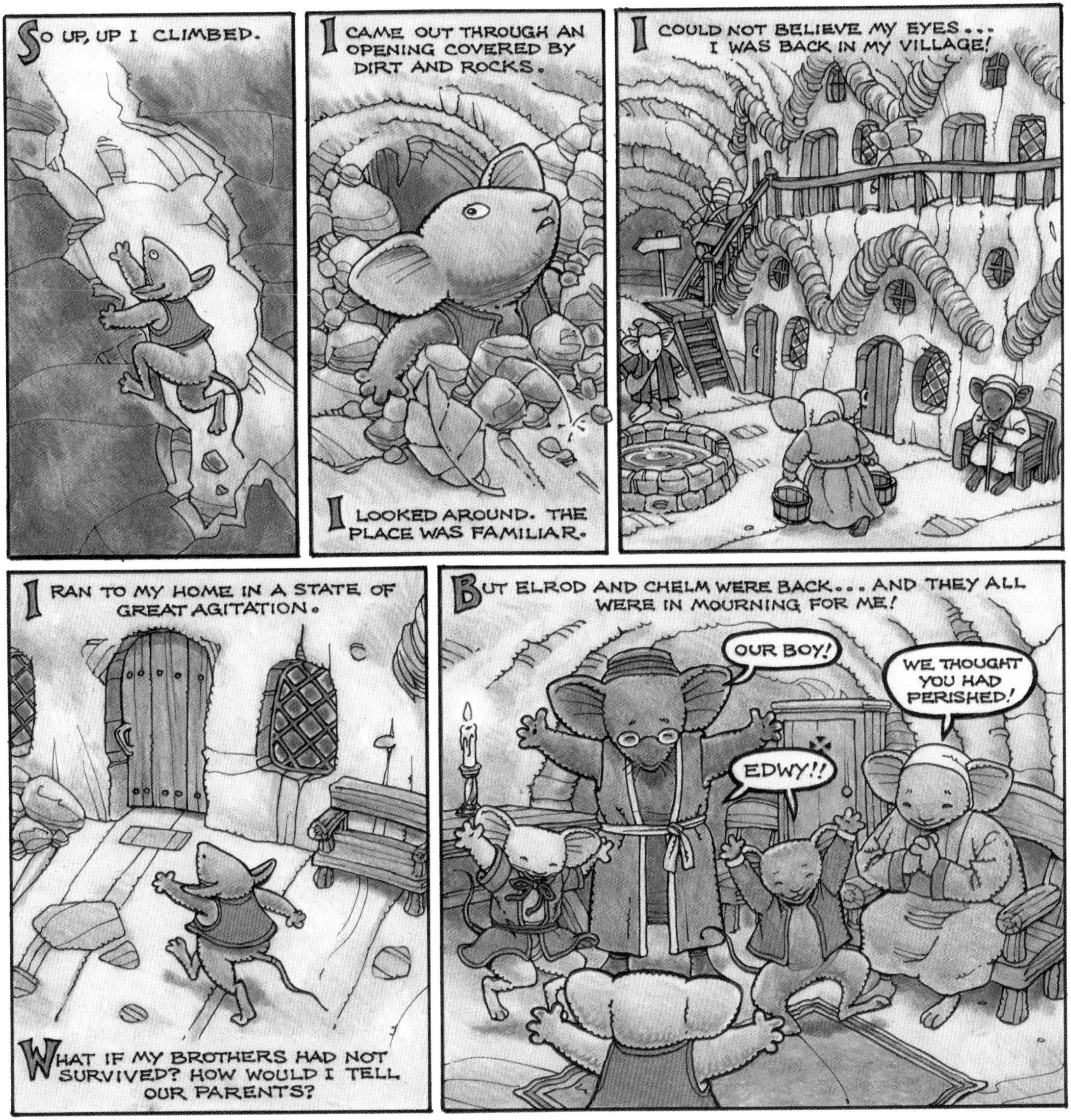
SO UP, UP I CLIMBED.
I CAME OUT THROUGH AN OPENING COVERED BY DIRT AND ROCKS.
I LOOKED AROUND. THE PLACE WAS FAMILIAR.
I COULD NOT BELIEVE MY EYES... I WAS BACK IN MY VILLAGE!
I RAN TO MY HOME IN A STATE OF GREAT AGITATION.
WHAT IF MY BROTHERS HAD NOT SURVIVED? HOW WOULD I TELL OUR PARENTS?
BUT ELROD AND CHELM WERE BACK... AND THEY ALL WERE IN MOURNING FOR ME!
OUR BOY!
WE THOUGHT YOU HAD PERISHED!
EDWY!!

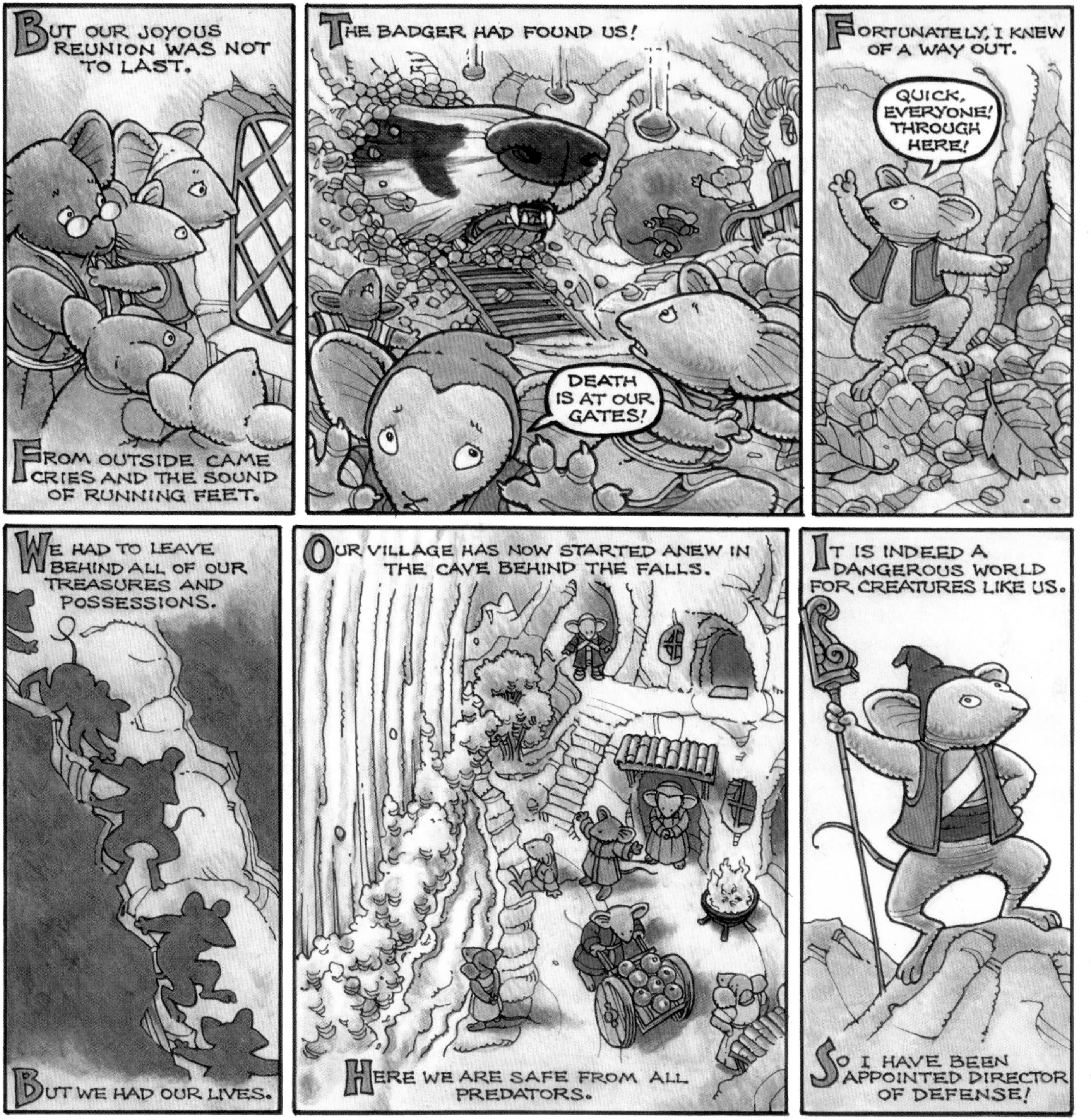
BUT OUR JOYOUS REUNION WAS NOT TO LAST.
FROM OUTSIDE CAME CRIES AND THE SOUND OF RUNNING FEET.
THE BADGER HAD FOUND US!
DEATH IS AT OUR GATES!
FORTUNATELY, I KNEW OF A WAY OUT.
QUICK, EVERYONE! THROUGH HERE!
WE HAD TO LEAVE BEHIND ALL OF OUR TREASURES AND POSSESSIONS.
BUT WE HAD OUR LIVES.
OUR VILLAGE HAS NOW STARTED ANEW IN THE CAVE BEHIND THE FALLS.
HERE WE ARE SAFE FROM ALL PREDATORS.
IT IS INDEED A DANGEROUS WORLD FOR CREATURES LIKE US.
SO I HAVE BEEN APPOINTED DIRECTOR OF DEFENSE!

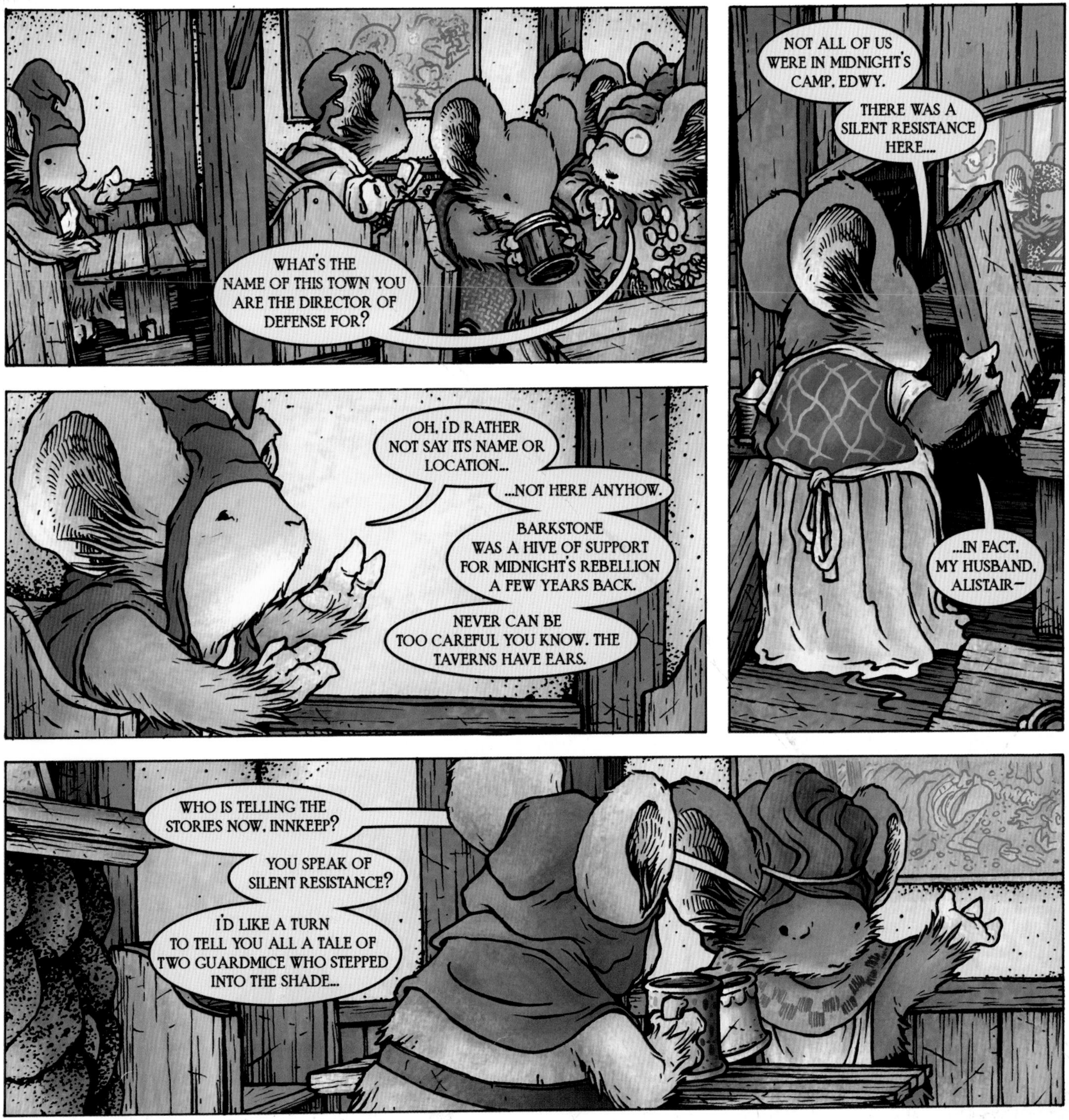
WHAT'S THE NAME OF THIS TOWN YOU ARE THE DIRECTOR OF DEFENSE FOR?
NOT ALL OF US WERE IN MIDNIGHT'S CAMP, EDWY.
THERE WAS A SILENT RESISTANCE HERE....
OH, I'D RATHER NOT SAY ITS NAME OR LOCATION...
...NOT HERE ANYHOW.
BARKSTONE WAS A HIVE OF SUPPORT FOR MIDNIGHT'S REBELLION A FEW YEARS BACK.
NEVER CAN BE TOO CAREFUL YOU KNOW. THE TAVERNS HAVE EARS.
...IN FACT, MY HUSBAND, ALISTAIR—
WHO IS TELLING THE STORIES NOW, INNKEEP?
YOU SPEAK OF SILENT RESISTANCE?
I'D LIKE A TURN TO TELL YOU ALL A TALE OF TWO GUARDMICE WHO STEPPED INTO THE SHADE...

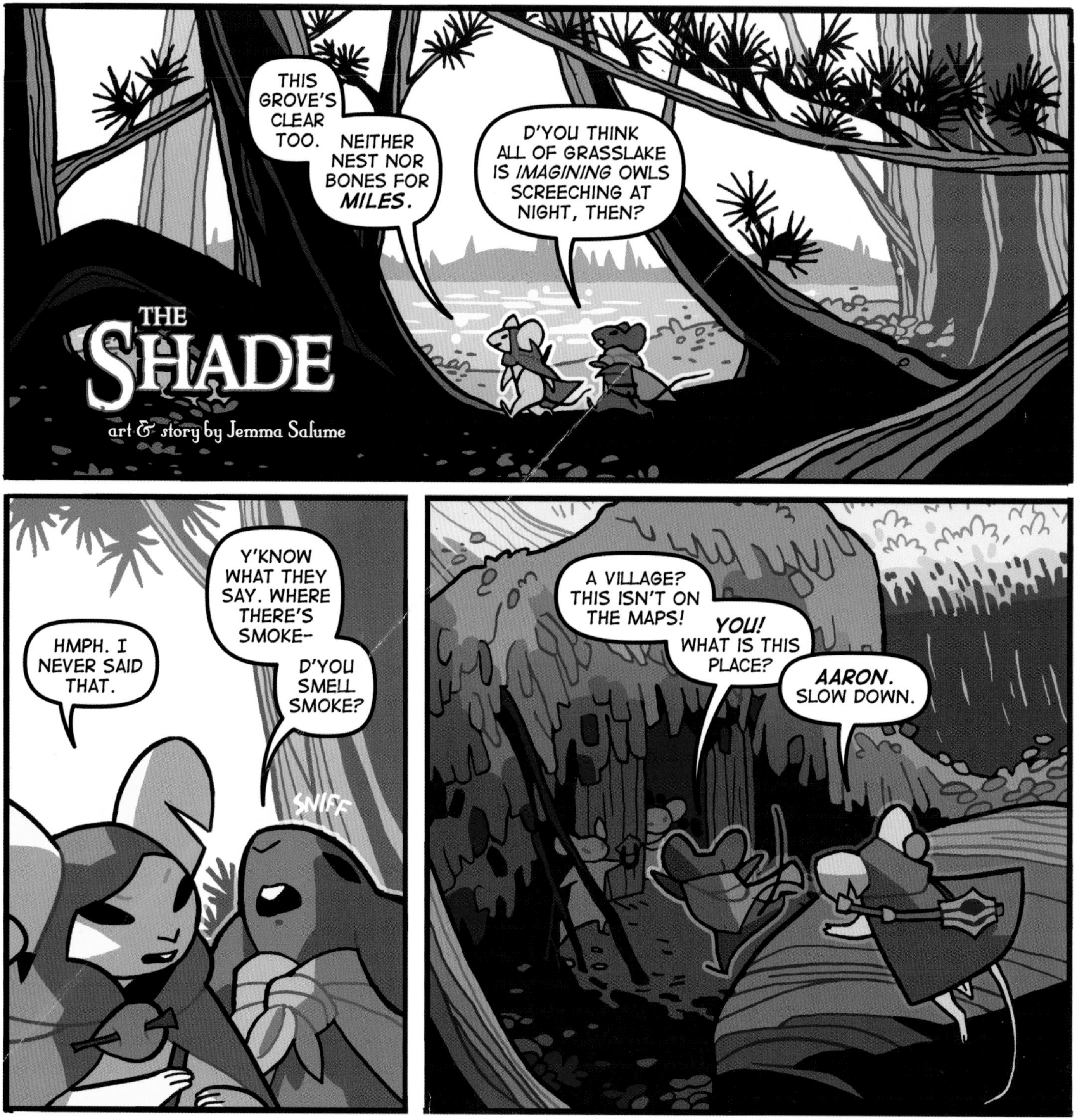
THE SHADE
art & story by Jemma Salume
THIS GROVE'S CLEAR TOO.
NEITHER NEST NOR BONES FOR *MILES*.
D'YOU THINK ALL OF GRASSLAKE IS *IMAGINING* OWLS SCREECHING AT NIGHT, THEN?
HMPH. I NEVER SAID THAT.
Y'KNOW WHAT THEY SAY. WHERE THERE'S SMOKE-
D'YOU SMELL SMOKE?
SNIFF
A VILLAGE? THIS ISN'T ON THE MAPS!
YOU! WHAT IS THIS PLACE?
AARON. SLOW DOWN.

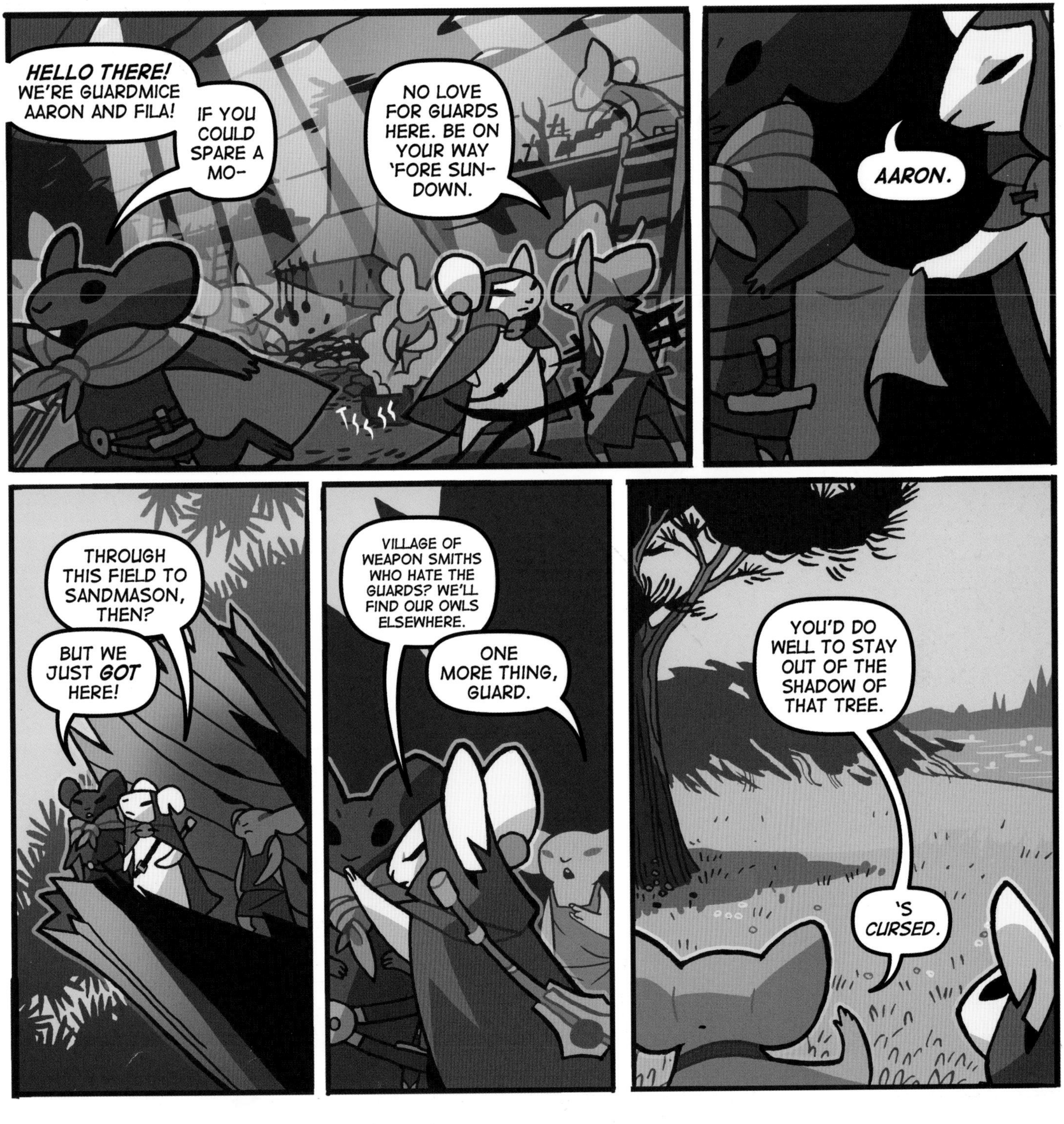
HELLO THERE! WE'RE GUARDMICE AARON AND FILA!
IF YOU COULD SPARE A MO-
NO LOVE FOR GUARDS HERE. BE ON YOUR WAY 'FORE SUNDOWN.
TSSSS
AARON.
THROUGH THIS FIELD TO SANDMASON, THEN?
BUT WE JUST GOT HERE!
VILLAGE OF WEAPON SMITHS WHO HATE THE GUARDS? WE'LL FIND OUR OWLS ELSEWHERE.
ONE MORE THING, GUARD.
YOU'D DO WELL TO STAY OUT OF THE SHADOW OF THAT TREE.
'S CURSED.

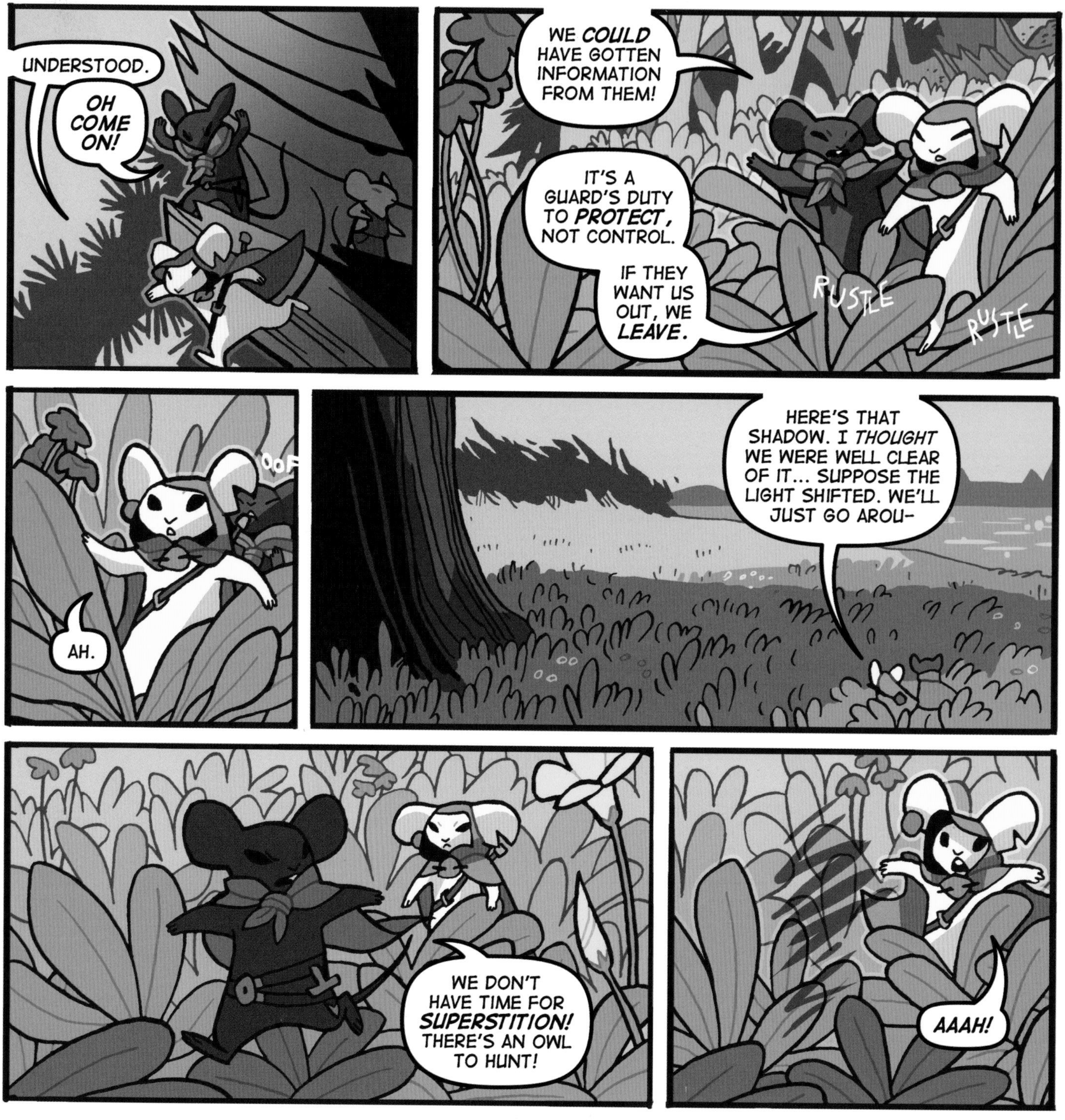
UNDERSTOOD.
OH COME ON!
WE COULD HAVE GOTTEN INFORMATION FROM THEM!
IT'S A GUARD'S DUTY TO PROTECT, NOT CONTROL.
IF THEY WANT US OUT, WE LEAVE.
RUSTLE
RUSTLE
OOF
AH.
HERE'S THAT SHADOW. I THOUGHT WE WERE WELL CLEAR OF IT... SUPPOSE THE LIGHT SHIFTED. WE'LL JUST GO AROU-
WE DON'T HAVE TIME FOR SUPERSTITION! THERE'S AN OWL TO HUNT!
AAAH!

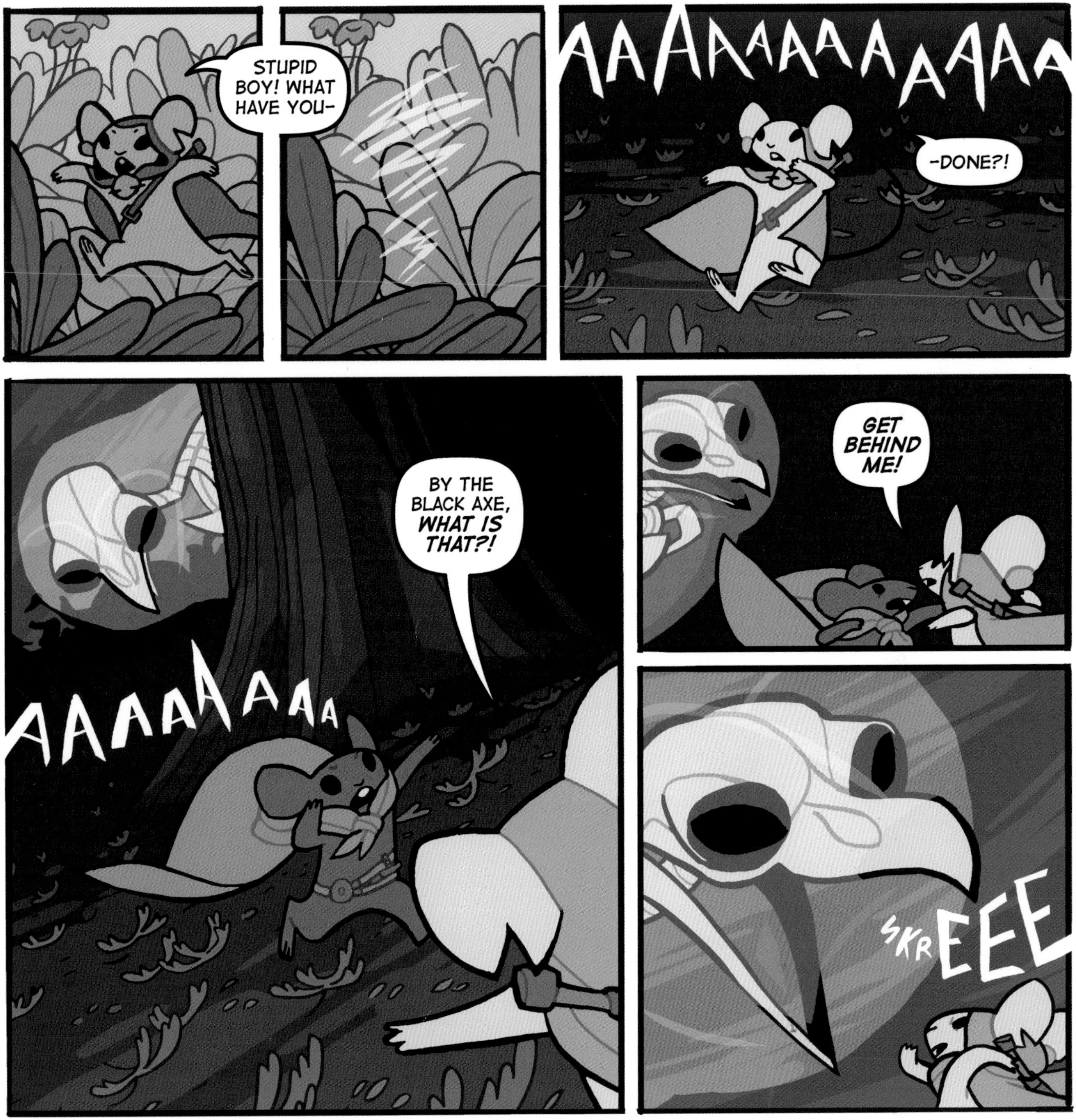

STUPID BOY! WHAT HAVE YOU-
AAAAAAAAAAAA
-DONE?!
BY THE BLACK AXE, *WHAT IS THAT?!*
AAAAAAAA
GET BEHIND ME!
SKREEE

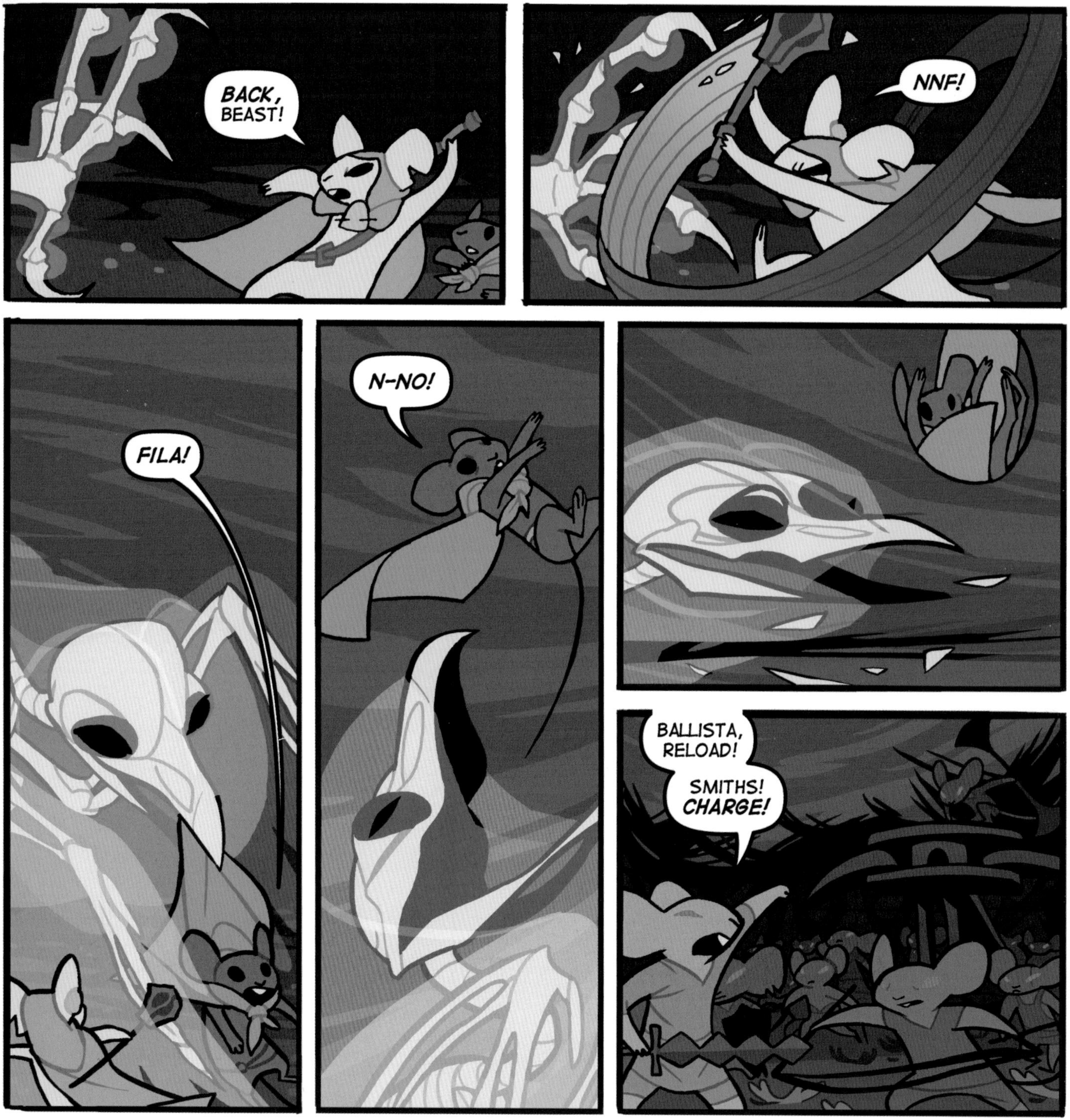
BACK, BEAST!
NNF!
FILA!
N-NO!
BALLISTA, RELOAD!
SMITHS! CHARGE!

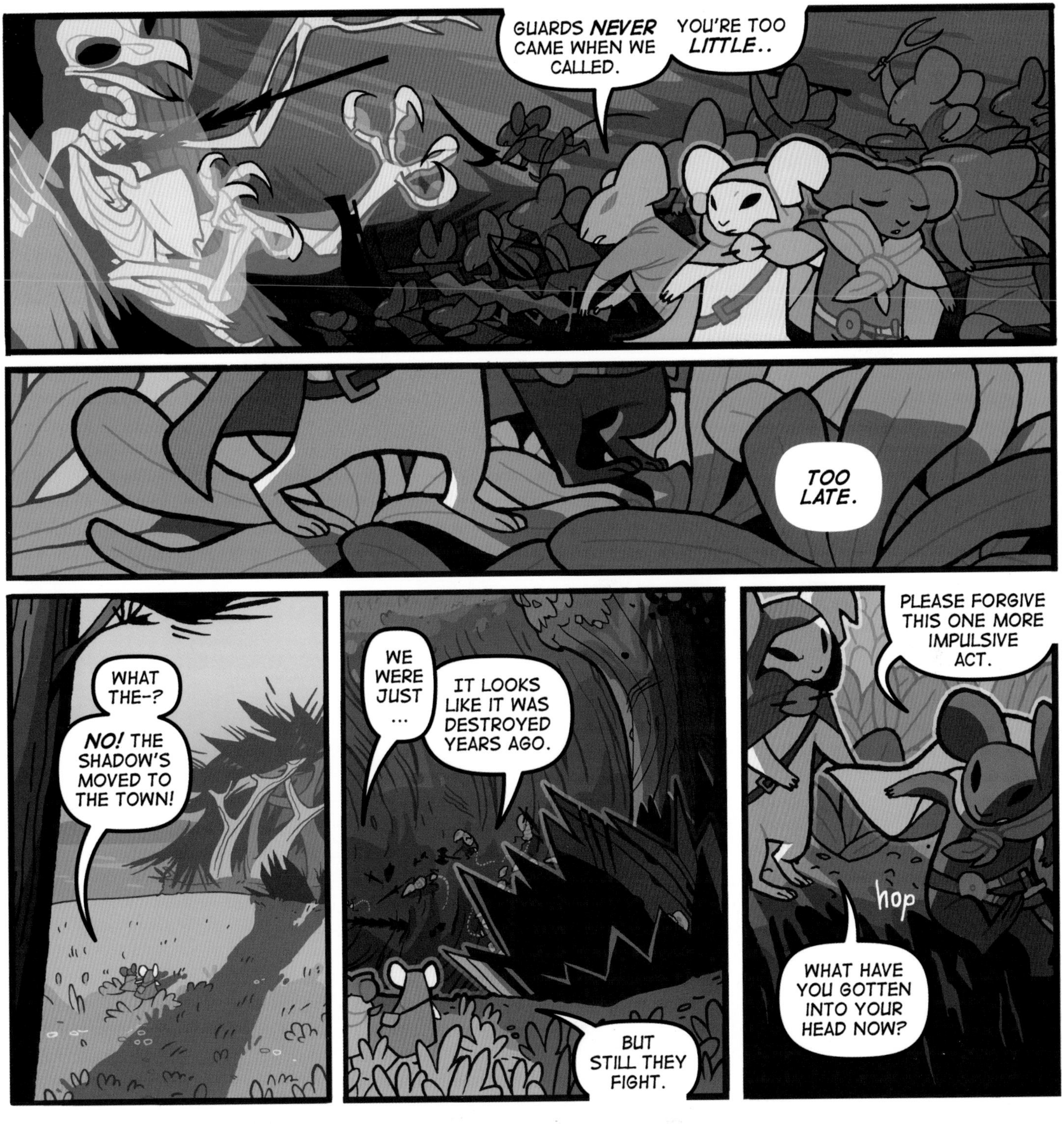
GUARDS *NEVER* CAME WHEN WE CALLED.
YOU'RE TOO *LITTLE*..
TOO LATE.
WHAT THE-?
NO! THE SHADOW'S MOVED TO THE TOWN!
WE WERE JUST ...
IT LOOKS LIKE IT WAS DESTROYED YEARS AGO.
BUT STILL THEY FIGHT.
PLEASE FORGIVE THIS ONE MORE IMPULSIVE ACT.
hop
WHAT HAVE YOU GOTTEN INTO YOUR HEAD NOW?

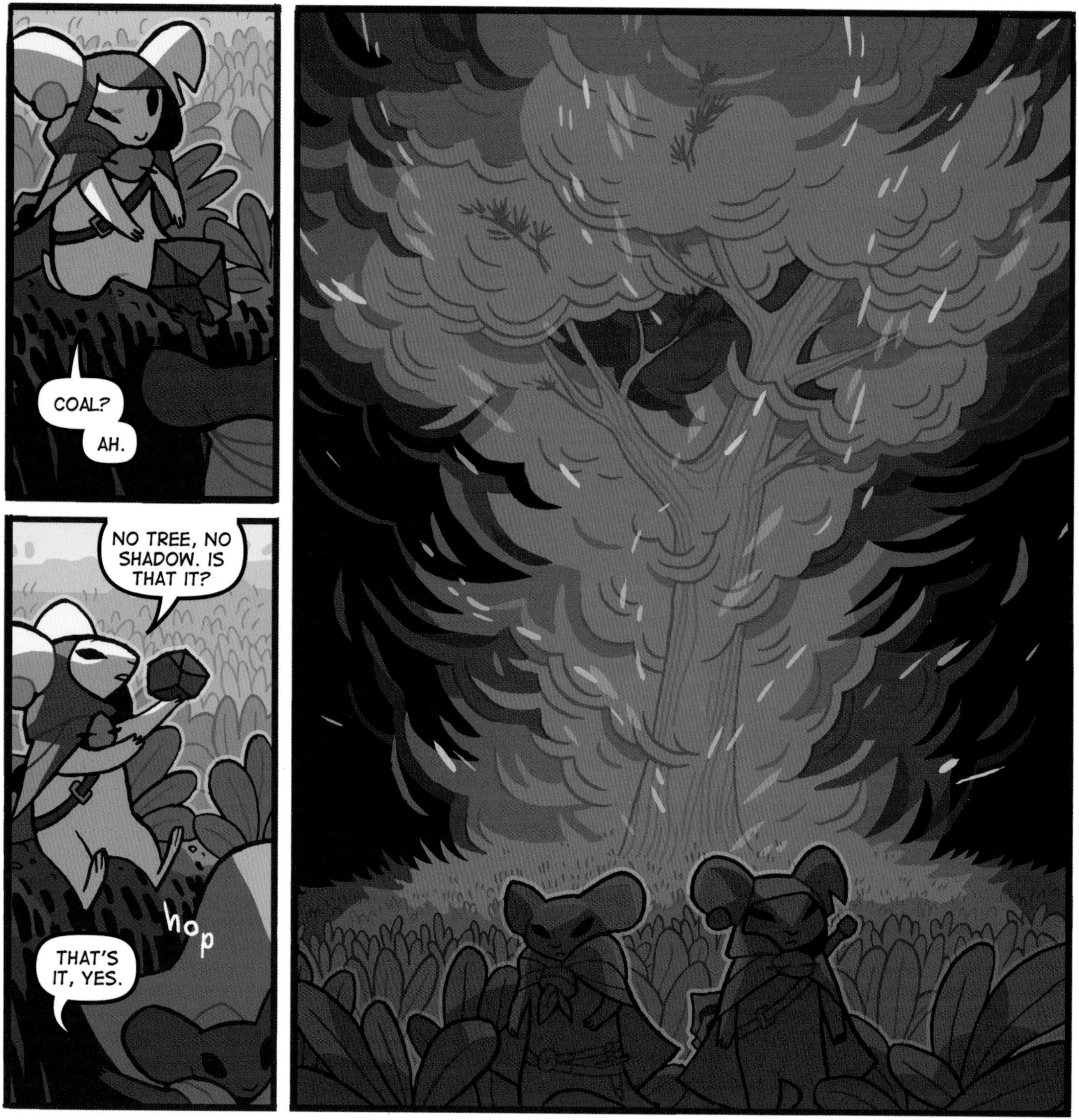
COAL?
AH.
NO TREE, NO SHADOW. IS THAT IT?
hop
THAT'S IT, YES.

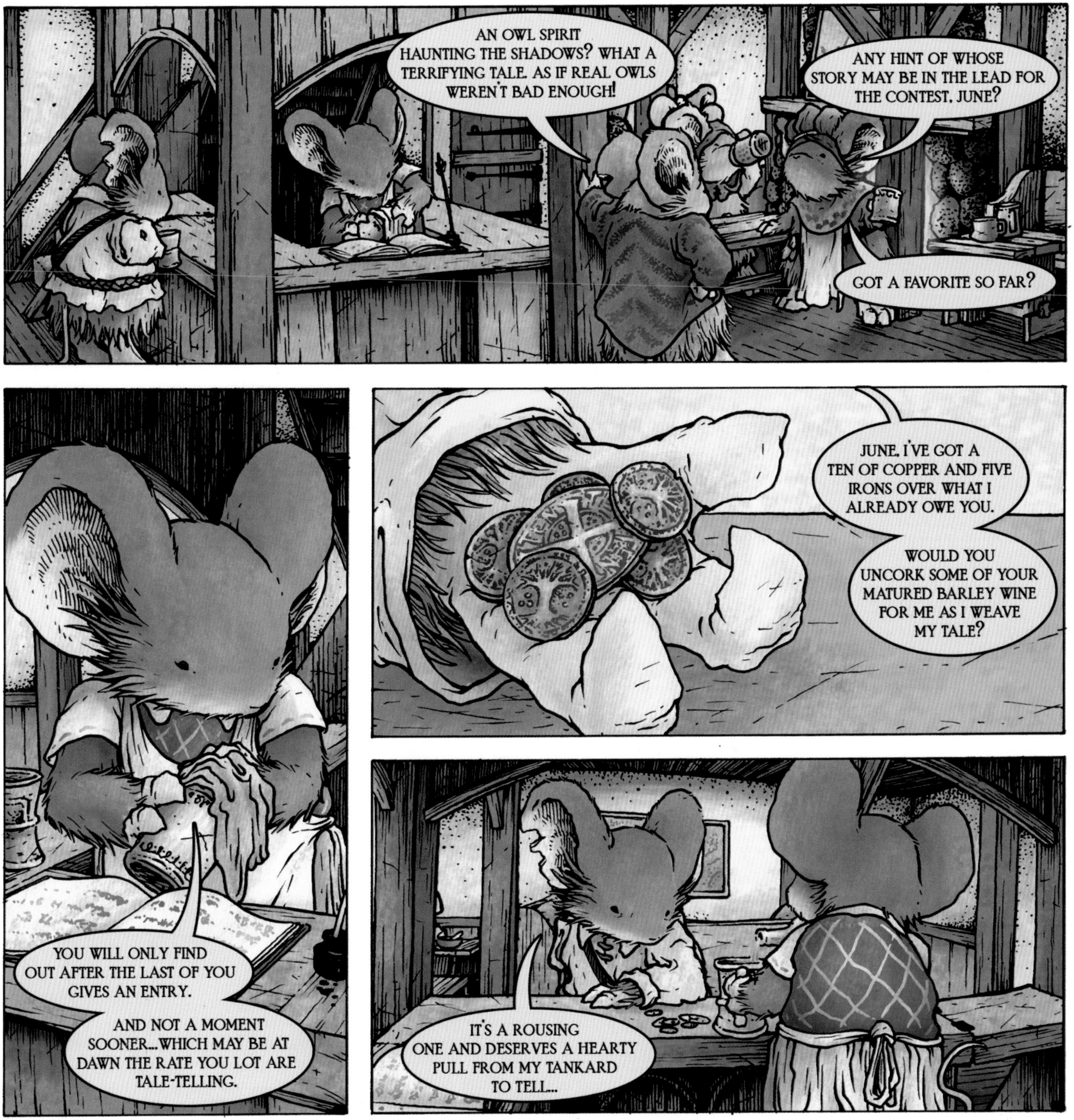
AN OWL SPIRIT HAUNTING THE SHADOWS? WHAT A TERRIFYING TALE. AS IF REAL OWLS WEREN'T BAD ENOUGH!
ANY HINT OF WHOSE STORY MAY BE IN THE LEAD FOR THE CONTEST, JUNE?
GOT A FAVORITE SO FAR?
YOU WILL ONLY FIND OUT AFTER THE LAST OF YOU GIVES AN ENTRY.
AND NOT A MOMENT SOONER...WHICH MAY BE AT DAWN THE RATE YOU LOT ARE TALE-TELLING.
JUNE, I'VE GOT A TEN OF COPPER AND FIVE IRONS OVER WHAT I ALREADY OWE YOU.
WOULD YOU UNCORK SOME OF YOUR MATURED BARLEY WINE FOR ME AS I WEAVE MY TALE?
IT'S A ROUSING ONE AND DESERVES A HEARTY PULL FROM MY TANKARD TO TELL...

BY ERIC CANETE

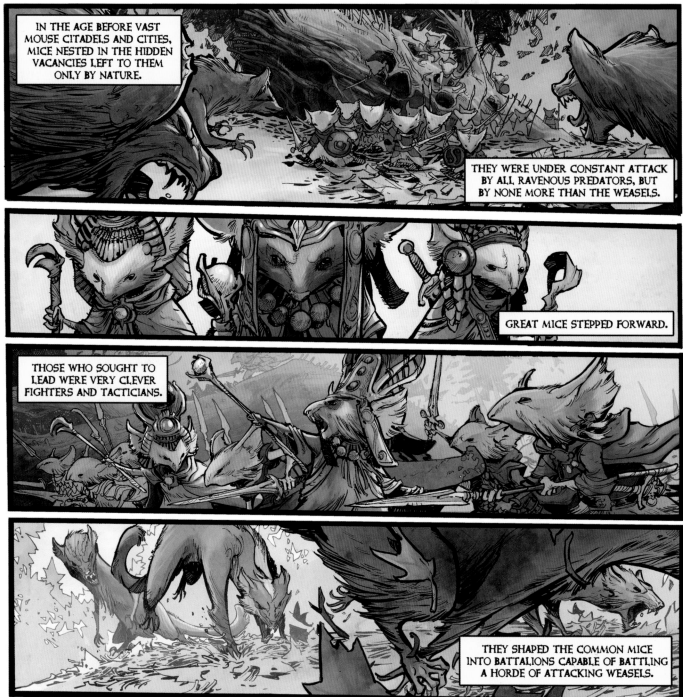

IN THE AGE BEFORE VAST MOUSE CITADELS AND CITIES, MICE NESTED IN THE HIDDEN VACANCIES LEFT TO THEM ONLY BY NATURE.

THEY WERE UNDER CONSTANT ATTACK BY ALL RAVENOUS PREDATORS, BUT BY NONE MORE THAN THE WEASELS.

GREAT MICE STEPPED FORWARD.

THOSE WHO SOUGHT TO LEAD WERE VERY CLEVER FIGHTERS AND TACTICIANS.

THEY SHAPED THE COMMON MICE INTO BATTALIONS CAPABLE OF BATTLING A HORDE OF ATTACKING WEASELS.

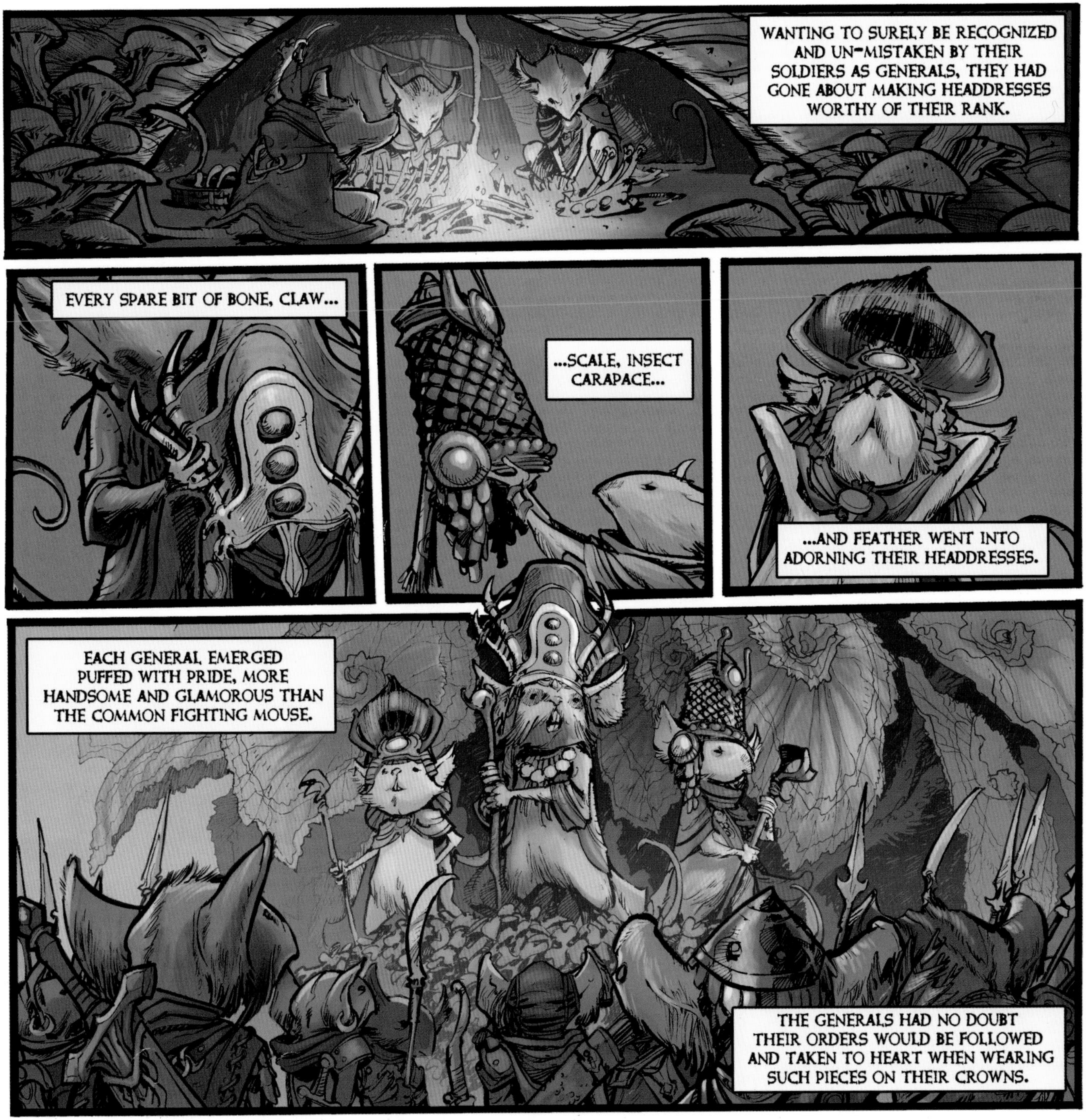
WANTING TO SURELY BE RECOGNIZED AND UN-MISTAKEN BY THEIR SOLDIERS AS GENERALS, THEY HAD GONE ABOUT MAKING HEADDRESSES WORTHY OF THEIR RANK.
EVERY SPARE BIT OF BONE, CLAW...
...SCALE, INSECT CARAPACE...
...AND FEATHER WENT INTO ADORNING THEIR HEADDRESSES.
EACH GENERAL EMERGED PUFFED WITH PRIDE, MORE HANDSOME AND GLAMOROUS THAN THE COMMON FIGHTING MOUSE.
THE GENERALS HAD NO DOUBT THEIR ORDERS WOULD BE FOLLOWED AND TAKEN TO HEART WHEN WEARING SUCH PIECES ON THEIR CROWNS.

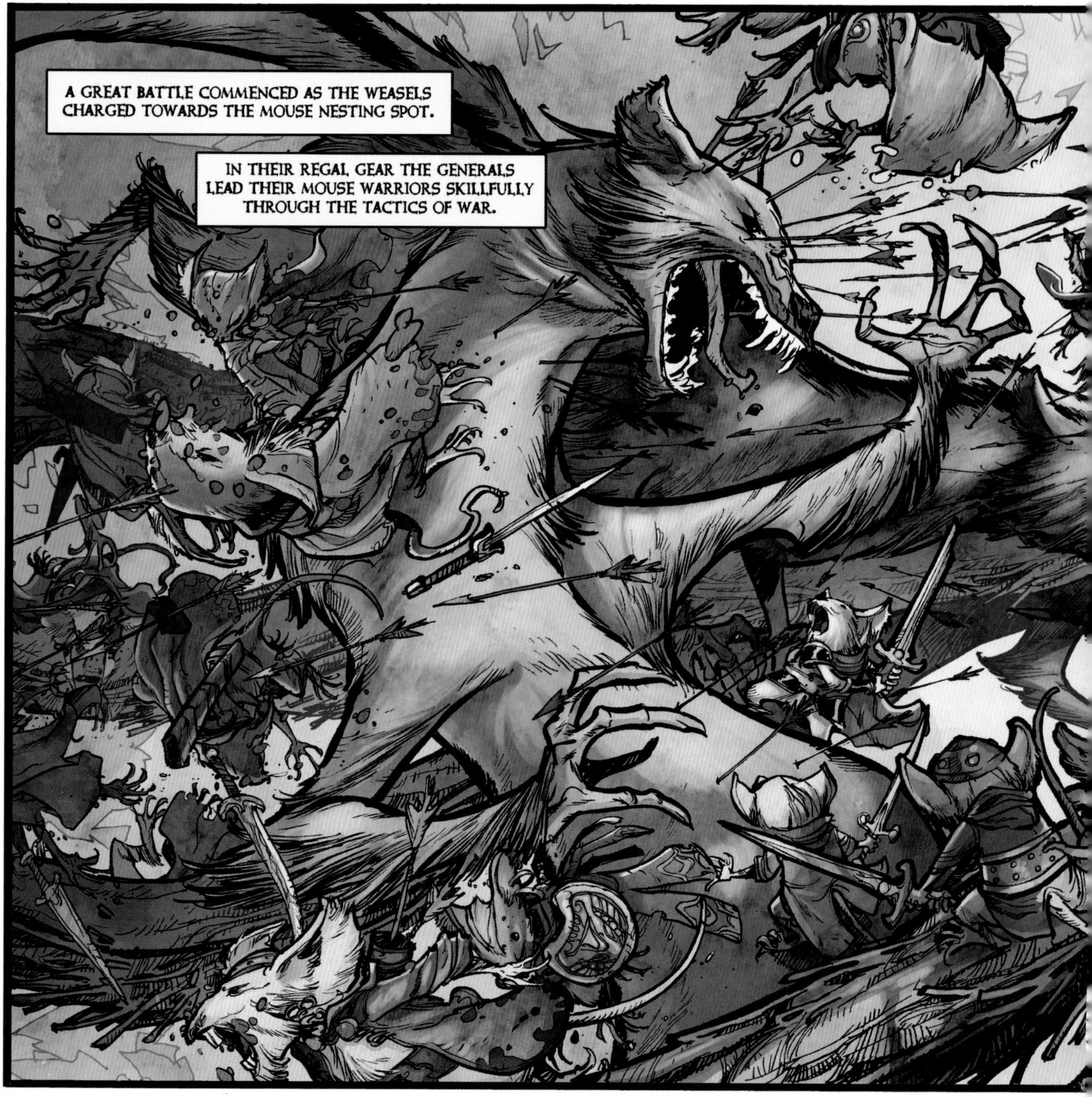
A GREAT BATTLE COMMENCED AS THE WEASELS CHARGED TOWARDS THE MOUSE NESTING SPOT.
IN THEIR REGAL GEAR THE GENERALS LEAD THEIR MOUSE WARRIORS SKILLFULLY THROUGH THE TACTICS OF WAR.

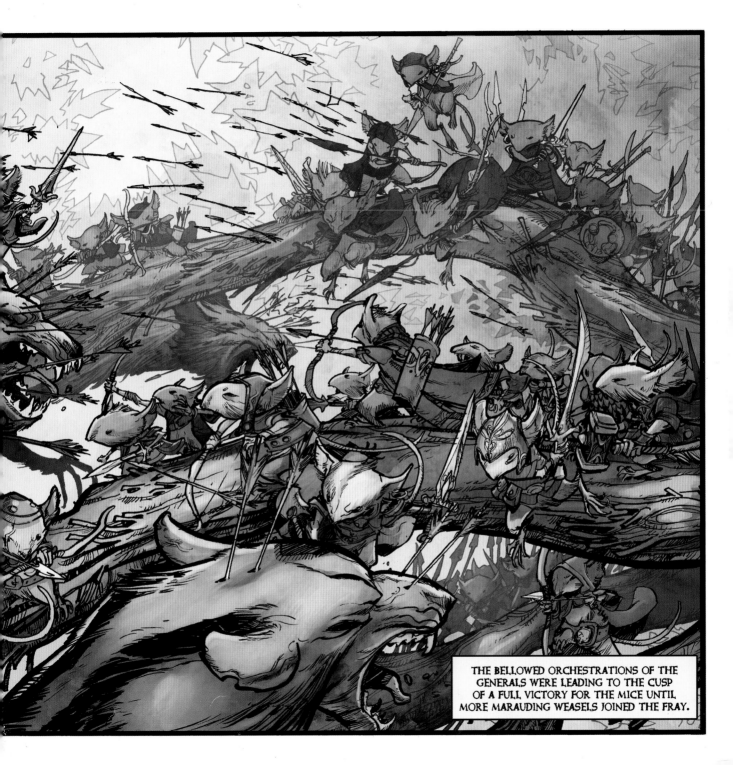

THE BELLOWED ORCHESTRATIONS OF THE GENERALS WERE LEADING TO THE CUSP OF A FULL VICTORY FOR THE MICE UNTIL MORE MARAUDING WEASELS JOINED THE FRAY.

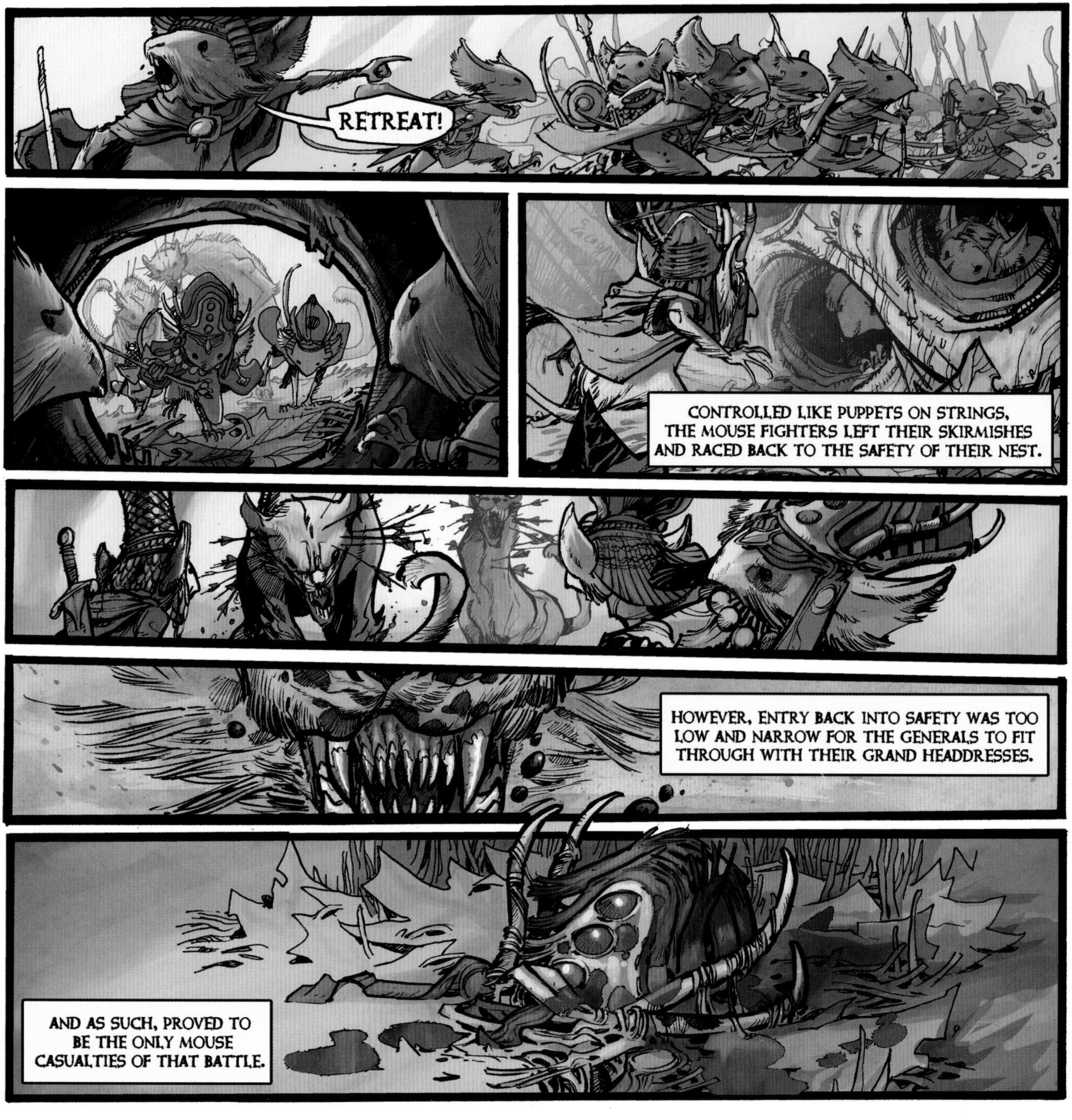
RETREAT!
CONTROLLED LIKE PUPPETS ON STRINGS, THE MOUSE FIGHTERS LEFT THEIR SKIRMISHES AND RACED BACK TO THE SAFETY OF THEIR NEST.
HOWEVER, ENTRY BACK INTO SAFETY WAS TOO LOW AND NARROW FOR THE GENERALS TO FIT THROUGH WITH THEIR GRAND HEADDRESSES.
AND AS SUCH, PROVED TO BE THE ONLY MOUSE CASUALTIES OF THAT BATTLE.

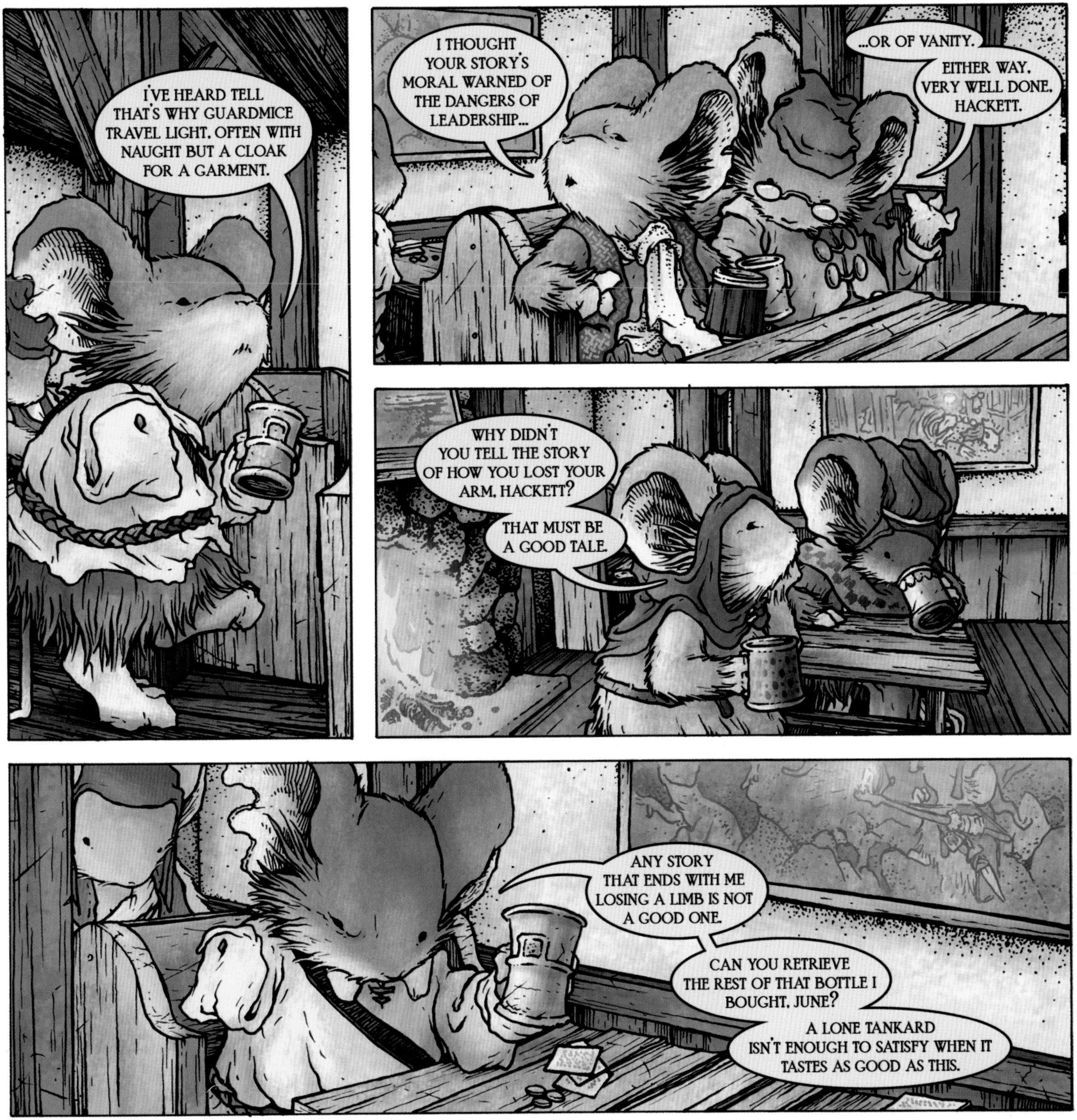
I'VE HEARD TELL THAT'S WHY GUARDMICE TRAVEL LIGHT, OFTEN WITH NAUGHT BUT A CLOAK FOR A GARMENT.
I THOUGHT YOUR STORY'S MORAL WARNED OF THE DANGERS OF LEADERSHIP...
...OR OF VANITY.
EITHER WAY, VERY WELL DONE, HACKETT.
WHY DIDN'T YOU TELL THE STORY OF HOW YOU LOST YOUR ARM, HACKETT?
THAT MUST BE A GOOD TALE.
ANY STORY THAT ENDS WITH ME LOSING A LIMB IS NOT A GOOD ONE.
CAN YOU RETRIEVE THE REST OF THAT BOTTLE I BOUGHT, JUNE?
A LONE TANKARD ISN'T ENOUGH TO SATISFY WHEN IT TASTES AS GOOD AS THIS.

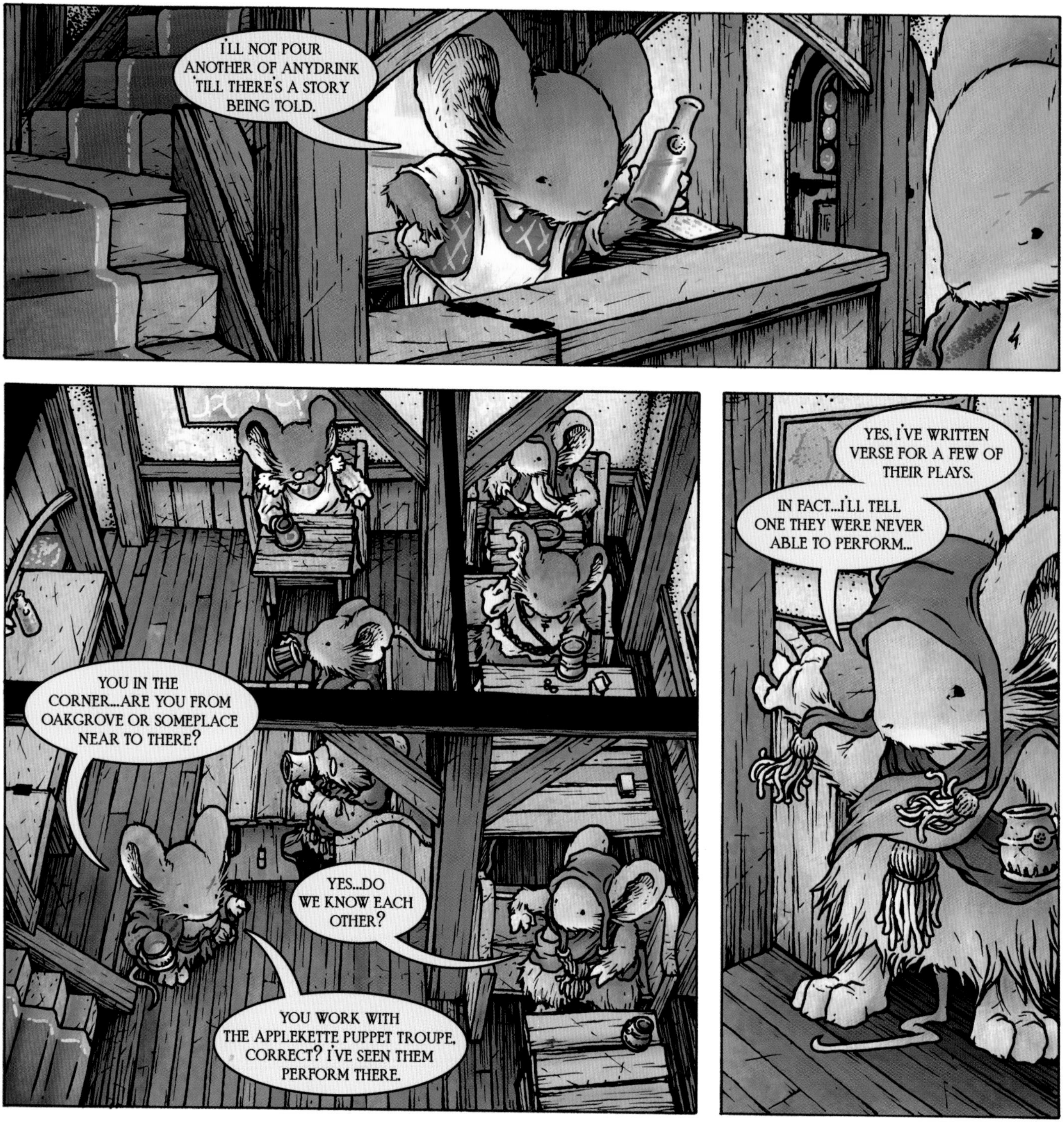

I'LL NOT POUR ANOTHER OF ANYDRINK 'TILL THERE'S A STORY BEING TOLD.
YOU IN THE CORNER...ARE YOU FROM OAKGROVE OR SOMEPLACE NEAR TO THERE?
YES...DO WE KNOW EACH OTHER?
YOU WORK WITH THE APPLEKETTE PUPPET TROUPE, CORRECT? I'VE SEEN THEM PERFORM THERE.
YES, I'VE WRITTEN VERSE FOR A FEW OF THEIR PLAYS.
IN FACT...I'LL TELL ONE THEY WERE NEVER ABLE TO PERFORM...

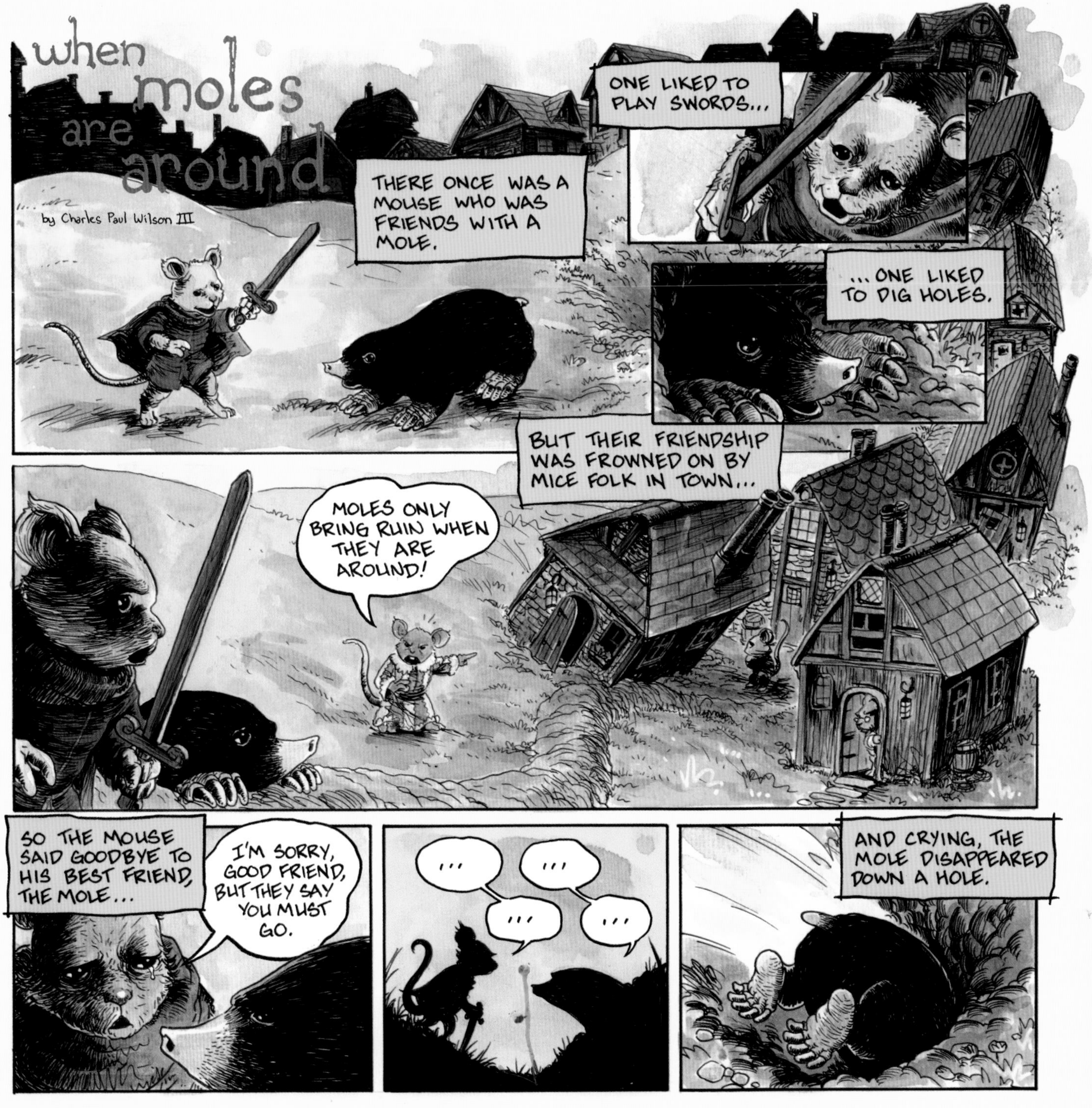
when moles are around
by Charles Paul Wilson III
THERE ONCE WAS A MOUSE WHO WAS FRIENDS WITH A MOLE.
ONE LIKED TO PLAY SWORDS...
...ONE LIKED TO DIG HOLES.
BUT THEIR FRIENDSHIP WAS FROWNED ON BY MICE FOLK IN TOWN...
MOLES ONLY BRING RUIN WHEN THEY ARE AROUND!
SO THE MOUSE SAID GOODBYE TO HIS BEST FRIEND, THE MOLE...
I'M SORRY, GOOD FRIEND, BUT THEY SAY YOU MUST GO.
...
...
...
...
AND CRYING, THE MOLE DISAPPEARED DOWN A HOLE.

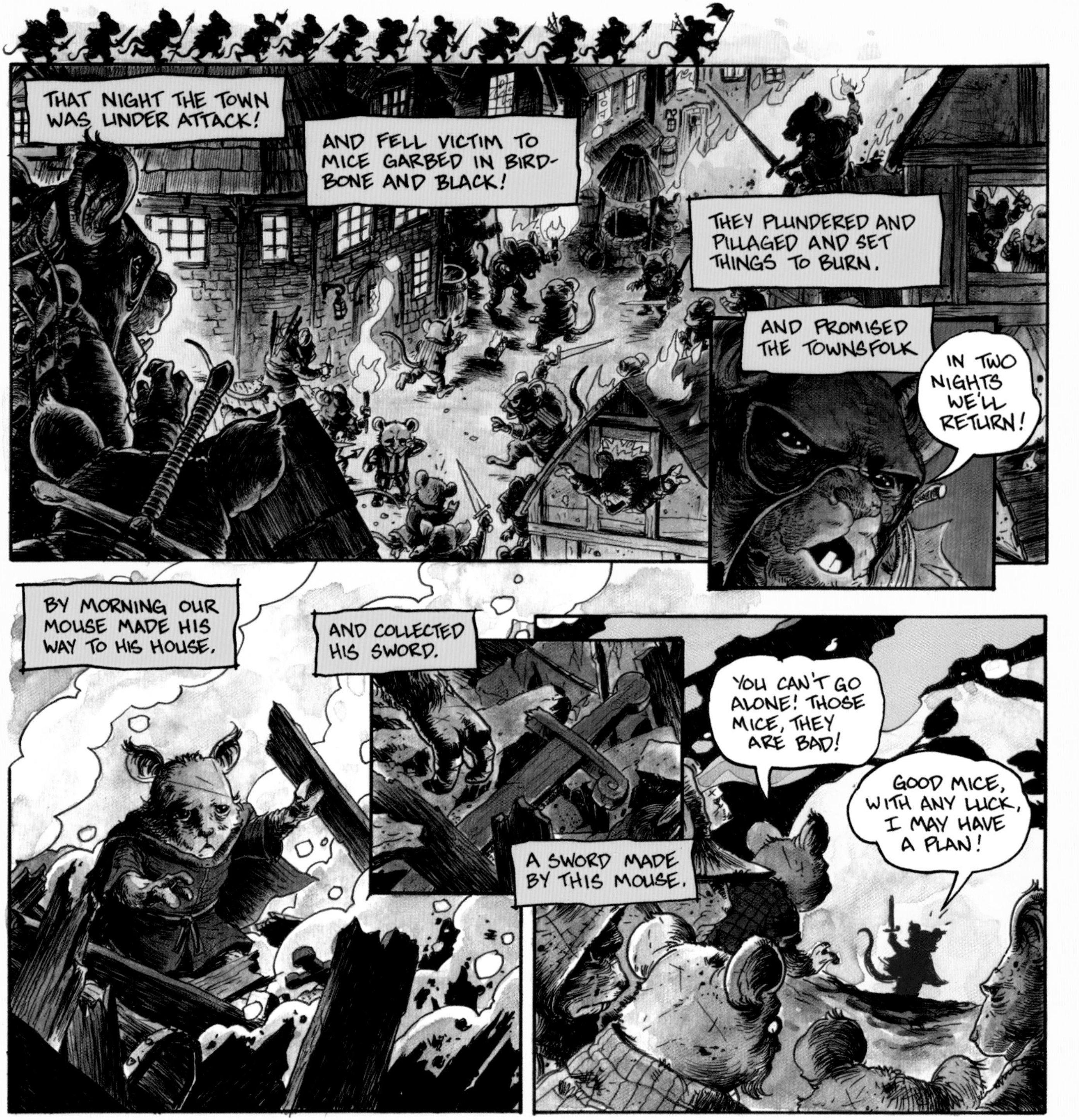
THAT NIGHT THE TOWN WAS UNDER ATTACK!
AND FELL VICTIM TO MICE GARBED IN BIRD-BONE AND BLACK!
THEY PLUNDERED AND PILLAGED AND SET THINGS TO BURN.
AND PROMISED THE TOWNSFOLK
IN TWO NIGHTS WE'LL RETURN!
BY MORNING OUR MOUSE MADE HIS WAY TO HIS HOUSE,
AND COLLECTED HIS SWORD.
A SWORD MADE BY THIS MOUSE.
YOU CAN'T GO ALONE! THOSE MICE, THEY ARE BAD!
GOOD MICE, WITH ANY LUCK, I MAY HAVE A PLAN!

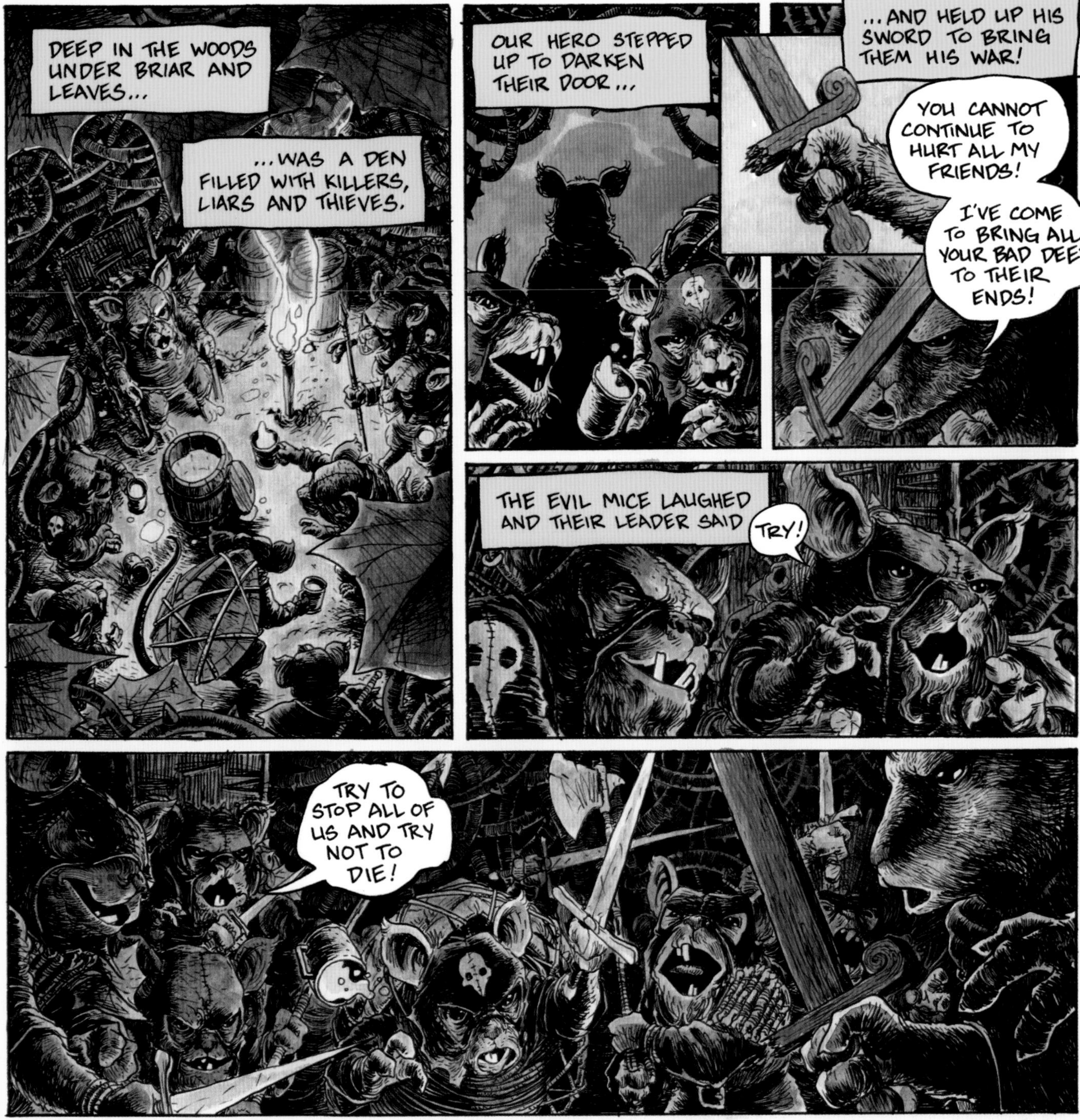

DEEP IN THE WOODS UNDER BRIAR AND LEAVES...
...WAS A DEN FILLED WITH KILLERS, LIARS AND THIEVES.
OUR HERO STEPPED UP TO DARKEN THEIR DOOR...
...AND HELD UP HIS SWORD TO BRING THEM HIS WAR!
YOU CANNOT CONTINUE TO HURT ALL MY FRIENDS!
I'VE COME TO BRING ALL YOUR BAD DEEDS TO THEIR ENDS!
THE EVIL MICE LAUGHED AND THEIR LEADER SAID
TRY!
TRY TO STOP ALL OF US AND TRY NOT TO DIE!

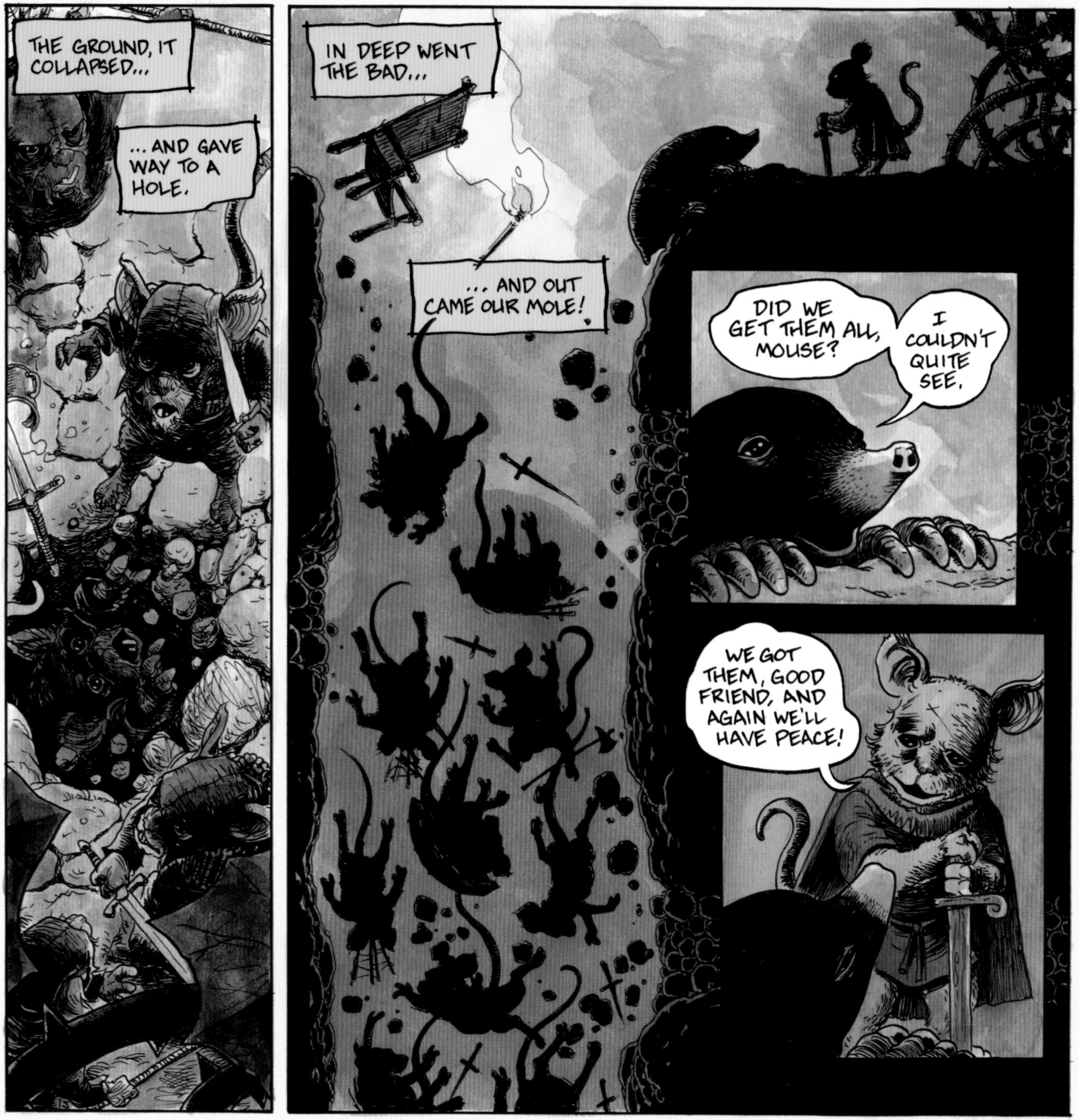
THE GROUND, IT COLLAPSED...
...AND GAVE WAY TO A HOLE.
IN DEEP WENT THE BAD...
...AND OUT CAME OUR MOLE!
DID WE GET THEM ALL, MOUSE?
I COULDN'T QUITE SEE.
WE GOT THEM, GOOD FRIEND, AND AGAIN WE'LL HAVE PEACE!

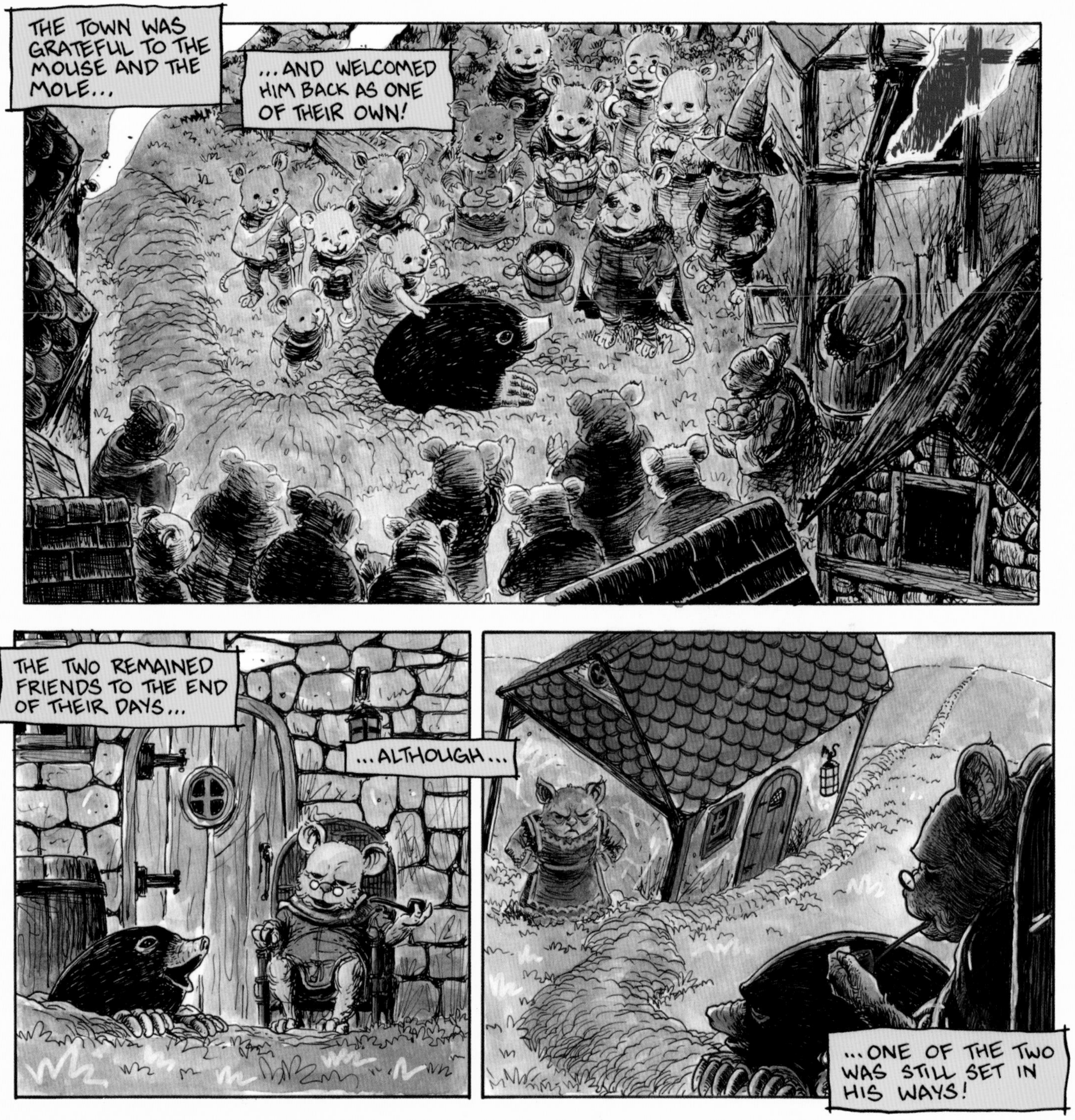
THE TOWN WAS GRATEFUL TO THE MOUSE AND THE MOLE...
...AND WELCOMED HIM BACK AS ONE OF THEIR OWN!
THE TWO REMAINED FRIENDS TO THE END OF THEIR DAYS...
...ALTHOUGH...
...ONE OF THE TWO WAS STILL SET IN HIS WAYS!

WHY WOULD THOSE PUPPET MICE NOT WANT TO RAISE THE CURTAIN ON SUCH A PLAY?
TOO MANY STRINGS, THEY SAID.
YOU ARE ALL THE FIRST AUDIENCE TO HAVE EVER HEARD THAT STORY.
THE ONLY THING I WISH TO KNOW MORE THAN HOW YOU KEEP WINNING AT THIS GAME...
...IS TO HEAR WHAT TALE YOU WILL TELL, BELLAH.
THERE IS ONLY ONE GOOD STORY I CAN TELL FROM MEMORY.
I KNOW IT NOT TO BE TRUE, BUT WHEN I WAS YOUNG, MY FATHER WOULD SAY THAT HE WAS ONE OF FOUR BROTHERS, AND THIS IS THE STORY HE'D TELL ME OF THEIR YOUTH.

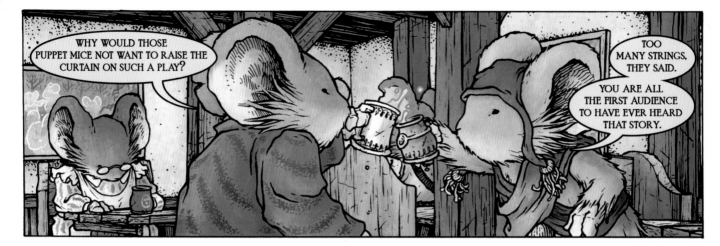

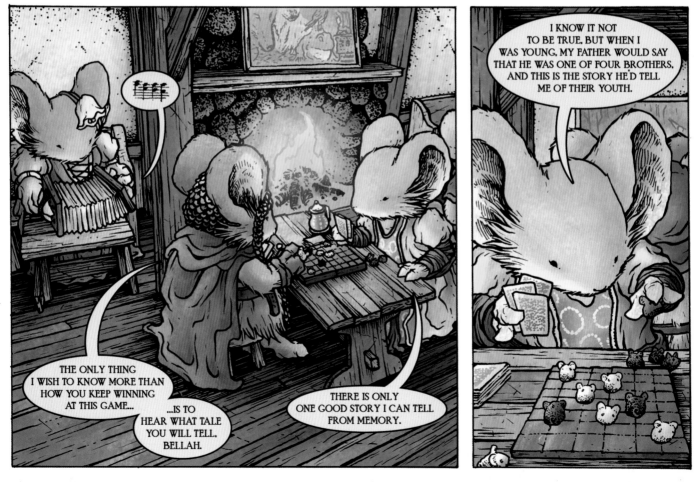

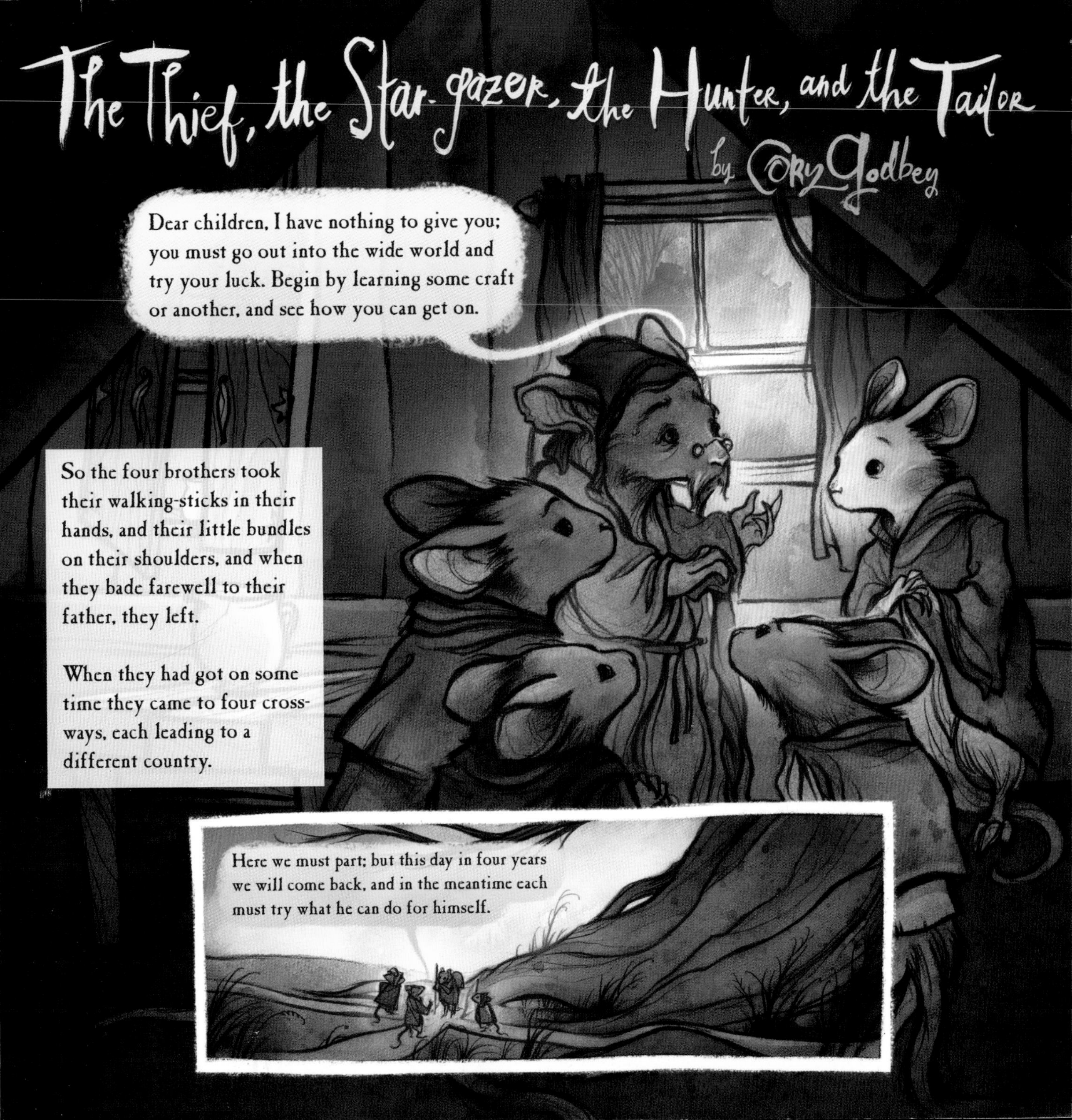
The Thief, the Star-gazer, the Hunter, and the Tailor
by Cory Godbey
Dear children, I have nothing to give you; you must go out into the wide world and try your luck. Begin by learning some craft or another, and see how you can get on.
So the four brothers took their walking-sticks in their hands, and their little bundles on their shoulders, and when they bade farewell to their father, they left.
When they had got on some time they came to four cross-ways, each leading to a different country.
Here we must part; but this day in four years we will come back, and in the meantime each must try what he can do for himself.

The first brother met an old mouse who was a cunning thief. Though he was hesitant to join, for the trade seemed dishonest.

Oh! You need not fear the gallows; for I will only teach you to steal what will be fair game.

The second brother met a star-gazer.

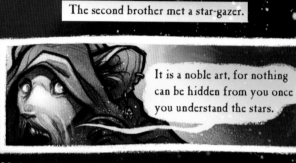

It is a noble art, for nothing can be hidden from you once you understand the stars.

He became a skillful star-gazer and his master gave him a glass.

"With this you can see all that is passing in the sky and on earth."

The third brother met a huntsmouse, who taught him the craft of the woods; and when he left his master gave him a bow.

Whatever you shoot at with this bow you will be sure to hit.

Not knowing what better to do, the youngest mouse learnt tailoring. By and by he was given a needle by his master.

You can sew anything with this, be it as soft as an egg or as hard as steel; and the joint will be so fine that no seam will be seen.

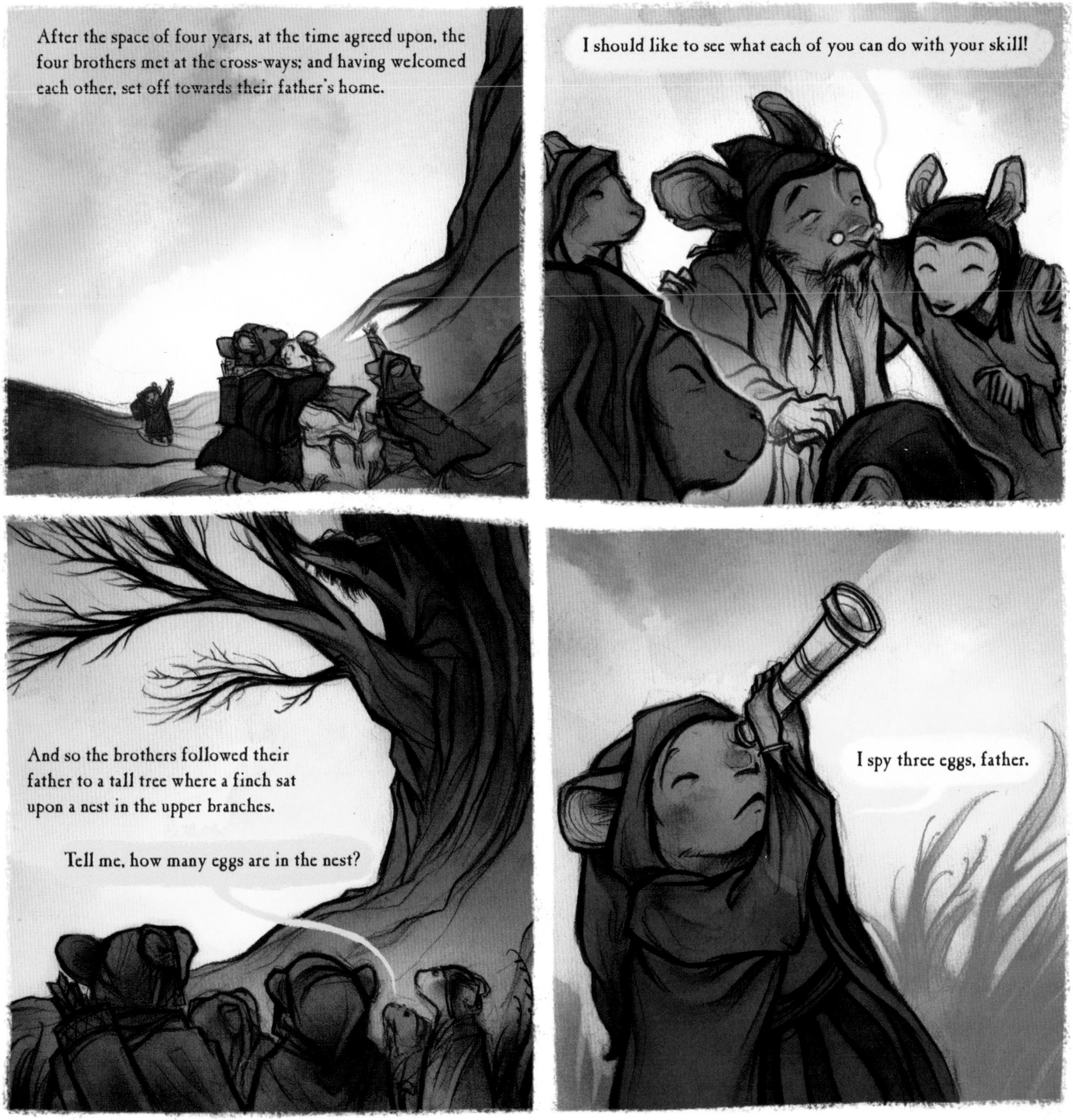
After the space of four years, at the time agreed upon, the four brothers met at the cross-ways; and having welcomed each other, set off towards their father's home.
I should like to see what each of you can do with your skill!
And so the brothers followed their father to a tall tree where a finch sat upon a nest in the upper branches.
Tell me, how many eggs are in the nest?
I spy three eggs, father.

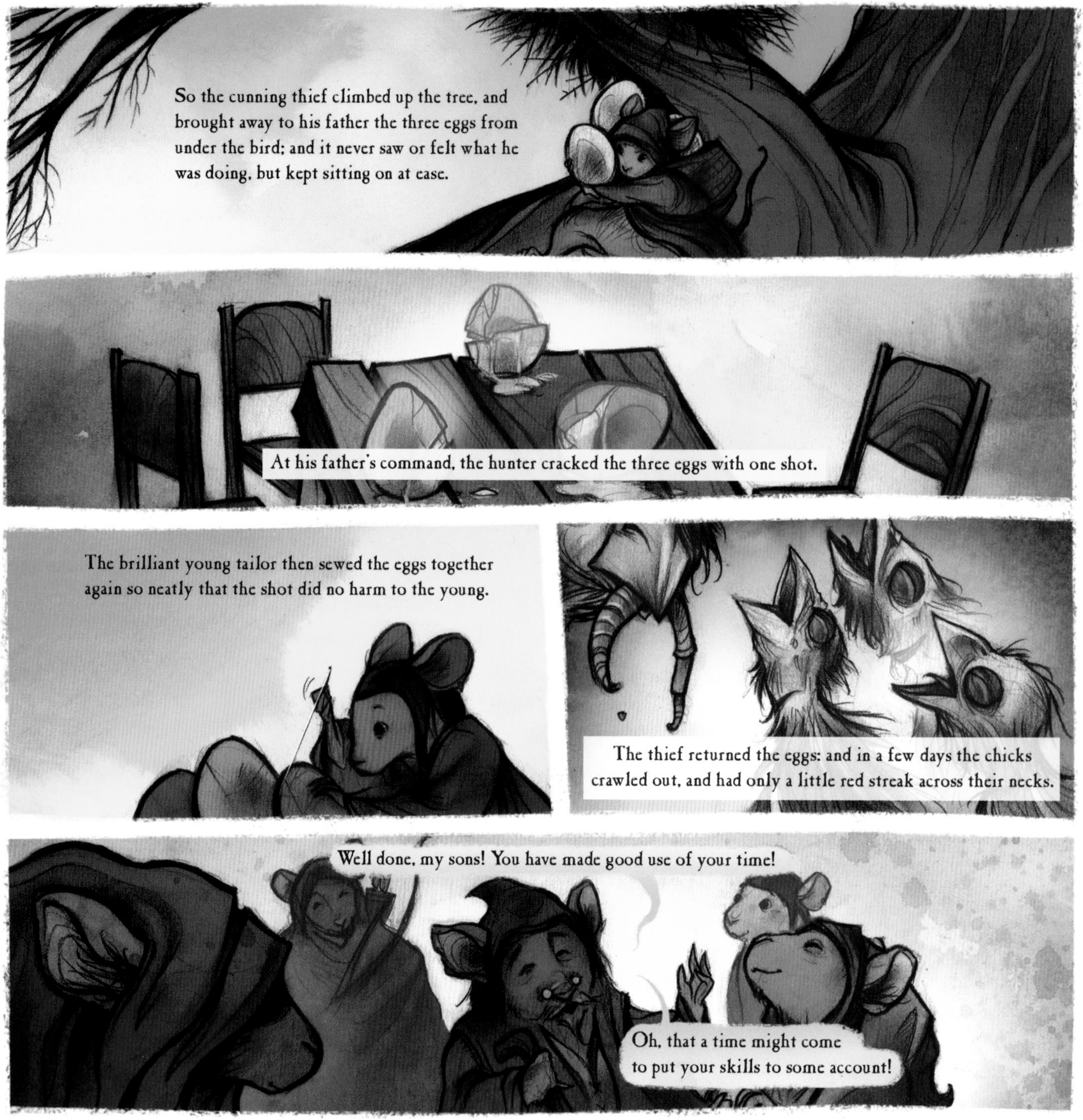

So the cunning thief climbed up the tree, and brought away to his father the three eggs from under the bird; and it never saw or felt what he was doing, but kept sitting on at ease.
At his father's command, the hunter cracked the three eggs with one shot.
The brilliant young tailor then sewed the eggs together again so neatly that the shot did no harm to the young.
The thief returned the eggs: and in a few days the chicks crawled out, and had only a little red streak across their necks.
Well done, my sons! You have made good use of your time!
Oh, that a time might come to put your skills to some account!

Not long after this there was a great bustle in the country; for the king's daughter had been carried off by a mighty creature, and the king mourned over his loss day and night, and made it known that whoever brought her back to him should have her for a wife.

Then the four brothers said to each other, "Here is a chance for us; let us try what we can do!"

And they agreed to see whether or not they could set the princess free.

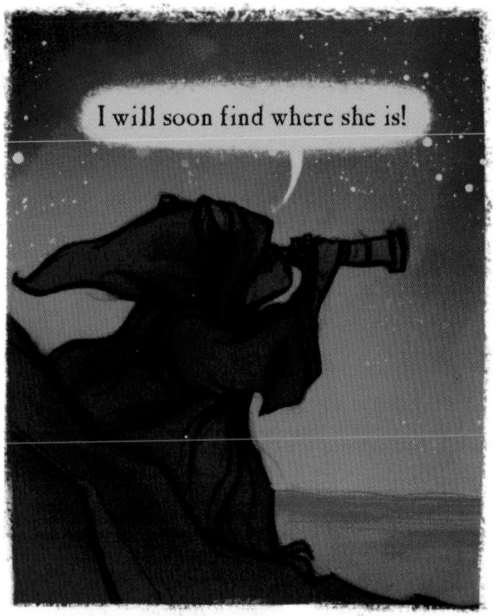
I will soon find where she is!

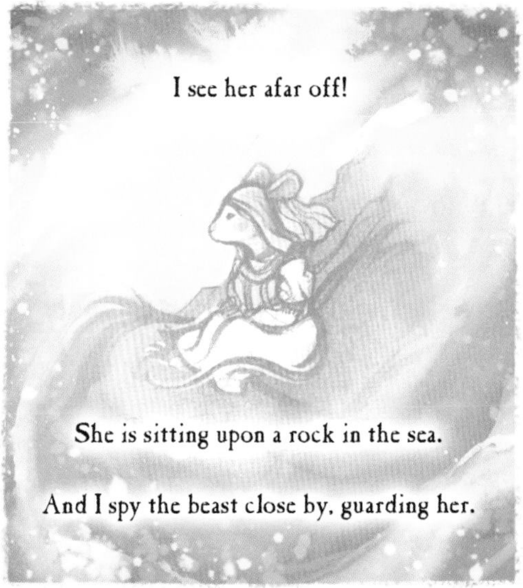
I see her afar off!
She is sitting upon a rock in the sea.
And I spy the beast close by, guarding her.

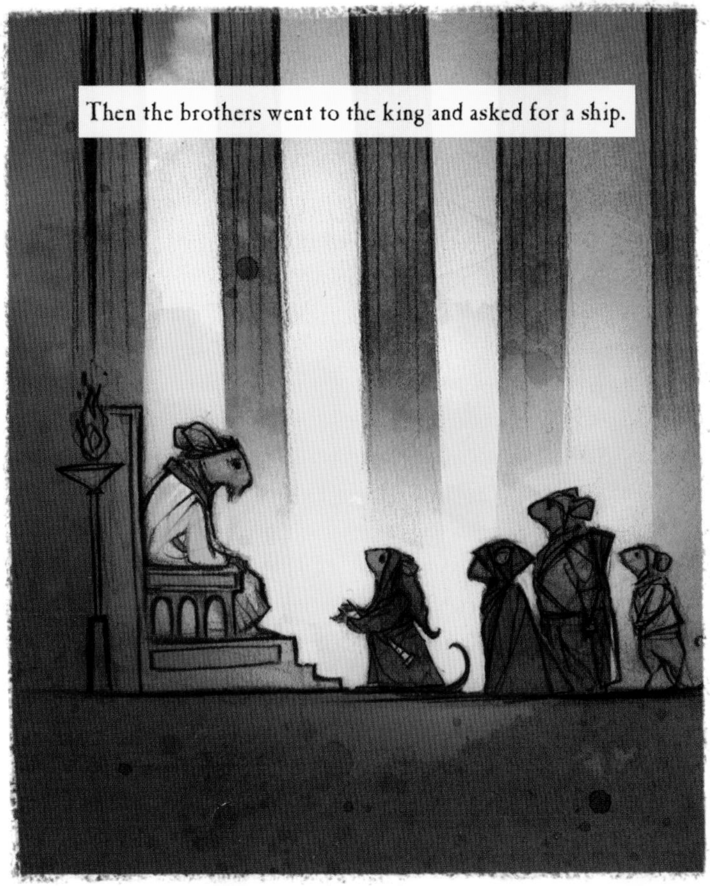
Then the brothers went to the king and asked for a ship.

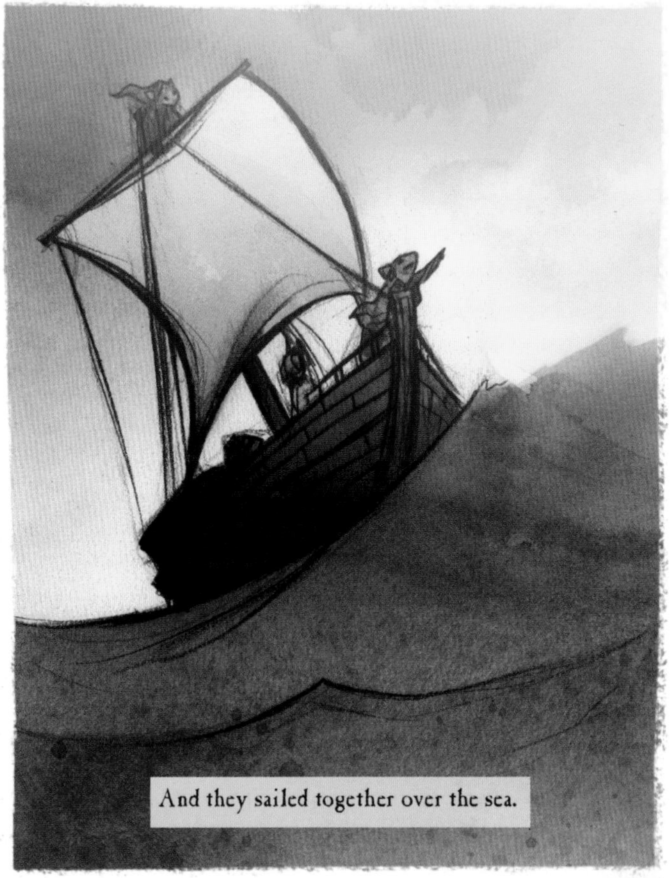
And they sailed together over the sea.

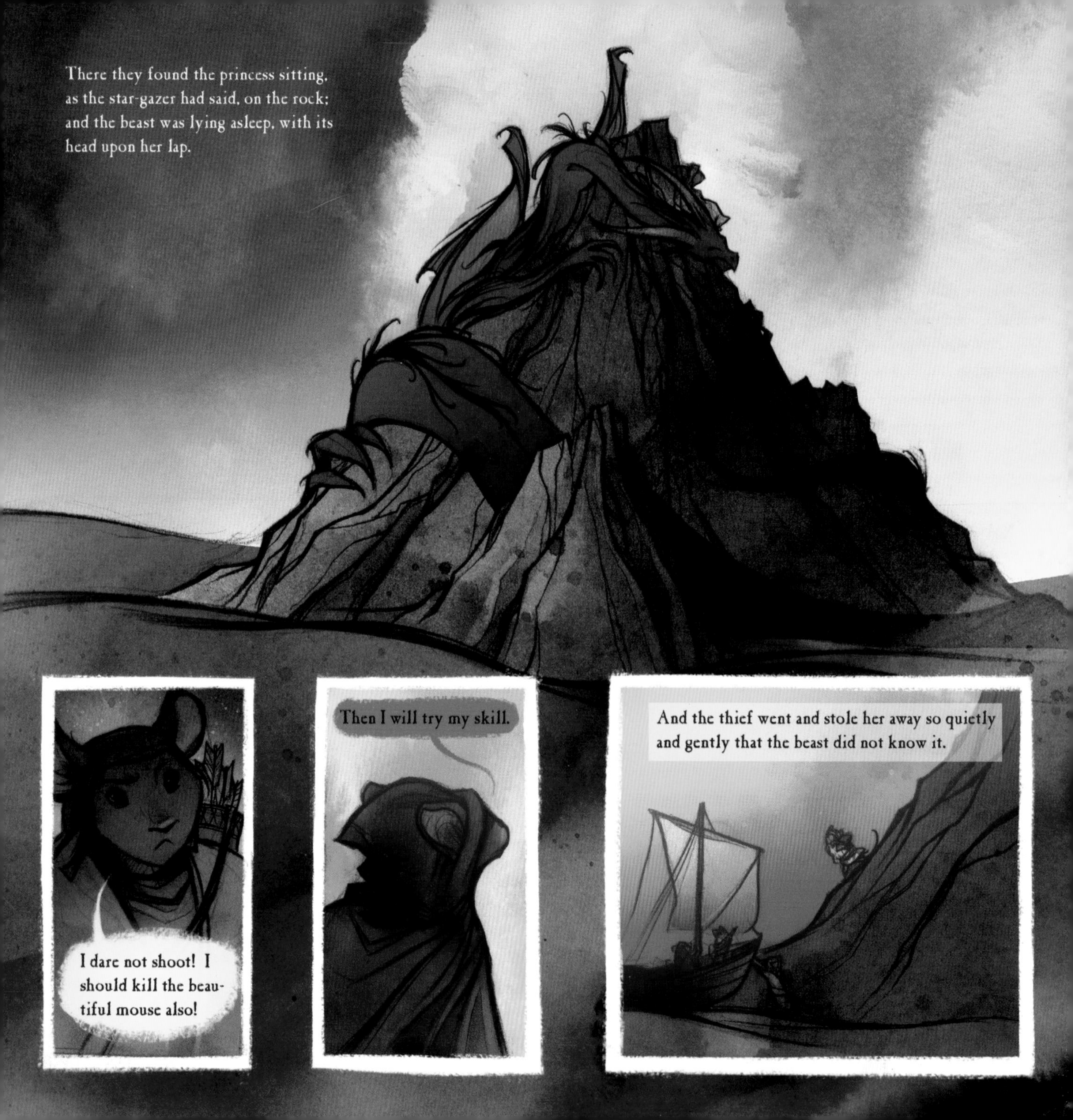
There they found the princess sitting, as the star-gazer had said, on the rock; and the beast was lying asleep, with its head upon her lap.
I dare not shoot! I should kill the beau-tiful mouse also!
Then I will try my skill.
And the thief went and stole her away so quietly and gently that the beast did not know it.

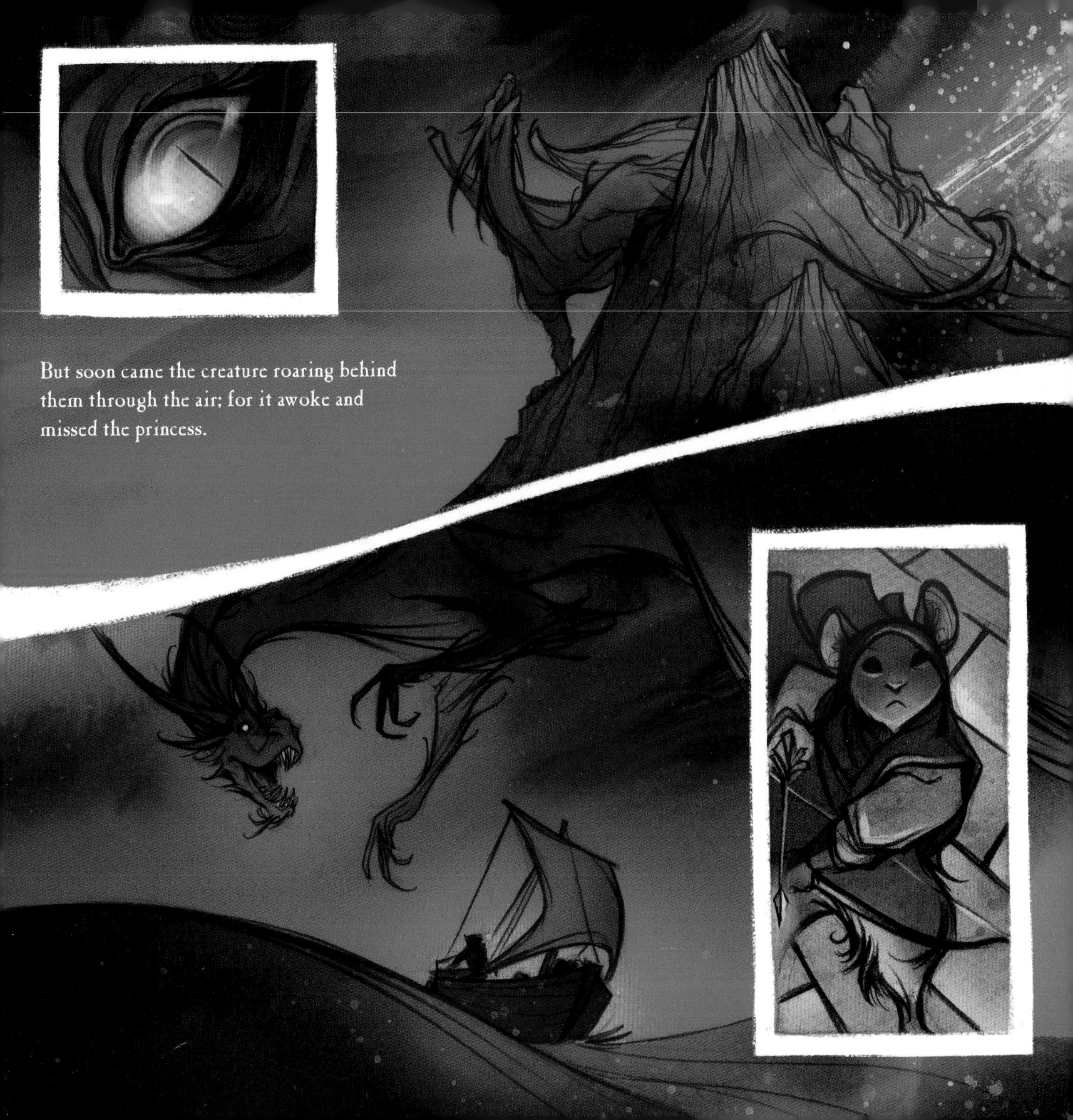

But soon came the creature roaring behind them through the air; for it awoke and missed the princess.

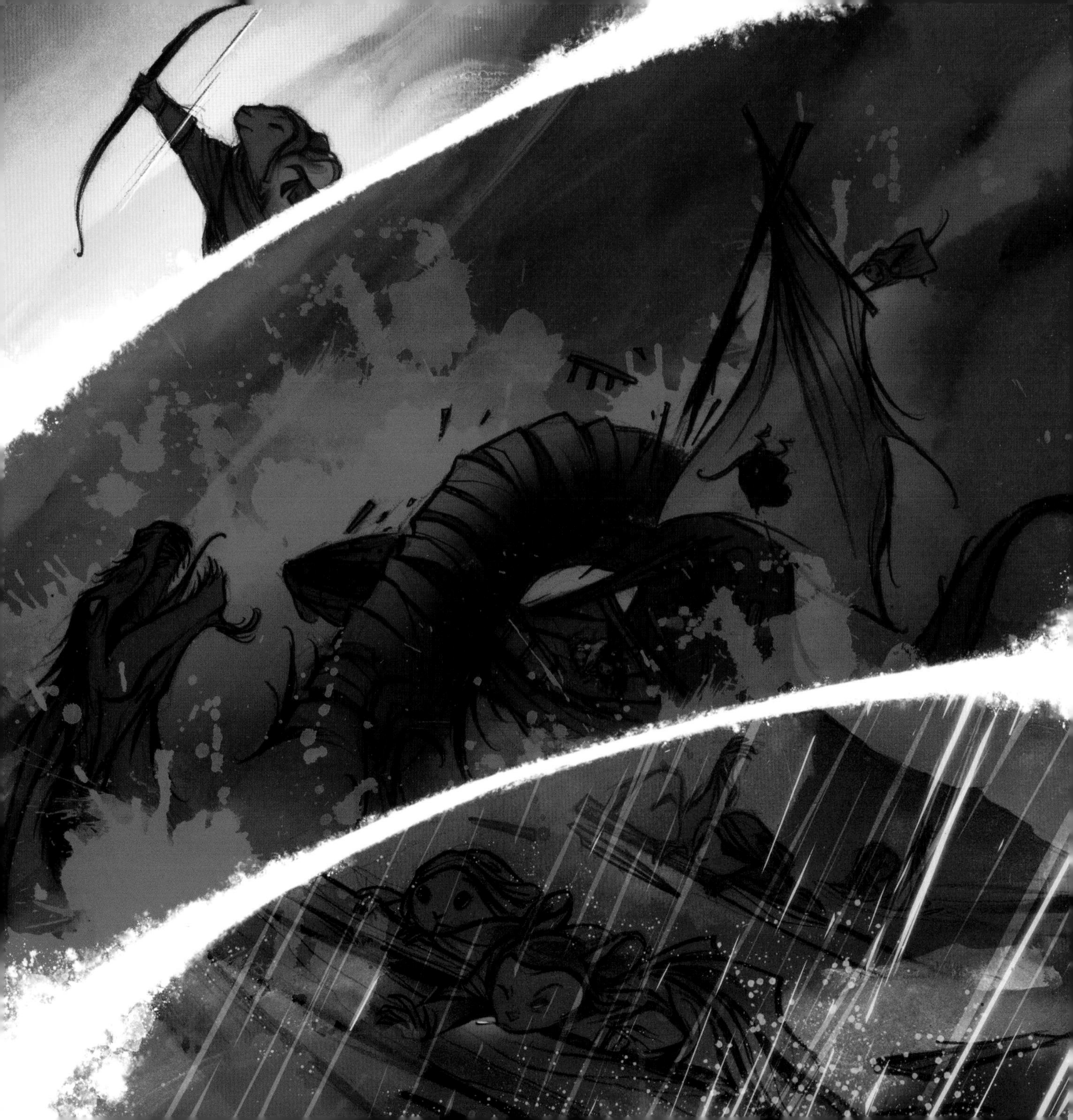

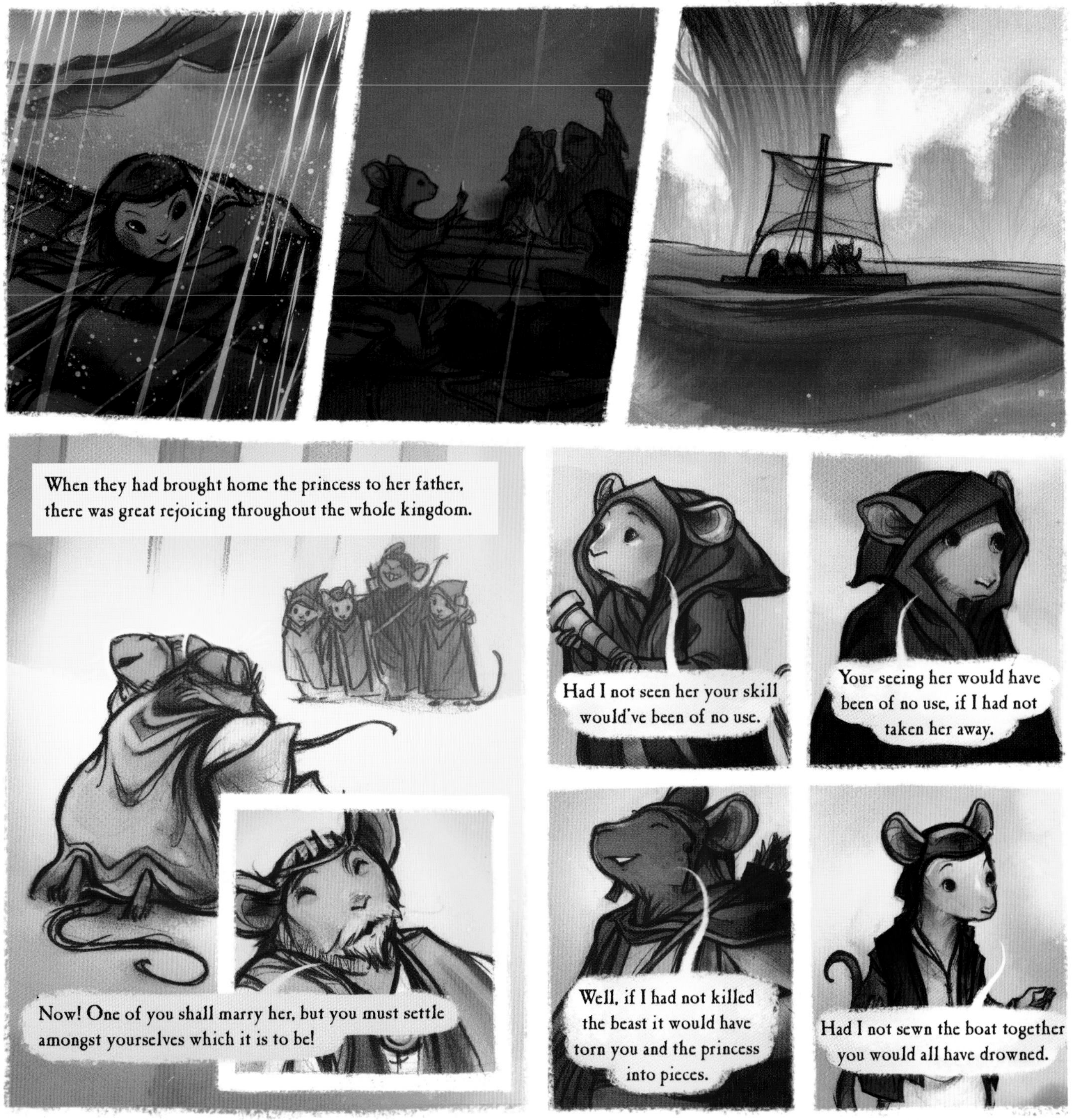
When they had brought home the princess to her father, there was great rejoicing throughout the whole kingdom.
Now! One of you shall marry her, but you must settle amongst yourselves which it is to be!
Had I not seen her your skill would've been of no use.
Your seeing her would have been of no use, if I had not taken her away.
Well, if I had not killed the beast it would have torn you and the princess into pieces.
Had I not sewn the boat together you would all have drowned.

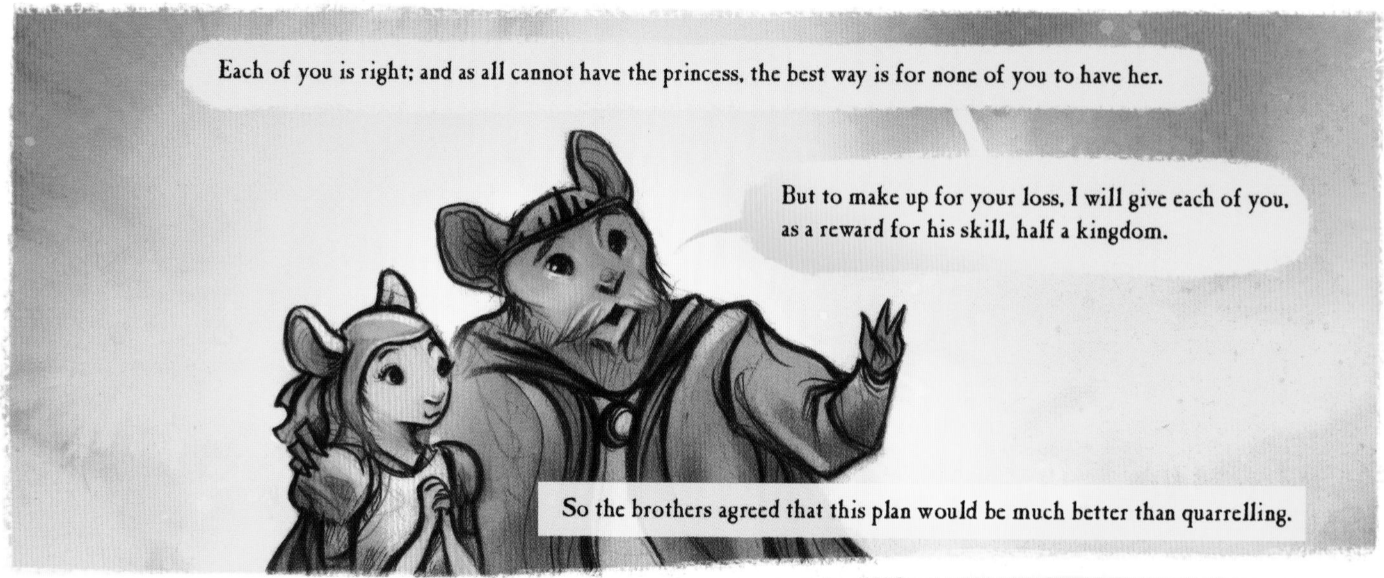
Each of you is right; and as all cannot have the princess, the best way is for none of you to have her.
But to make up for your loss, I will give each of you, as a reward for his skill, half a kingdom.
So the brothers agreed that this plan would be much better than quarrelling.

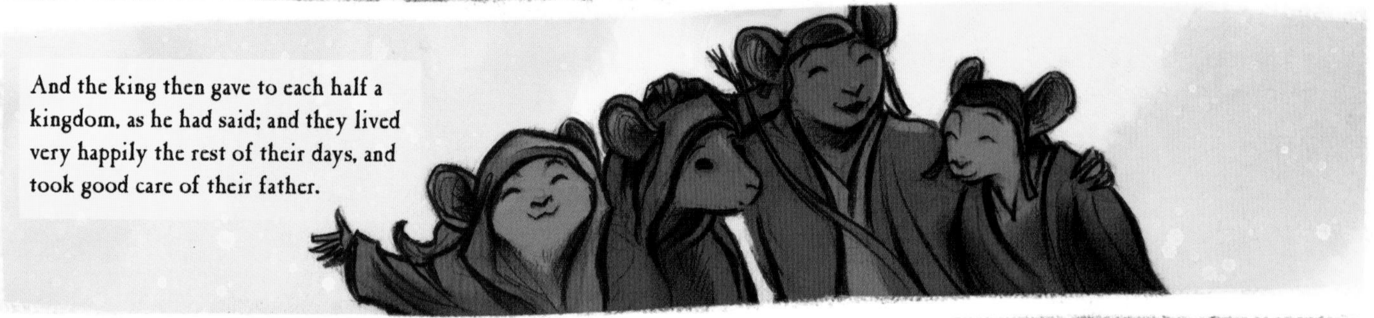
And the king then gave to each half a kingdom, as he had said; and they lived very happily the rest of their days, and took good care of their father.

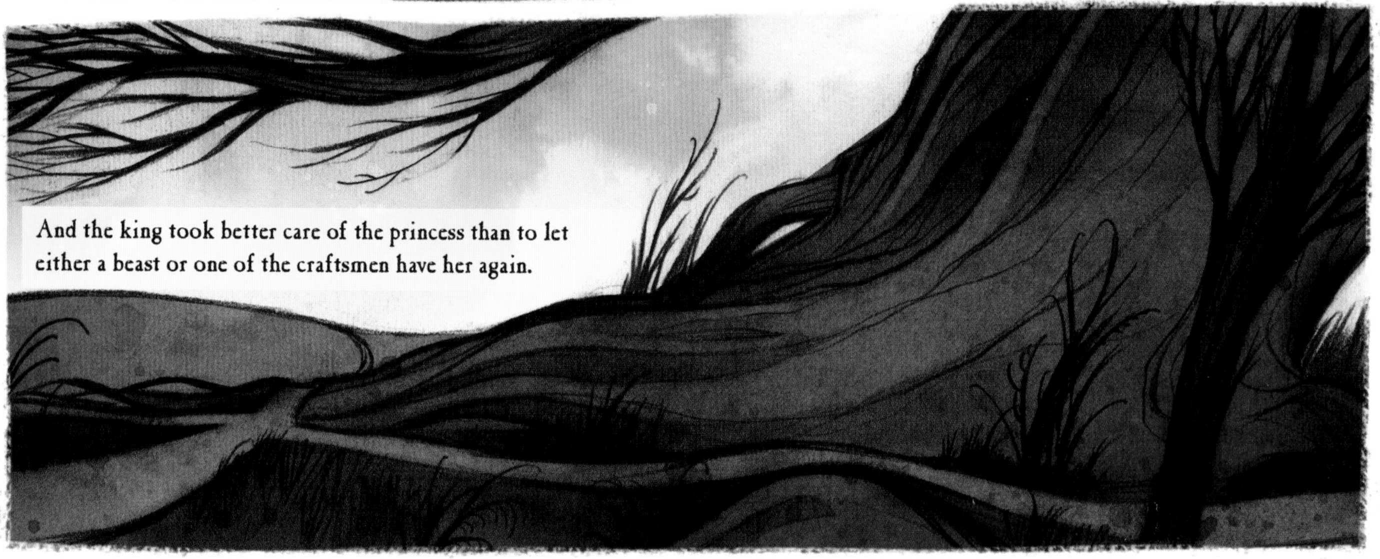
And the king took better care of the princess than to let either a beast or one of the craftsmen have her again.

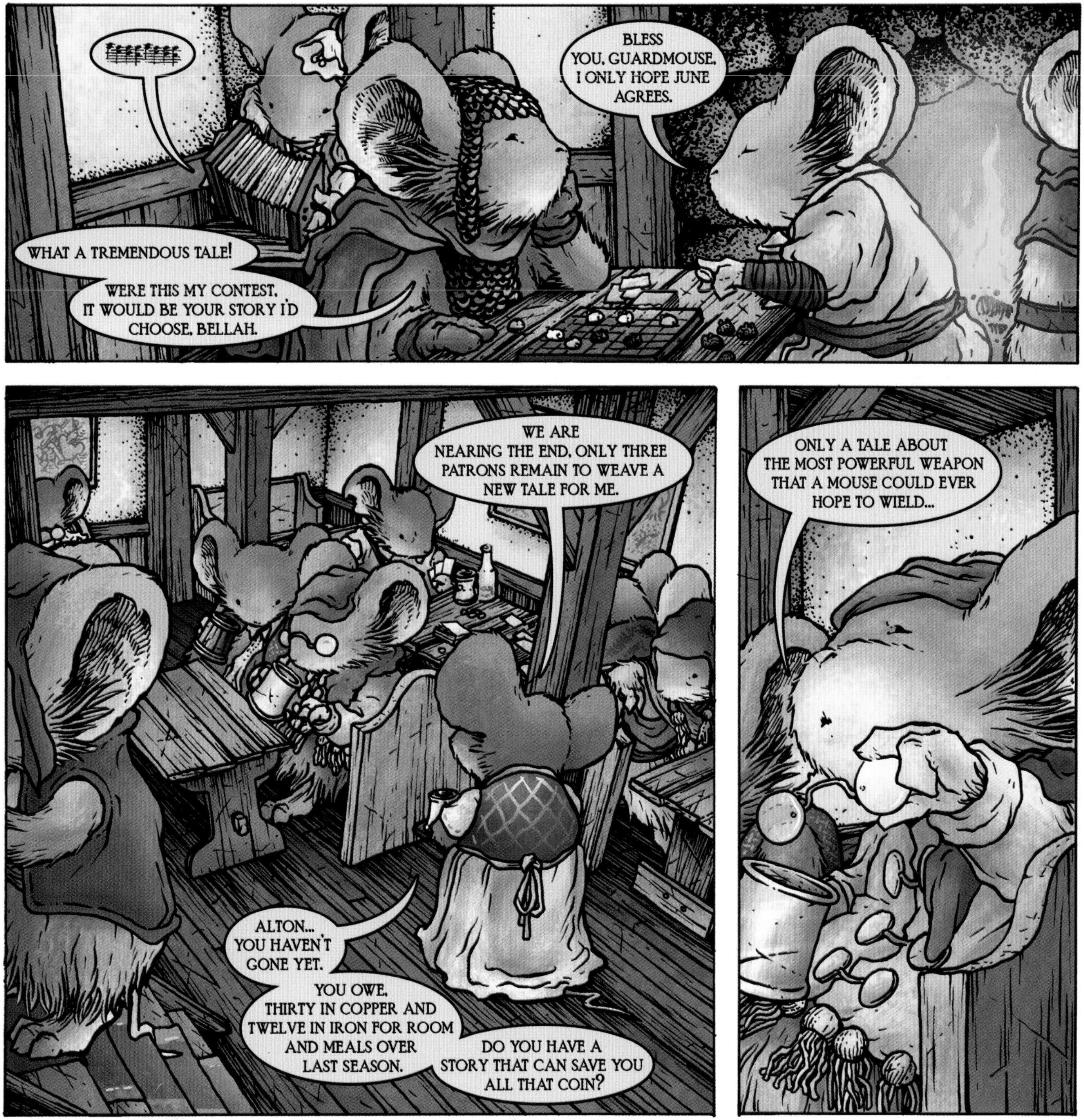

WHAT A TREMENDOUS TALE!
WERE THIS MY CONTEST, IT WOULD BE YOUR STORY I'D CHOOSE, BELLAH.
BLESS YOU, GUARDMOUSE. I ONLY HOPE JUNE AGREES.
WE ARE NEARING THE END. ONLY THREE PATRONS REMAIN TO WEAVE A NEW TALE FOR ME.
ALTON... YOU HAVEN'T GONE YET.
YOU OWE, THIRTY IN COPPER AND TWELVE IN IRON FOR ROOM AND MEALS OVER LAST SEASON.
DO YOU HAVE A STORY THAT CAN SAVE YOU ALL THAT COIN?
ONLY A TALE ABOUT THE MOST POWERFUL WEAPON THAT A MOUSE COULD EVER HOPE TO WIELD...

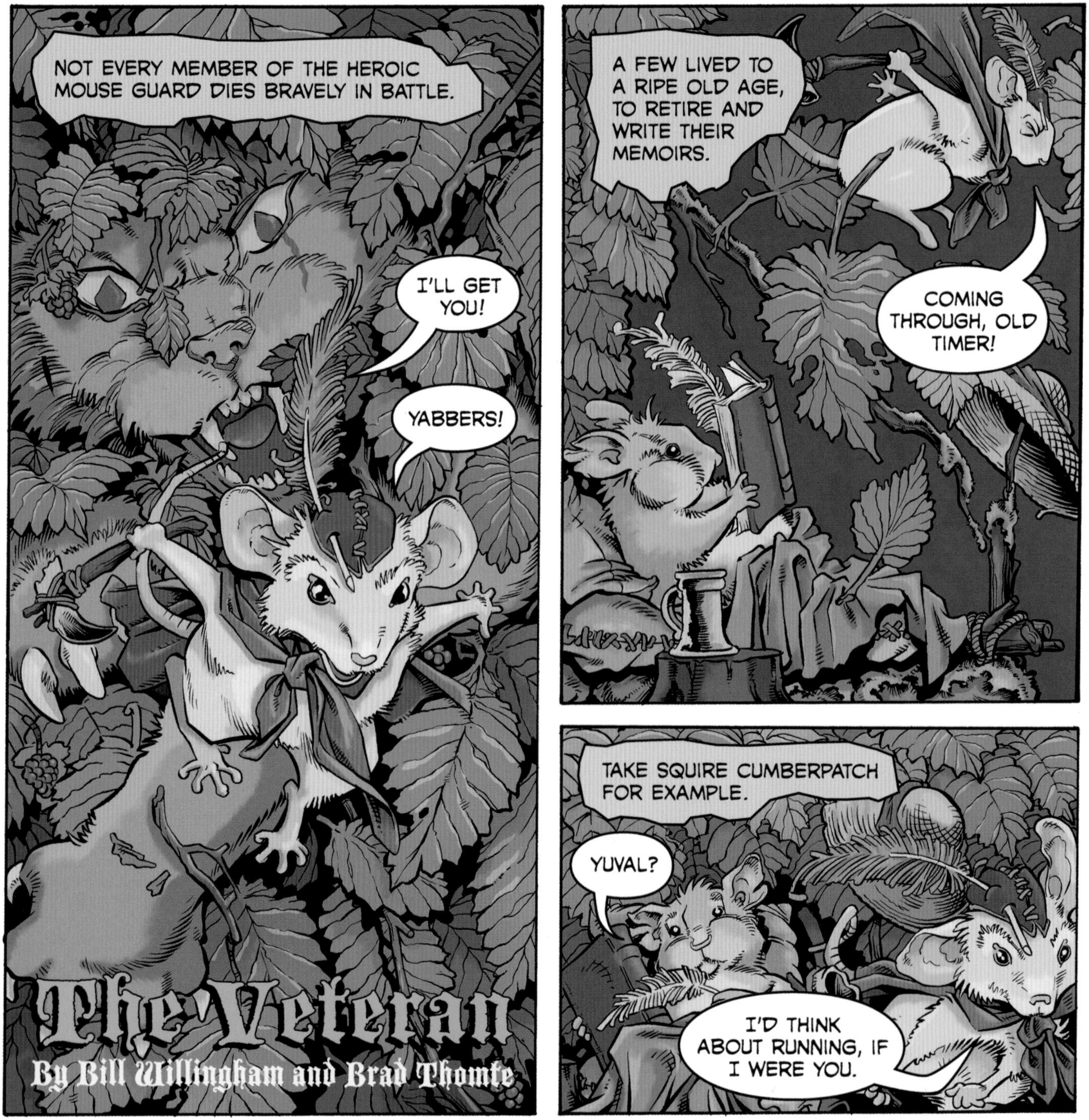
NOT EVERY MEMBER OF THE HEROIC MOUSE GUARD DIES BRAVELY IN BATTLE.
I'LL GET YOU!
YABBERS!
The Veteran
By Bill Willingham and Brad Thomte
A FEW LIVED TO A RIPE OLD AGE, TO RETIRE AND WRITE THEIR MEMOIRS.
COMING THROUGH, OLD TIMER!
TAKE SQUIRE CUMBERPATCH FOR EXAMPLE.
YUVAL?
I'D THINK ABOUT RUNNING, IF I WERE YOU.

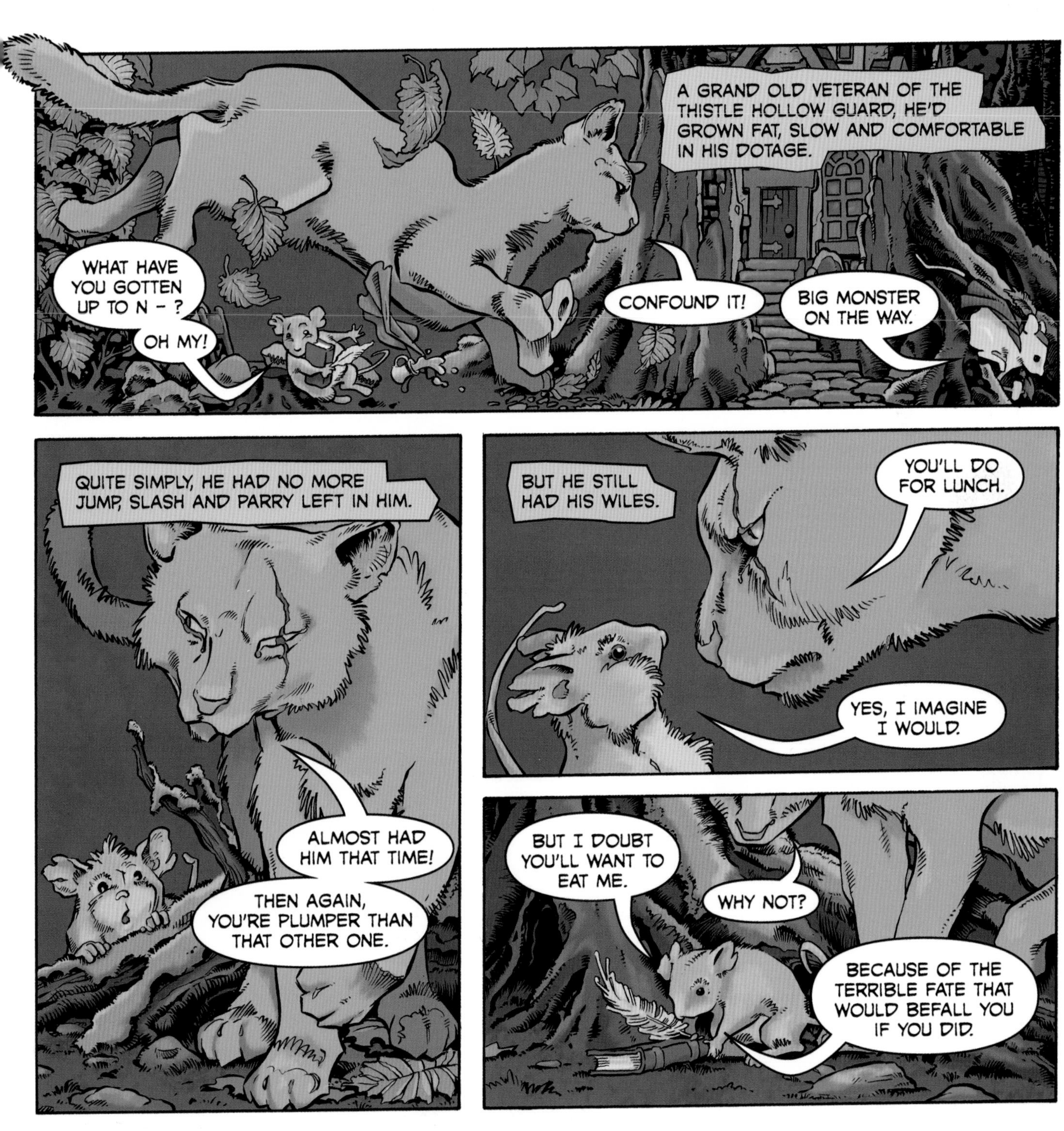
A GRAND OLD VETERAN OF THE THISTLE HOLLOW GUARD, HE'D GROWN FAT, SLOW AND COMFORTABLE IN HIS DOTAGE.
WHAT HAVE YOU GOTTEN UP TO N – ?
OH MY!
CONFOUND IT!
BIG MONSTER ON THE WAY.
QUITE SIMPLY, HE HAD NO MORE JUMP, SLASH AND PARRY LEFT IN HIM.
ALMOST HAD HIM THAT TIME!
THEN AGAIN, YOU'RE PLUMPER THAN THAT OTHER ONE.
BUT HE STILL HAD HIS WILES.
YOU'LL DO FOR LUNCH.
YES, I IMAGINE I WOULD.
BUT I DOUBT YOU'LL WANT TO EAT ME.
WHY NOT?
BECAUSE OF THE TERRIBLE FATE THAT WOULD BEFALL YOU IF YOU DID.

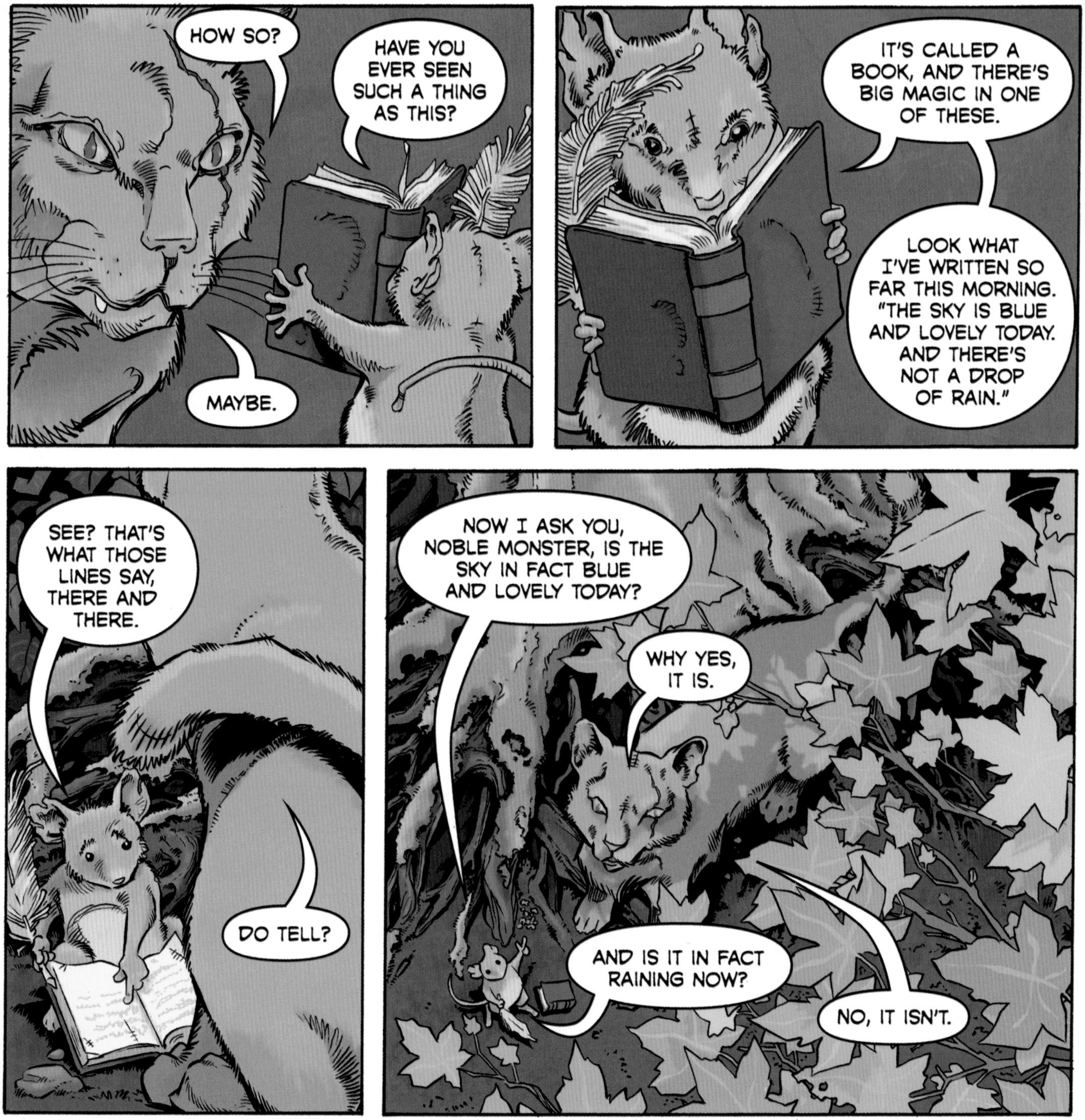
HOW SO?
HAVE YOU EVER SEEN SUCH A THING AS THIS?
MAYBE.
IT'S CALLED A BOOK, AND THERE'S BIG MAGIC IN ONE OF THESE.
LOOK WHAT I'VE WRITTEN SO FAR THIS MORNING. "THE SKY IS BLUE AND LOVELY TODAY. AND THERE'S NOT A DROP OF RAIN."
SEE? THAT'S WHAT THOSE LINES SAY, THERE AND THERE.
DO TELL?
NOW I ASK YOU, NOBLE MONSTER, IS THE SKY IN FACT BLUE AND LOVELY TODAY?
WHY YES, IT IS.
AND IS IT IN FACT RAINING NOW?
NO, IT ISN'T.

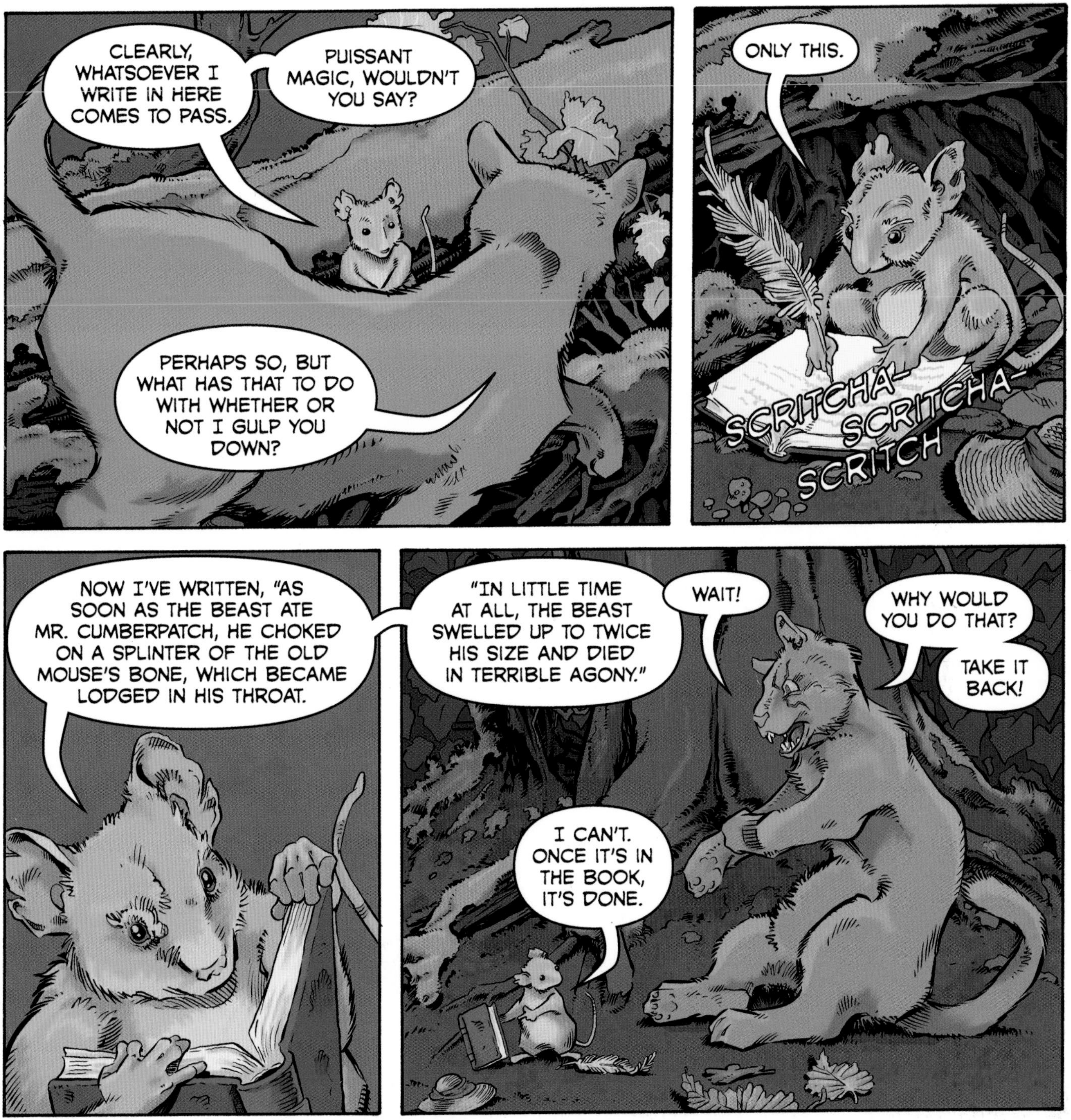
CLEARLY, WHATSOEVER I WRITE IN HERE COMES TO PASS.
PUISSANT MAGIC, WOULDN'T YOU SAY?
PERHAPS SO, BUT WHAT HAS THAT TO DO WITH WHETHER OR NOT I GULP YOU DOWN?
ONLY THIS.
SCRITCHA-SCRITCHA-SCRITCH
NOW I'VE WRITTEN, "AS SOON AS THE BEAST ATE MR. CUMBERPATCH, HE CHOKED ON A SPLINTER OF THE OLD MOUSE'S BONE, WHICH BECAME LODGED IN HIS THROAT.
"IN LITTLE TIME AT ALL, THE BEAST SWELLED UP TO TWICE HIS SIZE AND DIED IN TERRIBLE AGONY."
WAIT!
WHY WOULD YOU DO THAT?
TAKE IT BACK!
I CAN'T. ONCE IT'S IN THE BOOK, IT'S DONE.

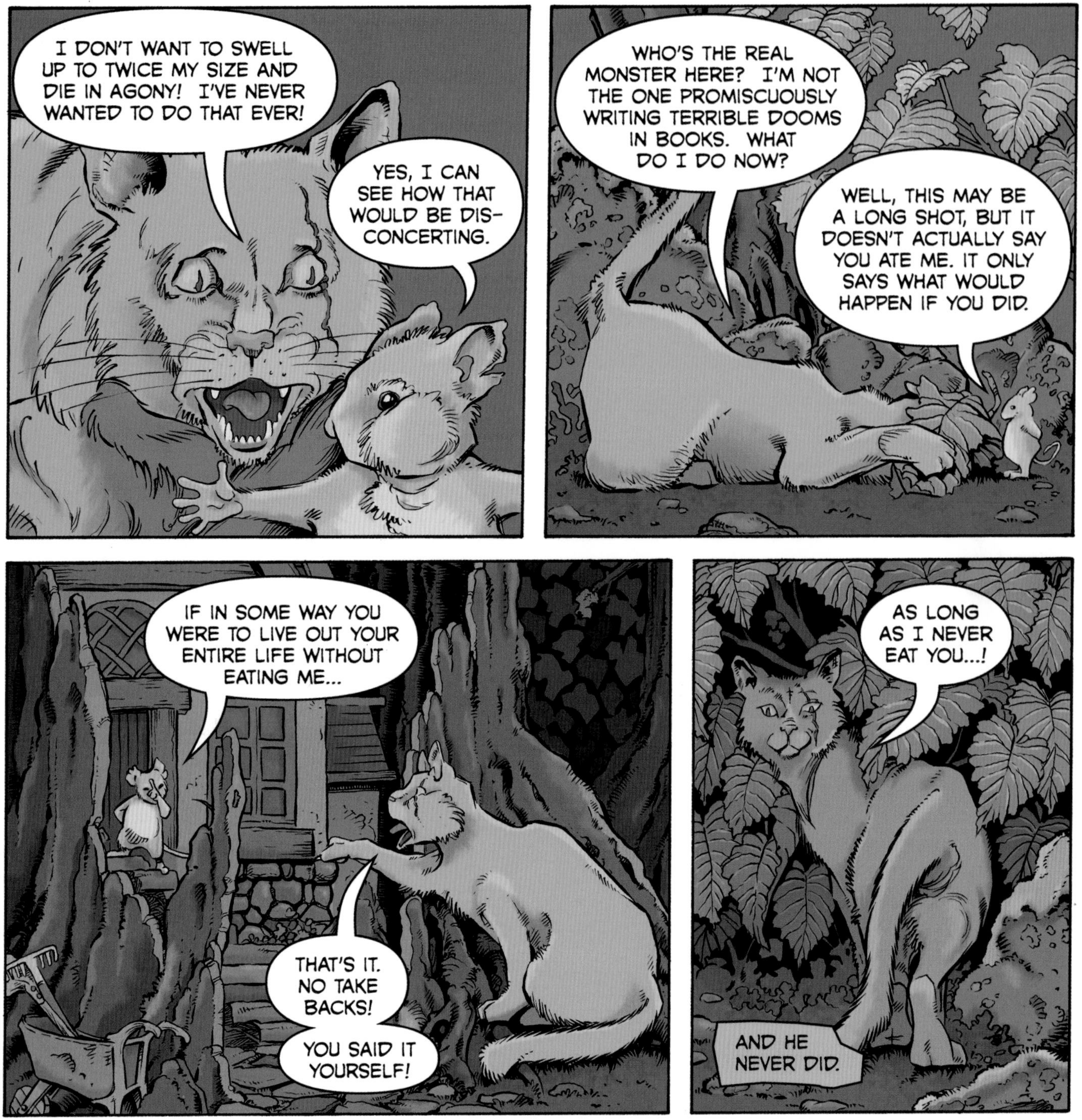
I DON'T WANT TO SWELL UP TO TWICE MY SIZE AND DIE IN AGONY! I'VE NEVER WANTED TO DO THAT EVER!
YES, I CAN SEE HOW THAT WOULD BE DIS-CONCERTING.
WHO'S THE REAL MONSTER HERE? I'M NOT THE ONE PROMISCUOUSLY WRITING TERRIBLE DOOMS IN BOOKS. WHAT DO I DO NOW?
WELL, THIS MAY BE A LONG SHOT, BUT IT DOESN'T ACTUALLY SAY YOU ATE ME. IT ONLY SAYS WHAT WOULD HAPPEN IF YOU DID.
IF IN SOME WAY YOU WERE TO LIVE OUT YOUR ENTIRE LIFE WITHOUT EATING ME...
THAT'S IT. NO TAKE BACKS!
YOU SAID IT YOURSELF!
AS LONG AS I NEVER EAT YOU...!
AND HE NEVER DID.

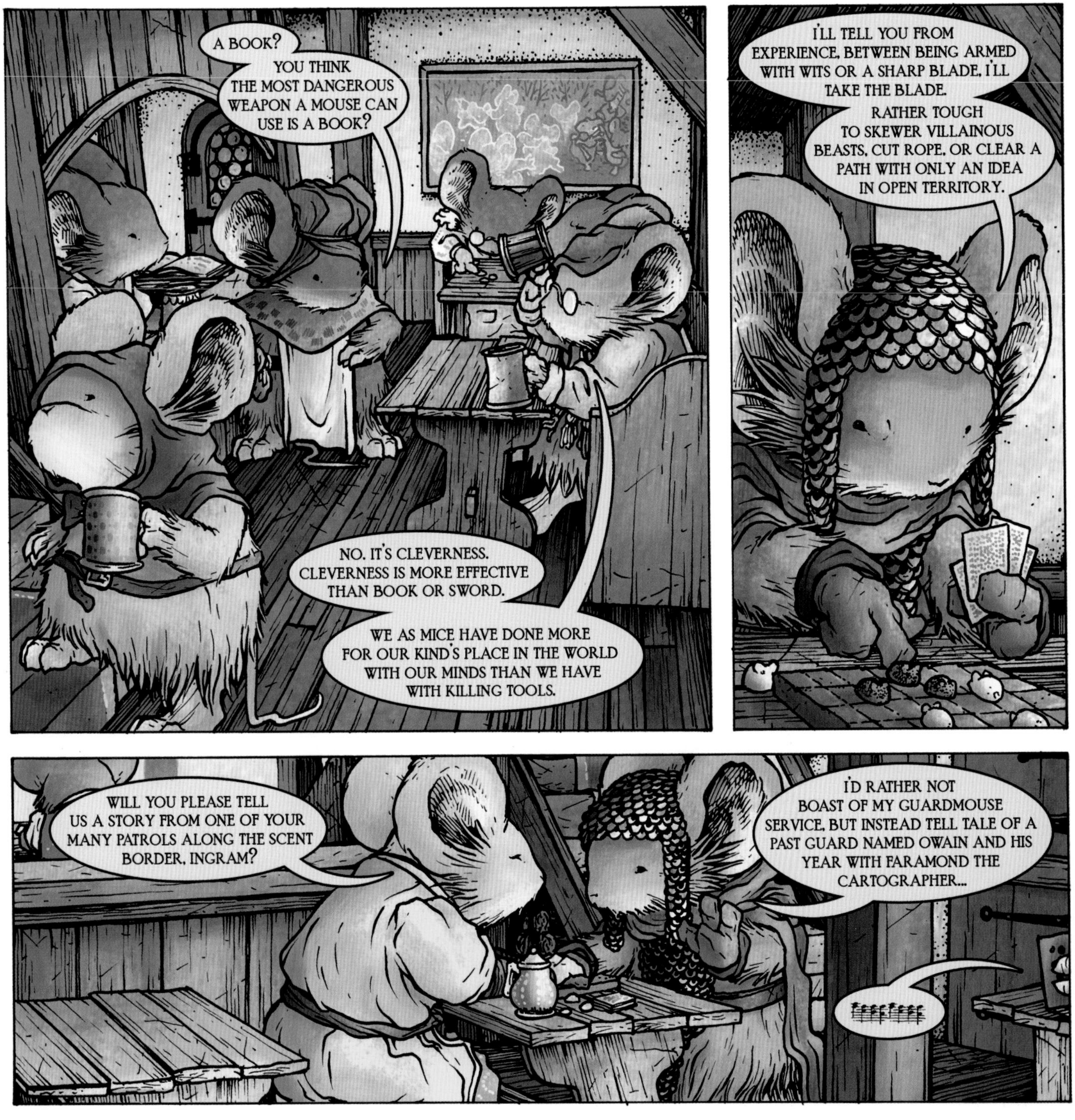
A BOOK?
YOU THINK THE MOST DANGEROUS WEAPON A MOUSE CAN USE IS A BOOK?
NO. IT'S CLEVERNESS. CLEVERNESS IS MORE EFFECTIVE THAN BOOK OR SWORD.
WE AS MICE HAVE DONE MORE FOR OUR KIND'S PLACE IN THE WORLD WITH OUR MINDS THAN WE HAVE WITH KILLING TOOLS.
I'LL TELL YOU FROM EXPERIENCE, BETWEEN BEING ARMED WITH WITS OR A SHARP BLADE, I'LL TAKE THE BLADE.
RATHER TOUGH TO SKEWER VILLAINOUS BEASTS, CUT ROPE, OR CLEAR A PATH WITH ONLY AN IDEA IN OPEN TERRITORY.
WILL YOU PLEASE TELL US A STORY FROM ONE OF YOUR MANY PATROLS ALONG THE SCENT BORDER, INGRAM?
I'D RATHER NOT BOAST OF MY GUARDMOUSE SERVICE, BUT INSTEAD TELL TALE OF A PAST GUARD NAMED OWAIN AND HIS YEAR WITH FARAMOND THE CARTOGRAPHER...

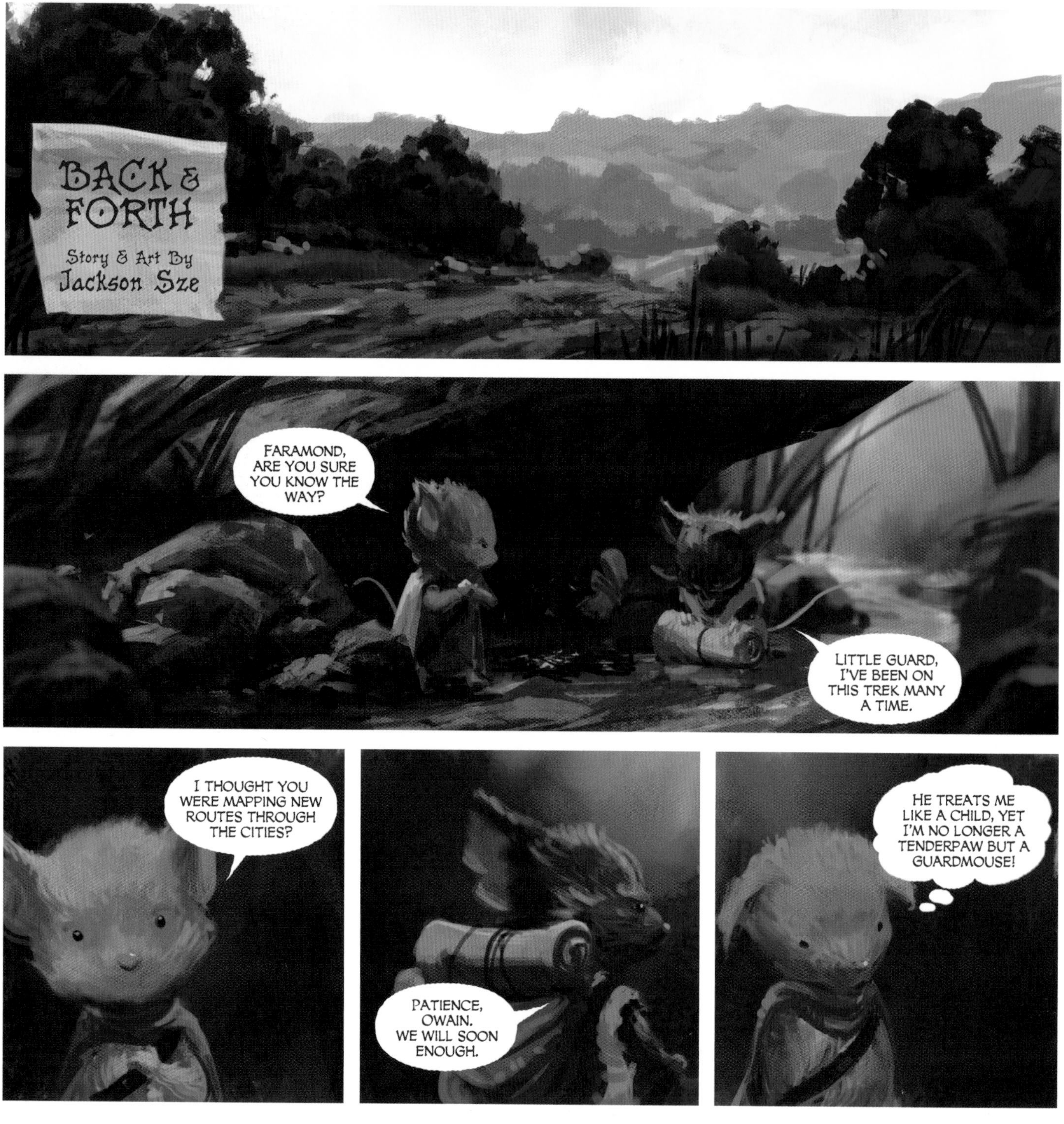
BACK & FORTH
Story & Art By
Jackson Sze
FARAMOND, ARE YOU SURE YOU KNOW THE WAY?
LITTLE GUARD, I'VE BEEN ON THIS TREK MANY A TIME.
I THOUGHT YOU WERE MAPPING NEW ROUTES THROUGH THE CITIES?
PATIENCE, OWAIN. WE WILL SOON ENOUGH.
HE TREATS ME LIKE A CHILD, YET I'M NO LONGER A TENDERPAW BUT A GUARDMOUSE!

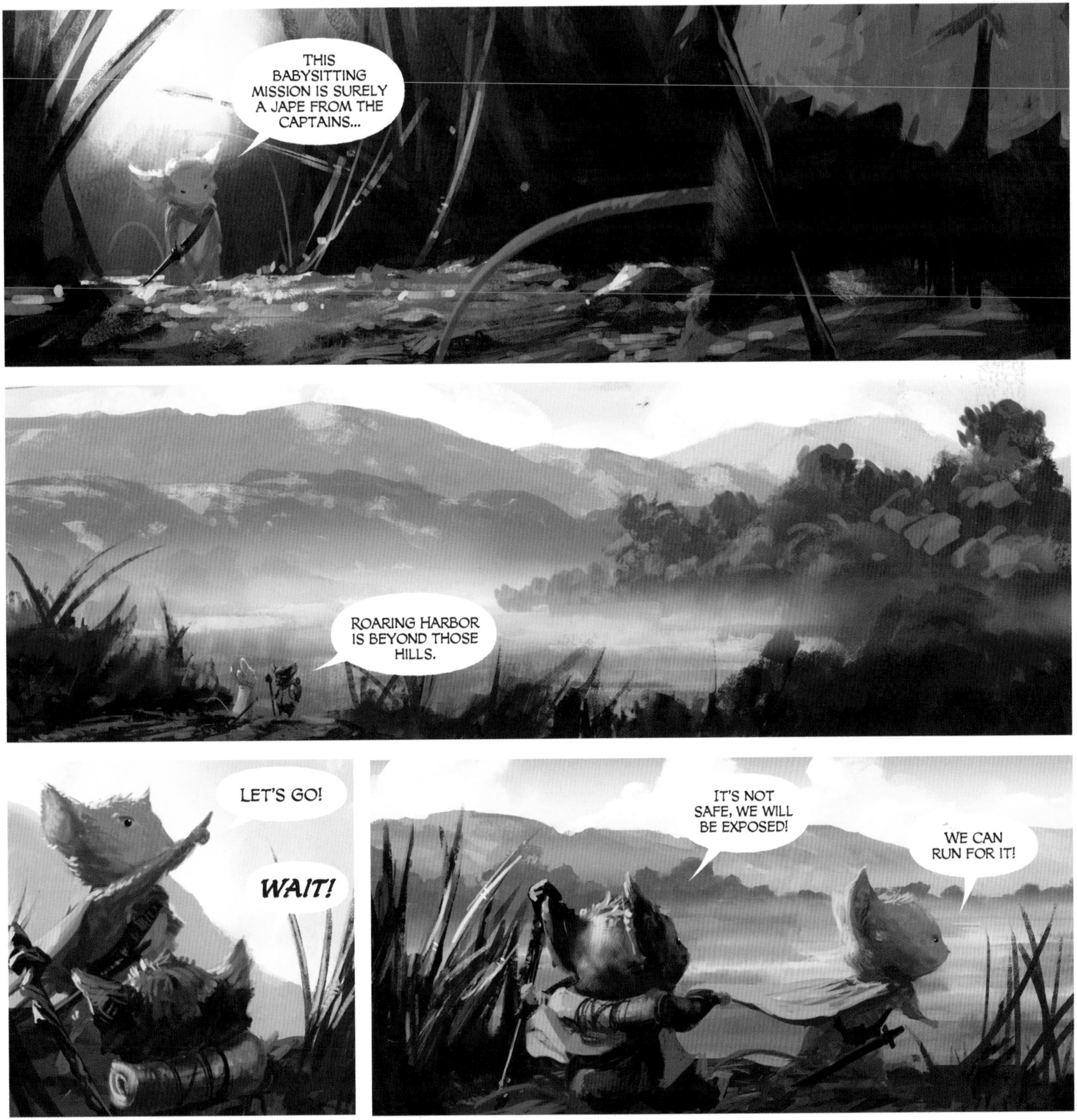
THIS BABYSITTING MISSION IS SURELY A JAPE FROM THE CAPTAINS...
ROARING HARBOR IS BEYOND THOSE HILLS.
LET'S GO!
WAIT!
IT'S NOT SAFE, WE WILL BE EXPOSED!
WE CAN RUN FOR IT!

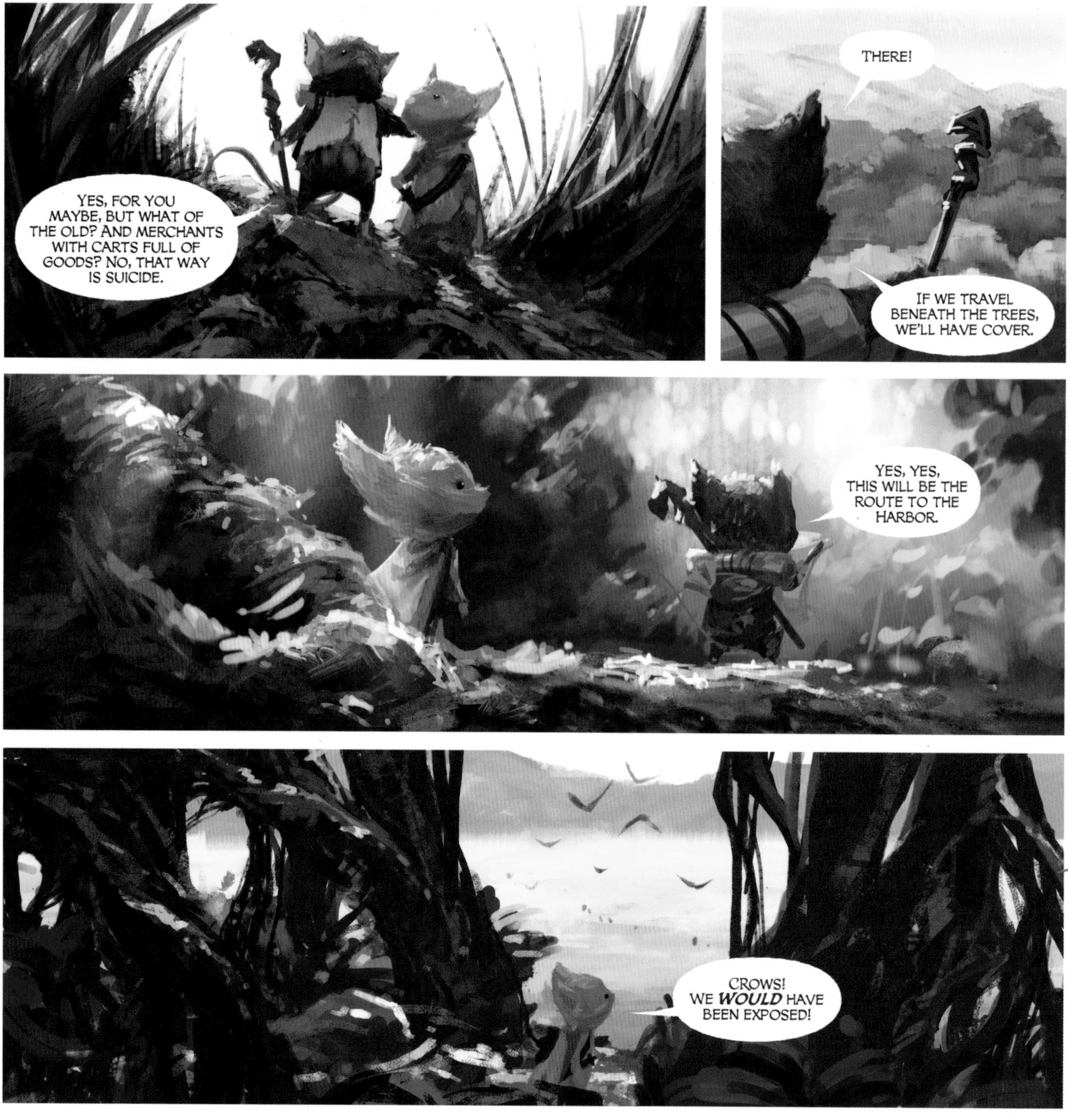
YES, FOR YOU MAYBE, BUT WHAT OF THE OLD? AND MERCHANTS WITH CARTS FULL OF GOODS? NO, THAT WAY IS SUICIDE.
THERE!
IF WE TRAVEL BENEATH THE TREES, WE'LL HAVE COVER.
YES, YES, THIS WILL BE THE ROUTE TO THE HARBOR.
CROWS! WE ***WOULD*** HAVE BEEN EXPOSED!

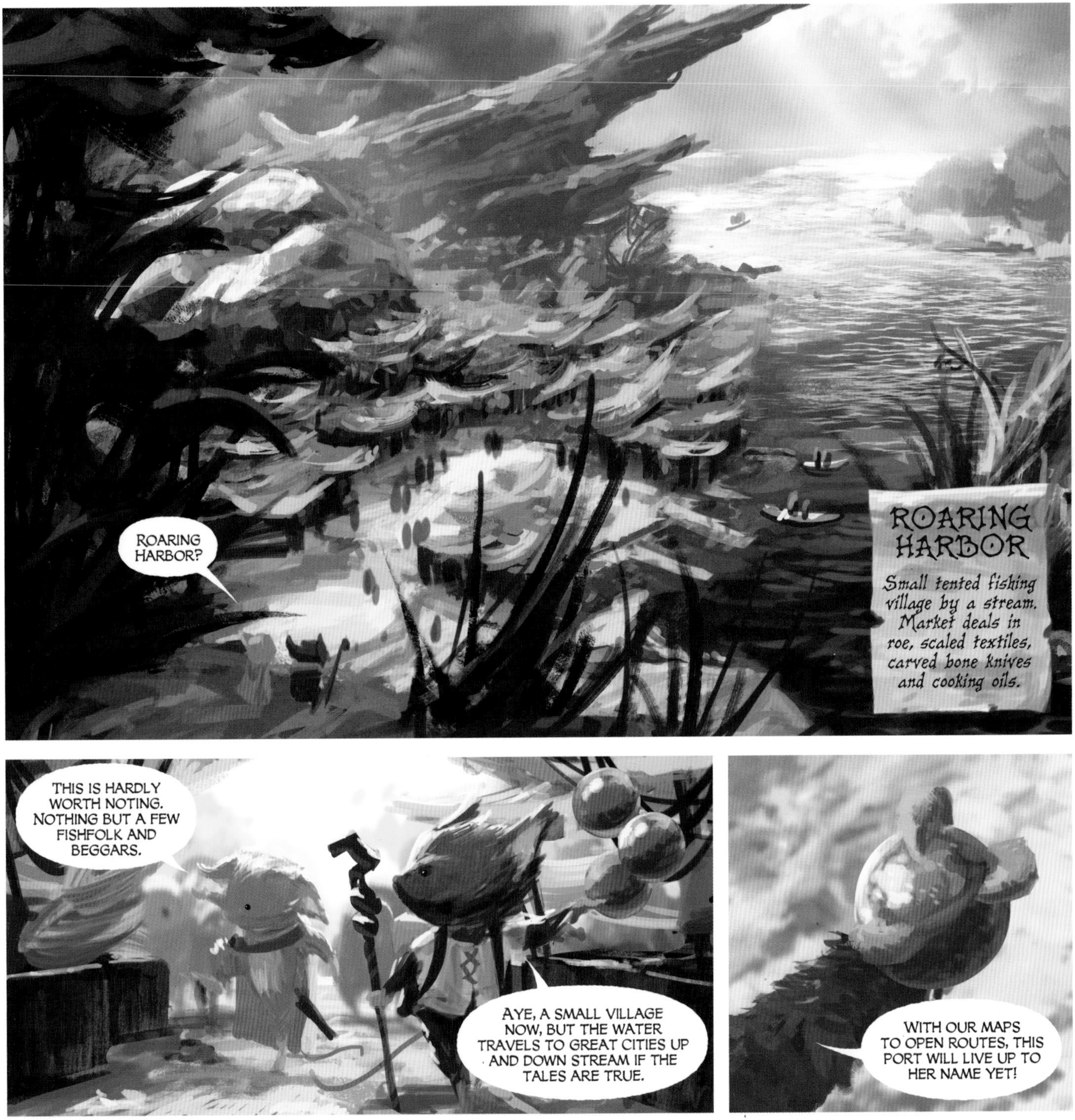
ROARING HARBOR?
ROARING HARBOR
Small tented fishing village by a stream. Market deals in roe, scaled textiles, carved bone knives and cooking oils.
THIS IS HARDLY WORTH NOTING. NOTHING BUT A FEW FISHFOLK AND BEGGARS.
AYE, A SMALL VILLAGE NOW, BUT THE WATER TRAVELS TO GREAT CITIES UP AND DOWN STREAM IF THE TALES ARE TRUE.
WITH OUR MAPS TO OPEN ROUTES, THIS PORT WILL LIVE UP TO HER NAME YET!

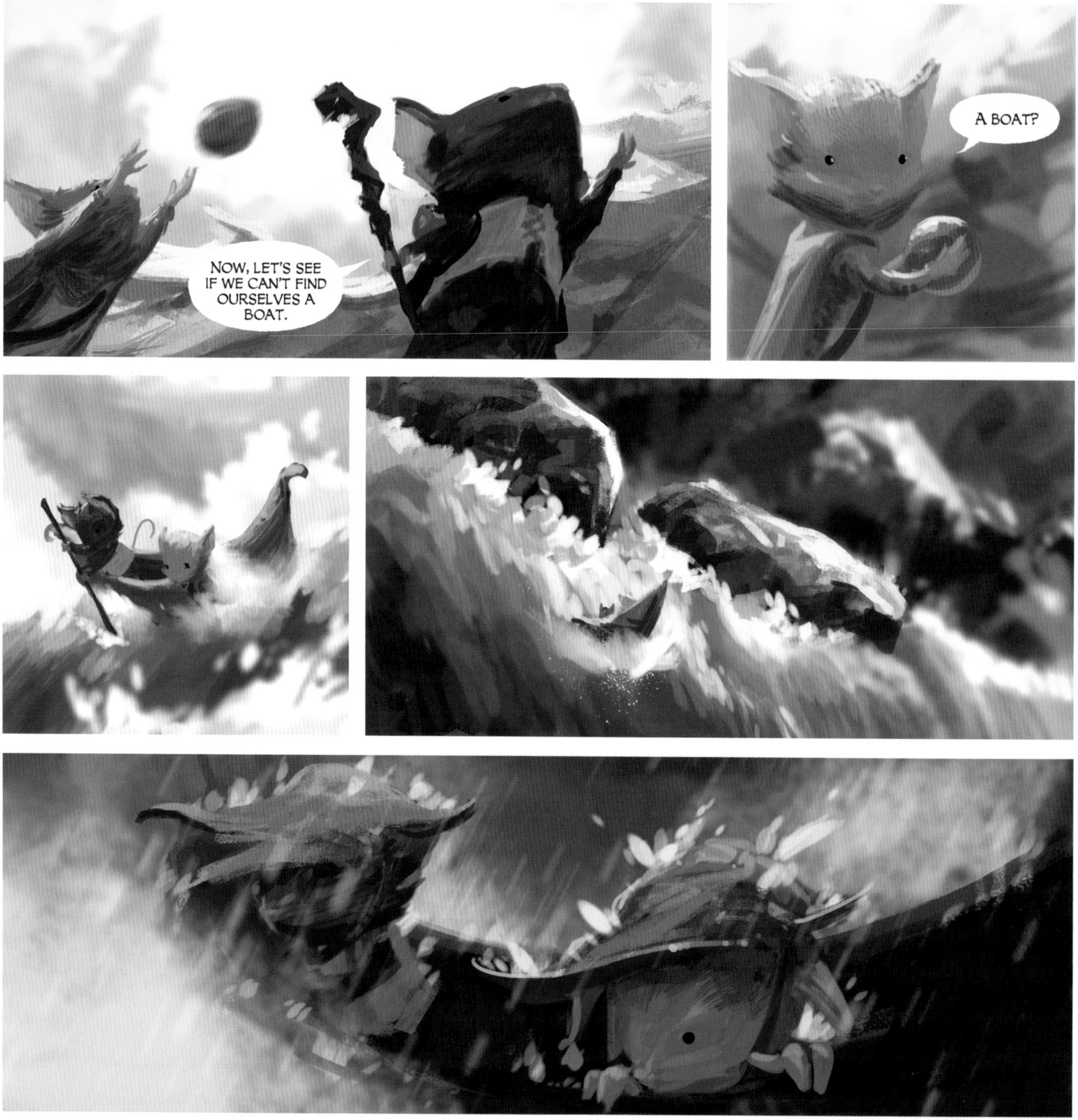
NOW, LET'S SEE IF WE CAN'T FIND OURSELVES A BOAT.
A BOAT?

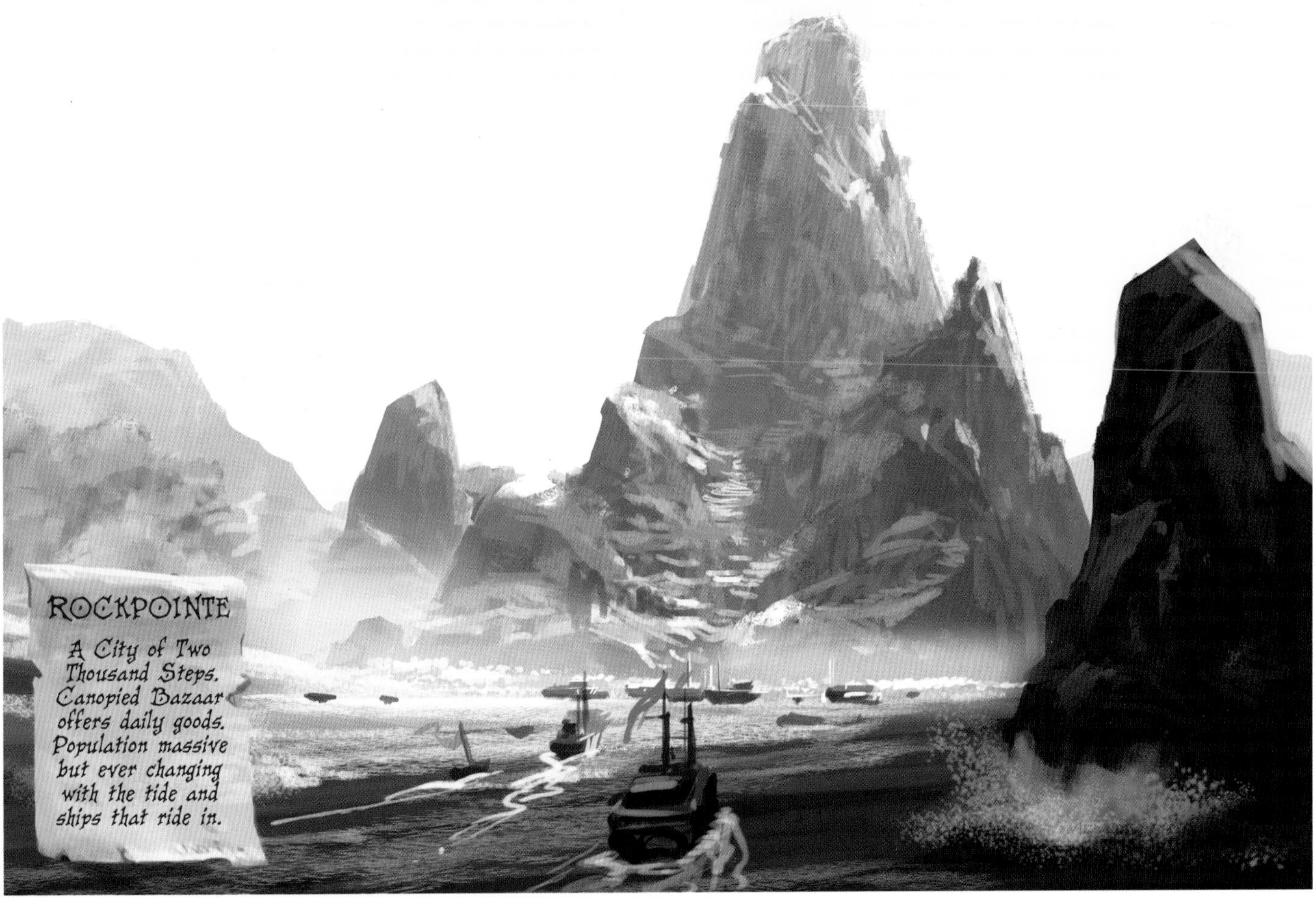
ROCKPOINTE
A City of Two Thousand Steps. Canopied Bazaar offers daily goods. Population massive but ever changing with the tide and ships that ride in.

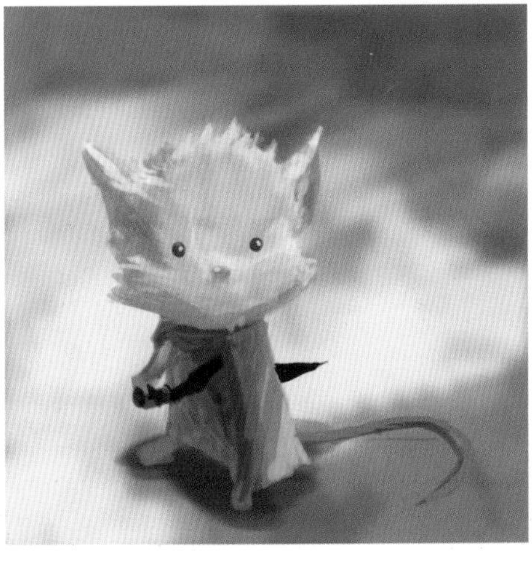

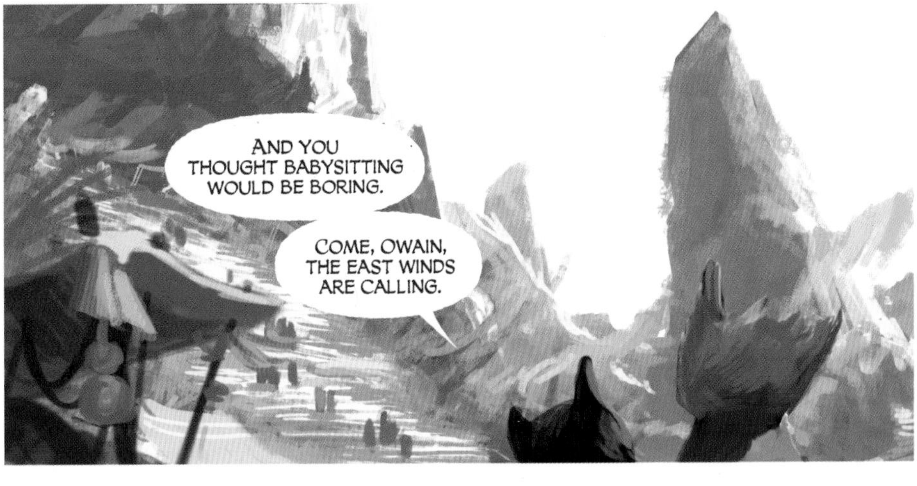
AND YOU THOUGHT BABYSITTING WOULD BE BORING.
COME, OWAIN, THE EAST WINDS ARE CALLING.

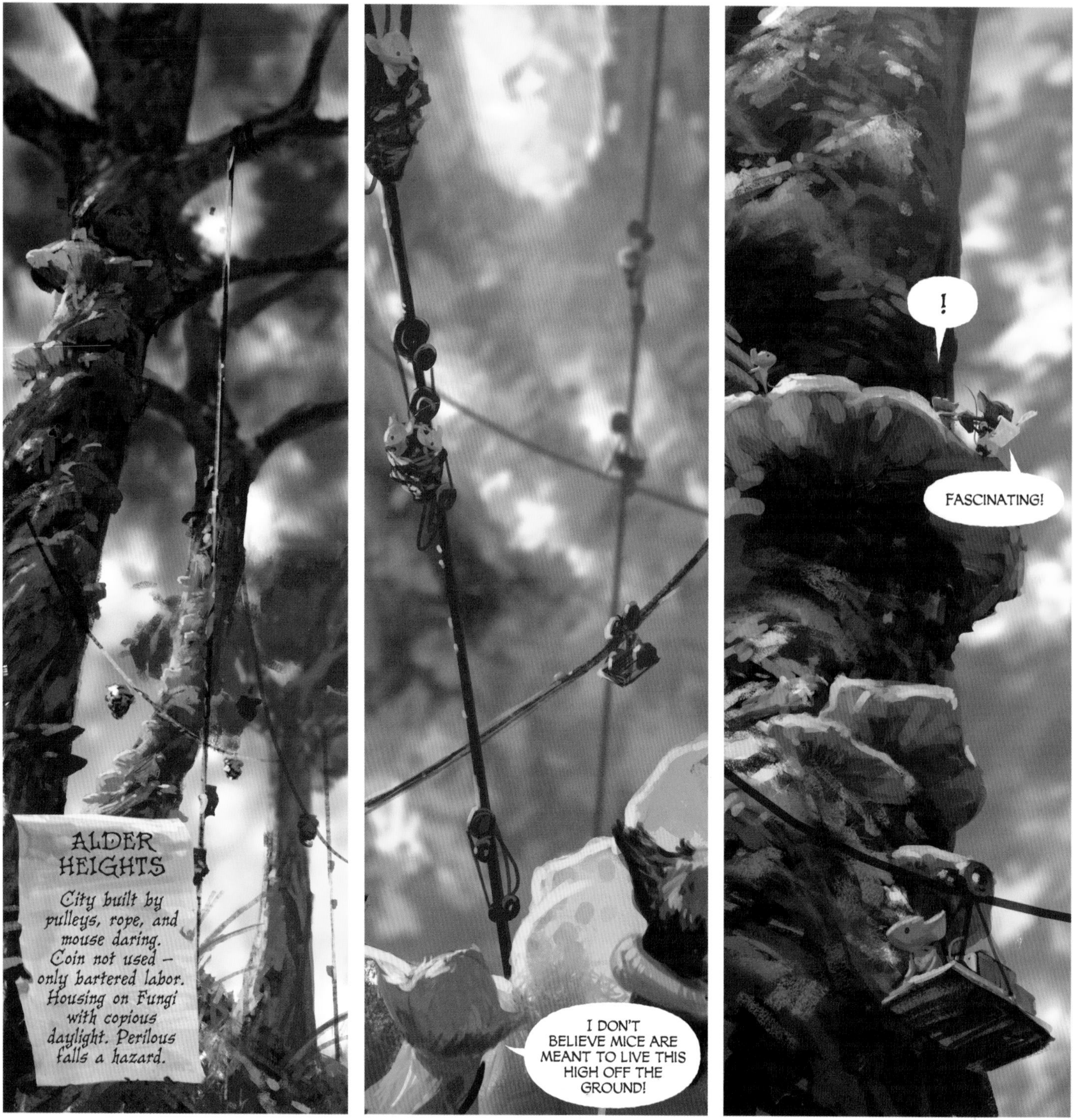
ALDER HEIGHTS
City built by pulleys, rope, and mouse daring. Coin not used – only bartered labor. Housing on Fungi with copious daylight. Perilous falls a hazard.
I DON'T BELIEVE MICE ARE MEANT TO LIVE THIS HIGH OFF THE GROUND!
!
FASCINATING!

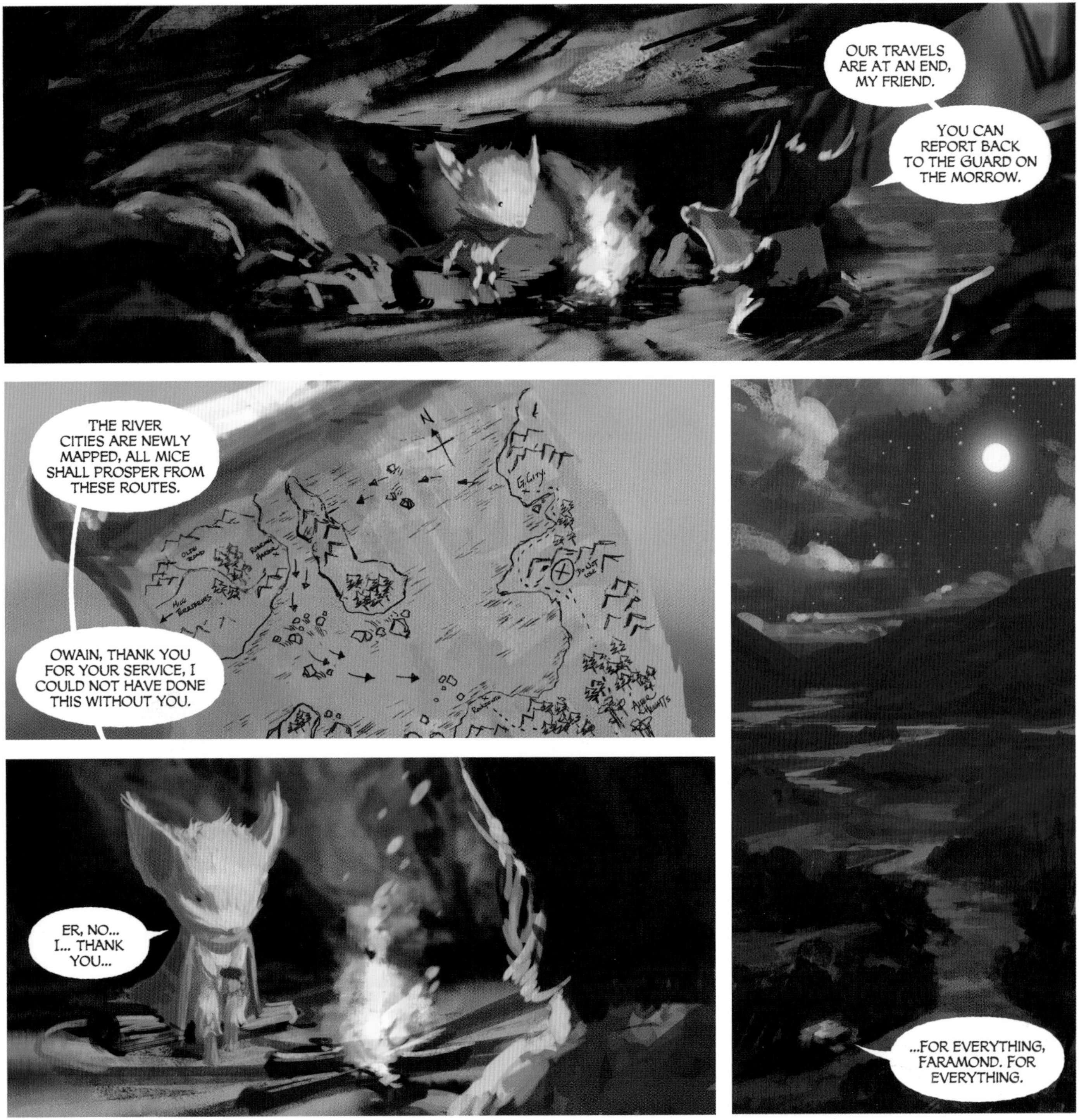
OUR TRAVELS ARE AT AN END, MY FRIEND.
YOU CAN REPORT BACK TO THE GUARD ON THE MORROW.
THE RIVER CITIES ARE NEWLY MAPPED, ALL MICE SHALL PROSPER FROM THESE ROUTES.
OWAIN, THANK YOU FOR YOUR SERVICE, I COULD NOT HAVE DONE THIS WITHOUT YOU.
ER, NO... I... THANK YOU...
...FOR EVERYTHING, FARAMOND. FOR EVERYTHING.

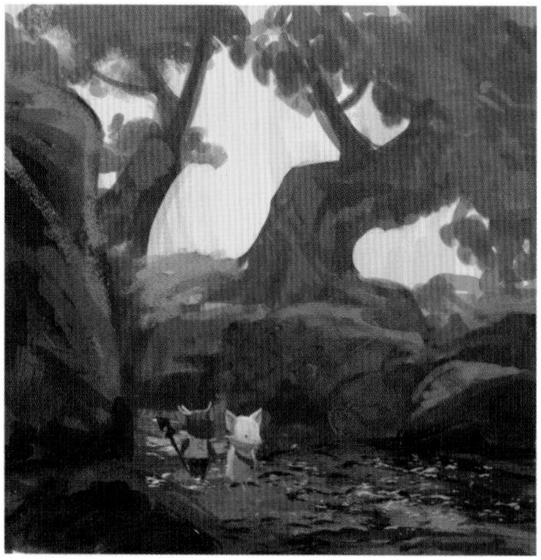
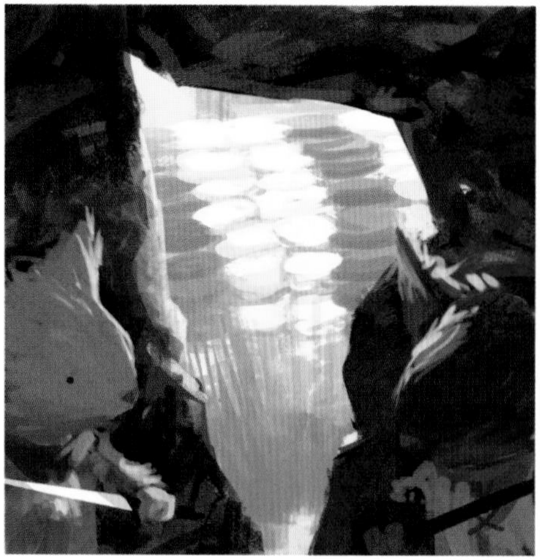
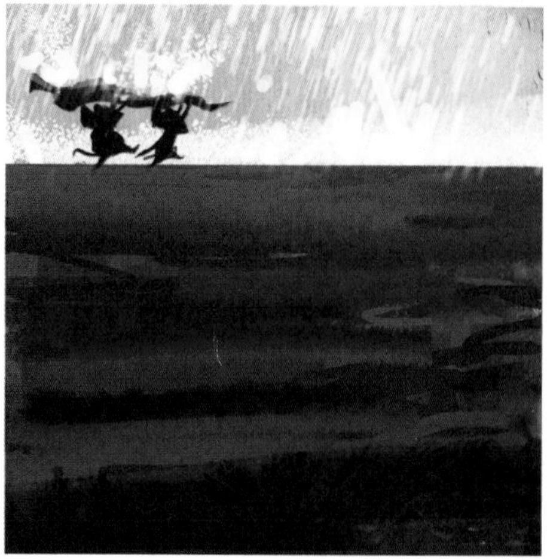
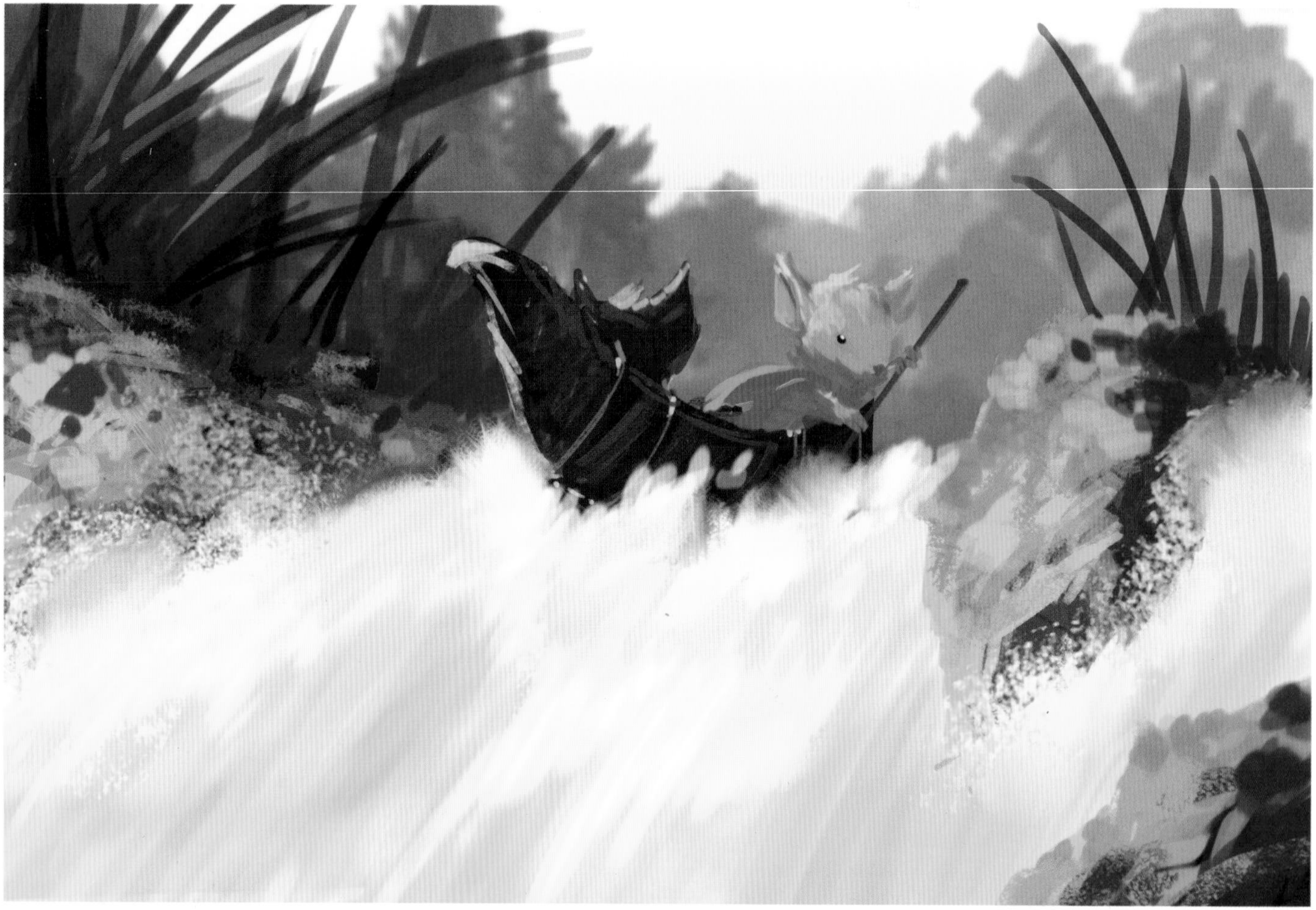

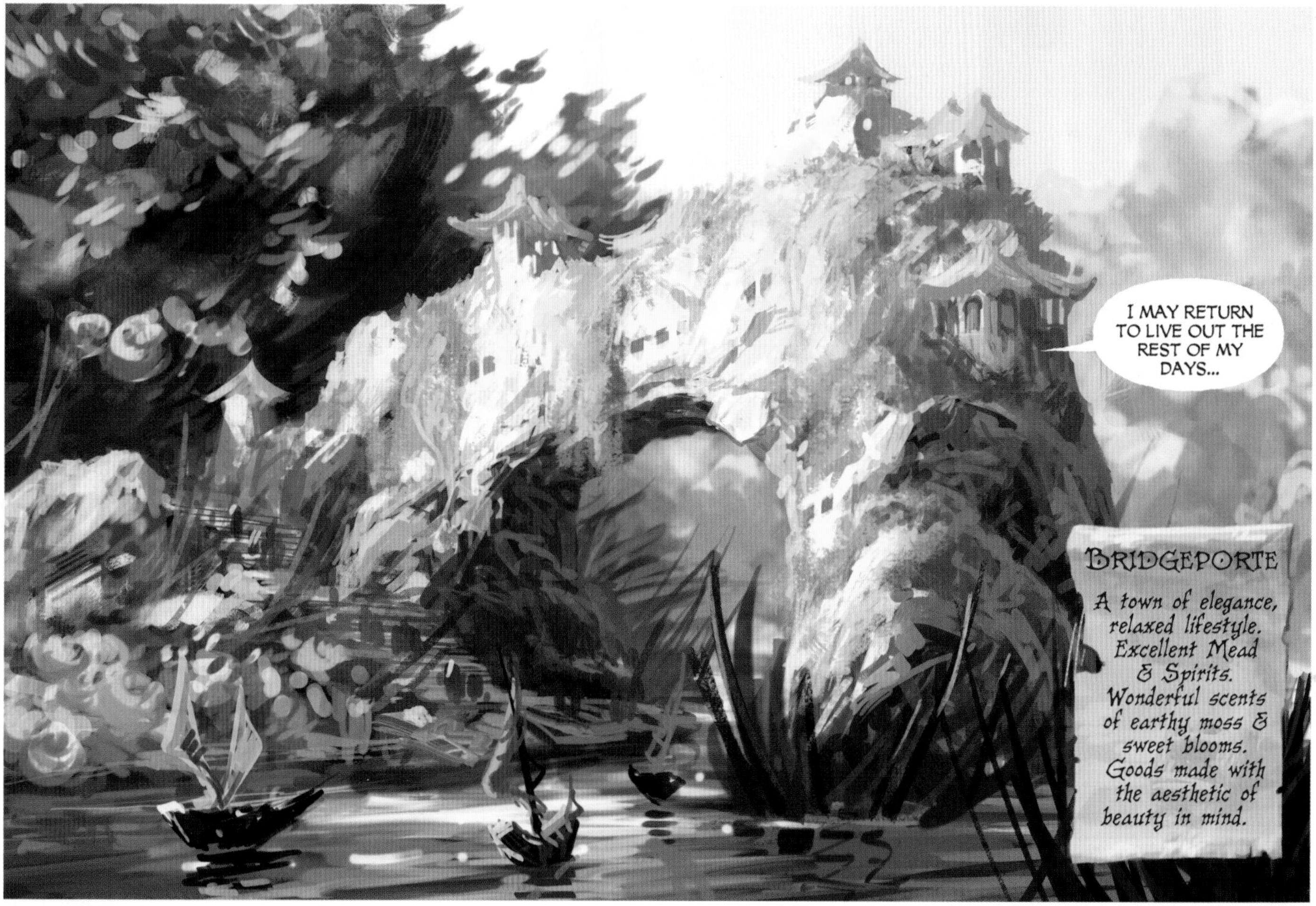
I MAY RETURN TO LIVE OUT THE REST OF MY DAYS...
BRIDGEPORTE
A town of elegance, relaxed lifestyle. Excellent Mead & Spirits. Wonderful scents of earthy moss & sweet blooms. Goods made with the aesthetic of beauty in mind.

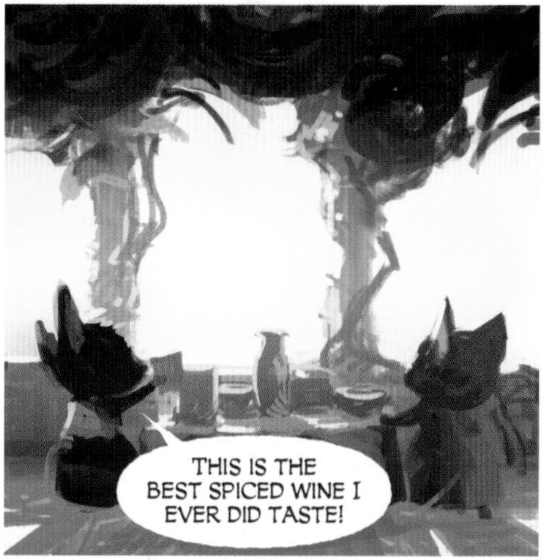
THIS IS THE BEST SPICED WINE I EVER DID TASTE!

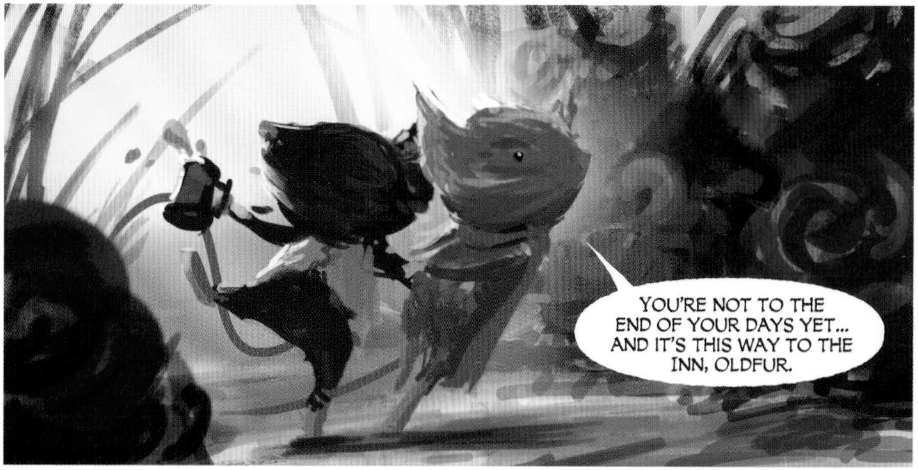
YOU'RE NOT TO THE END OF YOUR DAYS YET... AND IT'S THIS WAY TO THE INN, OLDFUR.

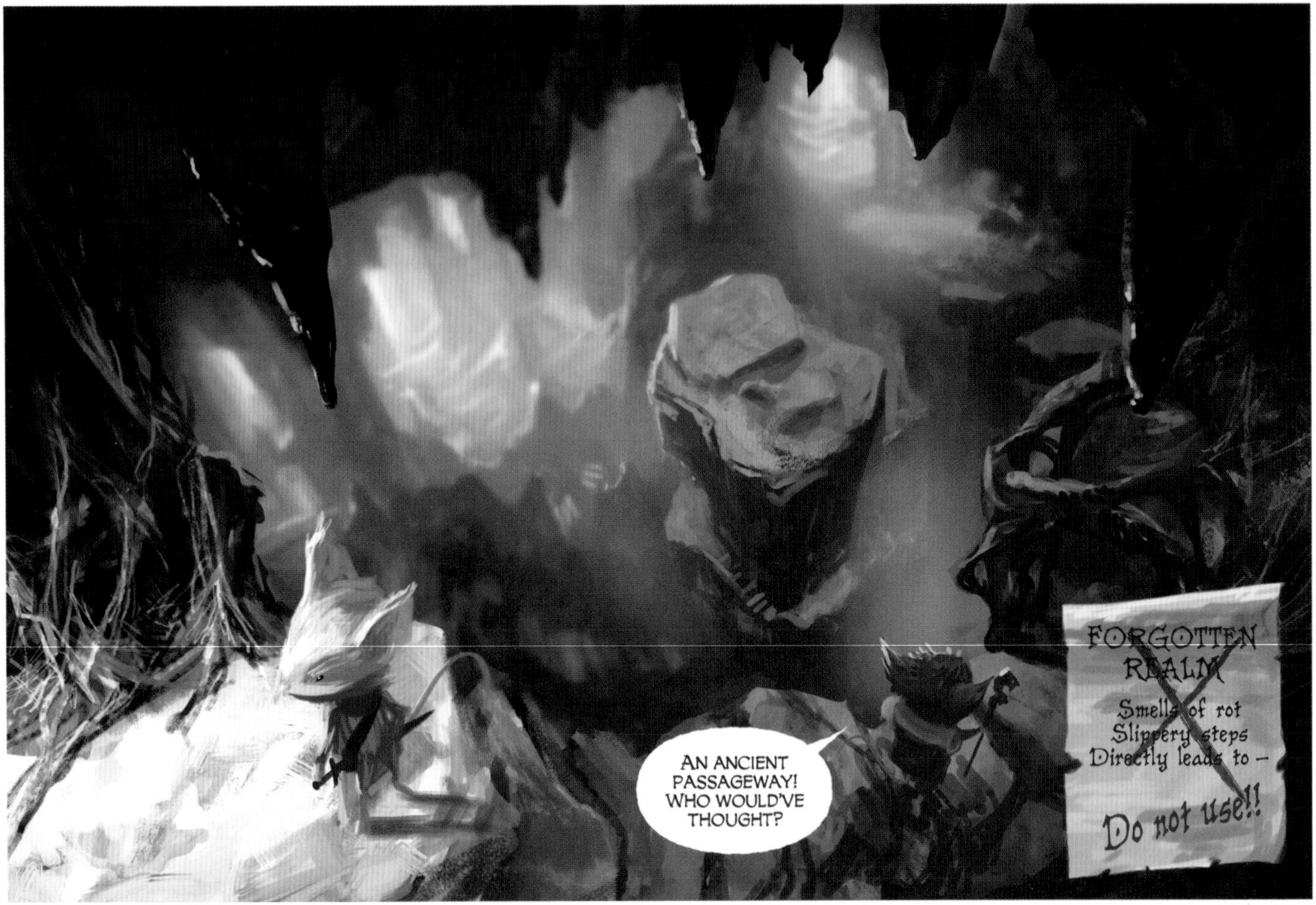
AN ANCIENT PASSAGEWAY! WHO WOULD'VE THOUGHT?
FORGOTTEN REALM
Smells of rot
Slippery steps
Directly leads to –
Do not use!!

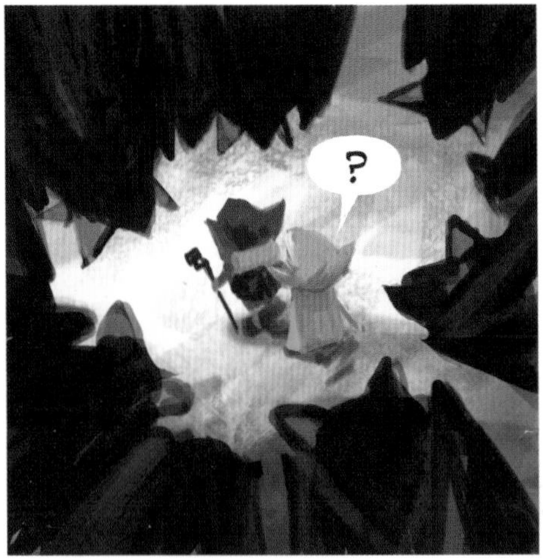
?

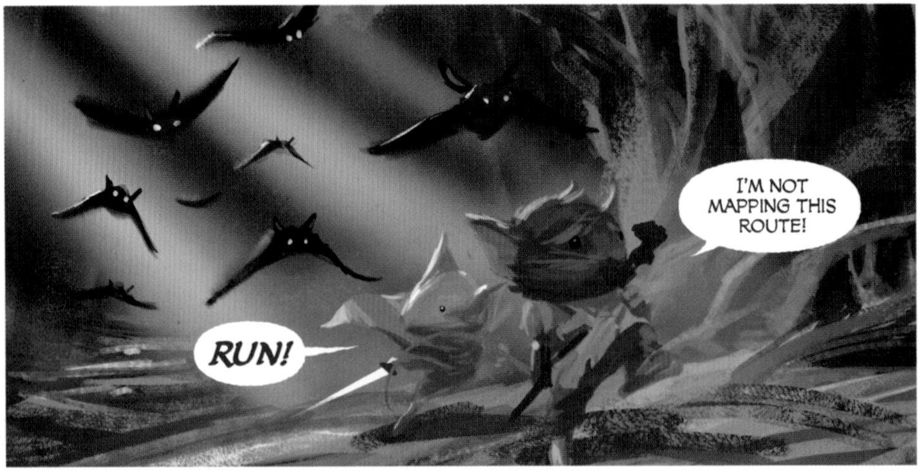
I'M NOT MAPPING THIS ROUTE!
RUN!

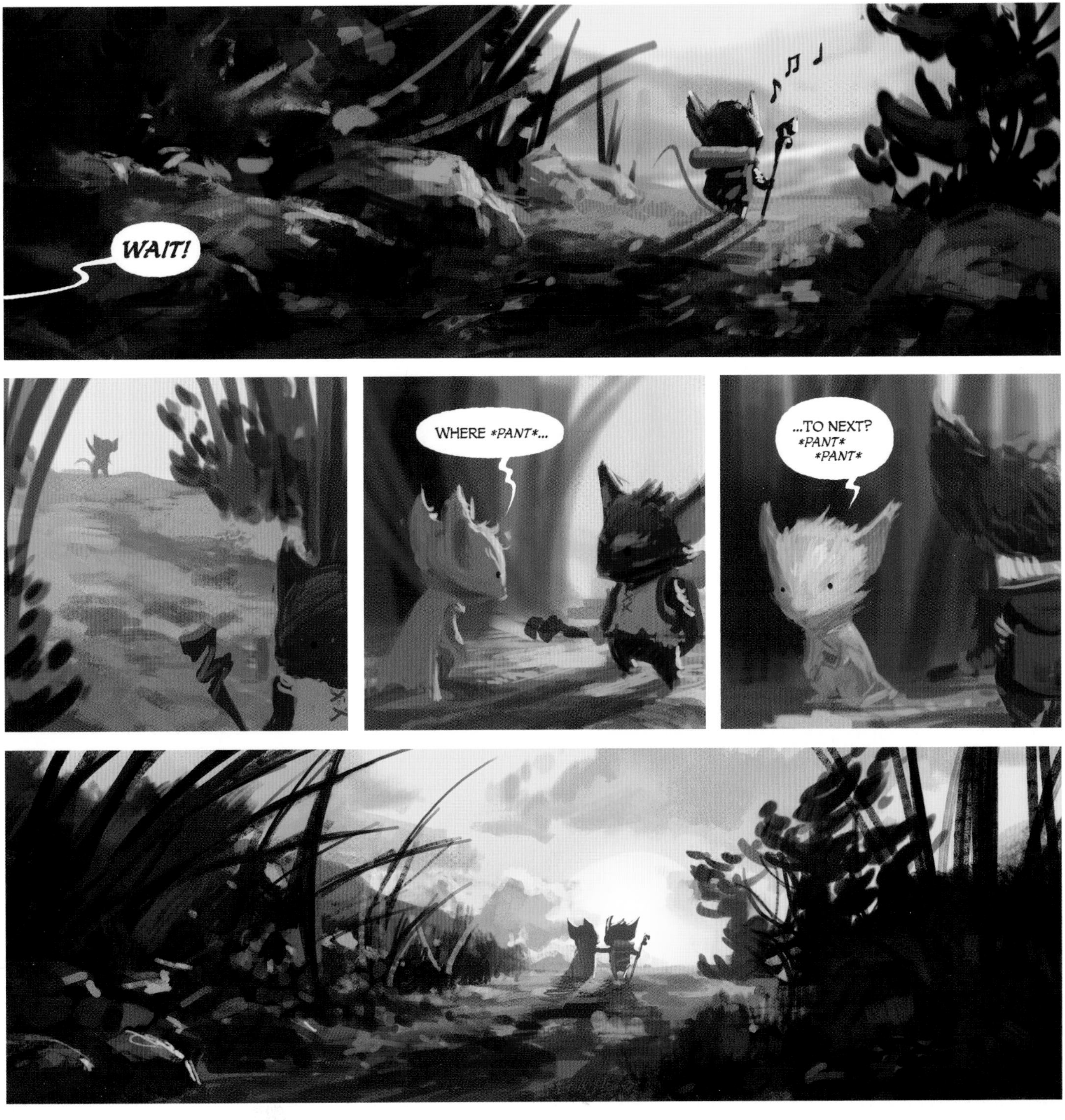
WAIT!
WHERE *PANT*...
...TO NEXT? *PANT* *PANT*

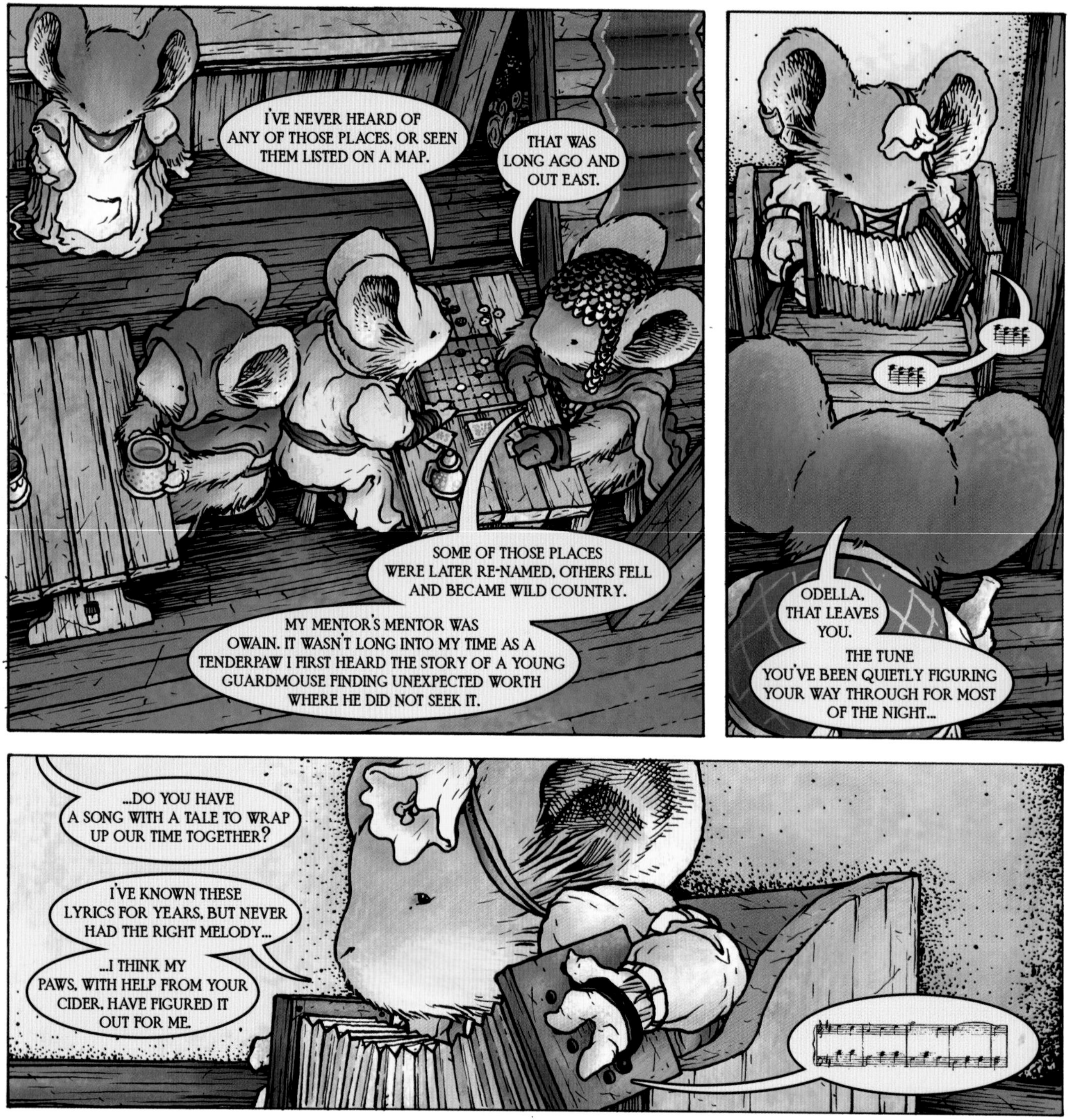
I'VE NEVER HEARD OF ANY OF THOSE PLACES, OR SEEN THEM LISTED ON A MAP.
THAT WAS LONG AGO AND OUT EAST.
SOME OF THOSE PLACES WERE LATER RE-NAMED, OTHERS FELL AND BECAME WILD COUNTRY.
MY MENTOR'S MENTOR WAS OWAIN. IT WASN'T LONG INTO MY TIME AS A TENDERPAW I FIRST HEARD THE STORY OF A YOUNG GUARDMOUSE FINDING UNEXPECTED WORTH WHERE HE DID NOT SEEK IT.
ODELLA, THAT LEAVES YOU.
THE TUNE YOU'VE BEEN QUIETLY FIGURING YOUR WAY THROUGH FOR MOST OF THE NIGHT...
...DO YOU HAVE A SONG WITH A TALE TO WRAP UP OUR TIME TOGETHER?
I'VE KNOWN THESE LYRICS FOR YEARS, BUT NEVER HAD THE RIGHT MELODY...
...I THINK MY PAWS, WITH HELP FROM YOUR CIDER, HAVE FIGURED IT OUT FOR ME.

THE TIMBER MICE

MUSIC: CLIFF MONEAR
ILLUSTRATIONS: JUSTIN GERARD
LYRICS: MOUSE TRADITIONAL

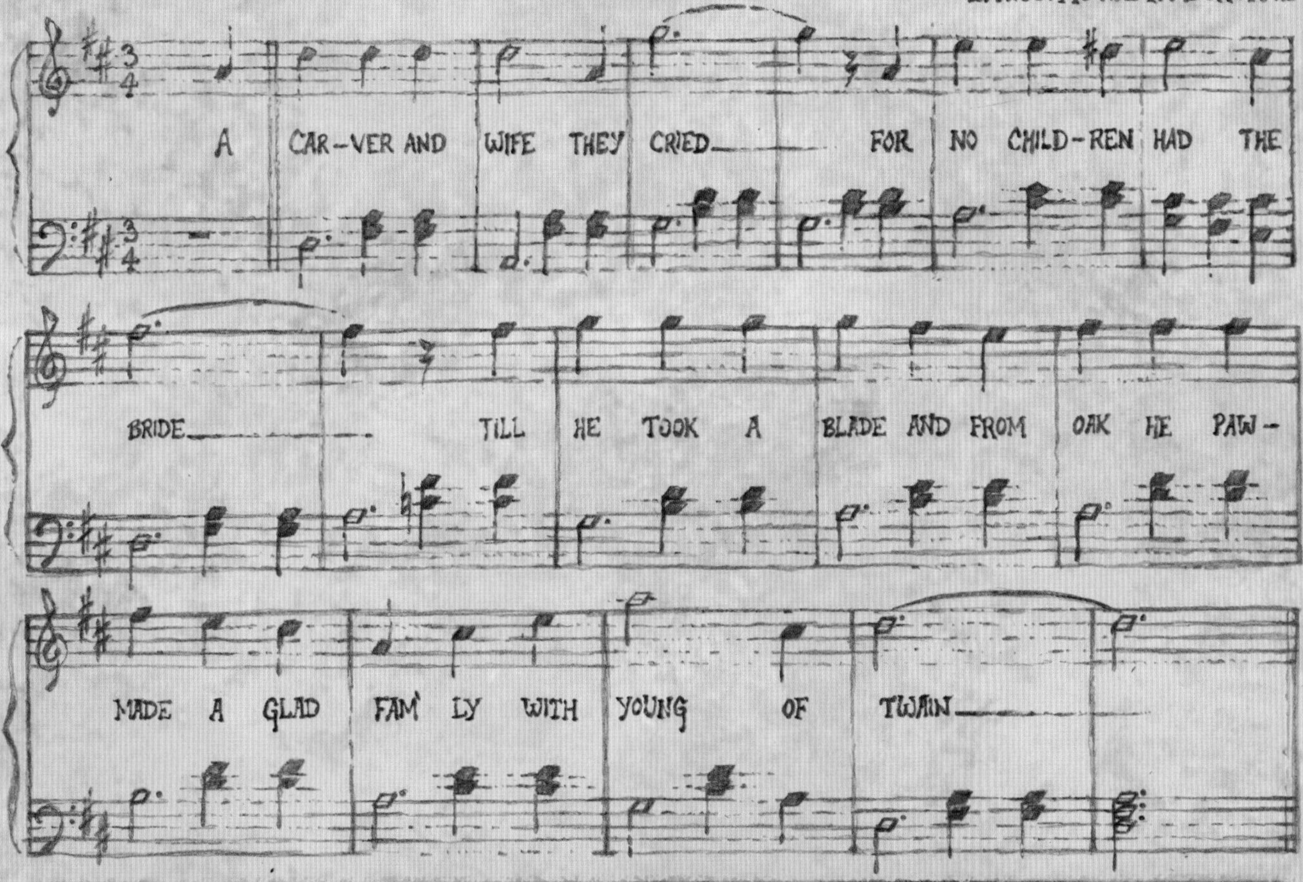
A CAR-VER AND WIFE THEY CRIED___ FOR NO CHILD-REN HAD THE
BRIDE___ TILL HE TOOK A BLADE AND FROM OAK HE PAW-
MADE A GLAD FAM' LY WITH YOUNG OF TWAIN___

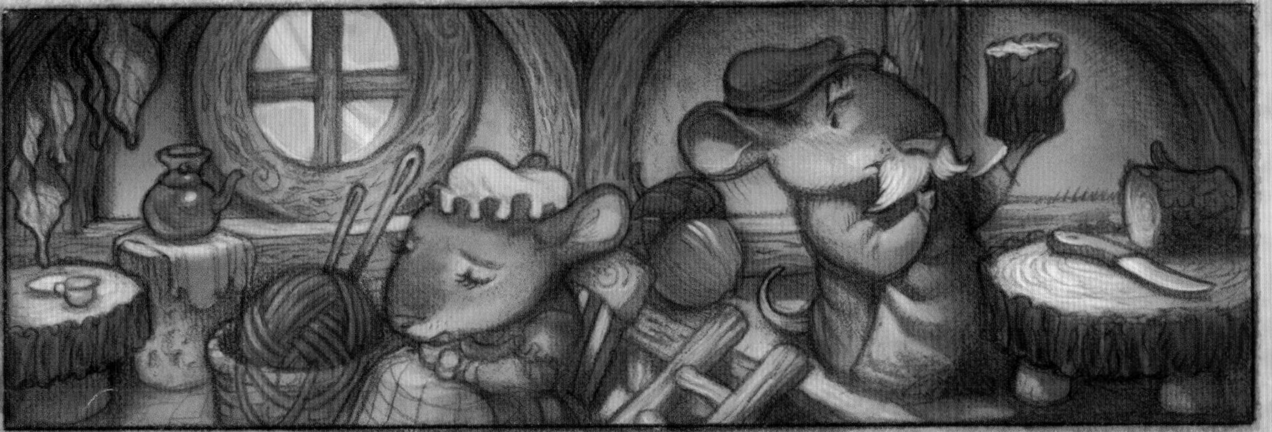

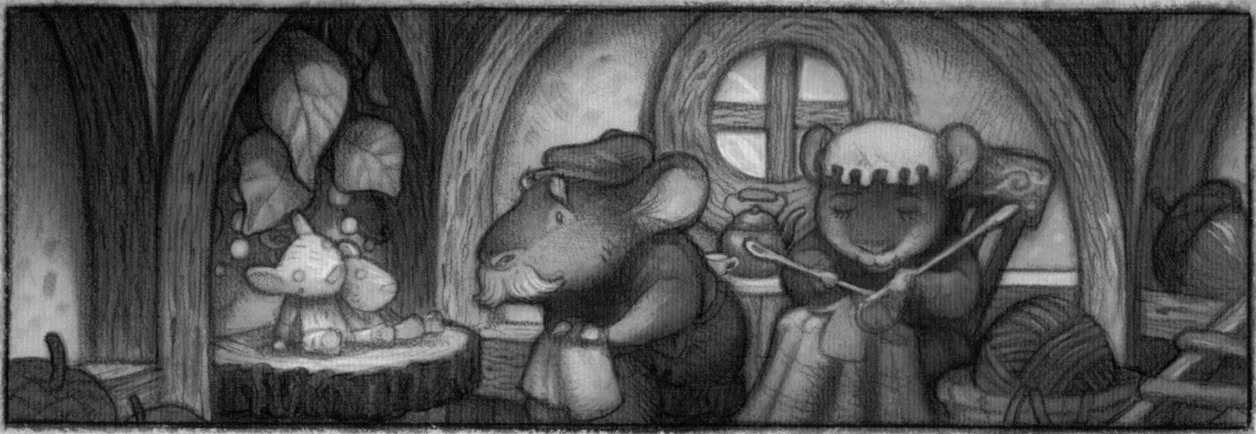

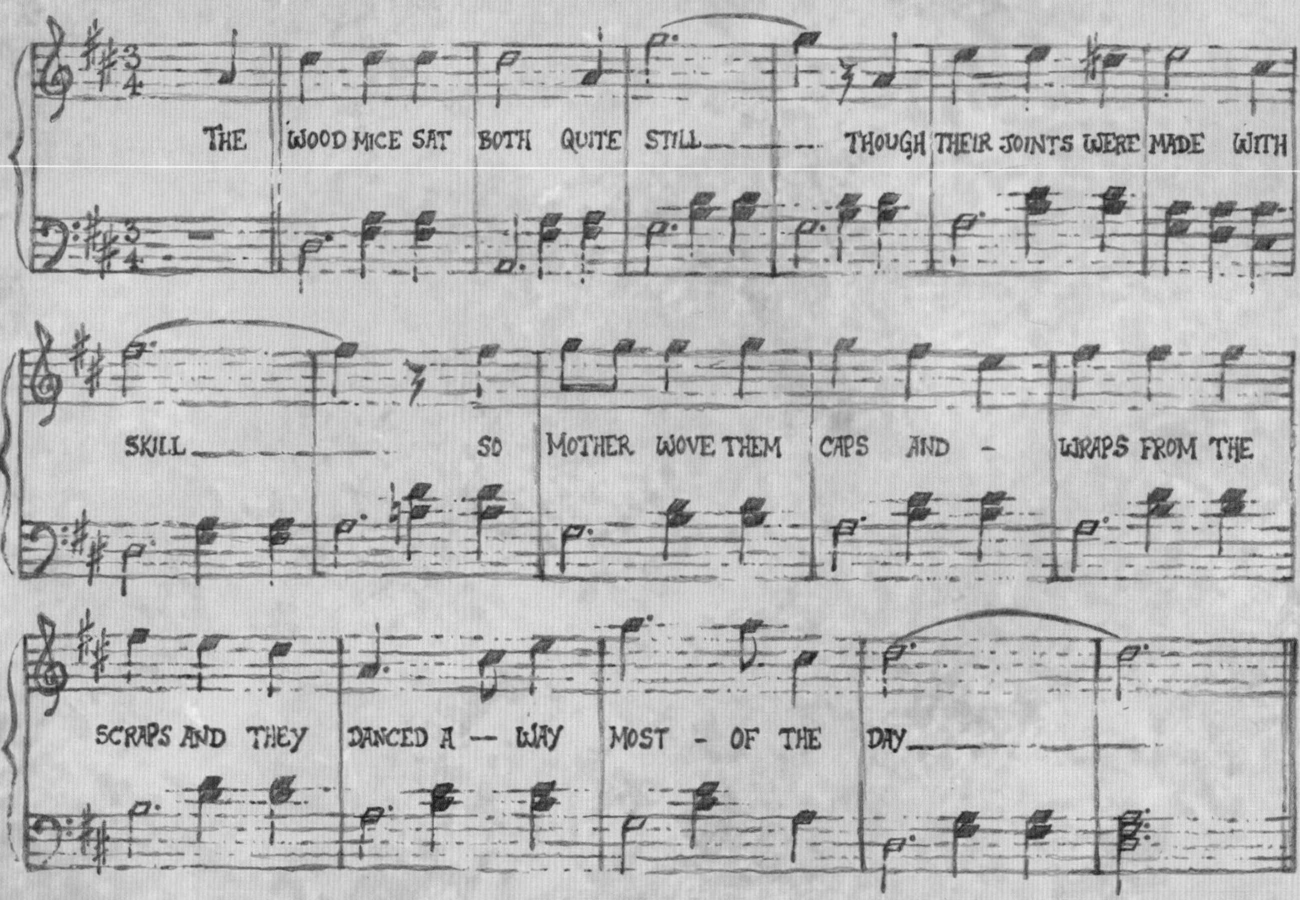
THE WOOD MICE SAT BOTH QUITE STILL — THOUGH THEIR JOINTS WERE MADE WITH
SKILL — SO MOTHER WOVE THEM CAPS AND - WRAPS FROM THE
SCRAPS AND THEY DANCED A — WAY MOST - OF THE DAY —

TRUE BLISS THE PAR-ENTS SHARED___ BOTH TAL-ENTS TO-GETH-ER

PAIRED___ TOOK TIM-BER AND LOOM TO BRING LIFE IN-TO

BLOOM AND JOY FOR - THE REST - OF THEIR DAYS

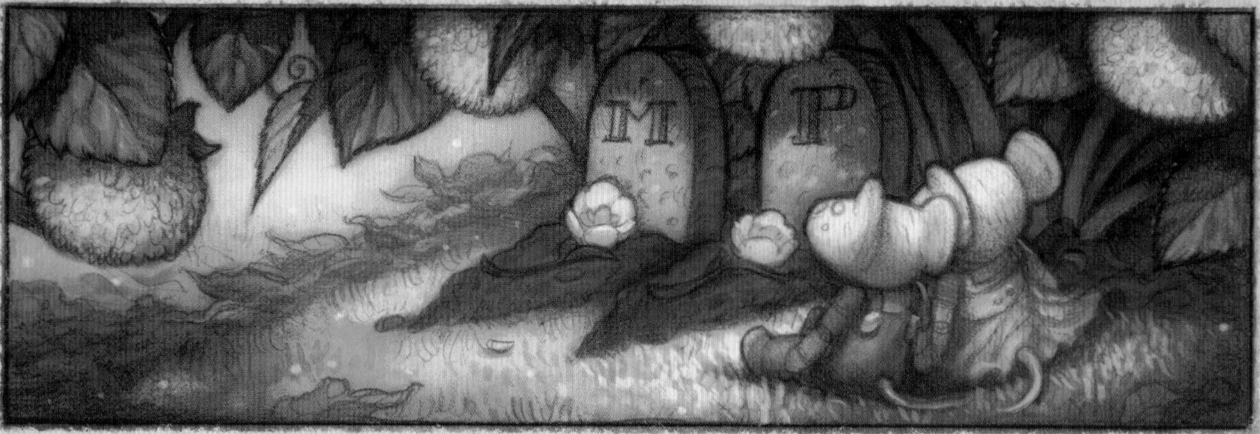
M
P

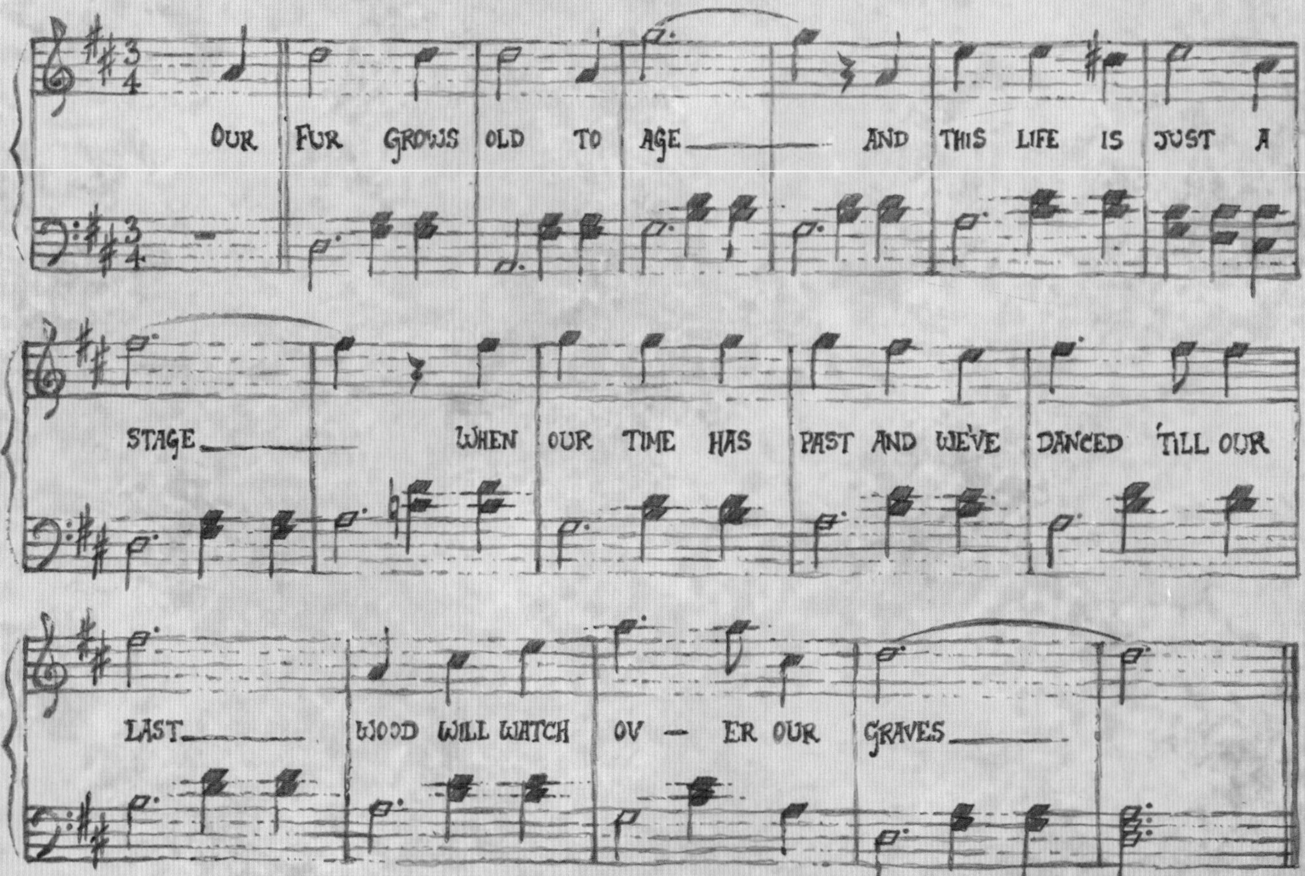
OUR FUR GROWS OLD TO AGE___ AND THIS LIFE IS JUST A
STAGE___ WHEN OUR TIME HAS PAST AND WE'VE DANCED 'TILL OUR
LAST___ WOOD WILL WATCH OV — ER OUR GRAVES___

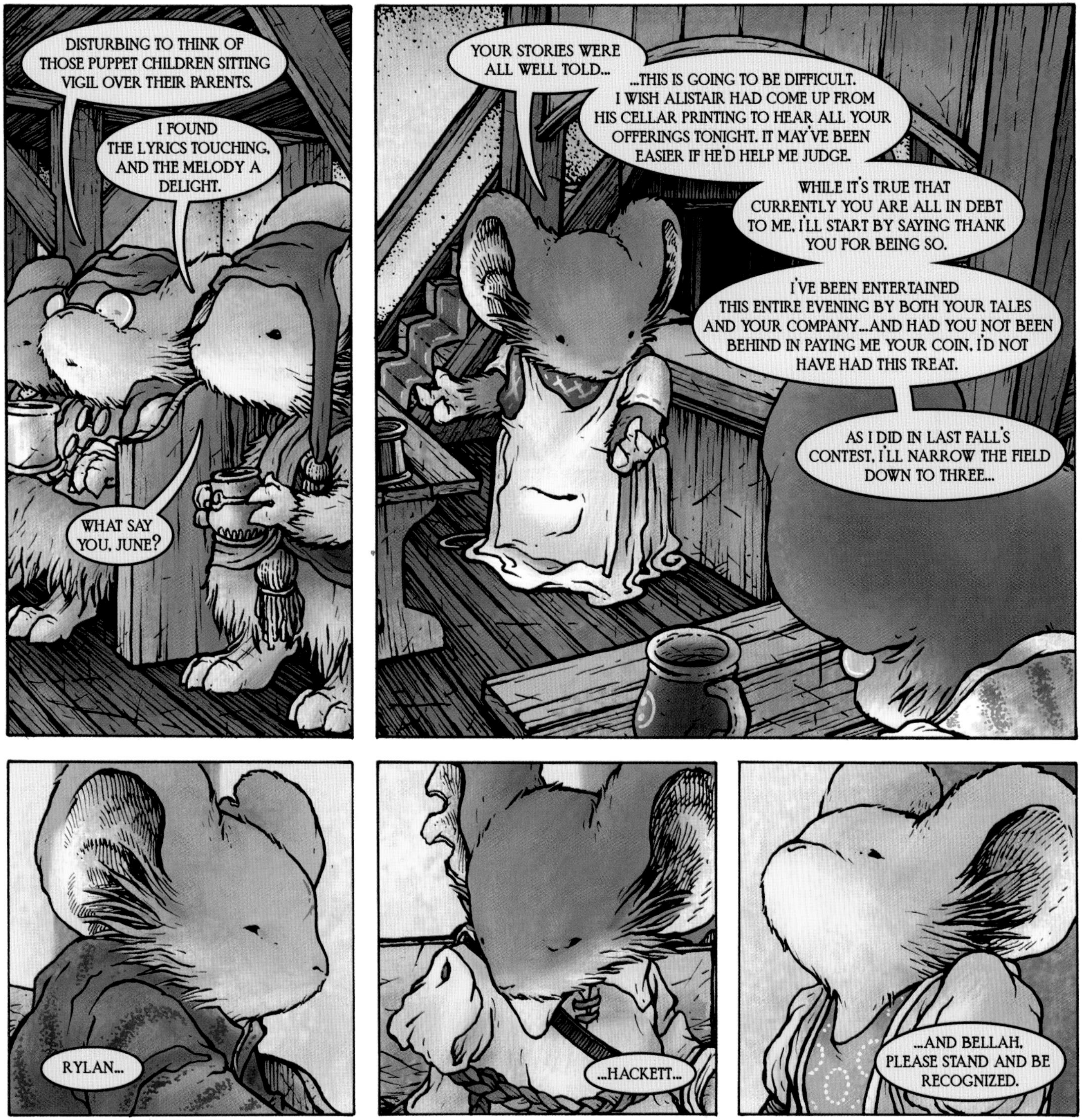
DISTURBING TO THINK OF THOSE PUPPET CHILDREN SITTING VIGIL OVER THEIR PARENTS.
I FOUND THE LYRICS TOUCHING, AND THE MELODY A DELIGHT.
WHAT SAY YOU, JUNE?
YOUR STORIES WERE ALL WELL TOLD...
...THIS IS GOING TO BE DIFFICULT. I WISH ALISTAIR HAD COME UP FROM HIS CELLAR PRINTING TO HEAR ALL YOUR OFFERINGS TONIGHT. IT MAY'VE BEEN EASIER IF HE'D HELP ME JUDGE.
WHILE IT'S TRUE THAT CURRENTLY YOU ARE ALL IN DEBT TO ME, I'LL START BY SAYING THANK YOU FOR BEING SO.
I'VE BEEN ENTERTAINED THIS ENTIRE EVENING BY BOTH YOUR TALES AND YOUR COMPANY...AND HAD YOU NOT BEEN BEHIND IN PAYING ME YOUR COIN, I'D NOT HAVE HAD THIS TREAT.
AS I DID IN LAST FALL'S CONTEST, I'LL NARROW THE FIELD DOWN TO THREE...
RYLAN...
...HACKETT...
...AND BELLAH, PLEASE STAND AND BE RECOGNIZED.

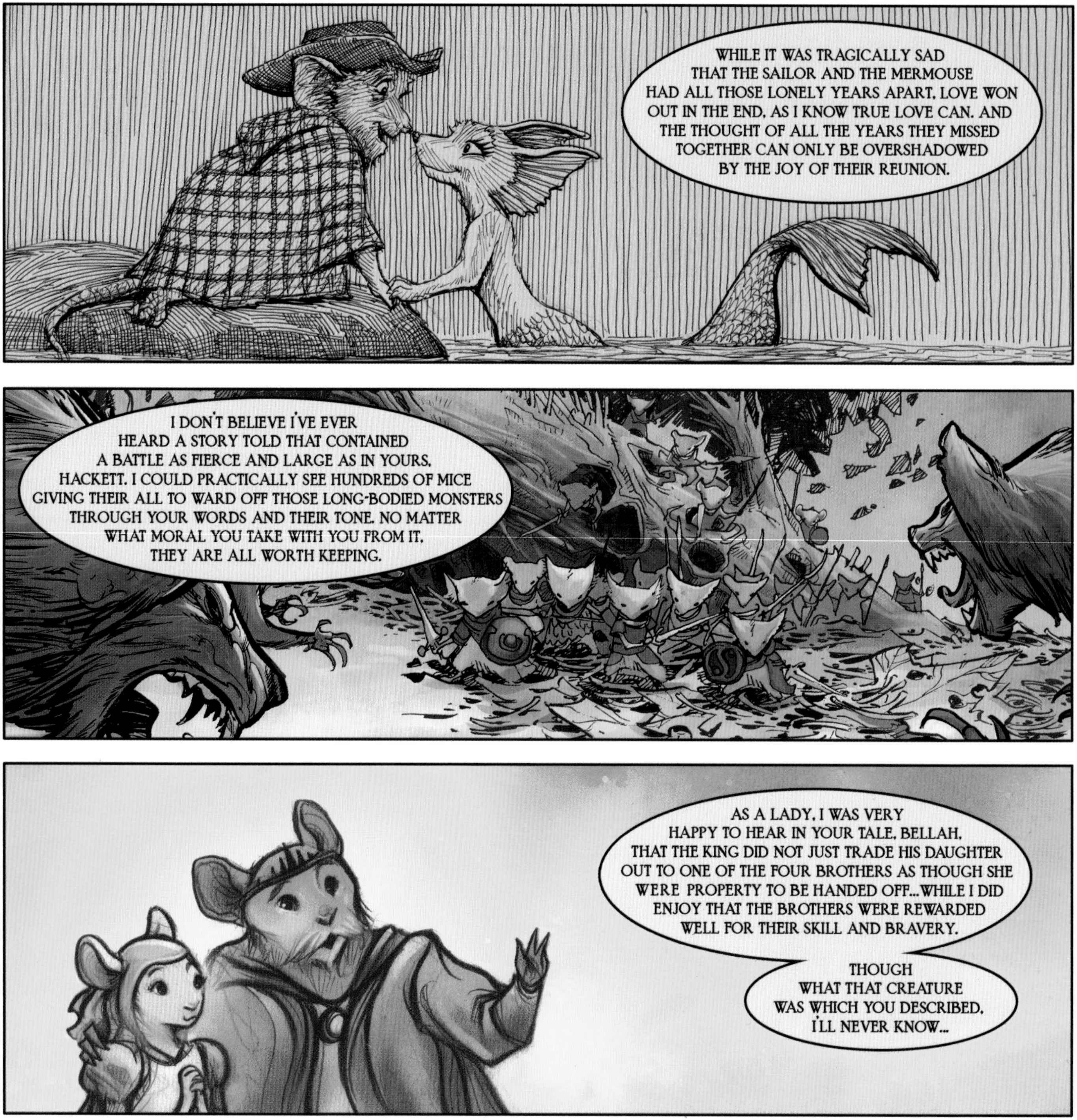
WHILE IT WAS TRAGICALLY SAD THAT THE SAILOR AND THE MERMOUSE HAD ALL THOSE LONELY YEARS APART, LOVE WON OUT IN THE END, AS I KNOW TRUE LOVE CAN. AND THE THOUGHT OF ALL THE YEARS THEY MISSED TOGETHER CAN ONLY BE OVERSHADOWED BY THE JOY OF THEIR REUNION.
I DON'T BELIEVE I'VE EVER HEARD A STORY TOLD THAT CONTAINED A BATTLE AS FIERCE AND LARGE AS IN YOURS, HACKETT. I COULD PRACTICALLY SEE HUNDREDS OF MICE GIVING THEIR ALL TO WARD OFF THOSE LONG-BODIED MONSTERS THROUGH YOUR WORDS AND THEIR TONE. NO MATTER WHAT MORAL YOU TAKE WITH YOU FROM IT, THEY ARE ALL WORTH KEEPING.
AS A LADY, I WAS VERY HAPPY TO HEAR IN YOUR TALE, BELLAH, THAT THE KING DID NOT JUST TRADE HIS DAUGHTER OUT TO ONE OF THE FOUR BROTHERS AS THOUGH SHE WERE PROPERTY TO BE HANDED OFF...WHILE I DID ENJOY THAT THE BROTHERS WERE REWARDED WELL FOR THEIR SKILL AND BRAVERY.
THOUGH WHAT THAT CREATURE WAS WHICH YOU DESCRIBED, I'LL NEVER KNOW...

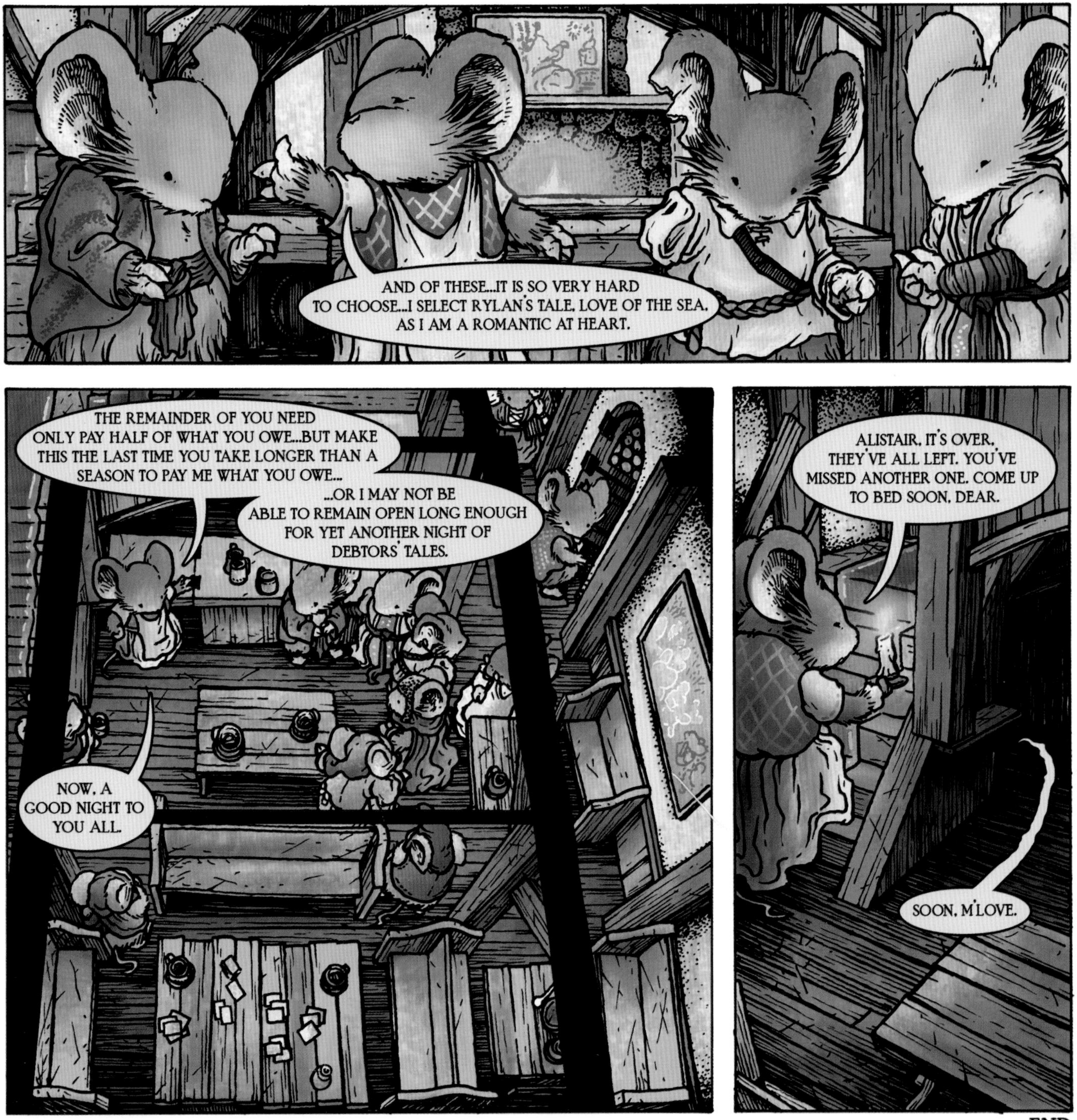
AND OF THESE...IT IS SO VERY HARD TO CHOOSE...I SELECT RYLAN'S TALE, LOVE OF THE SEA, AS I AM A ROMANTIC AT HEART.
THE REMAINDER OF YOU NEED ONLY PAY HALF OF WHAT YOU OWE...BUT MAKE THIS THE LAST TIME YOU TAKE LONGER THAN A SEASON TO PAY ME WHAT YOU OWE...
...OR I MAY NOT BE ABLE TO REMAIN OPEN LONG ENOUGH FOR YET ANOTHER NIGHT OF DEBTORS' TALES.
NOW, A GOOD NIGHT TO YOU ALL.
ALISTAIR, IT'S OVER, THEY'VE ALL LEFT. YOU'VE MISSED ANOTHER ONE. COME UP TO BED SOON, DEAR.
SOON, M'LOVE.

END

Alley Inn

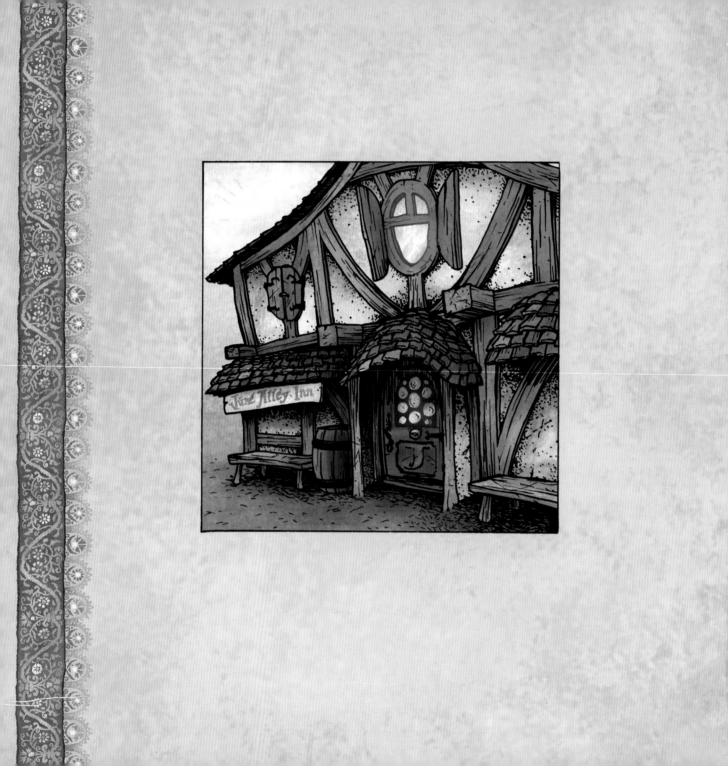

EPILOGUE

ART & STORY: DIRK SHEARER
& DAVID PETERSEN

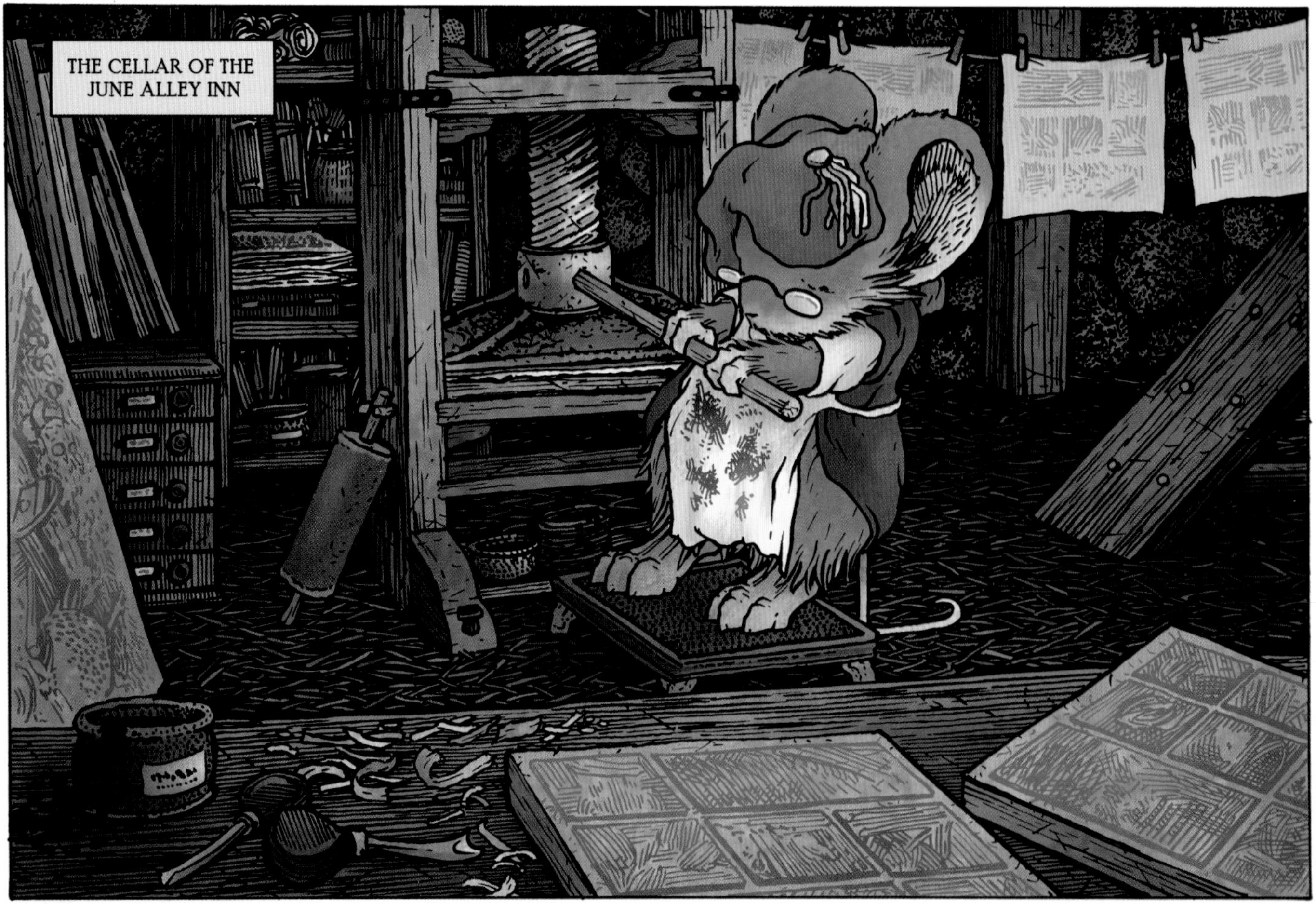
THE CELLAR OF THE
JUNE ALLEY INN

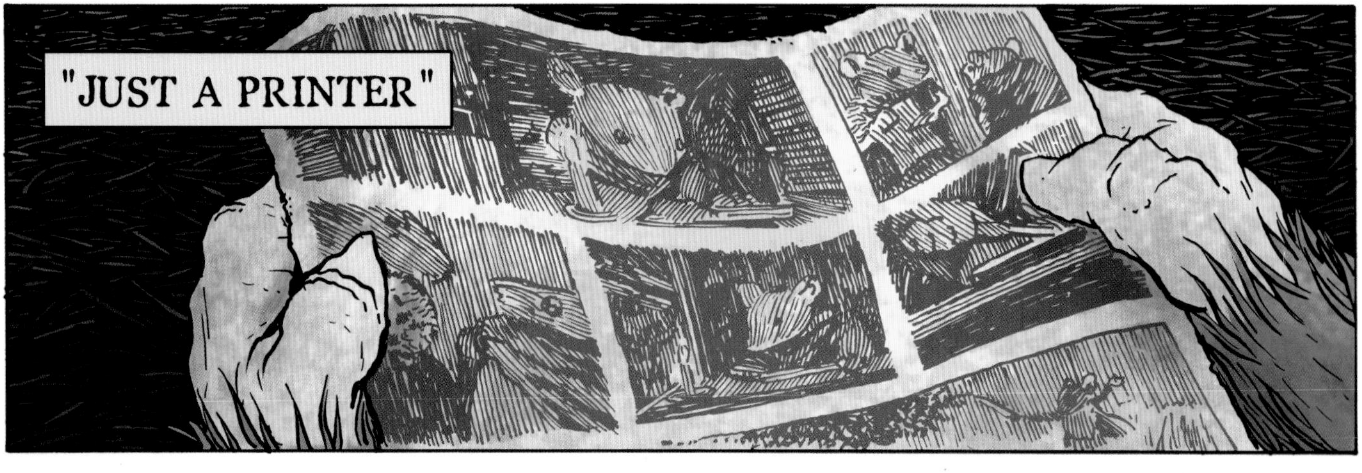
"JUST A PRINTER"

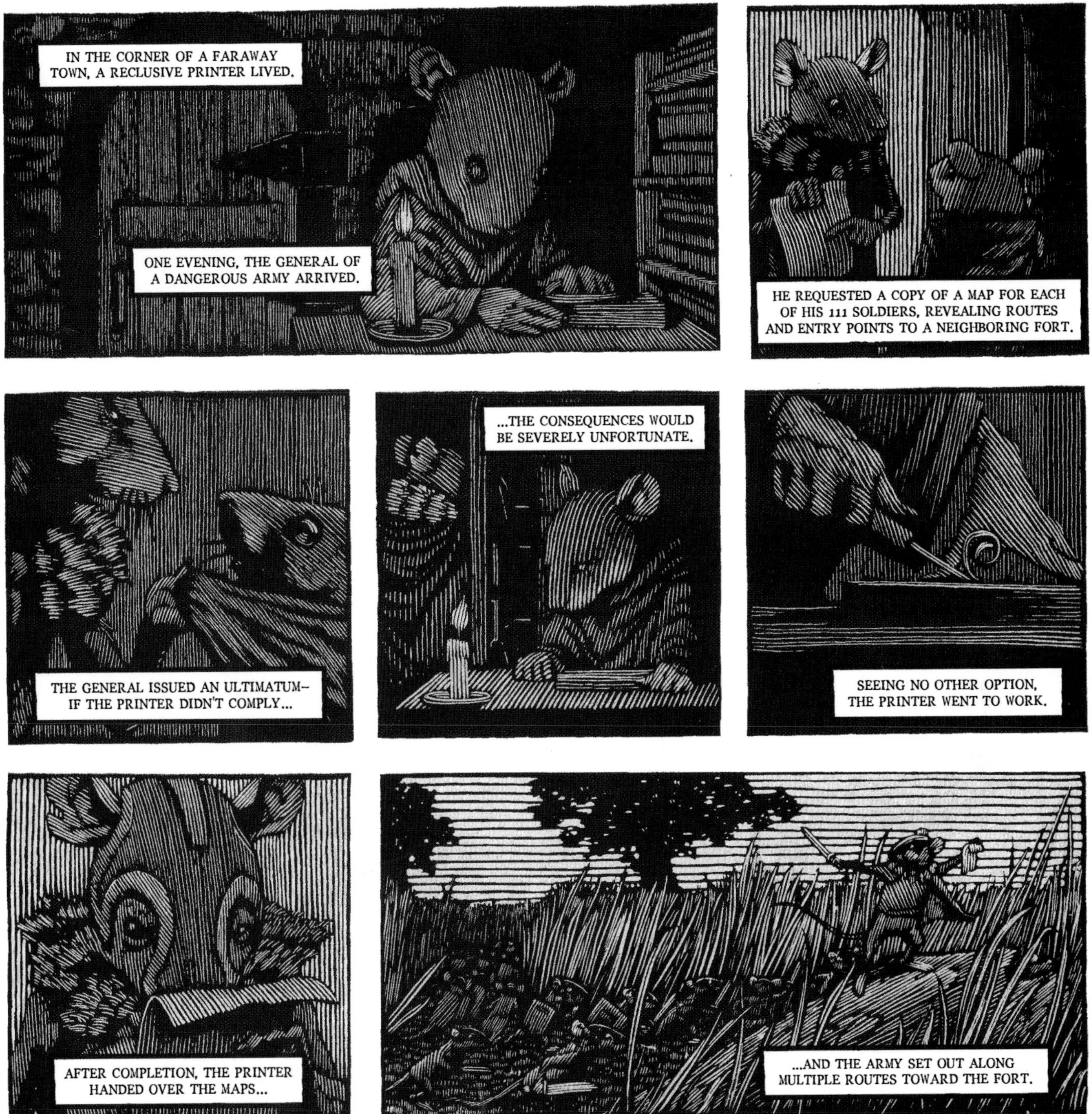
IN THE CORNER OF A FARAWAY TOWN, A RECLUSIVE PRINTER LIVED.
ONE EVENING, THE GENERAL OF A DANGEROUS ARMY ARRIVED.
HE REQUESTED A COPY OF A MAP FOR EACH OF HIS 111 SOLDIERS, REVEALING ROUTES AND ENTRY POINTS TO A NEIGHBORING FORT.
THE GENERAL ISSUED AN ULTIMATUM– IF THE PRINTER DIDN'T COMPLY...
...THE CONSEQUENCES WOULD BE SEVERELY UNFORTUNATE.
SEEING NO OTHER OPTION, THE PRINTER WENT TO WORK.
AFTER COMPLETION, THE PRINTER HANDED OVER THE MAPS...
...AND THE ARMY SET OUT ALONG MULTIPLE ROUTES TOWARD THE FORT.

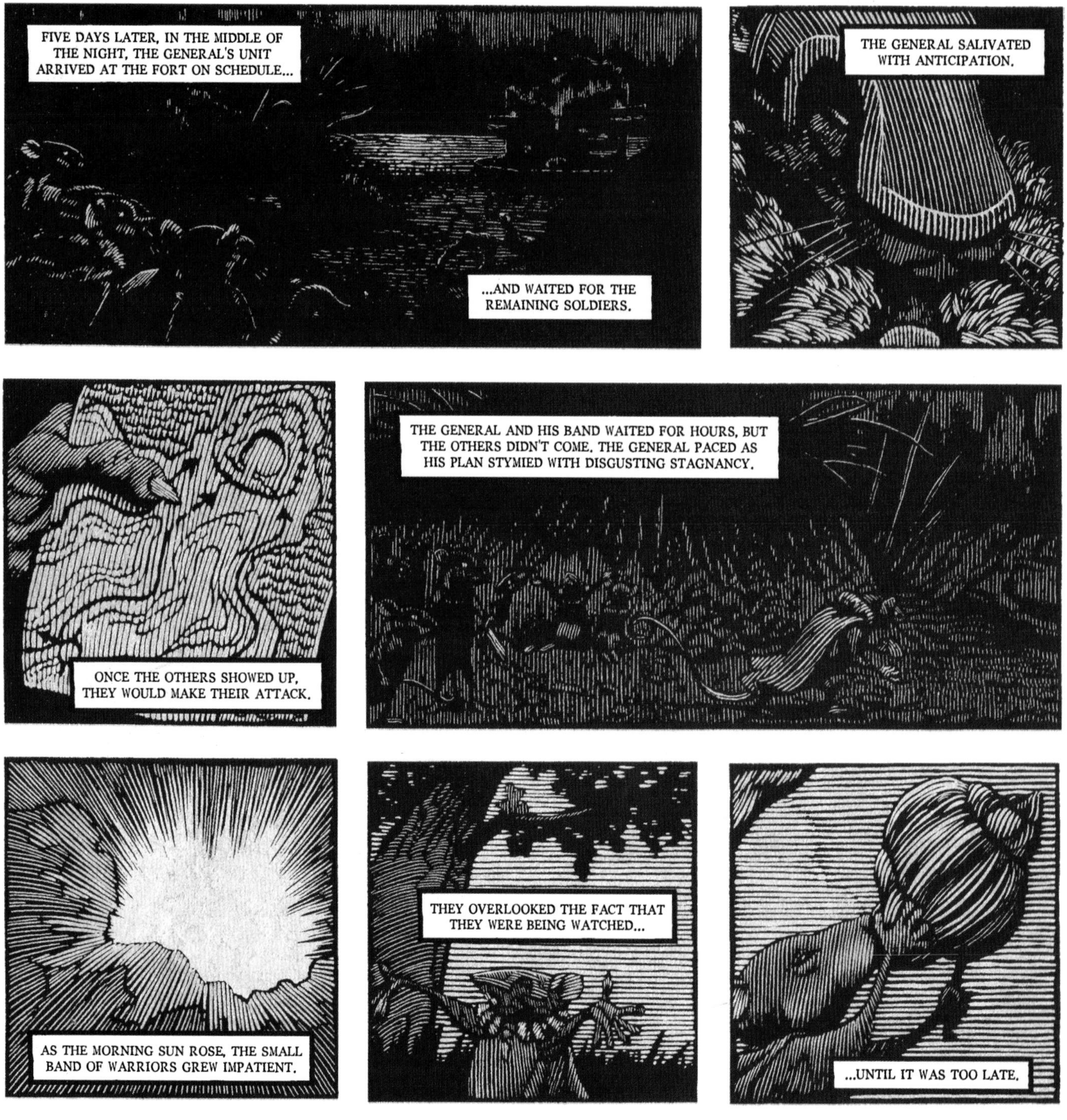
FIVE DAYS LATER, IN THE MIDDLE OF THE NIGHT, THE GENERAL'S UNIT ARRIVED AT THE FORT ON SCHEDULE...
...AND WAITED FOR THE REMAINING SOLDIERS.
THE GENERAL SALIVATED WITH ANTICIPATION.
ONCE THE OTHERS SHOWED UP, THEY WOULD MAKE THEIR ATTACK.
THE GENERAL AND HIS BAND WAITED FOR HOURS, BUT THE OTHERS DIDN'T COME. THE GENERAL PACED AS HIS PLAN STYMIED WITH DISGUSTING STAGNANCY.
AS THE MORNING SUN ROSE, THE SMALL BAND OF WARRIORS GREW IMPATIENT.
THEY OVERLOOKED THE FACT THAT THEY WERE BEING WATCHED...
...UNTIL IT WAS TOO LATE.

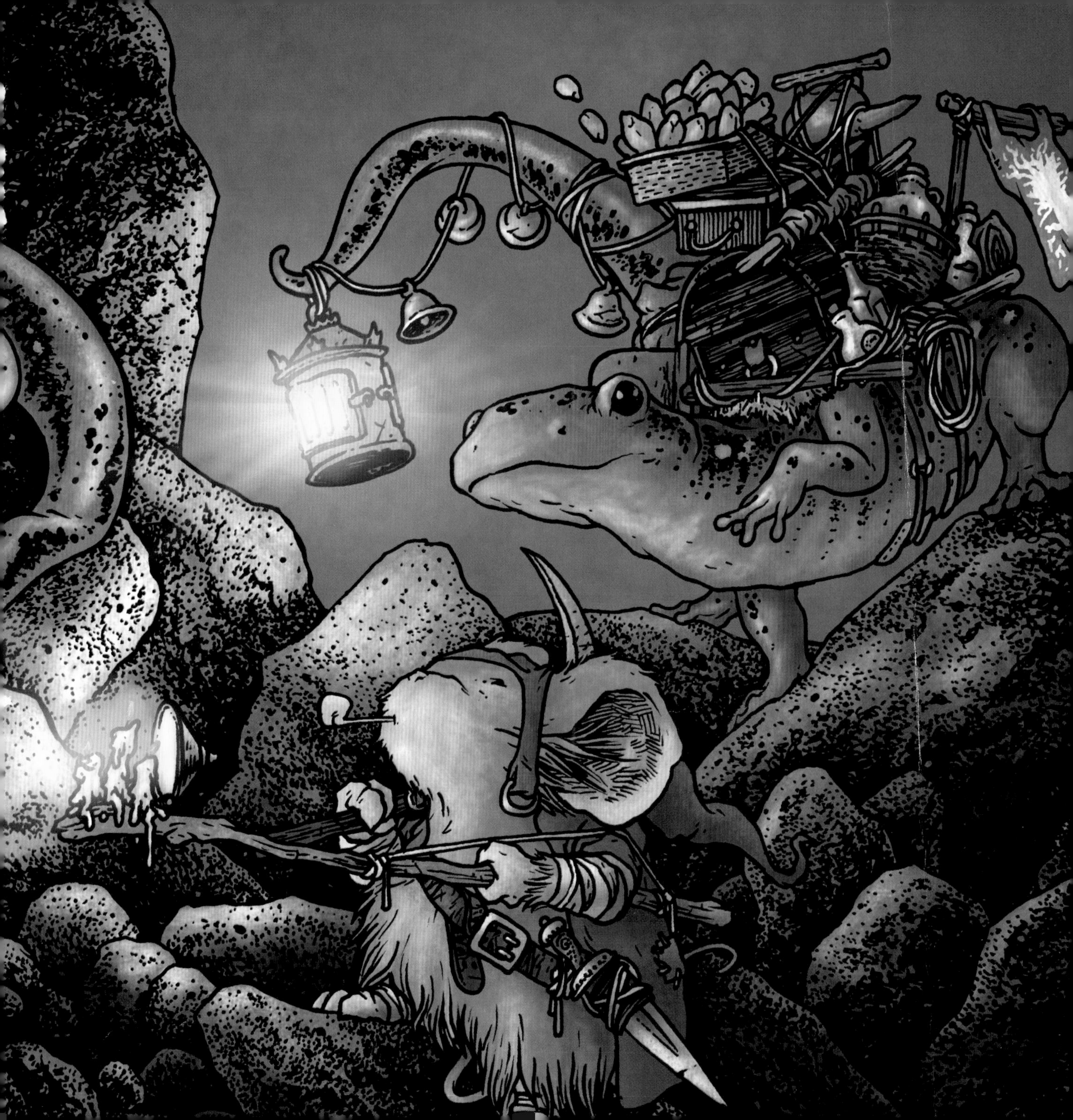

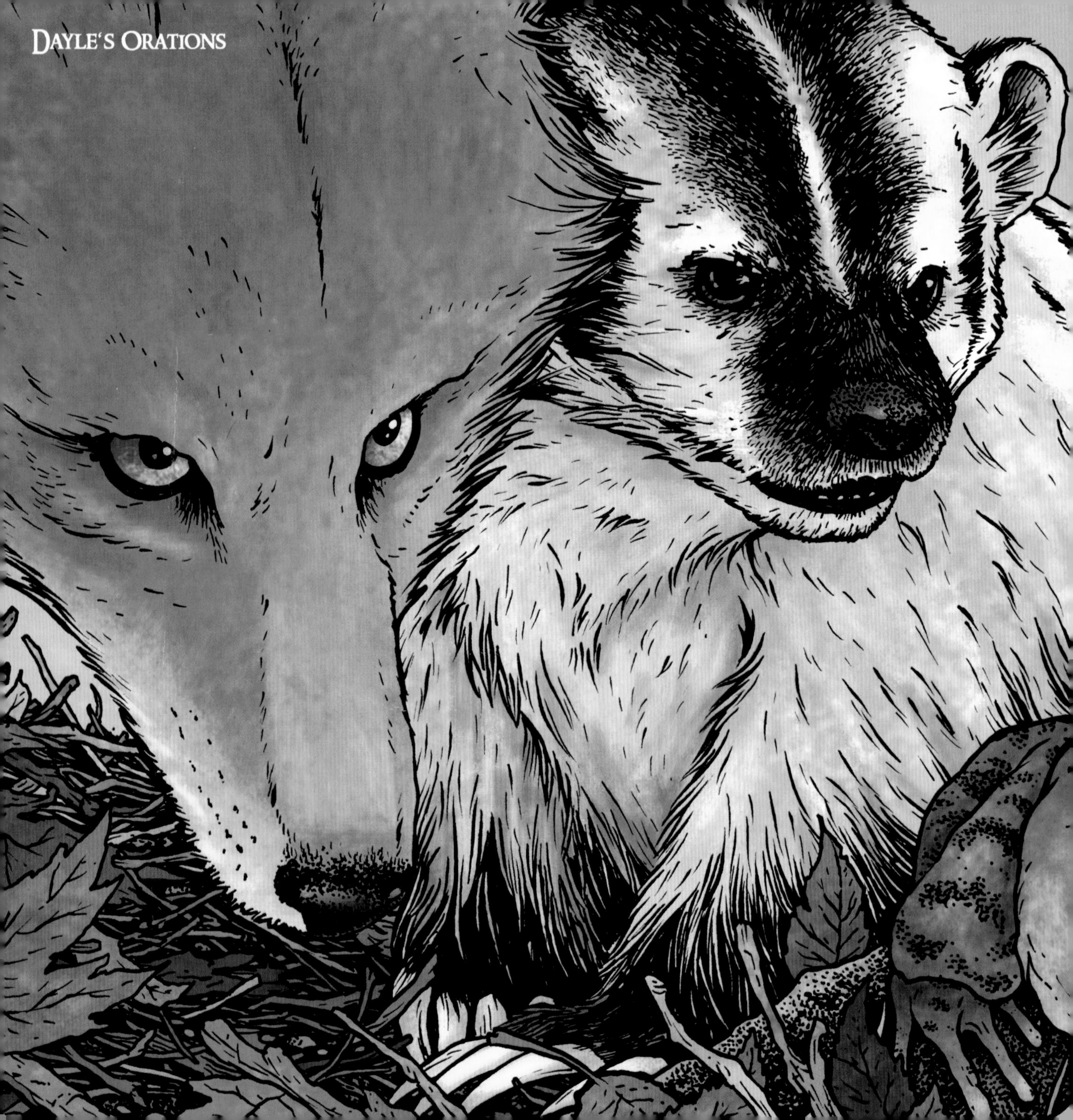

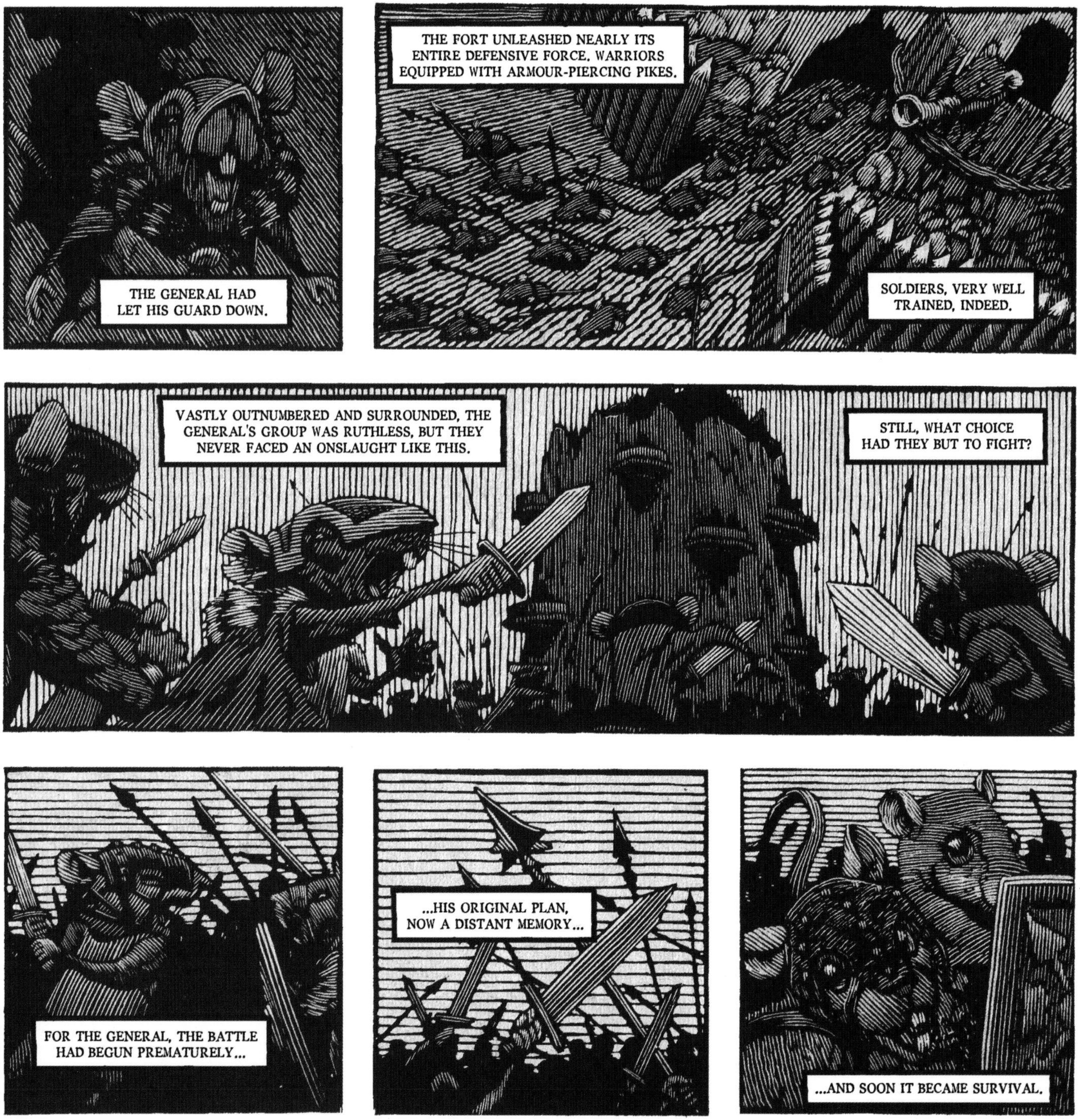
THE GENERAL HAD LET HIS GUARD DOWN.
THE FORT UNLEASHED NEARLY ITS ENTIRE DEFENSIVE FORCE. WARRIORS EQUIPPED WITH ARMOUR-PIERCING PIKES.
SOLDIERS, VERY WELL TRAINED, INDEED.
VASTLY OUTNUMBERED AND SURROUNDED, THE GENERAL'S GROUP WAS RUTHLESS, BUT THEY NEVER FACED AN ONSLAUGHT LIKE THIS.
STILL, WHAT CHOICE HAD THEY BUT TO FIGHT?
FOR THE GENERAL, THE BATTLE HAD BEGUN PREMATURELY...
...HIS ORIGINAL PLAN, NOW A DISTANT MEMORY...
...AND SOON IT BECAME SURVIVAL.

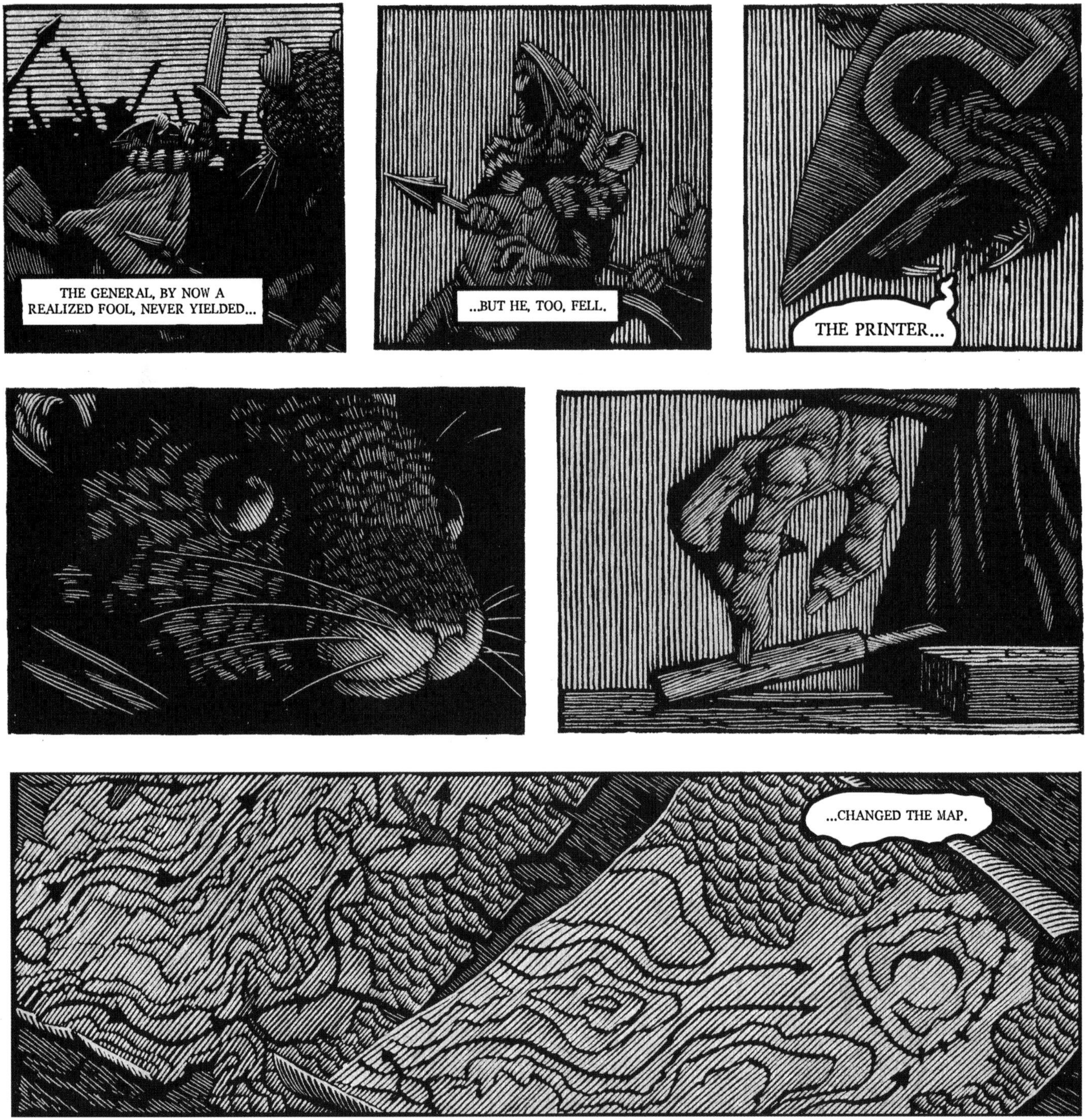
THE GENERAL, BY NOW A REALIZED FOOL, NEVER YIELDED...
...BUT HE, TOO, FELL.
THE PRINTER...
...CHANGED THE MAP.

END

Legend Cover Gallery

Legend of the Copperwood Mines:

In the years when Copperwood was known as Oakwood, a guardmouse named Othon ventured into a wet tunnel underneath the city's mighty tree. There he met and befriended three amiable salamanders who guided him beyond the oak's tangled root system and further into a rocky maze of caverns. When his candlelight hit the walls, his echo of "Wot-How!" startled the citizens far, far above, for everything his light shone on was a vein of untapped copper ore. This discovery led to the city's future wealth, prosperity, & renaming.

Legend of Dayle's Orations:

It was said that Dayle, chief orator in the third reign of Laria, could tame any beast of fur, scale, or feather with only his speech. He knew the old language of the trees, the language all creatures once spoke but none could remember. His words and timbre were moving and eloquent enough in his native voice, but when he whispered the same words in that ancient tongue, all beasts stopped to listen and were powerless to do anything more.

Legend of the Morten-Harvest Trio Dance:

The fabled mouse musical trio—Clyfford of Ivydale, Nichlas of Pebblebrook, and Bennett of Walnutpeck—were said to have played so perfectly together, made such beautiful harmonies, they could rouse even the long dead spirits of the mice in Seyan for a jig or three. And as tribute to the fallen, the trio did so on the eve before Morten-Harvest.

Legend of the Coin Horde Memorial:

A once fierce stoat huntress had bargained with her fellow kin to gain a single coin for every mouse she killed and delivered to them. So adept was she at the task that her fortune grew large enough for her to claim a role as their queen. She was said to have remorse late in life and starved herself in her treasure chamber as penance for the slaughter. A mouse-smith discovered the treasure horde & the queen's remains sixty years later, but left them all as a tribute to honor the lost lives.

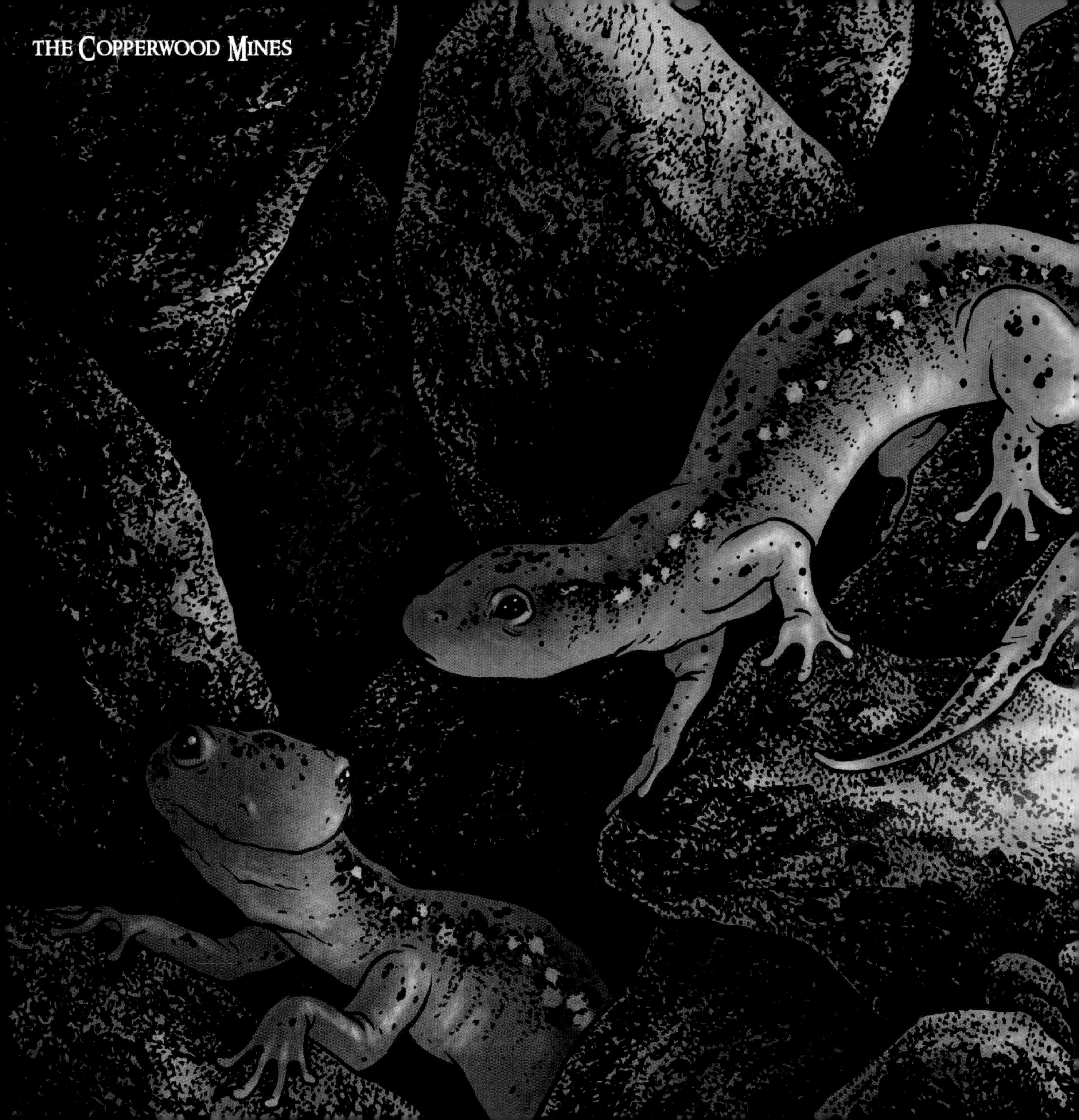

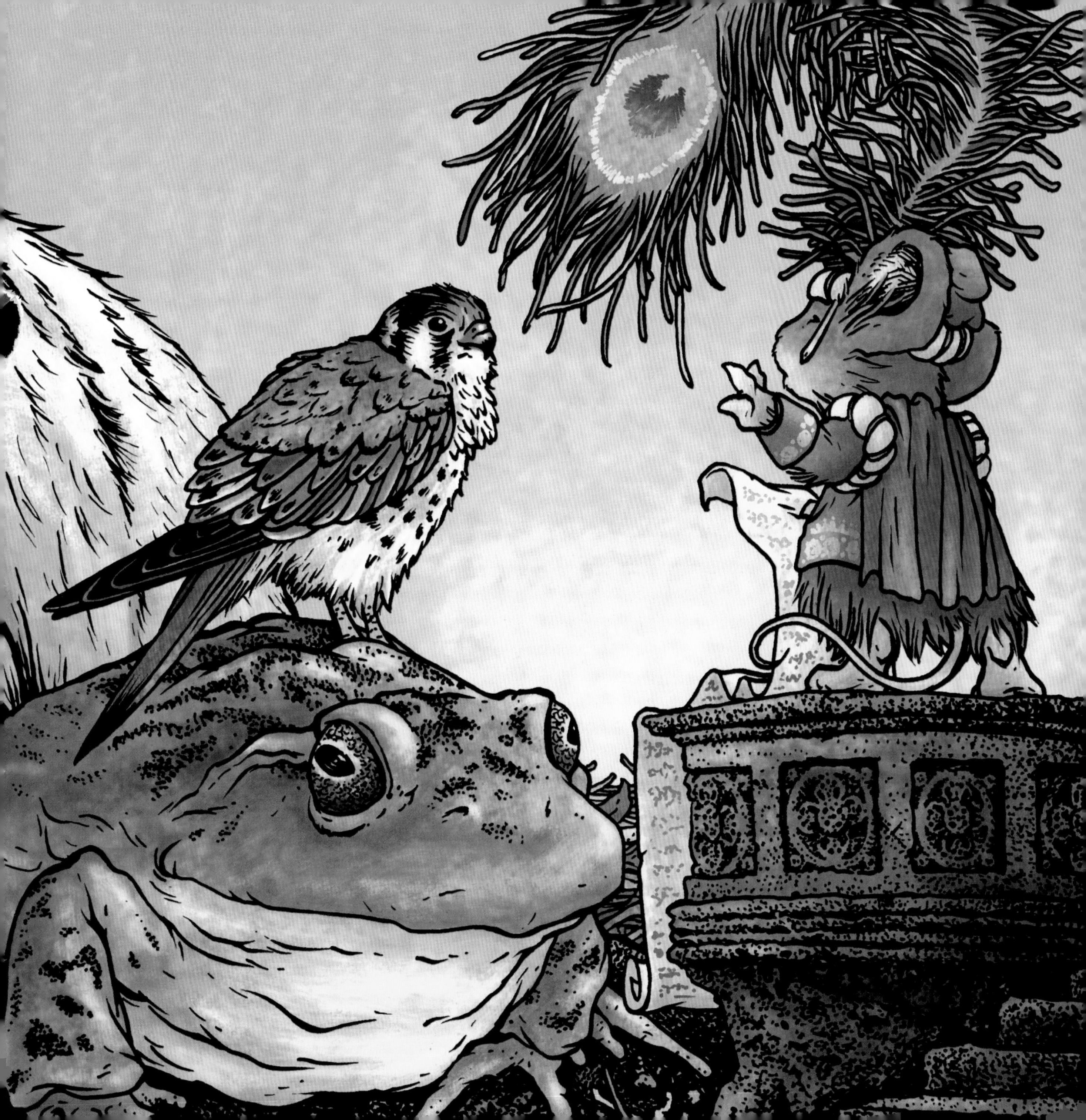

The Morten-Harvest Trio Dance

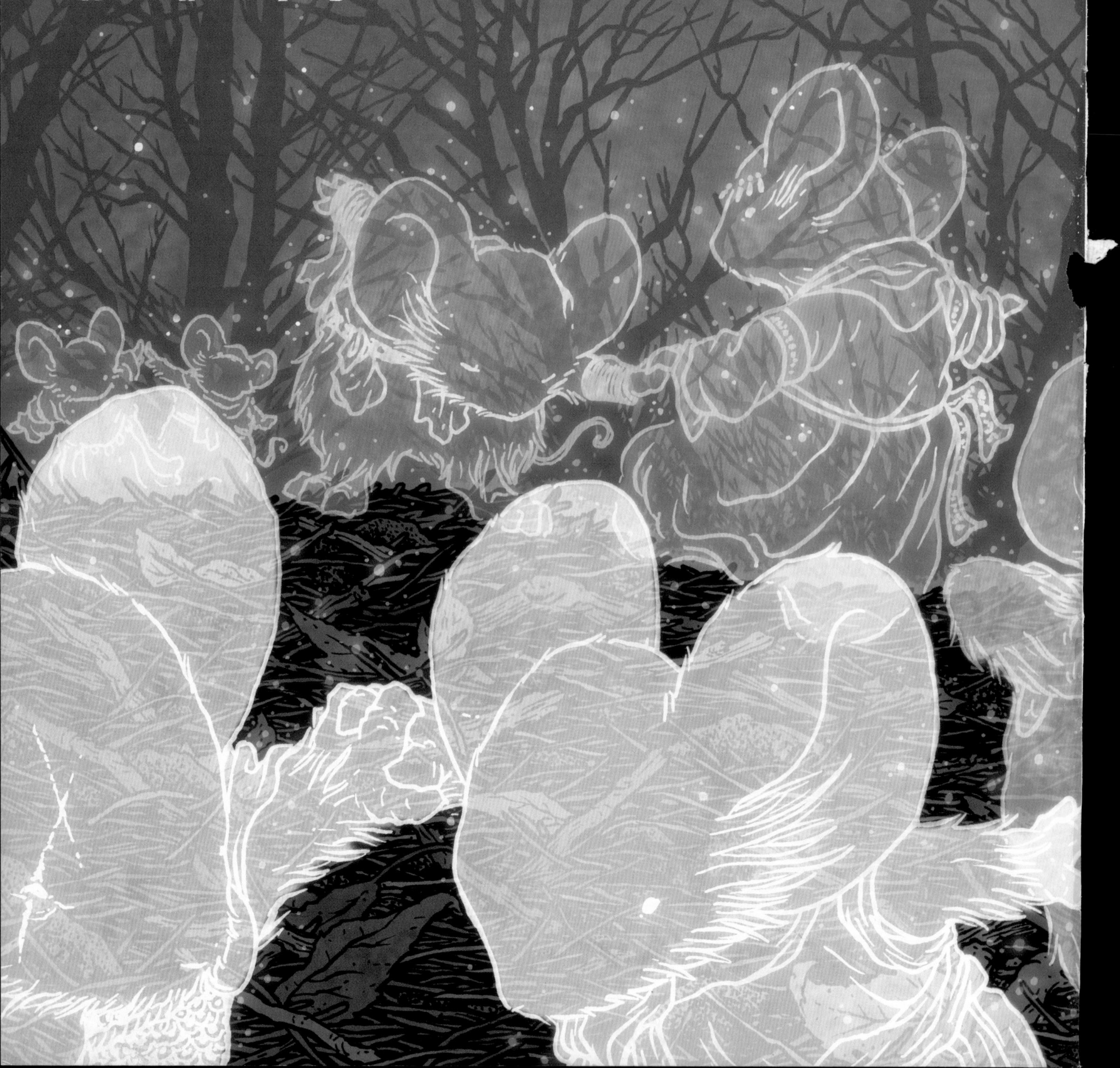

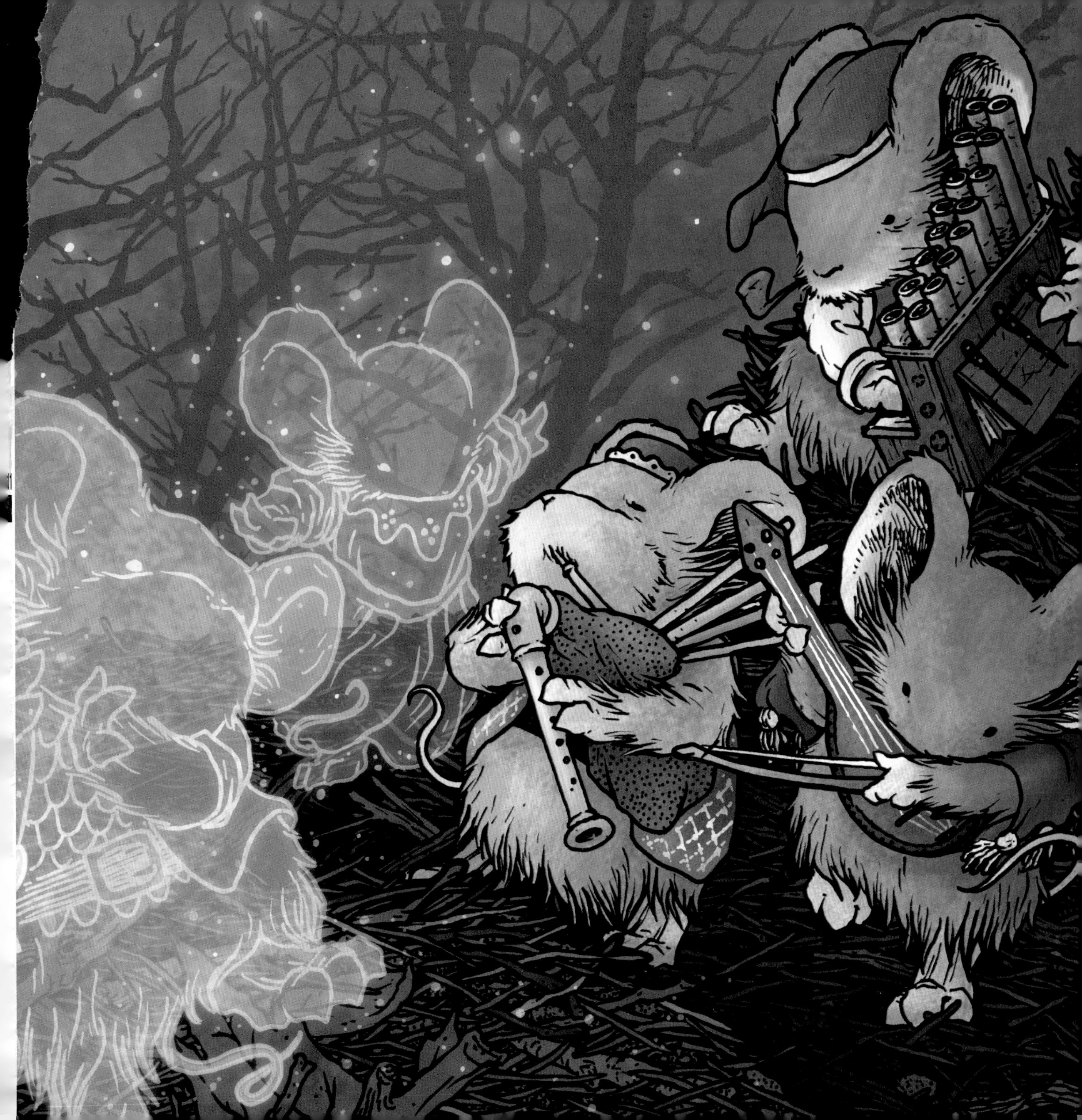

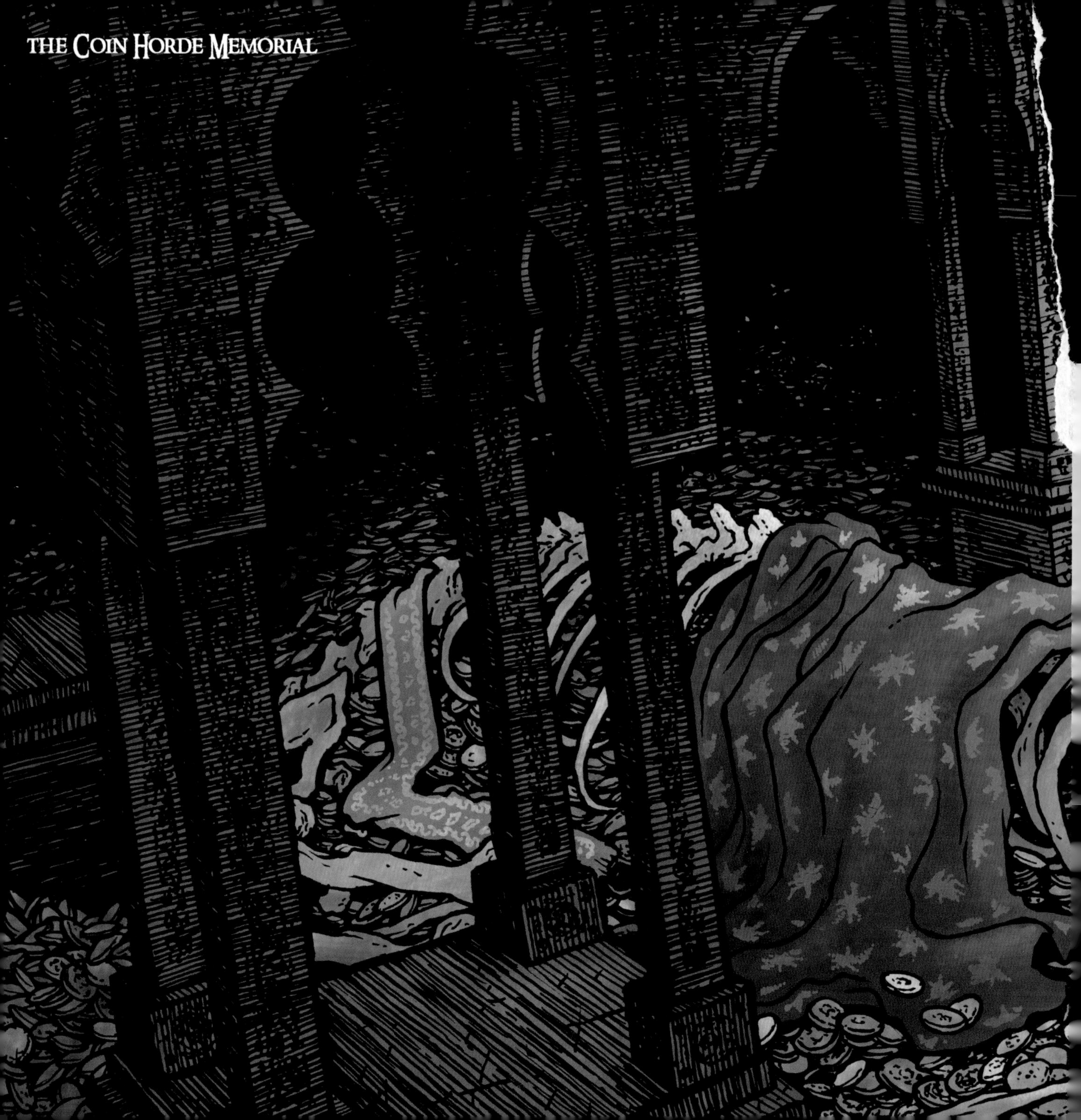

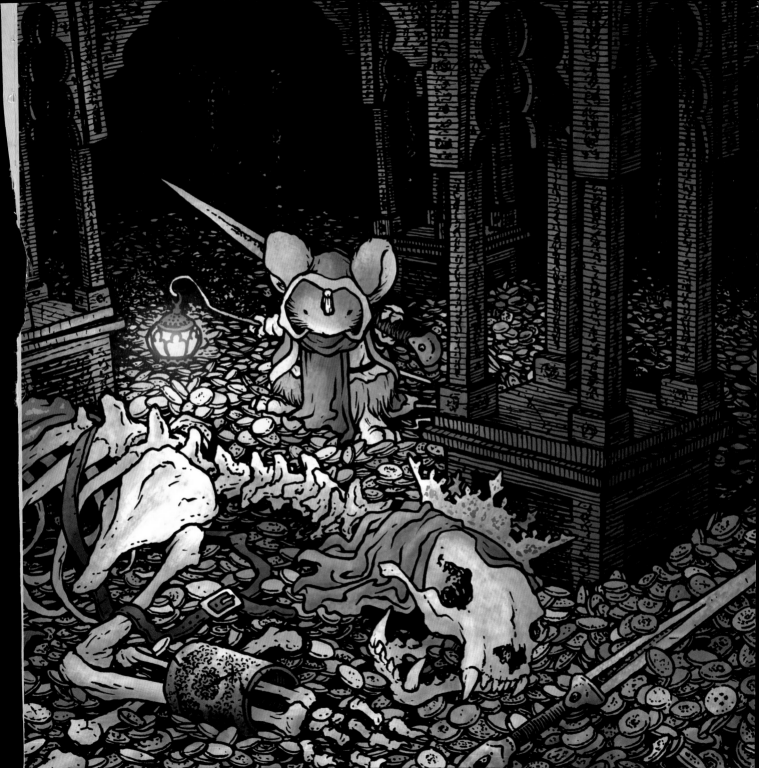

THE INN'S PATRONS:

June

Owner and operator of the June Alley Inn, which is known as the most hospitable inn on the west end of the Mouse Territories.

Kaleb

Lyrical writer of plays, most notably those performed by the Applekettle Puppet Troupe of Oakgrove.

Orwin

A peasant mouse who earns his keep tending & processing the harvests in Barkstone & Elmoss.

Hackett

A woodcutter who lost his arm to a mink while felling timber for the Barkstone gates.

Rylan

A seafaring mouse who traded goods between Rustleaf, Dawnrock & Darkwater.

Aemon

Chief object archivist in the city of Blackrock & known for hoarding his own private collection of historic goods.

Mira

Lives beyond Barkstone's walls mending clothes & mixing berry dyes.

ABOUT THE AUTHORS

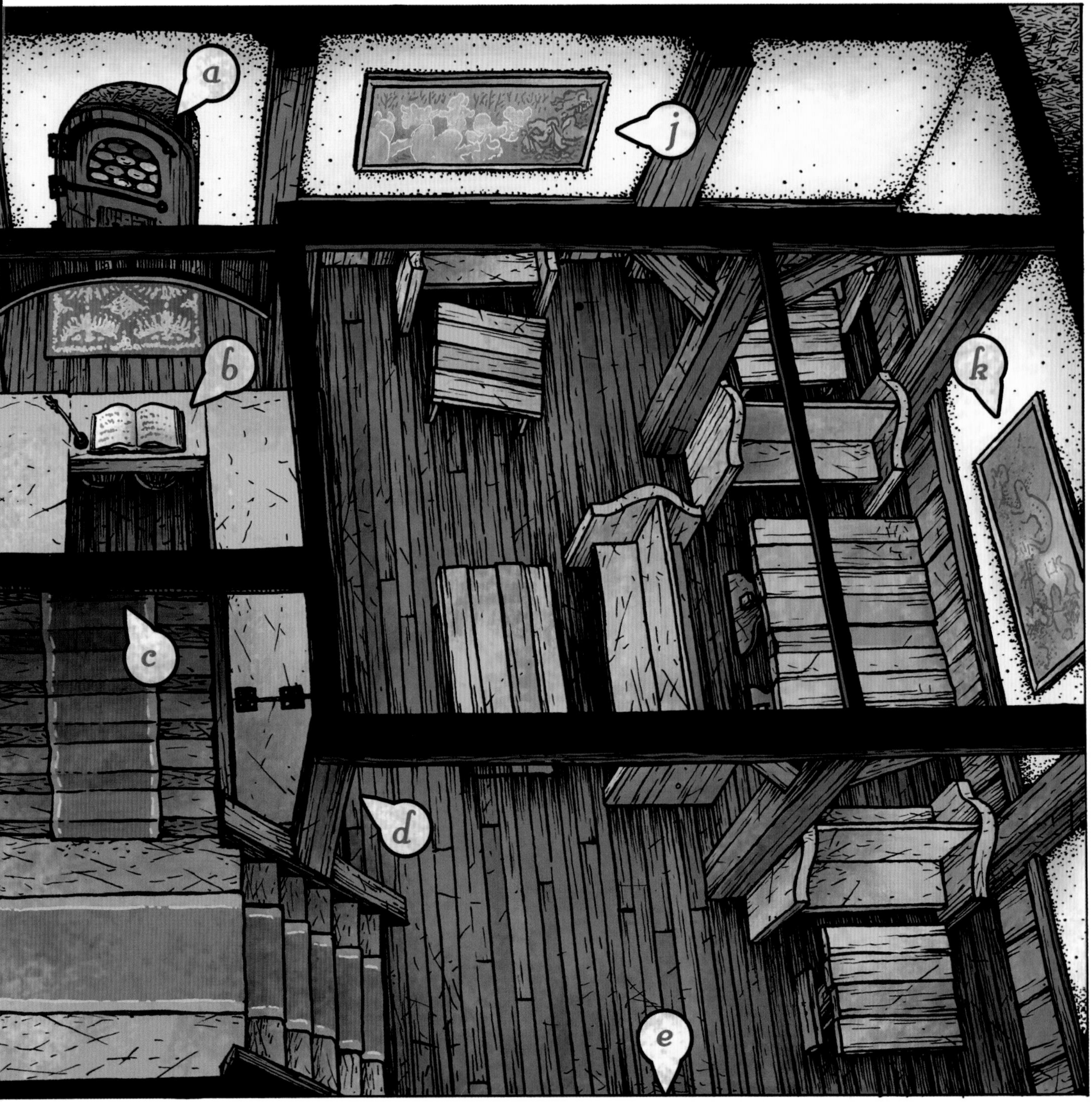
a
j
b
k
c
d
e

THE JUNE ALLEY INN

a: Entrance

b: June's Ledger

c: Stairs to Rooms

d: Back Bar Access

e: Doors to Kitchen

f: Firewood Storage

g: Stone Hearth

h: The Legend of Dayle's Orations

i: The Legend of the Coin Horde Memorial

j: The Legend of Morten-Harvest Trio

k: The Legend of the Copperwood Mines

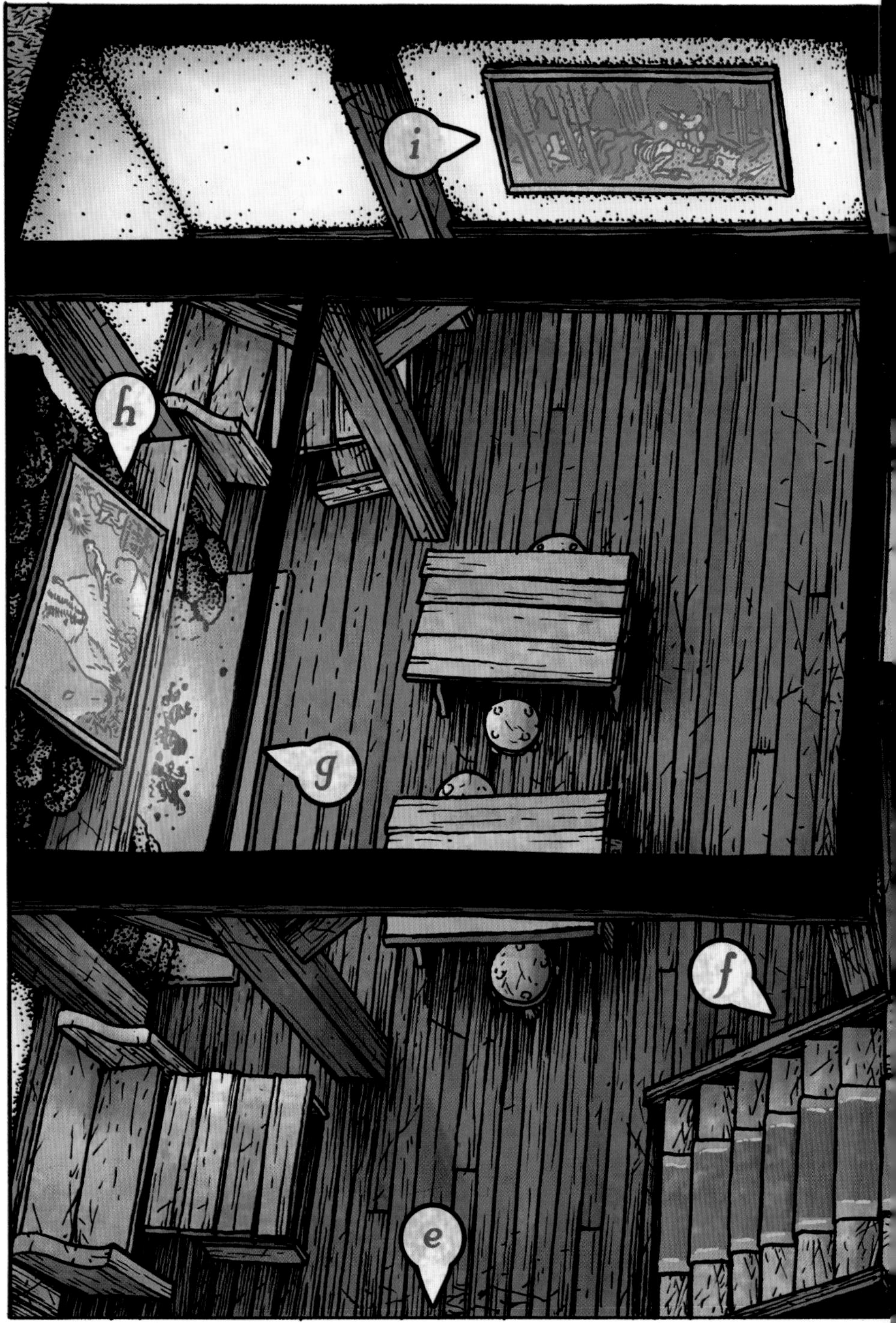
i
h
g
f
e

Ingram

A Guardmouse & patrol leader stationed to watch over the western Scent Border.

Alton

Studies & documents the skeletal anatomy of larger beasts after they perish.

Odella

Musician & songmouse who teaches the young and entertains the old with her melodies & lyrics.

Holton

A lantern-bearer who keeps the path well lit between Barkstone & Pebblebrook.

Edwy

Director of Defense of an unknown settlement which is believed to be west of Elmwood.

Bellah

The daughter of the famed star-mapper Zorian, she excels in the skill of tracking celestial patterns.

Alistair

June's husband & a printmaker who uses his craft to mass-produce images for greater mousekind.

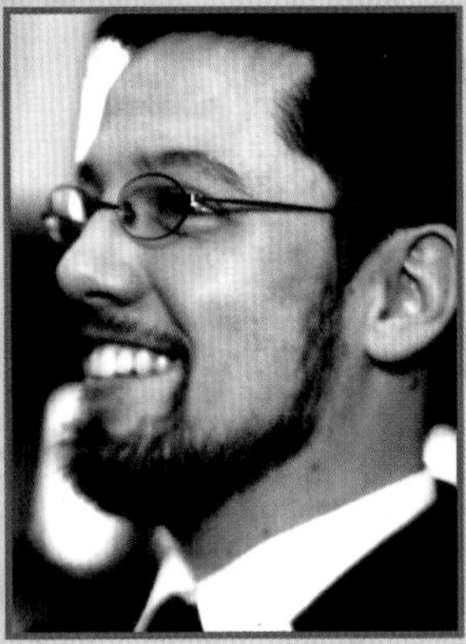

DAVID PETERSEN WAS BORN IN 1977. HIS ARTISTIC CAREER SOON FOLLOWED. A STEADY DIET OF CARTOONS, COMICS, AND TREE CLIMBING FED HIS IMAGINATION AND IS WHAT STILL INSPIRES HIS WORK TODAY. DAVID WAS THE 2007 RUSS MANNING AWARD RECIPIENT FOR MOST PROMISING NEWCOMER, AND IN 2008, WON EISNER AWARDS FOR BEST PUBLICATION FOR KIDS (*MOUSE GUARD FALL 1152* & *WINTER 1152*) AND BEST GRAPHIC ALBUM – REPRINT (*MOUSE GUARD FALL 1152* HARDCOVER). HE RECEIVED HIS BFA IN PRINTMAKING FROM EASTERN MICHIGAN UNIVERSITY, WHERE HE MET HIS WIFE, JULIA. THEY CONTINUE TO RESIDE IN MICHIGAN WITH THEIR DOG, AUTUMN.

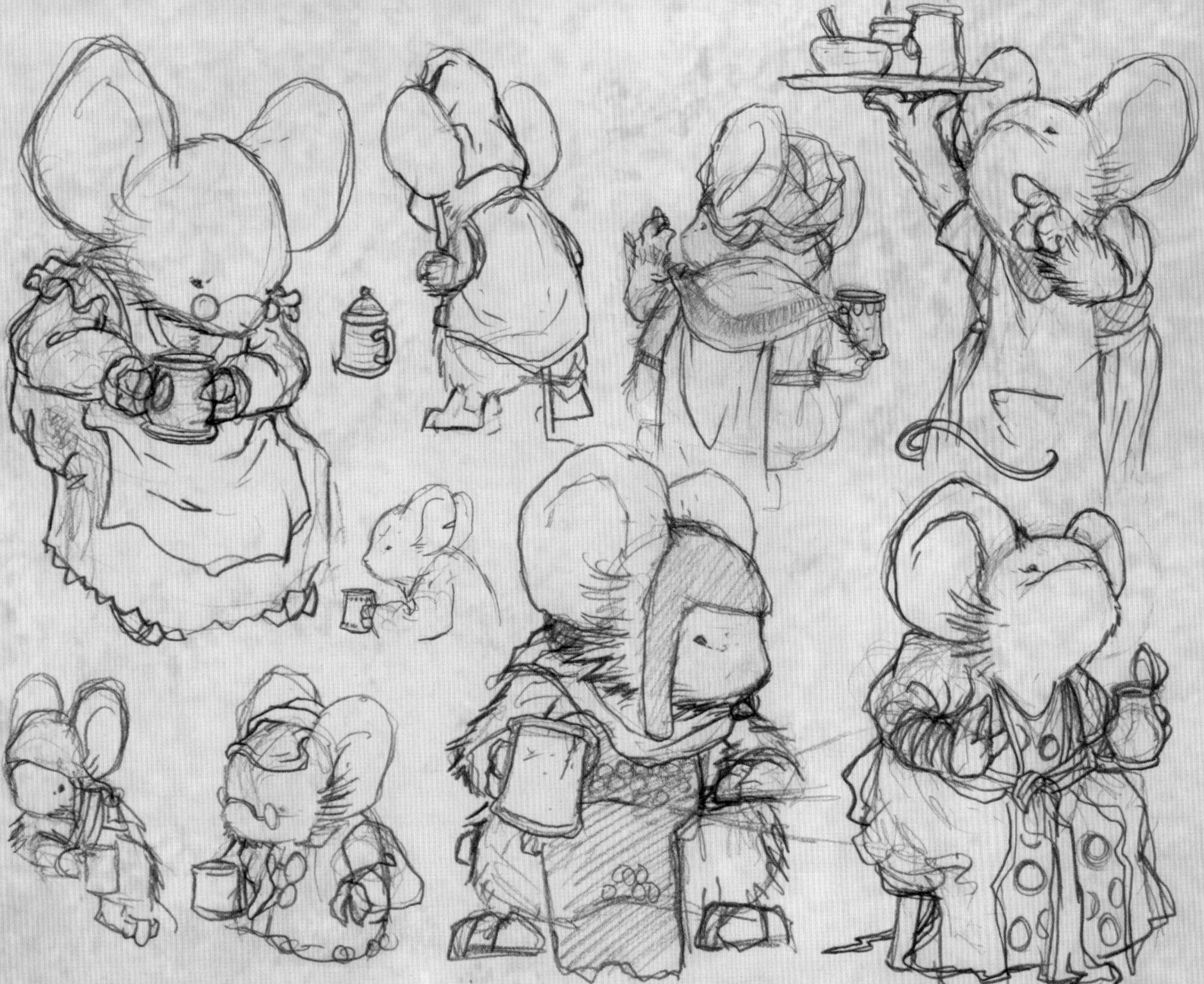

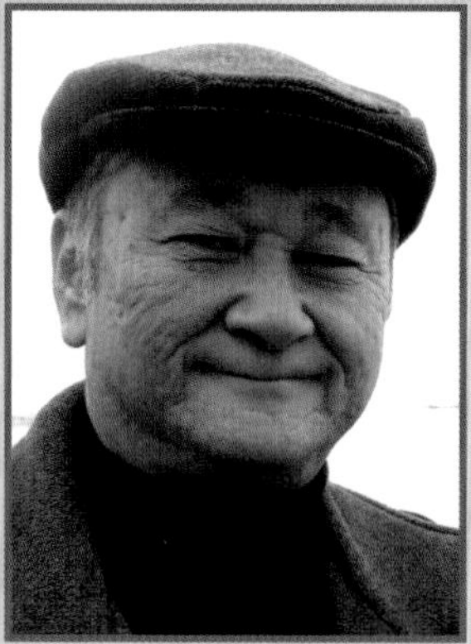

STAN SAKAI WAS BORN IN KYOTO, JAPAN, GREW UP IN HAWAII, AND NOW LIVES IN SOUTHERN CALIFORNIA. HIS CREATION, *USAGI YOJIMBO* THE SAMURAI RABBIT, WAS FIRST PUBLISHED IN 1984 AND CONTINUES TODAY. HE DOES EXTENSIVE RESEARCH FOR HIS STORIES AND HAS RECEIVED NUMEROUS RECOGNITIONS, INCLUDING A FEW EISNER AWARDS, A HARVEY, A NATIONAL CARTOONISTS SOCIETY AWARD, AMERICAN LIBRARY ASSOCIATION AWARD, AND THE JAPANESE-AMERICAN NATIONAL MUSEUM CULTURAL AMBASSADOR AWARD.

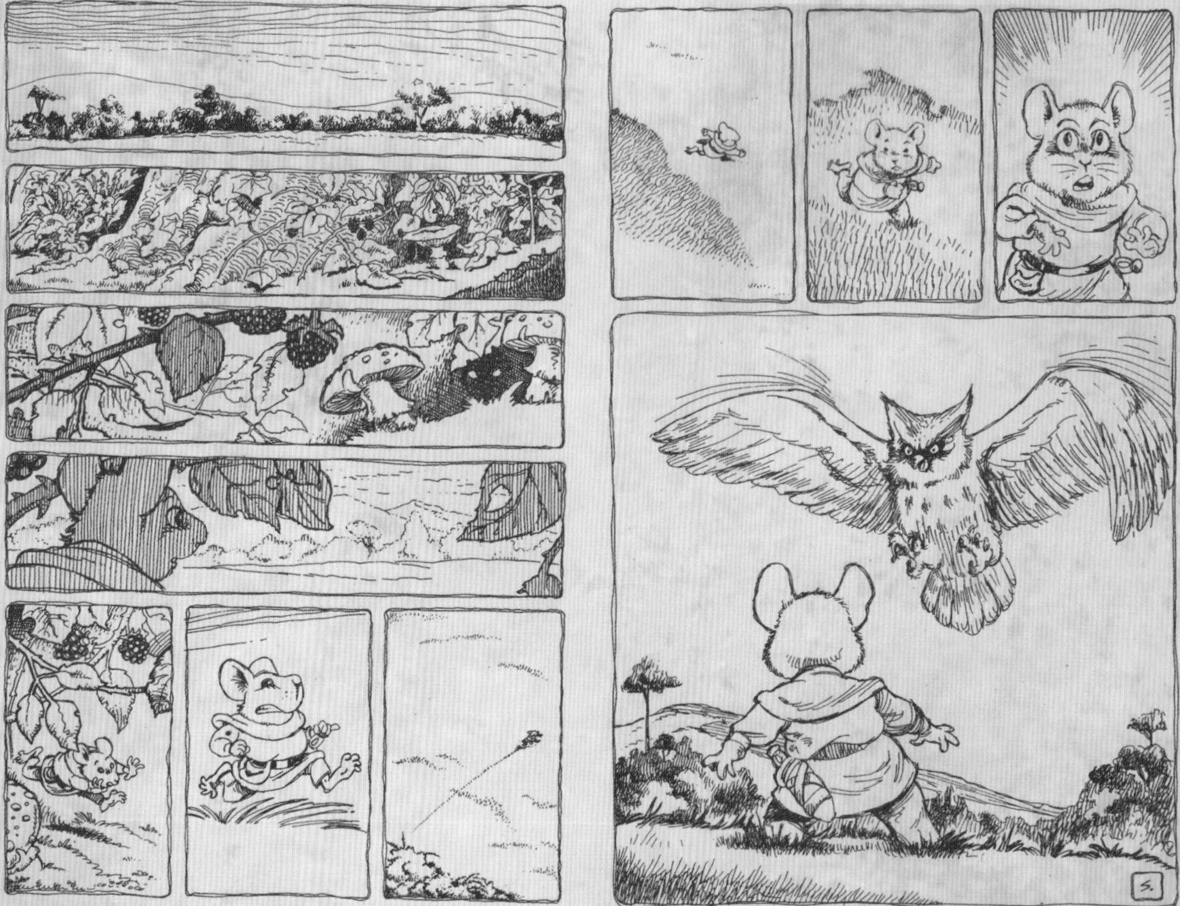

NICK TAPALANSKY IS THE AUTHOR OF MULTIPLE GRAPHIC NOVELS, INCLUDING *AWAKENING* (ARCHAIA/BOOM! STUDIOS) AND *CAST NO SHADOW* (FIRST SECOND), WITH MORE ON THE WAY. HIS WORK HAS ALSO BEEN FEATURED IN THE HARVEY AWARD-WINNING *POPGUN* VOL. 4 ANTHOLOGY AND *THE PERHAPANAUTS* (BOTH PUBLISHED BY IMAGE COMICS), AS WELL AS THIS VERY BOOK. SINCE YOU'RE ALREADY UP TO THE AUTHOR PAGES, AND WELL OUT OF THE STORIES, HE ENCOURAGES YOU TO SEEK OUT ALL SORTS OF ODDS AND ENDS AND UNIVERSAL SECRETS, AND EVEN SOME FREE COMICS, AT WWW.NICKTAPALANSKY.COM/BLOG.

Mouse Guard: Legends of the Guard Volume Two -- "Leviathan"

PAGE 01

Panel 1: Wide panel with space for story title; TIERNAN, all black but for a slash of white across his cheek, stands on the beach looking out toward the lapping ocean. The sun beats down, sparkling off of the waves. He has an ornate sword at his side and a rucksack sits in the sand next to him. He wears a gray hooded cloak, the hood lowered around his shoulders, as well as a charmed amulet around his neck, a chiseled blue stone with various runes inscribed upon it.

1 CAP (NARRATOR):
You've no doubt heard tell of Tiernan the Brave's Quest, and of the many adventures therein.

2 CAP (NARRATOR):
His search for a cure to save his ailing queen has been retold the land over for generations.

Panel 2: TIERNAN stands firm as he faces a wild FOX who is back on its haunches, defeated.

3 CAP (NARRATOR):
His battle, and subsequent friendship, with AIDEN THE STRONG,

4 TIERNAN:
Is that all you have, fox? I was ready for a fight!

Panel 3: TIERNAN inside a great room within a stone temple, studying sigils and glyphs on the wall. He holds a torch in one paw, his other tracing the lines of anancient mouse etched into the wall.

5 CAP (NARRATOR):
Deciphering the mysteries of the ancients in the OLD ISLAND TEMPLE,

olume Two -- "Leviathan"

above a beautiful sleeping QUEEN
ere's a flicker of stars within the
t fading away.

(NARRATOR):
ough the LAND OF DREAMS.

the introduction; TIERNAN is liftin the
has come to rest next to him. The SEAGULL

RRATOR):
wn as Tiernan the Brash, a mouse who
n fate could have a hand in his quest,
rgotten as the trial that changed it.

RATOR):
one time TIERNAN'S wit and strength
LD ISLAND TEMPLE is an exciting tale
wn...

TOR):
s the stuff of legends.

IRA):
Tiernan? Storm's in the air.

11 TIERNAN:
Aye, let's be off. A little rain and thunder doesn't scare you, right Keira?
For I know there is nothing which can stop my noble quest,
be it beast or nature!

ALEX ECKMAN-LAWN IS A PHILADELPHIA ILLUSTRATOR WHO HAS BEEN LIVING THE DREAM SINCE 1984. HE HAS WORKED PRIMARILY IN MUSIC ILLUSTRATION AND COMICS, SPLITTING HIS TIME BETWEEN ALBUM COVERS AND THE HEART-STOPPING THRILLS OF SEQUENTIAL STORYTELLING. CURRENTLY, ALEX IS HARD AT WORK ON A NEW COMIC PROJECT WITH WRITER NICK TAPALANSKY. IN HIS OWN TIME, ALEX IS WORKING TO SLOWLY TEAR THE SUN OUT OF THE SKY ONE DAY AT A TIME.

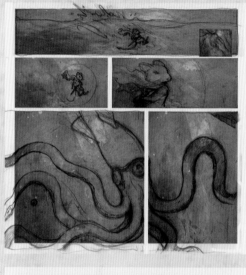

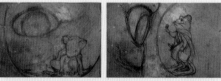

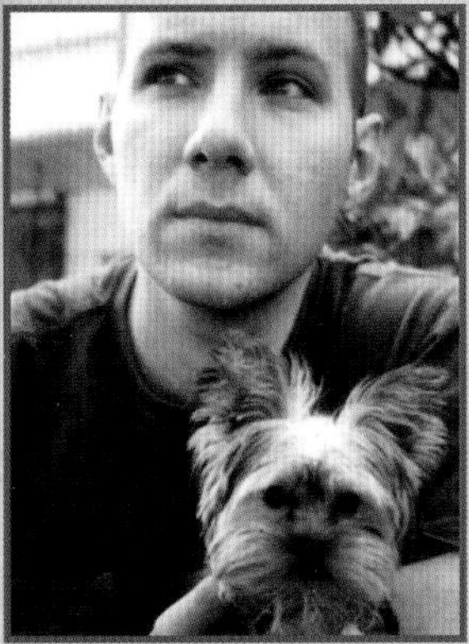

BEN CALDWELL GRADUATED FROM THE PARSONS SCHOOL OF DESIGN FOR ILLUSTRATION, AND EUGENE LANG COLLEGE FOR ANCIENT HISTORY. HE LIVES IN NEW YORK WITH HIS WIFE, BABY DAUGHTERS, DOG, AND LARGE COLLECTION OF CHINESE MURDER MYSTERIES. HE ALSO WROTE A SERIES OF GRAPHIC NOVELS CALLED *DARE DETECTIVES*.

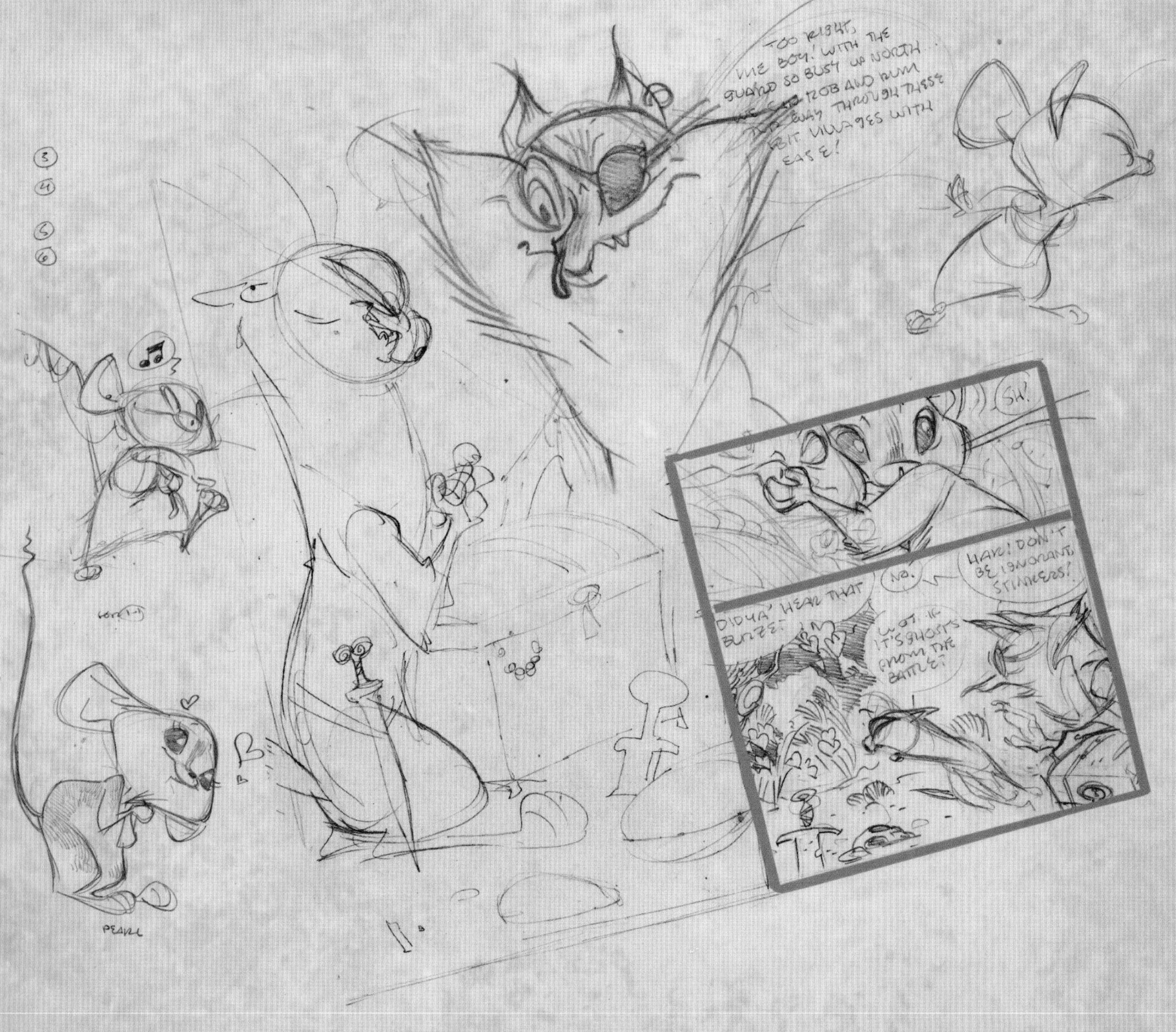

TOO RIGHT, ME BOY! WITH THE GUARD SO BUSY UP NORTH
ROB AND BURN
WAY THROUGH THESE
VILLAGES WITH EASE!
SH!
DIDYA' HEAR THAT BUZZ?
NO.
HAH! DON'T BE IGNORANT, STINKERS!
WOT IF IT'S GHOSTS FROM THE BATTLE?
PEARL

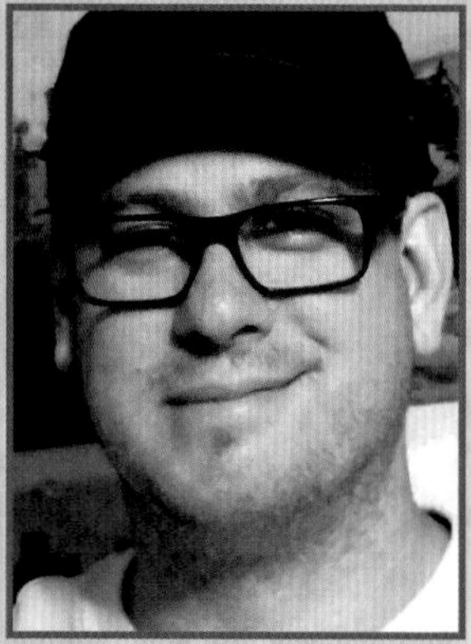

CHRISTIAN SLADE LOVES EVERYTHING ABOUT BEING AN ARTIST. SO FAR, HE HAS ILLUSTRATED SOME AMAZING PROJECTS THAT INCLUDE MAGAZINES, CHILDREN'S BOOKS, THEME PARKS, ANIMATED FILMS, AND NOW *MOUSE GUARD*! OVER THE LAST FIVE YEARS, CHRISTIAN HAS BEEN THE ILLUSTRATOR OF THE *RICKY AND PALS* STORY IN *RANGER RICK JR.*, PUBLISHED BY THE NATIONAL WILDLIFE FEDERATION. HE HAS A HEALTHY BOX OF COMIC BOOKS, A TON OF *STAR WARS* TOYS, AND A GIANT RUBBER TARANTULA. HE KEEPS ALL OF THESE THINGS IN HIS HOME STUDIO IN WINTER GARDEN, FLORIDA, WHERE HE LIVES WITH HIS WONDERFUL WIFE, ANN, THEIR TWIN CHILDREN, KATE AND NATE, AND WELSH CORGIS, PENNY AND LEO. TO SEE MORE OF HIS COMIC WORK, CHECK OUT HIS ALL-AGES GRAPHIC NOVEL SERIES *KORGI*, PUBLISHED BY TOP SHELF.

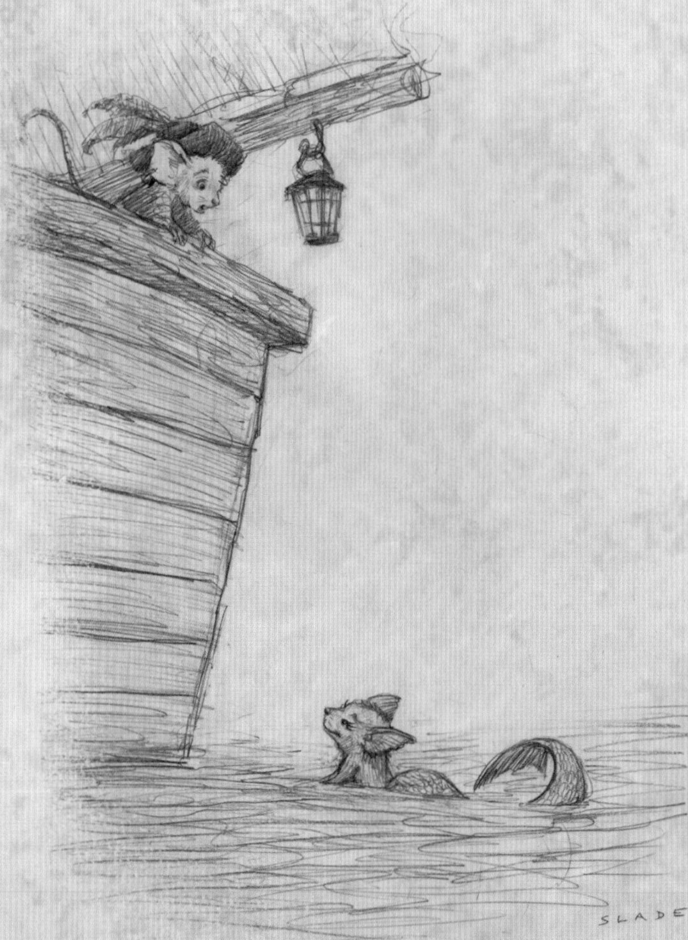
SLADE

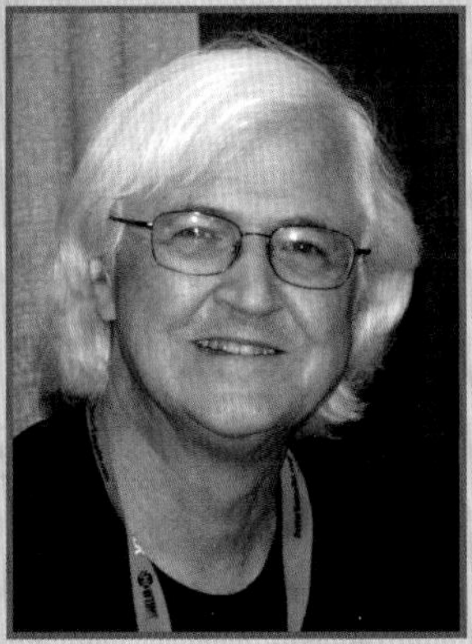

RICK GEARY WAS BORN IN 1946 IN KANSAS CITY AND GREW UP IN WICHITA. AFTER GETTING A DEGREE IN ART AND FILM, HE MOVED TO SAN DIEGO IN 1975. HE BECAME KNOWN BY PUBLISHING IN *HEAVY METAL*, *EPIC*, AND *NATIONAL LAMPOON*. GEARY IS PERHAPS BEST KNOWN FROM HIS ONGOING REAL-CRIME COMICS SERIES DEDICATED TO FAMOUS HOMICIDE CASES OF THE 19TH CENTURY, *A TREASURY OF VICTORIAN MURDER*.

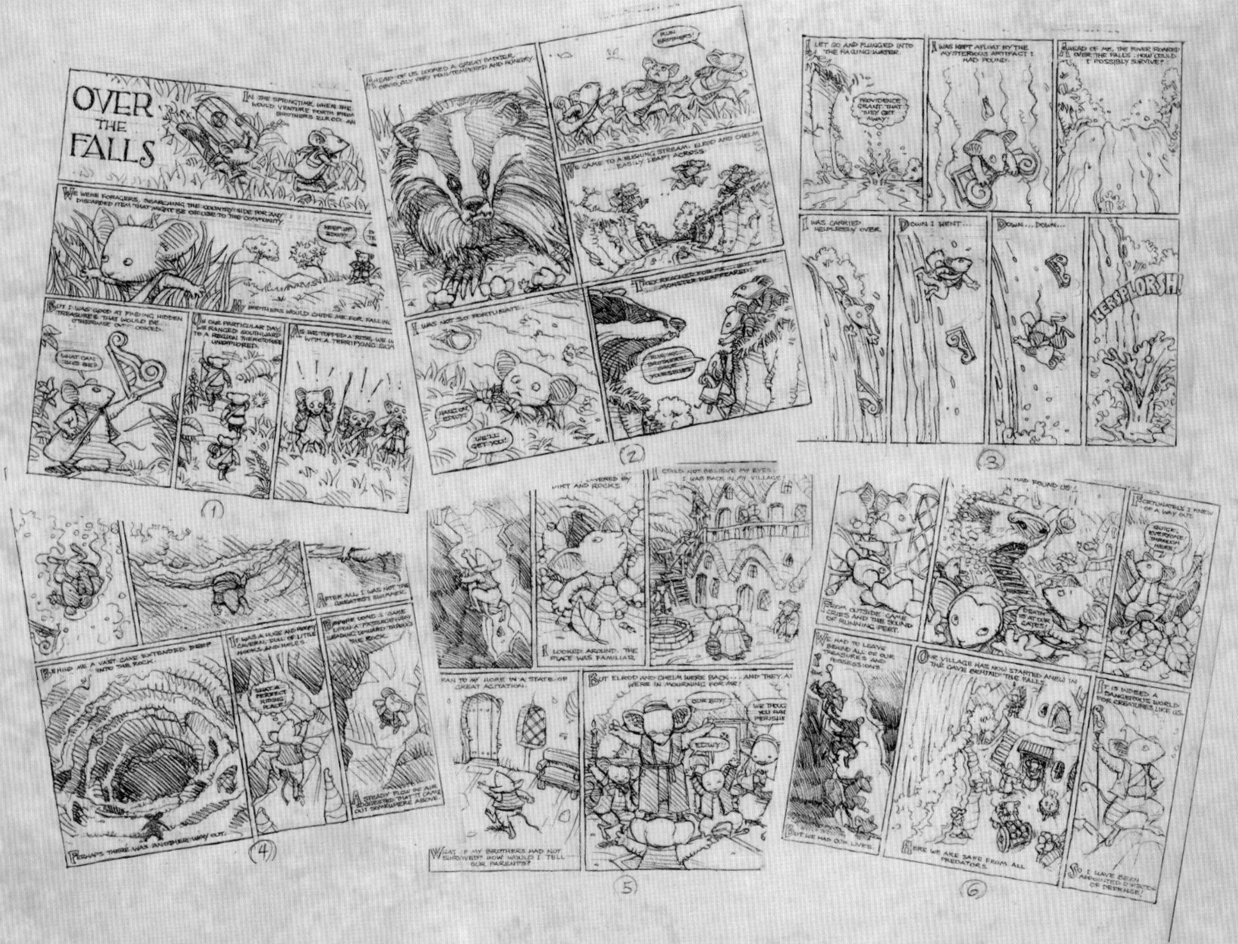
OVER THE FALLS
KERSPLORSH!
(1)
(2)
(3)
(4)
(5)
(6)

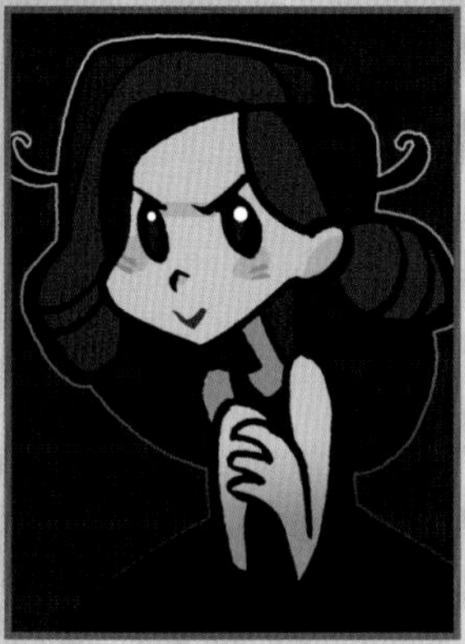

JEMMA SALUME GREW UP IN SAN FRANCISCO AND HAS BEEN DRAWING SINCE SHE FIGURED OUT CRAYONS WEREN'T FOOD. BETWEEN GETTING DIVE-BOMBED BY BLACKBIRDS AND FALLING DOWN HILLS, SHE'S SELF-PUBLISHED THE THREE-PART *CAPTAIN KITTEN* (IT RULES), DONE COVERS FOR *ADVENTURE TIME* COMICS (THEY RULE), DESIGNED A REALLY AWESOME POSTER FOR ADAM WARROCK (WHO RULES), AND SOME OTHER STUFF. SHE ENJOYS THE HECK OUT OF *MOUSE GUARD*, LONG WALKS ON THE BEACH, RUINING EVERYTHING YOU HOLD DEAR, AND WRITING BIOS IN THE THIRD PERSON.

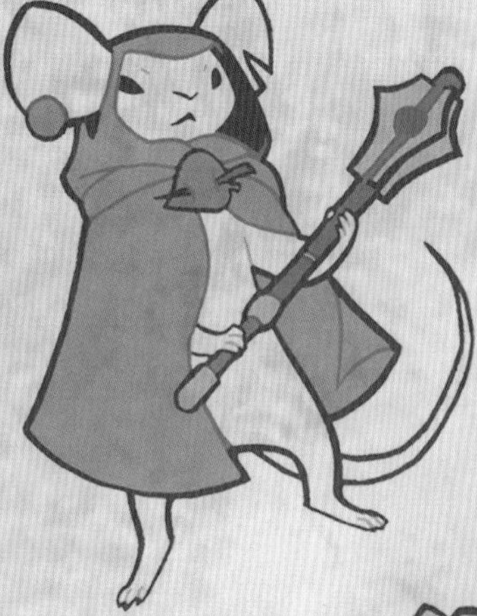

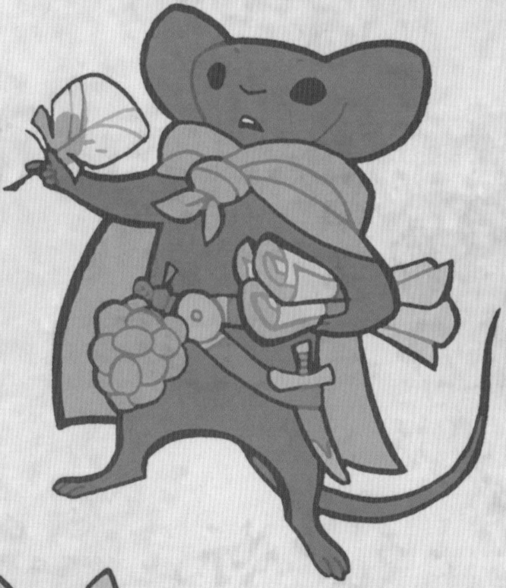

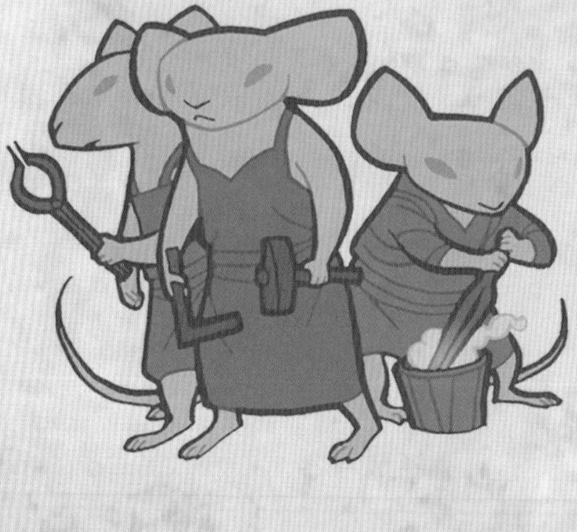

ERIC CANETE IS AN ILLUSTRATOR, DESIGNER, AND STORYBOARD ARTIST BASED IN LOS ANGELES, CA. HIS COMICS WORK INCLUDES *CYBERNARY 2.0, IRON MAN: ENTER THE MANDARIN, THE END LEAGUE, LUKE CAGE, SPIDER-MAN,* AND *SUPERBOY.*

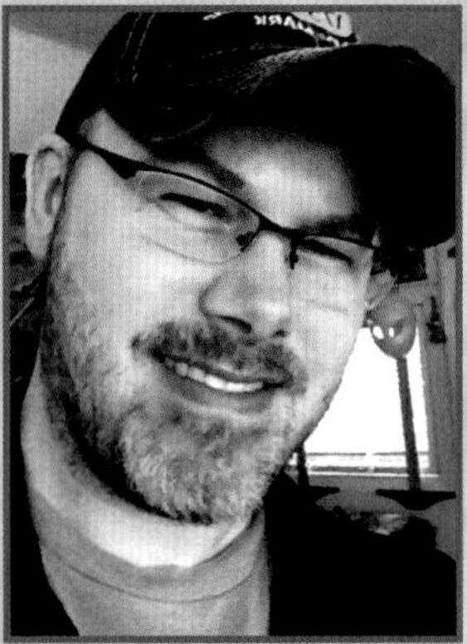

C.P. WILSON III IS AN ILLUSTRATOR AND CO-CREATOR OF THE *NEW YORK TIMES* BEST-SELLING GRAPHIC NOVEL *THE STUFF OF LEGEND*, PUBLISHED BY TH3RD WORLD STUDIOS. HE CURRENTLY RESIDES IN NEW JERSEY WITH HIS WIFE, STEPHANIE, THEIR DOG, TWO CATS, AND A GOLDFISH NAMED CHARLIE FISH.

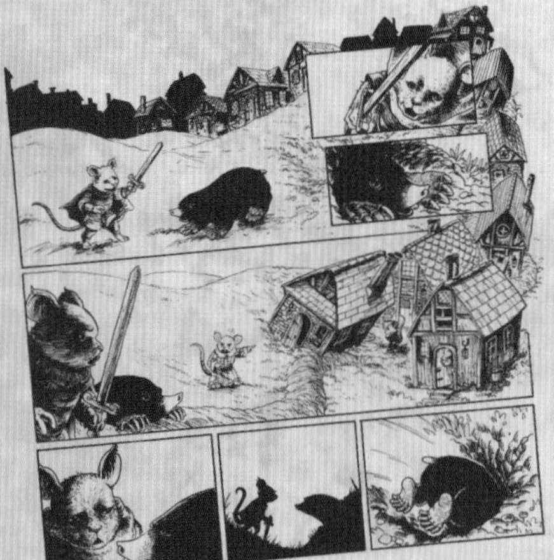

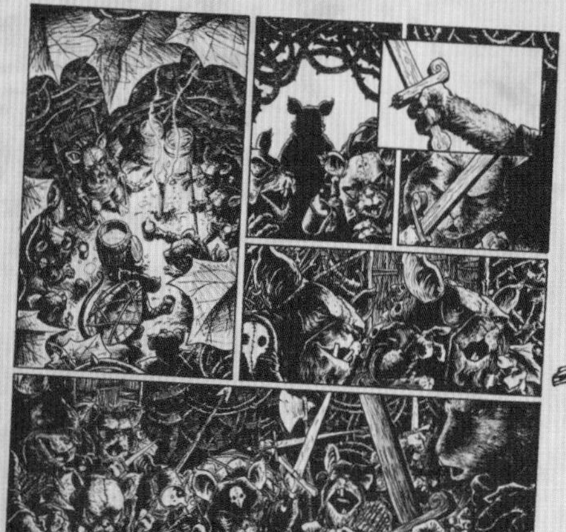

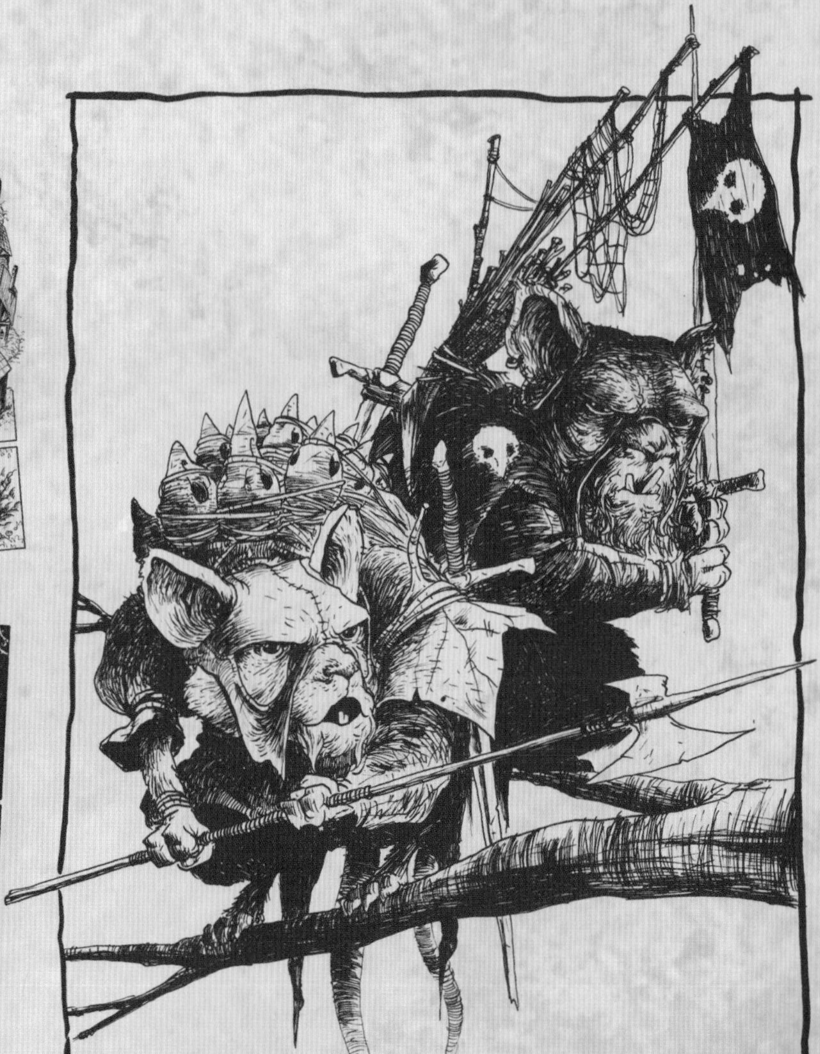
C.P. WILSON III

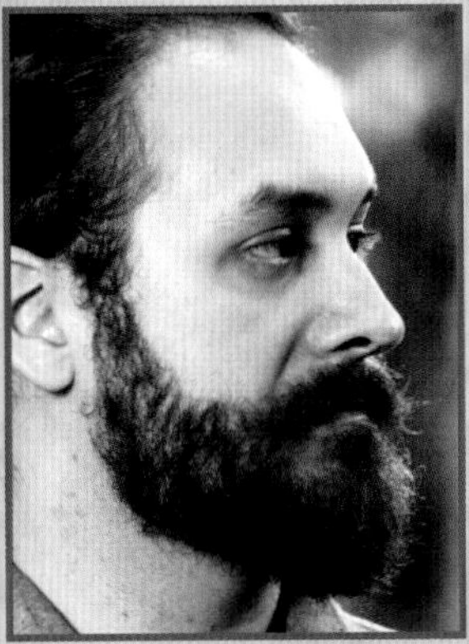

CORY GODBEY LIVES IN SOUTH CAROLINA WITH HIS WIFE, ERIN, AND THEIR MANY CATS. HE CREATES FANCIFUL ILLUSTRATIONS FOR PICTURE BOOKS, COVERS, COMICS, ADVERTISING, ANIMATED SHORTS, AND FILMS. CORY'S WORK HAS BEEN FEATURED IN A VARIETY OF ESTEEMED ANNUALS, PUBLICATIONS, AND GALLERIES. SOME OF HIS FAVORITE PAST PROJECTS INCLUDE WORKING WITH THE JIM HENSON CO. AND ARCHAIA ON *FRAGGLE ROCK* AND *LABYRINTH* COMICS, AS WELL AS CREATING THE ART AND ANIMATION FOR THE AWARD-WINNING DOCUMENTARY FILM *THE LAST FLIGHT OF PETR GINZ*. HE SHARES HIS CREATIVE PROCESS AND EXPERIENCE WITH EMERGING ARTISTS THROUGH ONLINE CLASSES, WORKSHOPS, AND MENTORSHIPS.

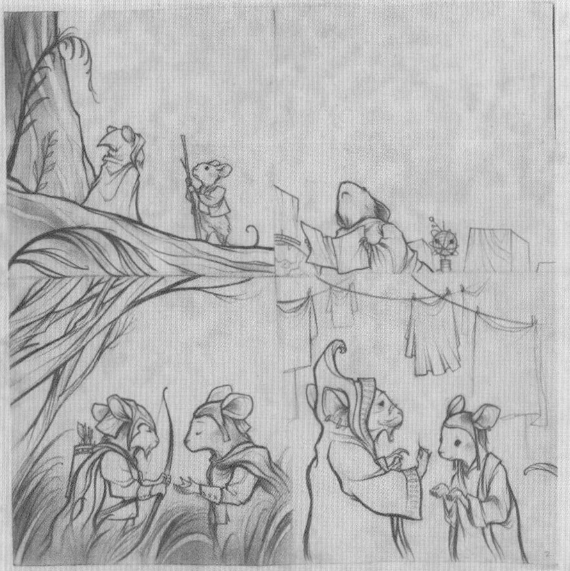

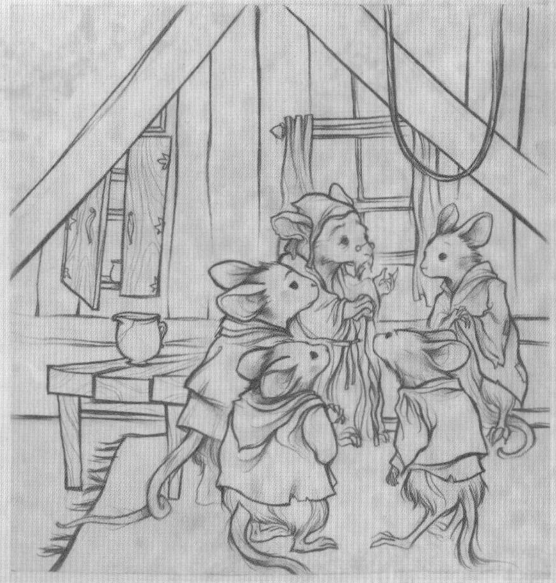

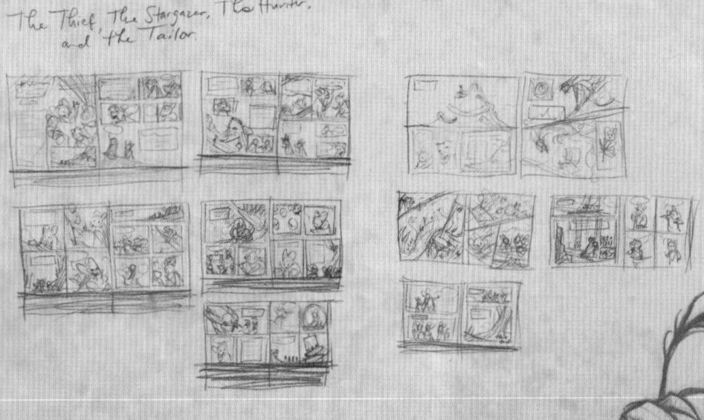
The Thief, The Stargazer, The Hunter, and the Tailor.

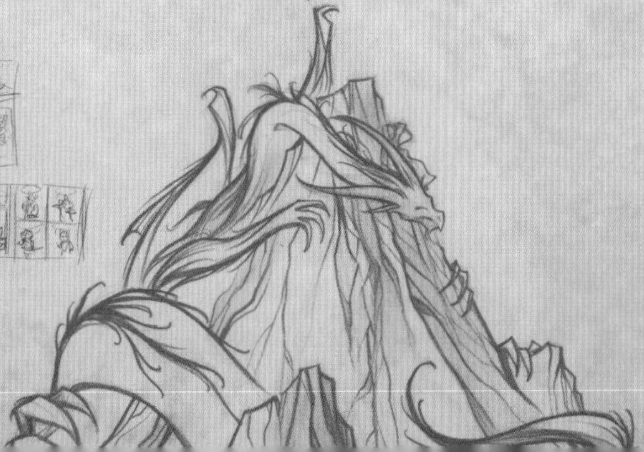

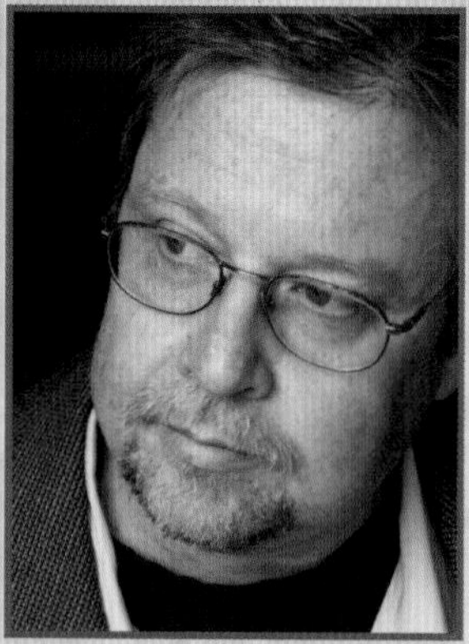

BILL WILLINGHAM HAS WRITTEN AN ADVENTUROUS MOUSE OR TWO IN HIS PAST, WHAT WITH THE MOUSE POLICE BEING SUCH A BELOVED PART OF HIS SWEEPING *FABLES* SAGA. AND HE MAY HAVE DRAWN AN ADVENTUROUS MOUSE AT LEAST ONCE BEFORE. BUT THIS IS CERTAINLY HIS FIRST TIME BOTH WRITING AND DRAWING (AND INKING) WARRIOR MICE. HE ALSO WRITES NOVELS AND COMIC BOOKS, BUT HAS NEVER COMPLETED ANY JOB ON OR BEFORE DEADLINE. TRUST THAT HIS SHAME IS VAST ABOUT THAT.

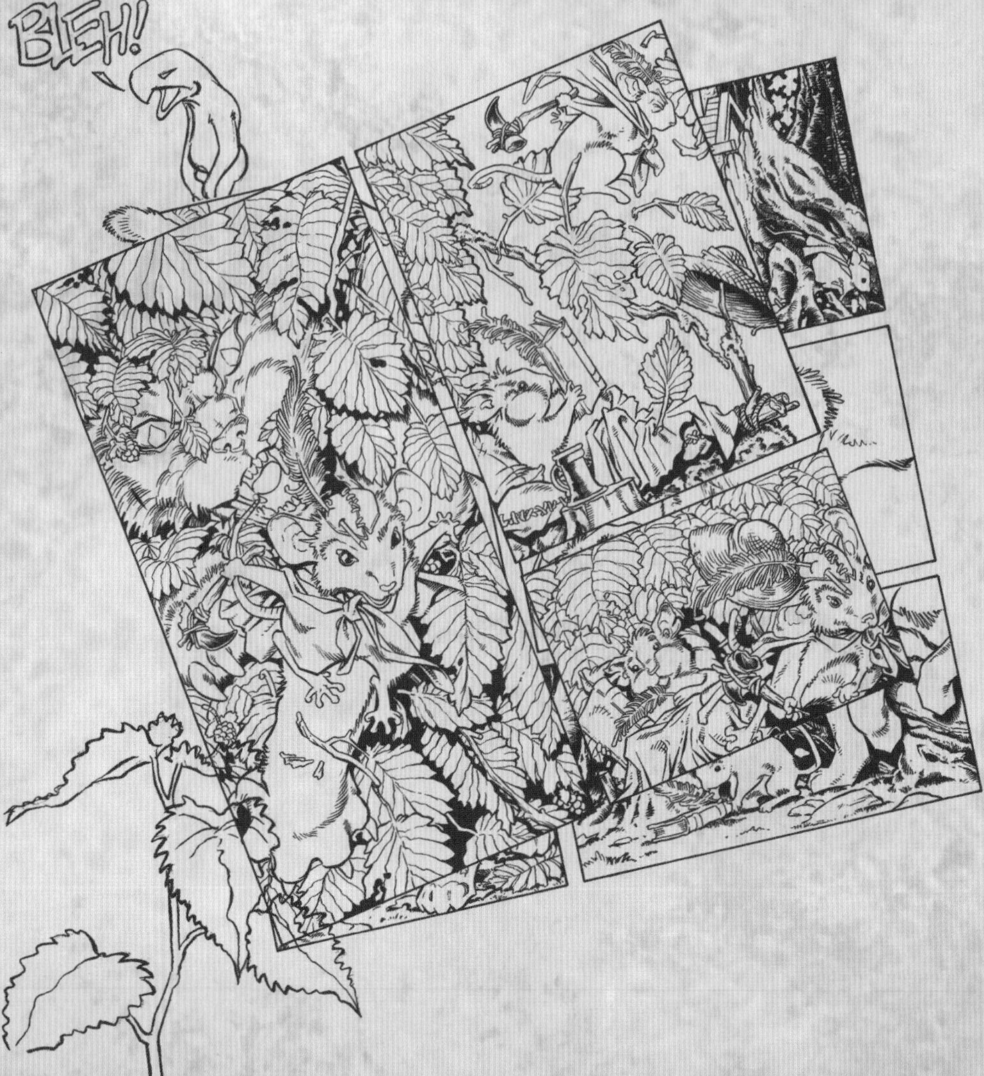
BLEH!

JACKSON SZE HAS WORKED AS A CONCEPT ARTIST IN ADVERTISING, VIDEO GAMES, TELEVISION AND FILM. HE IS CURRENTLY A SENIOR CONCEPT ILLUSTRATOR AT MARVEL STUDIOS, CONTRIBUTING TO MOVIES SUCH AS MARVEL'S *THE AVENGERS*, *THOR: THE DARK WORLD*, AND *GUARDIANS OF THE GALAXY*. HE IS ALSO A FOUNDING MEMBER OF THE *BATTLEMILK* SERIES OF ART BOOKS.

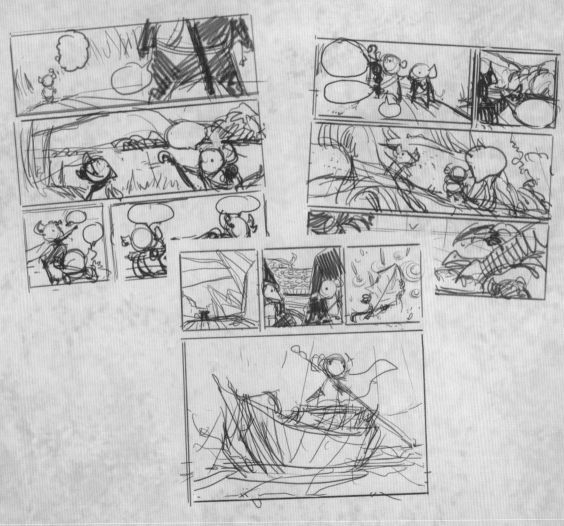

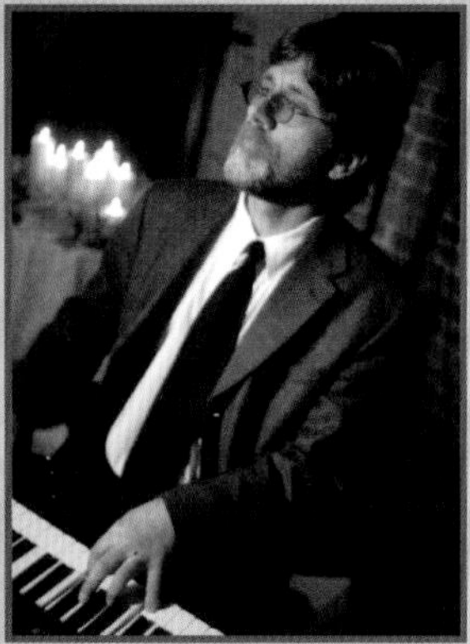

CLIFF MONEAR IS A PROFESSIONAL MUSICIAN AND COMPOSER. A PRODUCT OF THE BERKLEE COLLEGE OF MUSIC – CLIFF'S JAZZ GROUP, "THE CLIFF MONEAR TRIO," IS ONE OF THE BUSIEST PERFORMING RHYTHM SECTIONS IN THE MIDWEST. IN ADDITION TO THIS VERY FULL PRIVATE AND PUBLIC PERFORMANCE SCHEDULE, AND TEACHING COMMITMENTS AT WAYNE STATE UNIVERSITY, CLIFF IS THE EXCLUSIVE STEINWAY & SONS REPRESENTATIVE FOR THE MICHIGAN JAZZ COMMUNITY. FOR BOOKING INFORMATION, EMAIL: INFO@CLIFFMONEAR.COM.

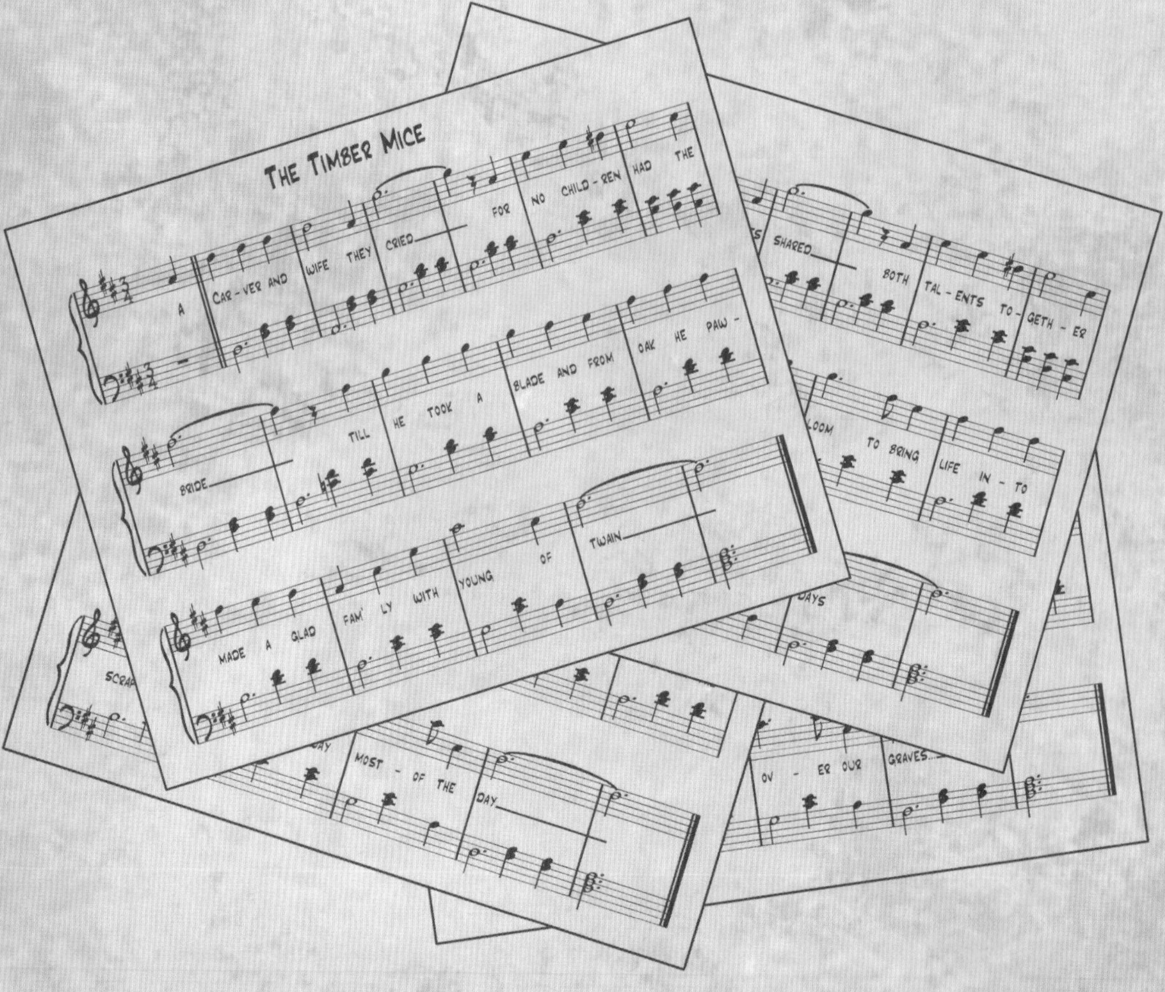
THE TIMBER MICE
A CAR - VER AND WIFE THEY CRIED FOR NO CHILD - REN HAD THE
BRIDE TILL HE TOOK A BLADE AND FROM OAK HE PAW -
MADE A GLAD FAM' LY WITH YOUNG OF TWAIN
SHARED BOTH TAL - ENTS TO - GETH - ER
LOOM TO BRING LIFE IN - TO
DAYS
MOST - OF THE DAY
OV - ER OUR GRAVES

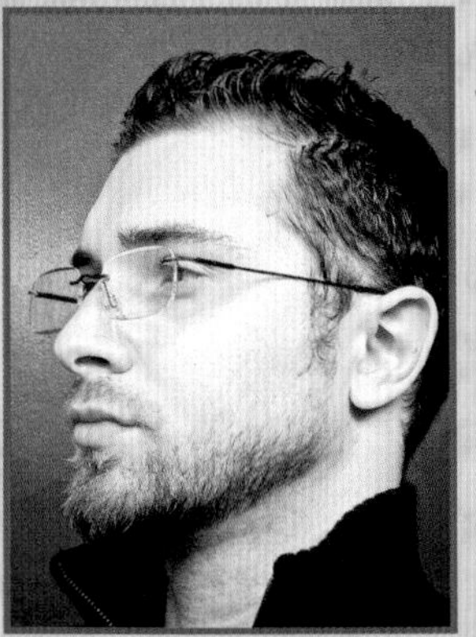

JUSTIN GERARD'S WORK HAS BEEN REGULARLY FEATURED IN *SPECTRUM FANTASTIC ART* AND HAS APPEARED IN THE SOCIETY OF ILLUSTRATORS' ANNUALS, *EXPOSE*, AND *FLIGHT*. JUSTIN ALSO CONTRIBUTES ARTICLES TO VISUAL DESIGN MAGAZINES SUCH AS *IMAGINEFX* AND TO BLOGS SUCH AS MUDDYCOLORS. HIS WORK HAS WON SEVERAL AWARDS: AN IPPY AWARD FOR HIS WORK IN *BEOWULF, BOOK 1: GRENDEL THE GHASTLY*, THE CHESLEY AWARD IN 2009, AND A SILVER AWARD FROM SPECTRUM IN 2012.

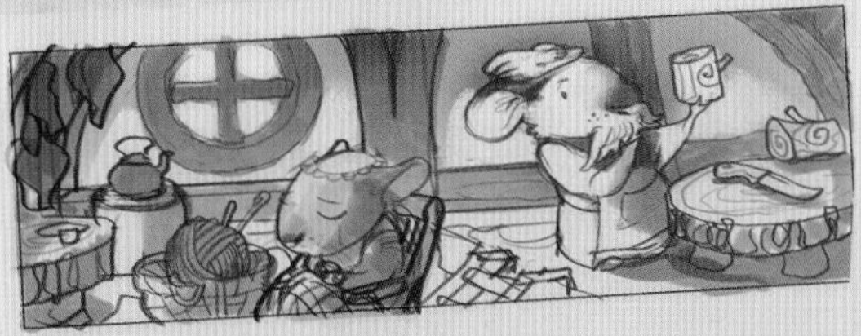

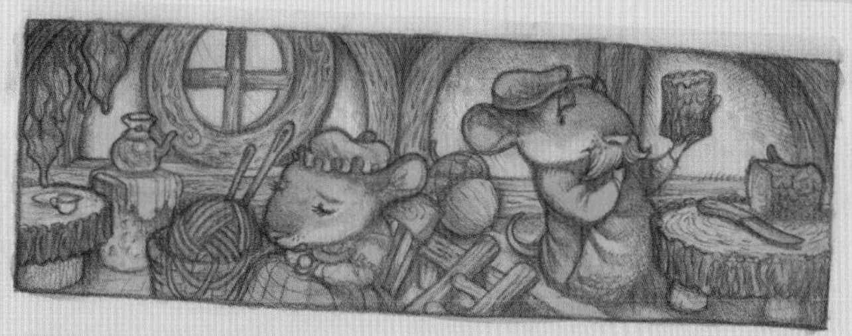

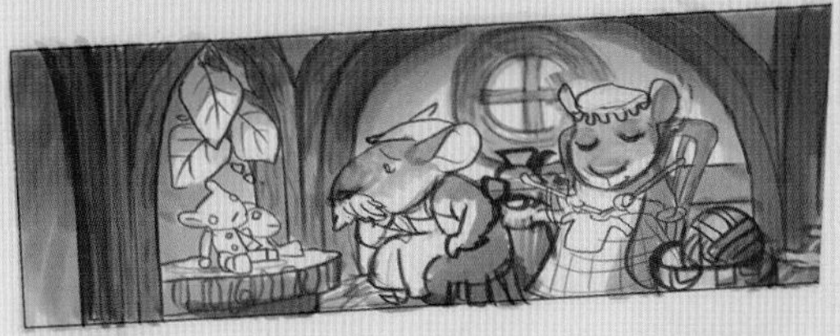

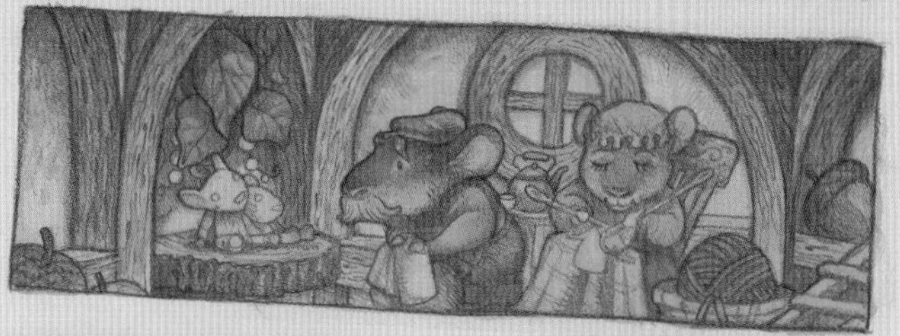

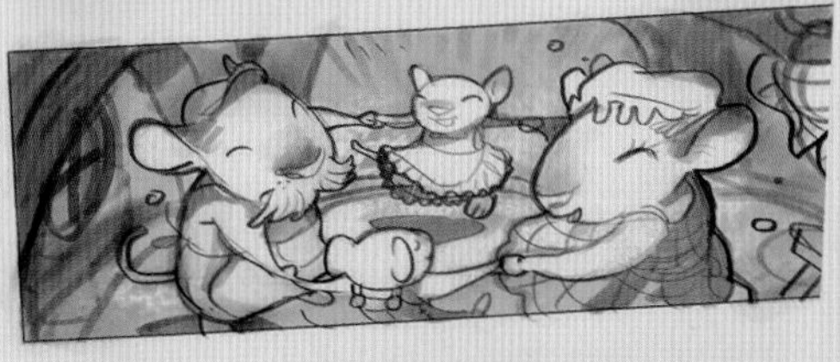

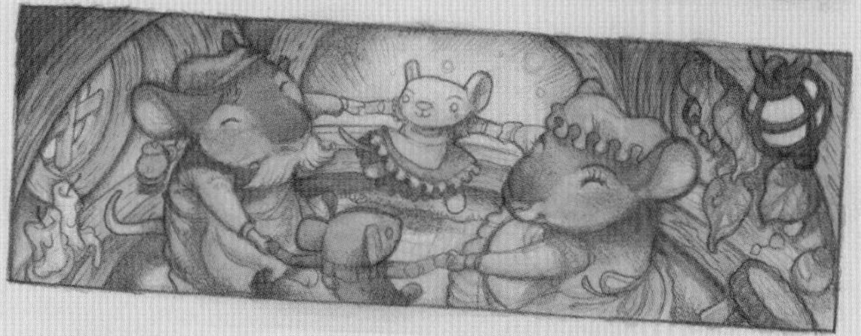

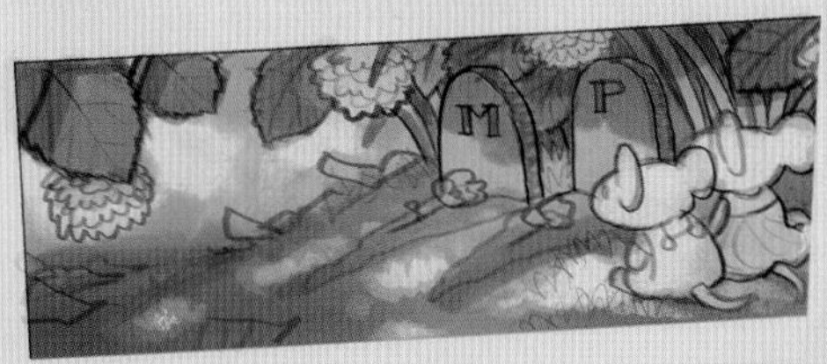

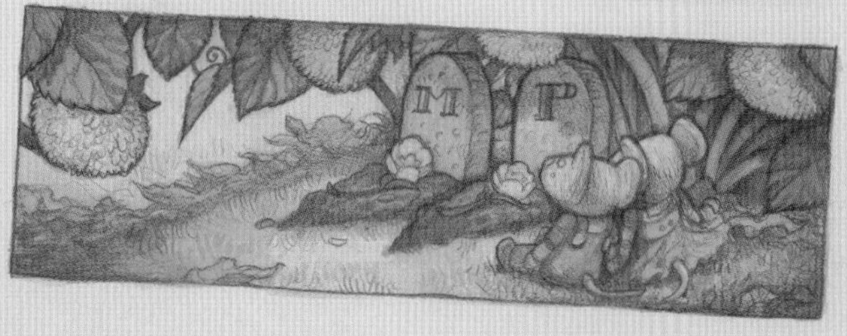

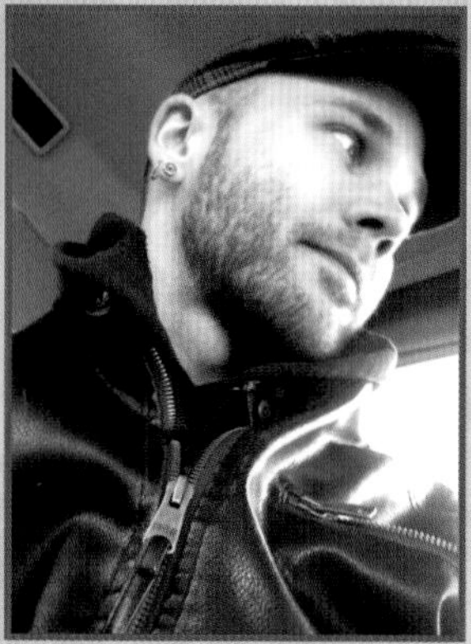

DIRK SHEARER ENJOYS VERSATILITY AS A COMMERCIAL ARTIST. HIS SCRATCHBOARD ILLUSTRATIONS CAN BE SEEN IN ANDREW GASKA'S *CONSPIRACY OF THE PLANET OF THE APES*, BRYAN GLASS AND MIKE OEMING'S *MICE TEMPLAR: VOLUME 1*, AND MIKE OLIVERI'S *THE PACK: WINTER KILL*. HE ILLUSTRATED SAM COSTELLO'S "PIECES OF MEAT" WEBCOMIC ONE-SHOT, AND OUTSIDE GENRE FICTION, HE'S CONTRIBUTED EDITORIAL ARTWORK FOR *POPULAR SCIENCE MAGAZINE*, PRODUCT DESIGN FOR ROOMMATES PEEL & STICK, AND LOGOS FOR VARIOUS COMPANIES.

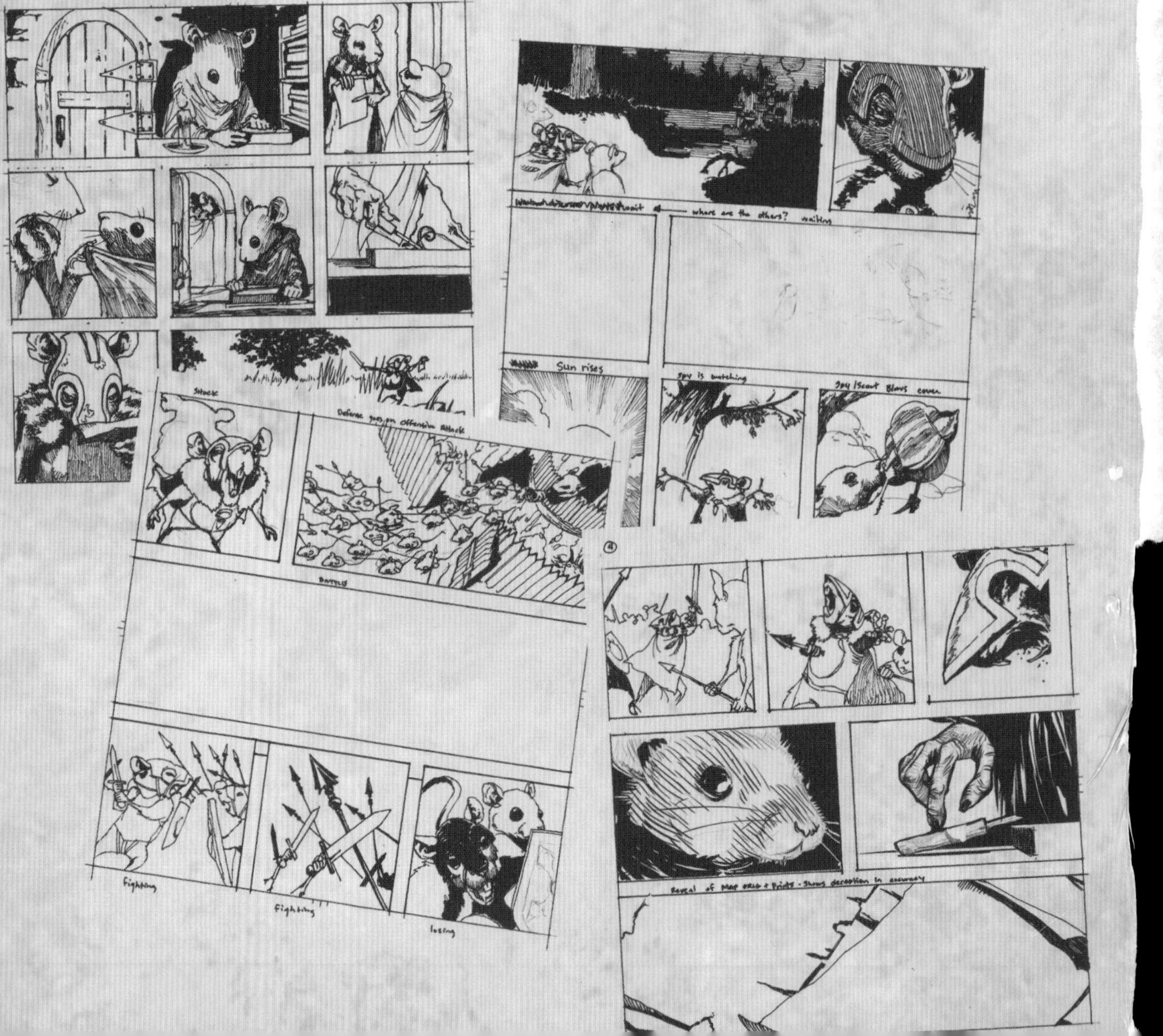
where are the others? waiting
Sun rises
Spy is watching
fighting
fighting
losing

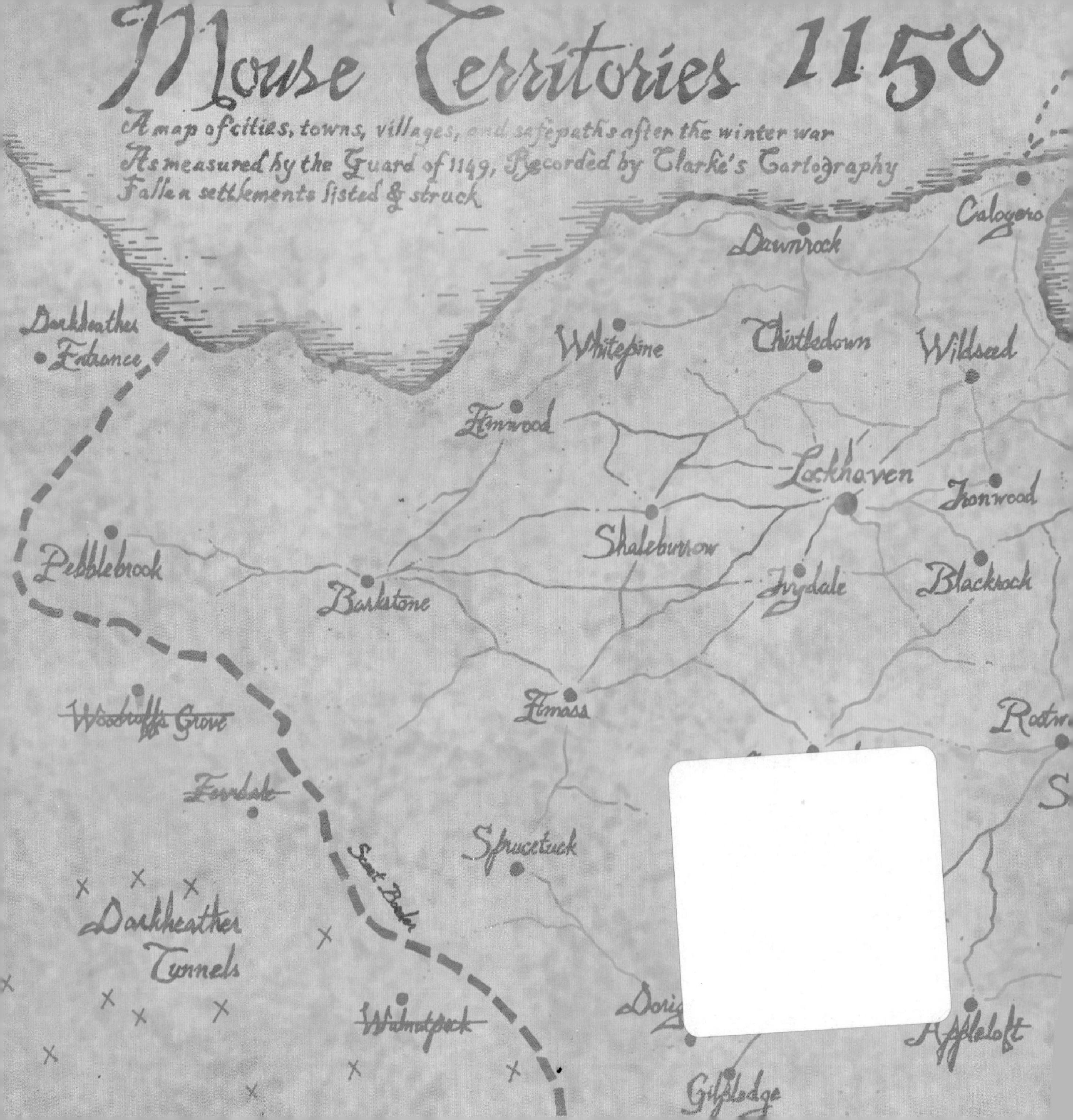

Mouse Territories 1150

A map of cities, towns, villages, and safe paths after the winter war
As measured by the Guard of 1149, Recorded by Clarke's Cartography
Fallen settlements listed & struck

Calogero

Dawnrock

Darkheather
Entrance

Whitepine   Thistledown   Wildseed

Elmwood

Lockhaven   Ironwood

Shaleburrow

Pebblebrook

Ivydale   Blackrock

Barkstone

Elmoss

Rootw~

~Woodruff's Grove~

S~

~Ferndale~

Sprucetuck

Scent Border

Darkheather
Tunnels

×   ×   ×

×

×   ×   ×

×

~Walnutpeck~

Dorig~

Appleloft

×

Gilsledge